About the author

Peter Keating read Ancient and Medieval History at Royal Holloway College, London. After obtaining a 2.1 Honours degree, he worked in a variety of industries, lectured at evening classes, taught history at secondary school and self-published several history study guides for students (GCSE, A-level). Simultaneously, he continued researching the early Byzantium Empire and wanted to pass on his passion for the period using the medium of fiction. He felt that while historical figures can be rather daunting for a reader, they could be brought to life in historical fiction. *Belisarius: Military Master of The West* is the first of five novels covering this exciting but little-known era in European history.

BELISARIUS: MILITARY MASTER OF THE WEST
BOOK ONE: NIKA

Peter Keating

BELISARIUS: MILITARY MASTER OF THE WEST
BOOK ONE: NIKA

Vanguard Press

VANGUARD PAPERBACK

A CIP catalogue record for this title is
available from the British Library.

ISBN 978-1-80016-021-7

*Vanguard Press is an imprint of
Pegasus Elliot MacKenzie Publishers Ltd.*
www.pegasuspublishers.com

First Published in 2021

**Vanguard Press
Sheraton House Castle Park
Cambridge England**

Printed & Bound in Great Britain

Dedication

To my mentor, Julian (Iouliane) Chrysostomides, Emeritus Reader in Byzantine History, University of London. (21 April 1928 – 18 October 2008): Greek historian of Byzantium and citizen of the world.

Acknowledgements

To my mother, Jean Keating, who never gave up and taught me to read and write, the second-best gift after life.

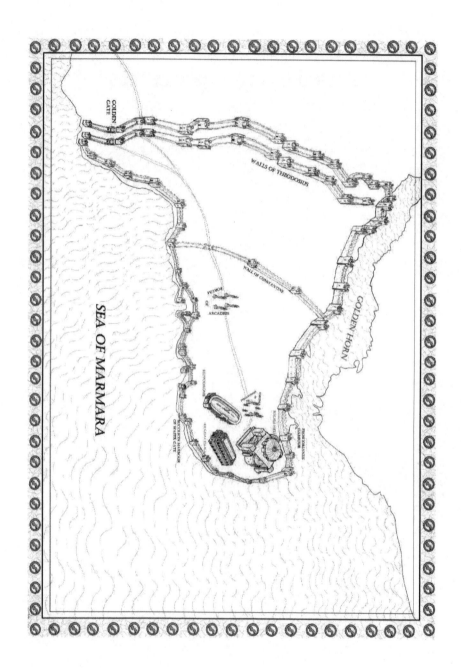

GOLDEN GATE

WALLS OF THEODOSIUS

WALL OF CONSTANTINE

FORUM OF ARCADIUS

SEA OF MARMARA

GOLDEN HORN

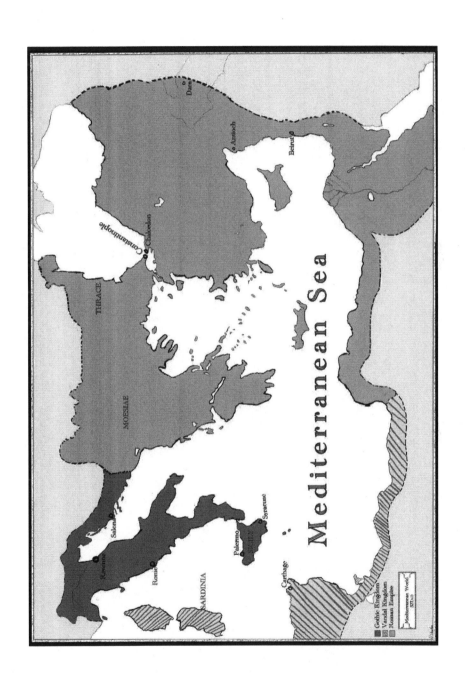

Chapter One

The warm wind blew across the Golden Horn, collecting moisture as it drifted over the Sea of Marmara nearby; it only served to increase my awareness of the afternoon humidity. The older I had become, the less I enjoyed the damp heat. As I sat at my desk, the paper lying before me, perilously empty, my thoughts flooded the room. Questions nipped at my mind. How to start a history of my campaigns and not talk about my personal life? It had been weeks since I had attended the magistrates' court to answer charges of corruption, and I was sure I knew who had organised the affair. I also had a good idea why.

"Papa, are you in your study?" I recognised the voice of my daughter, Johanna, her question dispelling the thoughts clinging to me. I knew she required my response.

"Yes, I am in the study," I replied, vaguely distracted but not unwelcoming, as her familiar shadow stood in the doorway.

"Any luck starting your magnum opus?" She came into my study, carrying a small basket of bread and some cheese, judging by the smell. I hadn't eaten since I had woken that morning. Judging by the light, it was late afternoon already. I hadn't managed to write anything, though there was much to try to pen. I welcomed the break from the blank paper, I hadn't seen Johanna for several days since I started trying to write my personal history. Calmly, she sat down next to me. She moved the paper out of the way and served the bread and cheese in its place. She was the spitting image of her mother. She also had her willpower — she had waited before marriage, taking her own time and making her own choice. Her mother, before she had died, had done her utmost to marry Johanna off to one of Justinian's family. But she had refused the arranged marriage, and she had refused to speak to her mother over the matter. She kept it up till the day Antonina died, an example of her determination. Antonina blamed me even on her deathbed, she still informed me that this is what happened when you educated a daughter. Well, Johanna was my daughter, and I intended that she should be as independent as she wanted. When I died, she would inherit everything, her half-brother and sisters would receive nothing, just a small bequest.

She looked over at me, and her bright eyes investigated mine. She had a way of reading my moods.

"Papa… think of this as a task! It's your chance to tell your side of the story, not just what happened." There was a look in those eyes that prompted me to think on her words, to think about what was going on, and I curled an eyebrow as I considered how to reply to her on this matter.

"Yes, I suppose you're right." I paused, waiting to see if she would notice before I mused on the matter myself. "Why do you think Procopius asked me to write a history of my wars?"

"You always said he understood politics and how the system worked. Look how he has progressed since he worked for you. I was just a child when you hired him," Johanna said, a slight sigh of nostalgia or perhaps even amusement in her tone, but it brought me back to my thoughts. She laid out the food for me, kissed my forehead and sat down.

I pondered over what Procopius and I had talked about after the recent court case; Justinian, our Basileus, had called an investigation into the actions of a few of my old staff. They had been rumoured to have taken bribes in Italy and sold food at exorbitant prices during the Siege of Rome; the case had seemed quite strong against them. But this time it had failed; largely because he'd picked the wrong judge, my old secretary, Procopius. He had won favour with the emperor recently, thanks to his panegyric on the 'Buildings' that the emperor had commissioned — to further glorify his realm. From this, Procopius had been given evermore powerful and rewarding roles within the government; loyalty has its rewards. But this time he had seemingly failed to bring the proscribed judgement against me. He found the evidence, dragged out of former slaves — even after the procedural torture — false and malicious and so closed the case in my favour. After the verdict, he had called me into his chambers and explained in a hushed tone, just in case we were overheard, his reasons.

"My dear General, this time I could save you. The case was weak and deliberately so, Justinian knew it. I feel it was another warning for you to disappear from public view. I would further add that maybe a pilgrimage to some remote location soon will save you and give the appearance of public contrition."

He had been as honest but cautious in his words as any would, and I whispered back, slightly confused by the statement.

"I thought he'd had his pounds of gold and silver from me, what else is there?"

"You are a face from the past, and even without your knowledge, you are, or could be, a focus for revolt against his waning grip on power," Procopius had whispered, his tone firm and voice steady.

"But I have never challenged him, even when we thought he was dying from the plague. We all looked around for a strong figure to succeed him; with no heirs and no sign of his guidance in the matter, we couldn't be left alone. Luckily, he recovered, and all was set right."

I had almost scoffed at the words but for the caution requested and in hindsight remembering my surprise appeared foolish.

"Yes, but you forget that the empress lived then. She balanced his personal demons and held them in check, guiding him. When she couldn't guide him, as with Divinity questions, she bypassed him and gave her personal support to the other side. So, you were safe."

"Yes, I was drawn into the controversy, but she had such force and insight. I am getting old. I was never a politician. You always saw the intrigue, and I have missed your advice. But as I am out of service, I thought after he had taken my wealth and estates, he had vented his rage." Still, I had been oblivious, reluctant to believe that there would be any reason for the emperor to be vindictive.

"When was the last time you saw him or even spoke to the Basileus?" he said, and for a while, I fell silent as I thought it over.

"It's been years since he recalled me and sent me north. You, on the other hand, see him more; so, I bow to your knowledge. God Almighty, I served in the guard with the man, socialised, and you think you know the man, only to learn that power changes all.

"Look, my friend, you must stop living in the past, the now is more dangerous than you could believe. The longer he lives on his own, the stranger and more paranoid his behaviour becomes. You are a danger because you once were his best general and friend. Without the late empress and dare I say it, your ex-wife, you have no one to protect you.

This case should have shown you how little you understand what is happening at Court!"

"So, the pilgrimage is a ruse to escape the capital and his fears?" I sighed regretfully.

"Of course, anyway you are older now, and it is common for ex-officials to seek solace in God, as well as seeking forgiveness for actions in life. He will see it that way, as his religiosity dominates his thinking. But you can do one thing for me before you leave, say next summer after you announce your pilgrim intentions. Write me an account of the wars we fought together, so I have a record. Even I will need to leave the capital in a few years. If I plan it right, I will gain a posting back to my home in Caesarea. It should be out of his reach and palace intrigue. So, leaving me free to write a history of our times," he said as if relieved by the thought.

"Well, I can trust no one else. I have little to lose except my life, I suppose. A record of what we have done and failed to do will serve as a lesson for those to come. It is traditional for so-called great men to write their accounts, or as you used to say 'histories'. I will take your advice and use the autumn and winter to write as much as I can before I leave. Thank you for your kindness."

We parted, he back to the palace and me to my small estate across the water from the capital to contemplate all he had said.

It was the urging of my only daughter that persuaded me that Procopius was right, that I should tell my story, as much as I can remember of it. She had been good to me, visiting me when she could, making excuses to her husband to see me. She also agreed that leaving the old house and going on a spiritual retreat would be a good idea. It would give me time to recover and prepare my soul for the next life.

So here I sit, looking at blank paper again.

I was never one for letters, but I suppose the best way is to begin with a brief mention of my life. Then of what I think is worthy of my time with the emperor-to-be, Flavius Petrus.

"So, Johanna, here I am facing the blank paper again, where do you start your story?" I said as I considered my life all over again, the thoughts floating about like clouds thrown around on a stormy day. She looked up from her food.

I was rather bemused by the grin she suddenly wore as she practically teased me with the simplicity of her advice.

"Well, I suppose the easiest way is to begin from the beginning. From there, try and explain yourself through your story."

It seemed perhaps the correct answer for a child to give, though, of course, she was hardly that any more. But there was so much to discuss, so much to filter through and some of the topics were too difficult to even attempt to divulge. Some stories from the past had only recently begun to stick as a lump in the throat and rot away all the pleasant thoughts of the time before, and when I responded with a simple, "some of it is still too hard to discuss," she practically snorted at me as if I were being foolhardy.

"Look, when it comes to Lady Antonina, just say what you're happy about."

"You mean *your* mother?" I chided her, slightly irritated to hear her speak so disrespectfully, but then I held my tongue. I remembered their recent past — her death- and calmed down before I could sound unfair. Without missing a beat, she passed me the bread and cheese, and we ate in silence, my mind clouded with my thoughts before they seemed to untangle from one another. A different matter popped to the front of my mind, and I turned towards my daughter and said, "All I knew were the rumours that Phocas told me. She, Antonina was a convinced Alexandrian, just like the late Augusta Theodora and she was determined to force my godson to become one. She took it too far!"

"Well, Papa, if that's what you feel was behind it, I would leave any mention of Lady Antonina's indiscreet actions out of your history. After all, it's about your wars, not hers and better to say what you know rather than to speculate," she said wisely, and I informed her I was happy to have spoken it over with her and I would begin at the start. She seemed pleased and began to clear the remains of the food, leaving me to my writing.

"Good. I'll see you in the morning. I have things to do in the house. Don't stay up all night — your eyes aren't as good as they were, especially in the lamplight."

"I'll make a start, and I'll go to bed once the lamps are lit," I said,

17

then turned to the great sheets of nothingness where I would have to explain my entire life and once more, I felt the room and the world take in a deep breath and wait for me to start.

I reached for the pen and dipped it in the fresh ink. For a moment, I pondered the smell of the parchment; I wondered what animal had given up its skin for my project. I had thought about using Egyptian paper, but it was expensive, and in the mixed climate, I wondered if it would last. The animal skin lasted and was available here in the capital and cheaper. The smell of the ink reminded me of being back in a military headquarters, there, someone like Procopius would do the writing, I would just tell him what I wanted written, and he would compile a piece of poetry out of my words.

But the smell of the animal skins always reminded me of my childhood too; it triggered all sorts of memories. How long ago, it seemed now. I can still see the house and the farm; I can still daydream back to when being a child was so clear and free. Everything then was new and fresh; days seemed to last forever. Even sitting and looking out of a window during a boring class on Roman poetry didn't make the day any shorter and the blow from the teacher only reminded one of how trapped you were.

So, let's begin…

I was born in the province of Middle Dacia, in the town of Germania, in the ninth year of the Augustus Anastasius. My grandfather was granted the rank of most notable for his service under the Vicar of Dacia in the time of the godforsaken Attila's invasion of the province. He retired to Germania and bought a ruined estate outside of the town and rebuilt it. This was where my father grew up and served the town in the role of magistrate. With this status, I was well educated and prepared for government service. In other words, to not only follow my father but my grandfather and eventually reach the Senate in the capital city of many names, Constantinople, New Rome, the mother of all cities. But my uncles had served in the army and, from as far as I can remember, they told me tales of the campaigns they served in, the different regions and the excitement of being a soldier, which is what I wanted. Not just any soldier, of course, but one of the Imperial Schola Guards or Excubitors, who served in the presence of the emperor. This was the best route to becoming a commander, as you were more likely to catch the eye of the emperor. With my education, I would have a head start over the more experienced men, who couldn't read or write. So, I had them train me, and when my uncles were away, I paid for a coach to ensure I could ride as a cavalryman, use a bow and lance and fight with a sword.

The advantage of wealth allowed me to have this dual education and to round it off, after a hard day's training, I could relax in one of the few surviving hot baths that the town was famed for — even in the winter, the outside baths were still hot. These efforts were the only way to persuade my father that my path lay with the army, not the civil service. He was the only one who could allow this, as a family of our rank had to serve the government by law, and most chose the easy route rather than the hard and dangerous life of a soldier. Being seen to refuse my request for military service could place him under a cloud if the prefect of the province heard about my choice. Dishonour was something my father took seriously, unlike others who would pay their way out of problems, such as when the prefect demanded that officials send sons for military service as an example to the town. Some could bribe and have a provincial official issue a deferment or even claim their son was a priest or monk at the time. Money could buy anything one wanted or needed, but thankfully it was not my father's way. Nothing has changed since then though, money talks and about the only thing that can't be purchased is the Imperial throne.

Unlike the men of the town and countryside, I had a choice of one or the other; they could only escape to the army to avoid following their father's livelihood. So, if you wondered why our army was so dependent on mercenaries, that is why; the army could only recruit the sons of soldiers if they could find them. The pay was so low, but a mercenary was well paid from the start of his service. Yet, men were supposed to be free to join the army, but they were not. Some of our mercenaries were runaway citizens who joined the barbarians so that they could be paid a just wage. In a way, the state was its own worst enemy. Those tied to the land paid for the barbarians to defend them as they demanded more pay, so the people had to pay higher taxes. I first came across this in Italy, where we charged more to defend them than the barbarians charged them when they conquered them.

With age, they say, comes wisdom, so as I look back, I can now see the unjustness of the system I served; but what choice did we have? Our peoples had been conquered by barbarians such as the Vandals and Goths, who were not Catholic, and forced our lost citizens to worship their twisted false heretical barbarian Christ. We had a divine mission to release them from their living hell that endangered their souls. We did this, but the cost, in the end, was so high that when the 'bearded ones' came to Italy, we had little to stop them with. But that gets ahead of my history, and I will speak of this more in the right place.

So, when the winter snows had melted enough for travel on the roads, and I had reached manhood, my father wrote to one of his family's allies in the capital and arranged a place for me in one of the palace guard units. I would start at the bottom and earn my promotion. My father was strict about that; only through ability would I progress. I think this was his last test to ensure I was committed to my choice. Once the reply had been received, I was ready to leave. I was assigned to assist with guarding that year's tax returns, which that year were going direct to the capital, rather than the diocese capital. Each town was selected to make payments either to the province, diocese — a collection of provinces — or to the capital, depending on the wants of the capital; that is how much it demanded from each vicar. Each town collected from the citizens and the countryside and any shortfall was made up by people like my father, which meant that he had the hard task of extracting the yearly tax from the community. He did this as honestly as he could, but failure to collect meant people like him would be forced to sell up to cover the difference. No one liked the Imperial tax system. In lean years people could starve as they were forced to hand over their produce to cover the tax demand, leaving very little for them in the winter.

Now I see the system for what it was — a drain on the citizens of the Empire to pay for grandiose buildings that weren't to benefit the farmer in Thrace, but rather the grandeur of the capital and the Basileus. Yet it all failed to defend them from the ravages of the barbarian, as there was never enough money to pay for an army to defend them. What it paid for was a weak defence of the provinces, based on small hilltop forts with few defenders designed to offer a secure refuge for the countryside or small towns that didn't have a wall or a garrison. The frontier troops were poorly paid and spent more time growing food than training to be soldiers. The only saving grace was that the barbarians mainly raided, so were uninterested in besieging a garrisoned town or fort. Instead, they stripped the countryside bare, took anyone they could as slaves and retreated over the frontier, till the next harvest when they would strike again. For regions such as Thrace, the countryside closest to the frontiers were slowly depleted of peasants who fled into towns; only the very rich could survive there. The very large estates mostly farmed by slaves or landlocked peasants continued to operate, while the owner lived in the fortified towns or even in the capital. The only advantage they offered was protection. They had an investment to protect, so they paid for their own soldiers, the so-called 'biscuit eaters'. I had at one time as many as seven thousand cavalry that I personally paid and fed, hence the term, from the traditional military ration of the hard-baked biscuits.

So, in the second year of the late Emperor Justin's reign, I said my goodbyes to my mother and father and headed south towards the Military Road, escorting the tax convoy. I joined with ten other men, paid for by the town to protect the silver and gold coins in the wagon, along with a further wagon holding the food and other items for living on the road. The minor roads tended to be just usable, as there was little money to pay for their upkeep, and any heavy rain caused us to stop and pitch camp. We waited till the water had drained away, as the driver couldn't see the potholes with all the water sitting on the surface. Once we reached the main artery, the Military Road, we could travel in all weathers as the provinces were responsible for its upkeep. If they wanted a relief force sent quickly from the capital, this was the only route they could use. Dotted along at the distance of a day's march in good weather were small towers with guards and their families. They maintained the post and kept fresh horses and looked after the remounts of the postal service and offered water and limited shelter to users of the road. The closer we came to the capital, the larger these posts became, till they were a fort with a small garrison and accommodation for many travellers and food. On top of this, the road became more crowded, and the journey slowed, as we had to fall in behind other convoys heading for the capital, and when a military unit was on the road, we had to pull off the road to make way for them.

On this journey, I first saw cities such as Hadrianopolis with its mighty walls, the older sections made up of limestone with the new sections clearly visible with interlaced red and white brick walls, which had replaced the sections destroyed by the barbarians. We entered the city by crossing the bridge and then through the Western Military Gate. The city was laid out in the Roman style of a legionary fortress with straight roads leading to the forum and government buildings and barracks. We stayed a few days in the city, and it was even grander than Philippolis, which we had reached earlier. The place was heaving with people from all over the Empire. This is where I heard Greek being spoken as much as Roman. I had learnt a little Greek, but the accents were different. Closer to the capital, I noticed just how much Greek was preferred to Roman. Of course, in the army, we used a hybrid Roman-Greek-Goth language to enable us to give orders and understand our troops.

By the time we reached Heraclea on the coast of the Marble Sea, spring had fully arrived, and the area was awash with the colour of blossoms as the land returned to fertility. But with it came a new scent for me, salt from the sea. Heraclea, I always remember smelled of fish. We had fish sauce as a treat at home, but here it was freshly made from the early catch of gutted fish. It was pungent, but here it was the only smell, everything tasted of the sauce even fresh fish and vegetables. I never got used to the smell of fish that dominated the cities and towns on the coast, especially the capital, which in the heat of summer smelt just like a rancid pot of sauce. But the people here loved it and regarded it as the most natural smell, as a baker does of his freshly baked bread. I still hang garlic and onions and have grown plenty of herbs around the villa to compete with the stink of fish sauce. It's also one of the reasons I preferred to live outside the walls of the capital. The air moved around here, unlike in the capital where it was trapped. There it blew mostly from the Golden Horn across the city, carrying the stench of fish from the markets to every nook and cranny of every building.

Speaking of the sea, this was the first time I ever saw one. It was blue, just like I had been told it would be, wide and smooth-looking from a distance. Up close, as I would later learn, it was rough at the best of times, and when the wind changed, a storm could envelop it as fast as a sandstorm in the desert. Then it turned an angry boiling white, and the waves turned into a moving mountain range. Even in spring, it was warm along the road by the sea. During one of the first breaks after leaving Philippolis, I washed in it for the first time and learnt the difference between river water and the sea. With salt, I was left with a fine crust after drying, and it got into all the sores I had developed from riding and walking since leaving home, stinging in a manner one can hardly describe. On the other hand, it cleaned them, and the sores quickly cleared up and made the remaining part of the journey to the capital more comfortable. Since then, I have used either the sea, if I can, or salted water to clean myself after a day's marching or riding while on campaign. The trick was getting the right amount. Too much and it left salt in all my skin creases which acted like sand and caused just as many rubs; with experience, I learnt to balance the mixture. But nothing, even today in the capital, can beat the warmth and healing of the hot water pools of home.

Then finally we approached the capital after the road had joined and ran alongside one of the main aqueducts, which towered above us as its multiple tiers of arches allowed it to breach the small valleys, before reaching the great walls of the capital. They had been built by Theodosius, and I have never, in all my campaigns across the Empire, seen anything as splendid as those walls. Even from a distance, especially in the afternoon, when the sun catches the outer wall's brickwork and causes it to glow, one is reminded of Homer's description of Troy. The closer one came, the easier it was to see the grandeur and sheer power those walls projected. As we reached the first military gate close to the coast, we could see over to our left the great impressive Golden Gate, which was the colour of chalk.

Only the Basileus used it when entering the city in triumph. The first military gate only allowed access into the city, and it was only wide enough for a wagon to pass through. To leave the city and return the way we had come, one used the second military gate. Before we could enter, we had to cross the moat using a wooden bridge, the ditch was full after recent rain, but it was normally dry and only flooded in times of emergency. Then, we passed through the first customs post, which lay outside of the lower outer wall atop the inner side of the moat. Once through that post, we entered the gates of the middle wall, then we crossed an open area till we reached the last gate fitted into the third and highest wall. Finally, we were inside the capital and assigned accommodation till we could hand over the tax to the designated officer and receive a signed Imperial receipt. My fellow travellers would ensure this reached home safely, as their lives depended on this — this was the only proof we would have that we had not lost or stolen any of the tax we had conveyed from home to the capital.

For me, after my first night's sleep, I headed towards the Imperial quarter and the headquarters of the Master of all the Soldiers, the most senior of all army commanders ready to report for duty. It was quite a walk. As I was of no importance, I could not ride inside the capital. I walked with my two horses in tow. The road was paved and quite wide in sections of my journey, there were blocks of new buildings on either side while in other sections there was only parkland, orchards or vineyards with sheep and cows out to pasture. Closer to the Imperial quarter, the city built up, especially once I passed through the old walls and into the very heart of the Empire.

My first impressions were that every other building was a church of some kind, but with experience, I learnt that many of these were private houses of the elite of the city. Some were indeed churches and monasteries, but the extravagant nature of the private houses could make anyone confused. These sights remained the norm as I continued on through the Forum built by the Emperor Arcadius and finally reached the Forum of Theodosius, and hence to the military headquarters, where I presented myself. Once there, I was informed that I had been assigned to the Excubitors — the sentinels or personal guard of the Basileus. I had expected to be posted to the Schola and then possibly posted back to the army of the West, which was based in Thrace, and so closer to home, so it was quite the surprise.

Although the Excubitors were the main guards of the palace, they were based by the walls at the Gothic barracks, close to the second military gate. The barracks had gained this name as in times before the Gothic mercenary troops had been housed here. Later, under Emperor Leo, they became his power base and housed his fellow Isaurians whom he formed into his sentinels, trusted and pampered over the rest of the army. Under the last emperor, who fought a major war against them, the main Isaurian elements were purged, and it was now made up of a mix of Romans, like me, from the West and Greeks from the East. There were also a small number of Isaurians, who were tough mountain people from Asia-Minor, fiercely independent and prone to banditry when pressed to pay taxes, but good fighters.

So, my training began. The morning was spent at the Hippodrome, learning how to fight in armour with a variety of hand-held weapons. After lunch, we cleaned our kit, sharpened swords and repaired clothing and armour ready for the next day. At first, I thought this would be easy, but after running, climbing over obstacles and fighting mock battles with wooden weapons, I did not, and I was exhausted by the end of each day. But gradually it became habit and less tiring, in that I had enough energy to wander around the city when we were occasionally granted passes for the night. We were fed well, allowed wine with the evening meal of the usual bean stew or fish. We had meat on feast days and celebration days. After two months of infantry training, we began to train as cavalry.

The day started at dawn in the stables where we prepared our mounts for the day, ensuring they were healthy and smart. We groomed each mount before placing on its armour and then the saddle. After that, we paraded before the count of the sentinels. He would then choose a squadron to inspect formally, disciplining any man whose equipment or horse wasn't up to his standards. Then we were given our tasks — for me and other new boys that was more training. We would ride out of the city to the plains close by, and there began practising moving in formations. First, at a walking pace and as we improved gradually faster till we regularly charged over the plain. At noon we rested, first removing the equipment from our mounts, cleaning them, feeding and watering and then resting them. After that, we cleaned our equipment, and once that was done, we ate our lunch. All the time a section was allocated guard duty to protect us from a surprise attack. We trained for war and as if we were in a war. The afternoon was taken up with practising archery from horseback, first having the mount held so we could adjust to the position required for shooting. First forward, then to either side and lastly, the Hun shot, where we turned as fully as we could to the rear to fire well-aimed shots. Not as easy as it sounds and it just got harder as the horse moved, first at a walking pace and as we improved, faster till we could shoot while charging. We practised one at a time, aiming at a stuffed, mounted target. With time, we shot together in pairs and finally as a whole troop.

It took most of the summer to become at least competent at archery on the move. Later, once we had been sent to a squadron, we would train with the lance and then hand weapons. But archers were the most numerous in our cavalry, so we were trained first in that skill so that as soon as we were appointed, we could fight and be of use on the battlefield. It would take years, we were told, before we would be considered effective with all weapons.

Once sent to a squadron, we would regularly mount guard in the palace and at the city gates, as well as providing security at official occasions, including events at the Hippodrome. When not guarding, we would spend each day training as a unit and undertake more specialist training such as using the lance. I thought shooting from horseback was difficult, but using a lance was even more complicated. I spent most of the first weeks eating dirt, as I continually forgot to release the lance as I struck the target. The impact of hitting the target when at charge was enough to completely lift you off the saddle, at which point you either let go and crashed to the ground or were balanced for a moment in the air till the lance snapped and then you crashed to the ground. The other guards spent most of their time laughing at my exploits — they called me 'The Mole' for my efforts at digging holes in the ground.

My body felt each crash, and I had bruises that left most of my body a blue-grey patchwork. If nothing else, the pain quickly taught you to release just before impact, then you either reached for your sword or mace or axe, depending on which you preferred. Your target should have been unhorsed and either dead or dazed, at which point you clubbed or axed him to death to make sure. By then, you had either charged through most of the enemy or had come to an abrupt halt, the most dangerous moment for cavalry, and you needed to be able to fight your way out. While you swung left and right at the enemy, you urged your mount forward and as fast as possible. This was especially effective against infantry who either ran from you, ducked out of the way, or, if stupid, stood their ground and were mown down by the mass of the horse. It was hammered into us that movement was all that could save us on the battlefield; freezing would get you killed. Once through the enemy, you regrouped around the dragon standard and prepared for another charge, hopefully into the flanks of the enemy and victory.

I spent a further year developing my skills as well as learning the duties of a guard. What I hadn't known was that all the time, I was being watched by the deputy commander of the guards, Timostratus, a man constantly on the lookout for good soldiers. At the end of my second year in the guard, I was summoned into his office, a space cluttered with maps and documents. It looked like a mess, but I later learnt he had a keen memory and a curious system of order amongst the chaos and knew exactly where everything was. If you wanted to annoy him, of course, you moved something — then he would fly into a rage. It was a lesson I found out rather unfortunately when I once thought to tidy his office. The outcome of this first meeting was that I had been chosen to be promoted to the old rank of tribune and would work directly for him on his staff. He mentioned that I had impressed my instructors and fellow guardsman, as well as my officers. When he saw talent, he developed it.

I was going to spend several years on his staff, learning how to command an army, and eventually, he would promote me to lead a squadron of the guard to see how much I had learnt. If I did well, I would gradually rise to command a whole formation or legion as he liked to refer to them. When he went on campaign, I would go with him and learn the art of being a general. Unfortunately, we had very few major campaigns, and instead, I learnt most of my skills from major field exercises. As soon as I received the promotion, I wrote home to my family with the news. Eventually I had a reply, only to learn that both my parents had died in an outbreak of pestilence that had stricken the region during the last winter. I was heartbroken, as I could only have imagined how proud my father might have been at the news that I had become an officer. Now there was no one to tell, my uncles had long since retired from the army, and I had lost touch with them. On perhaps the brighter side, I had a larger income but very little to spend it on.

It was while I was on Timostratus's staff that I first met the future Emperor Justinian; he was of average height, heavy build — typical farming stock. On that day, my life changed completely. He wandered into the office and asked to speak to the general. I had recognised him as the son of Justin, the commander of the guards, and treated him like any other officer. He had looked me over for a time before replying to my answer that the general was at the palace.

"Ah, a native Roman speaker. By your accent, you're from Dacia?" he questioned with an eyebrow slightly raised and a look in his eyes as if he were daring me to prove him wrong and say different. But he was correct, and I spoke to him with all the politeness afforded to all officers.

"Yes, sir, you have a good ear for accents."

At that, he sat down in the general's chair and looked me up and down. A wide smile was on his face as he settled in the chair as if it were his own, and I could tell he was bemused by something.

"No, I only recognise those from my province. I came here to speak to the general about you, Belisarius." He laughed rather suddenly, looking to the desk thoughtfully as if he might be reading from a document, but I could hardly believe it. I was dumbstruck and could find nothing to say in reply to his statement. But he spoke again with a curious manner as if he were building up to something, I should be very keen to hear. "Belisarius, I have heard good things from Timostratus; the most important being loyalty. He knows he can trust you, and in the capital that is a rare gift. Also, you are from the provinces and have no bond to the palace or any of the senatorial families."

I nodded in agreement. With my parents' dead as well, I had little connection even to my home province. But I remained unsure where this conversation was leading — questions of loyalty and talking about palace connections could be dangerous if answered incorrectly. Was he trying to trick me into betraying the general, perhaps? I knew the general was loyal to the emperor and Justin, but there always seemed to be people out to question loyalty. And yet my possibly stupid expression of confusion served only to entertain him further.

"Belisarius, you look perplexed." His expression was all humorous as if he were suddenly afraid that I was perhaps some provincial simpleton and not as interesting a figure as he'd been led to believe. But I knew too that honesty in this kind of situation was of more importance, and so I just remained dutiful in my response, though it was little more than a question in return.

"Yes, sir, I am not sure what I can do for you?"

"First, you are being promoted to spear carrier. Then tomorrow, you will report to my quarters and become one of my personal bodyguards. I need officers who are loyal and have ability," he stated so plainly I could hardly recognise what he was actually saying at first. I swallowed hard. I wasn't sure about this; I wanted to stay with the general. I knew I had much to learn. But this was an order, and if Justinian gave it to me, then his uncle agreed. I had no choice but to salute and mumble my thanks, which gained a suddenly sharp, almost dangerous expression from him. "I am sorry, Belisarius you said something?"

"Yes, sir, thank you, sir." I corrected my impoliteness, and it seemed to please him, but I was not sure what to do next or even how appropriate it was to react to this sudden, and in my mind, unfounded promotion.

"Good, I'll see you in the morning." With that, he stood up and walked out of the office, and I remained standing there, stunned. Later, Timostratus returned, and I discussed the matter with him. I was relieved that he wanted me to stay, but Justin had decided that Justinian needed good men to watch over him, and there was no debating the matter. But he was swift to give me a warning — to keep whatever I saw from now on to myself and never discuss it, even with a girlfriend.

From now on, I would not be able to trust any of my colleagues or any new friends. I was to become the private gatekeeper to Justin's favourite nephew. In the capital, access to men of power normally came through connections and, of course, patronage; I was now linked to Justin's powerbase. If they fell from power, so would I.

Over several weeks, Justinian gradually began to use my services more and more. At first, I was posted to guard his quarters. The following week, I was named to join him on rides outside of the capital. Slowly, I was drawn in ever closer to him. Within a month, I was quartered in the same house as him. I was woken when he did and slept once he was in his bedroom. It was a relatively easy life compared to training, yet I was sure there was more going on than met the eye. I was certain that he slipped out of the house at night and returned in the early hours. But I remembered what the general had said and so never mentioned my suspicions. Anyway, who could I mention them to that would have any bearing upon Justinian?

Then one evening, after I had retired for the night and was sure that Justinian had also, the curtain to my room was swung open, and in strode Justinian. He was wearing non-military clothing and looked just like any other wealthy young man you would see strolling around the capital with an entourage in tow. He was carrying a bundle, which he casually chucked at me and then calmly gave me some rather unusual orders.

"Right, change into these and make sure you take your best sword and a couple of daggers with you."

It sounded dangerous and concerning, but I was not able to disobey and so automatically I got up. I dressed in the clothing, slightly coarser material than he wore, but still well cut and smart. I tucked my sword into the belt and the daggers into the top of the felt boots he had given me. I remained silent all through this. Once I was ready, he motioned me to follow him, and he led me out through a discreet doorway into the back alley of the house.

"Well, I think you are ready to join me on my little diversions. Just follow."

I did as I was bid. It had been a long time since I had bothered to venture out into the capital this late at night anyway. The alleyways and backstreets were still busy with soldiers, workers, and others looking for places to drink and for prostitutes. The nobility avoided these areas like the plague, or so I thought. That night I learnt that everyone who was anyone went out into the night to seek pleasure away from the tight grip of the palace and household. We trawled through a few seedy taverns, never quite stopping long enough to buy a drink. I occasionally thought I recognised a face or two in the crowds we travelled through, but I did not say anything, just observed.

Then we were at the rear of the Hippodrome, almost where we had started from. We had walked for some time, and I now assumed it was to make sure we lost anyone who thought about following us. We weren't furtive in our actions, and he led me into another alleyway, and suddenly we were outside a rather seedy-looking tavern named The Spinning Wool. He turned and looked at me, a wide grin on his face.

"Let's go in." he said — or rather ordered — as he marched straight in, without waiting for me to join him. Inside it was quiet — only the sounds of pleasure emanated from the stalls upstairs. Apart from that, the tavern was almost silent, save a few seasoned drinkers still hard at work with wine and chatting gently at their small tables. No faces looked up as I rushed in behind him. He made his way over to the L-shaped bar and leant on the flat wooden top. I walked over to join him, my right hand gently fiddling with the hilt of my sword underneath my cloak. A slightly taller than average woman appeared on the other side of the bar. She took one look at Justinian and shouted back behind her into the private area of the tavern.

"Theodora, special customer!"

"I am coming, I am coming." came a Greek sounding voice from the depths of the interior, sounding flustered but at the same time still in control.

By now, I had reached the counter where I noted Justinian's face had changed, and he looked completely different. His posture had completely relaxed, and he was actually what I would assume to be happy. The voice seemed to have caused this sudden reaction, and finally, the owner of it emerged. She had long, dark hair, was made up in the typical manner of a tavern owner, with jewellery on display, but of poor design, just shiny enough to catch the poor light of the tavern and sparkle. She swirled out from behind the counter with a suddenly coy look, but it seemed a rehearsed scenario as Justinian grabbed her by the waist, and they both embraced. Without a doubt, this wasn't his first encounter with this woman. He turned and looked at me with a big grin on his face and motioned for me to remain at the counter. He was led off to the rear by the woman and out of my sight. That was the first time I met the future Augusta, Theodora.

The woman at the counter looked at me and I at her. She was older than me, nearer Justinian's age than mine, and she had a full figure, slightly olive skin tone, dark hair, and brown eyes. She spoke in the natural Greek accent of the capital, and she looked back at me, almost surprised I had not really reacted. She suddenly twirled around on the spot, and her clothing did not cling to her body as she moved and gave a hint of what lay underneath.

"Like what you see, soldier boy?" She seemed to throw a kittenish expression towards me, but I will be the first to admit that in this situation, I was as clueless as any other. I was far more concerned with whether I was supposed just to sit and await Justinian's return or try to blend in — neither of which I was keen on.

"Um, yes, I think," I mumbled in reply, not exactly sure how I was supposed to respond in the situation and even rather shocked she'd ask such a thing. I felt my cheeks go a bright red. In hindsight, I was still very much a country boy in this big city, and there was a lot I still had to learn. I tried to clear my throat and speak a little more clearly as I requested wine, and she just gave me a rather dry expression.

"Oh, I thought you wanted something else. Cheap or good wine?"

I was not quite sure if I had offended her or not, the safest assumption being I probably had. Either way, she seemed to continue her work all the same as if such things never put her down, and I requested something decent with water to mix with it. I was feeling awkward all the same. In truth, these places were not as common outside of the larger cities.

But at that time, I knew the last thing I needed was to get drunk while Justinian was busy — I had no idea how long he would be. A good wine would take time to savour, and the water would dilute it further. The woman quickly filled a jug with water and then placed two cups on the tabletop, and wine was produced from below the counter. I placed several silver coins on the counter, and these disappeared with a quick sleight of her hand. She poured wine into both cups, leaving enough space for water. She then slowly poured the water in, till I motioned for her to stop, and we both drank our first cups in silence.

"So, what's your name, country boy?" she asked, leaning on the countertop, her brown eyes looking into mine demurely and making me feel anxious. Something about her manner felt as if she were probing for more than just my name, checking my credentials perhaps, or trying to figure out what kind of person I was.

"Belisarius, and your name?" I replied in my best Greek, toying with the idea of insulting her, but for some reason, not wanting to.

"Antonina," she replied. She stopped leaning on the bar and stood more upright. Her face was more rounded than Theodora's, and she had a very pleasant smile. She seemed rather more relaxed suddenly as if she'd gained all she needed to know just from the fact I was trying to be polite. "I am sorry, I thought you were just one of the normal heavies

Justinian brings in with him."

"I don't think so. I belong to the guard," I replied, realising I had said too much already. Then it occurred to me that she had probably guessed that. "I come from Dacia. I've been here in the capital for a few years. But I still have my accent."

"Well, I wouldn't have noticed." She smirked as she replied. There was something about her, even though she worked in a tavern. I was from a minor level of the bureaucracy and was considered to be of a higher station in society, but she had something that pulled me in from the very first time I met her.

"Who owns the tavern?" I asked, trying to think of something to keep the conversation going, although I knew it was probably a ridiculous question to ask, but it seemed to amuse her.

"We both do. Theodora and I set the place up. We had enough of working for others, and with a couple of wealthy patrons, we earned enough to buy the place."

I was impressed by the thought, and yet I was made uncomfortably aware of a sound from upstairs and the presence of other women. I dared to ask if those particular ladies were in their employ, but Antonina shook her head firmly with a stern expression. "No, they rent the spaces and what they earn, they keep. We make more than enough here, so we don't have to exploit the girls."

"That sounds unusual." I was sure it must have sounded a rather unkind thing to say, but Antonina seemed amused by it. She could tell my statement was made not necessarily because I thought it was abnormal, but rather if it were the norm for the city life, and she gave a soft and sweet chortle before giving a sudden sad little sigh.

"Well, we both know what it is like, and we can afford to be kinder."

I had to admit, I felt sorry for her, but I had no understanding of that kind of lifestyle, anyway. Just using such services was not really something I'd put much thought to. I'd always found myself far more preoccupied with training and begging to be trained, ever to give much thought to such matters. All the same, Antonina was very different from any woman I'd met before, and it was probably due to her straightforward manner, not to mention the fact she did not seem to feel it necessary to make up stories or tease my lack of knowledge as she spoke with me.

We chatted for the rest of the evening. Nothing of any more consequence was said between us, though I managed to keep chatting that night, hoping not only for the distraction until my master returned but also to keep her attention. Finally, Justinian came back with a smug expression that looked rather more like he was putting it on for the sake of pride than his true feelings. I stood up to meet him, and we said our goodbyes, but as we walked back, he said only one thing to me.

"So, you have been smitten by Antonina?"

I just went bright red and failed to reply. He didn't push for an answer. So, I too, met my future wife in a tavern, as poorly matched as it sounded. We returned there nightly, and Antonina entertained me with good wine, food, and conversation. During the many evenings we spent together, I learnt that she had three children already, two girls and a young son. I didn't enquire about the father or fathers. If she didn't want to tell me that was her business, I had fallen in love with her, and she knew it. I now looked forward to our evening trips. Justinian and I had a common secret, and that, more than anything else, formed a tight bond between us.

Since I was thought to be of a lower station, neither Justinian nor his uncle raised any objections when I asked for permission to marry Antonina. With my accumulated pay, I had ended up buying into the tavern business. The profit allowed us to extend to the tavern next door, and we converted part of the upstairs into flats for us to live in. We were married by a friendly priest, who raised no objections to Antonina's past life or fatherless children. Sadly, Justinian could not attend as Theodora would be present at a semi-public event, and it would be improper for them to be seen together. But now that I had quarters outside of Justinian's, which happened to be where Theodora lived, there was no longer any need for secrecy regarding our visits to the tavern. As far as anyone was concerned, he was coming to my tavern for the evening, and then I would escort him home.

This arrangement worked well until Justin became emperor. With this sudden elevation, Justinian was banned from seeing Theodora, let alone contemplating marriage with her. He was now the heir apparent, the Nobilissimus and only other royalty or senior senatorial daughters could be considered worthy of his attentions. Justinian's marriage to Theodora would have to wait till after he was emperor, and he could change the law of Constantine on societal weddings and permit it to take place. But even if it were the way of things, Justinian held a stubborn streak, and he seemed to truly love Theodora regardless of her status.

Did his uncle's ban stop him from visiting Theodora? Hardly! We just went back to subterfuge, and instead of visiting at night, I escorted him there during the day. As far as his uncle was concerned, he stopped off for lunch or late breakfast after a long ride in the countryside. I, in the meantime, settled down to a soldier's version of family life. Occasionally, I was sent to the East with a squadron of guards during times of tension with Persia. Apart from one minor raid, I saw little action. I was always back in the autumn once the campaign season was over and glad of it, as I would be back in the capital with my family.

It had been a long day at the palace waiting for Justinian the Nobilissimus to finish his work with his uncle the Basileus, when I was given the news that we had, in fact, been expecting and in little doubt over. I sat in an anteroom while the advisors moved in and out of the office. I was lucky to sit here. The rest of the detachment waited in the main entrance, which in winter was cold and in summer hot, till the later afternoon breeze entered the area and cooled it. Their spears and shields were stacked against the wall, while in the winter, they hung around braziers and in the summer, in the shadows. They were given water and food at noon; the rest of the day was spent rolling dice as they could not leave their post. I, on the other hand, could sit and read.

I had befriended one of the clerks in the Imperial office, and he regularly retrieved books for me from the Imperial library to study while I waited. He also helped if I got stuck on an obscure use of Roman, and most of all with Greek, I never really mastered reading it. The Nobilissimus often questioned me on my reading, and later, he assigned a reading list for me, and the clerk was instructed to ensure that I worked through the list. I gained quite a bit of knowledge reading the *Gallic Wars*, but I enjoyed the studies on the Punic Wars and Alexander's campaigns. In those days, they had huge armies and what appeared to be limitless resources to call upon. Generals, such as Scipio, even paid for their own armies which were larger than all our forces. They seemed to have an enormous amount of manpower to call upon. Even after the disaster of Cannae, Rome was still able to rebuild a replacement army within two years and continue a campaign in Hispania. Their enemies also had large resources and field armies of similar sizes. We could not match that, and even our enemies could not, which was fortunate. We all had a limited amount of manpower — continuous warfare and disease had drained us all.

This evening was different. Justinian came out of the office alone as the Basileus had already retired to his Imperial rooms. Now, I was expected to escort Justinian to his own section of the palace, but there seemed something odd in his expression as he approached. This time he had a smile on his face as he reached me. I bowed at his approach. He spoke softly but with real joy in his voice as he stood beside me.

"I thought I would tell you now rather than you learn tomorrow after the Senate meets, the Basileus has decided that the time is right and seven is a lucky number. So, as tomorrow marks the beginning of his seventh year, he decided that the Senate should announce my promotion officially to the rank of Caesar and become his official heir."

It had been expected news but was still exciting, and, of course, I had to perform the correct response at this knowledge. I bowed once again, picked up a piece of the hem of his cloak and kissed it.

"Hail, Caesar."

I stood up with my spear by my side and shield with the Chi-Rho Cross embossed on it, positioned across my left arm and chest, and presented a military salute bringing my spear aloft and shield raised to my forehead before returning them to the carry position. He smiled and continued out of the anteroom with me in tow, an expression of delight visible within his eyes. Inside the palace, I followed behind, as did the guards, but once outside, he moved into the centre of us. Now, as I led, the guards formed a box around him at a comfortable distance, but enough to stop an assassin from reaching him. When we reached his section of the palace, he halted abruptly, turned around, and signalled that we head for one of the smaller gates leading out of the palace. We automatically tightened the box formation.

"Where to, Caesar?" I called out to him firmly as we awaited his orders, but he seemed almost coy about answering at first. Then he replied, his voice still as cheerful as when he had first spoken to me.

"Take me to The Spinning Wool tavern."

That evening, sitting in the tavern close to the Hippodrome, following a jug full of local wine, the Caesar Justinian unexpectedly began to explain to me how his uncle Justin, had gained the throne. I had heard many stories from my fellow soldiers in the sentinels, and they all praised Justin, because he was "one of us," who'd gone on to rule the Empire. The young Caesar wasn't drunk, but for whatever reason, he needed to talk about his uncle and his place in the ruling of the Empire. I think now, in retrospect, that he felt the end was near for his uncle, and soon he would be ruling, and he was seeking allies for when he sat on the throne, and I was one of those chosen.

"Well, Belisarius, we are both from the West and speak Roman, unlike most of them here. We come from the land and know what work is like, and we follow the correct line of belief, the Chalcedon view on Christ, not the Alexandrian view, you understand what I mean?" he stated calmly and firmly before pausing, almost as if the statement was more to probe my belief than actually to tell me the story. I murmured agreement, not really understanding the difference at that time in the views of the so-called nature of Christ.

Later, I learnt that it was a difference over the understanding of a line of scripture from John, "the logos became flesh." Was Christ's nature split between the human nature of his flesh or the divine, logos, or was it one united nature? Even now to me, at my time in life, it seems like splitting a hair and then trying to split it again; after all, was Christ not the Son of God who came to redeem us, who died and rose at Easter? The hair was still hair, no matter how many times you split it in half.

But as I was from the West, we were followers of the Chalcedon vision, which, as the Caesar explained, was two natures in one and the correct view, while the late Emperor Anastasius had favoured the Alexandrian view of unity. It had been termed the Alexandrian view as one of its main centres was that of Egypt, and there the bishops fully supported this view; it was widespread in the East. While the West was Chalcedon, and that included Rome, but not being a scholar, I found the arguments confusing and miscellaneous. It caused major divisions within the Empire in the East and caused serious problems for us when, later on,

Justinian decided that all the Empire would only accept the Chalcedon view; even though the late Augusta had been a follower of Alexandrian unity.

I also tended to keep quiet when it came to talking about working hard on the land. Being of real working stock, as Justinian and his uncle had been, he was quite proud of not being from wealth or nobility, unlike myself, who had hidden my family connections to the lower rank of the nobility and so had never worked on the land or seen parents go hungry in the winter to allow their children to eat. Was I lying to him? No, because I never actually said my parents had worked on the land. He had assumed this, as I was from the countryside and had not gone into the sentinels as a junior officer, which was the normal route for anyone of the rank of the nobility.

Only the poor started at the bottom, but he had been surprised to discover that I could read and write and had an education. I explained, honestly, that my parents had paid for this. Again, Justinian stated only the poor knew the real value of education, which in his case was a bit rich as his uncle had summoned him and other nephews to the capital and once here Justinian had been raised to the rank of count of the sentinels gaining a 'really good' income. With this, he had paid for his nephews' education with the best scholars available in the capital. The current Caesar had outshone them in his abilities, and Justin had chosen him to be his successor. From what I later learnt, the best emperors of old had always adopted their heir. It had begun with Augustus, back when the Empire was first founded, and adoption of Caesars was seen to be the best way. Emperors, such as the Great Constantine, who had sons and not adopted heirs, had caused division and civil wars as the sons argued over the succession. Although the Caesar was blood-related, he was not a son who would have had the right to inherit the Empire directly. Instead, Justin had chosen who he thought could do the best job.

But back to my story, the Caesar continued his friendly talk, which was moving from talk to more of a lecture.

"The Basileus, had been clever and with success in the wars fought by the Emperor Anastasius, he had gained recognition as an effective military commander; honest and trustworthy. He even assisted in the defeat of Vitalian, the master of soldiers of Thrace who had forced

Anastasius to reject the Alexandrian doctrine and move towards the Chalcedon view. After Vitalian rebelled again and marched on the capital, he proved his loyalty, and he fought for the emperor who preferred another creed against a man who followed the same creed as he did. Defeating Vitalian once again, my uncle put loyalty over faith. He was his own man. And against protocol, he had secretly married my aunt, the Augusta Euphemia, before he gained the throne. You know her real name was Lupicina, and she was a slave, and like us was of peasant stock — he had brought her freedom. With his rank of count, the law forbade his marriage to that of a lesser. We call ourselves Christian, yet we have laws like this."

Again, I nodded. I had heard rumours muttered very quietly that the Augusta had once been a slave of the Basileus and in some quarters it was still considered a grave matter that they were both peasants and could hardly read or write, and yet they were our leaders. Having met some of the elite in the company of the Caesar, I can admit to preferring the company of soldiers and peasants. These elite were the very same group who sat around all day complaining about the state of the Empire and saying in the old days, things had been better. Yet, they were the very ones who sat there and did nothing except gossip when the barbarians surrounded us, complaining of how the army of old would never have let this happen. All the while sending their gold and silver out of the capital to a safe location or making preparations for fleeing.

"Anyway, Anastasius had no sons, but three nephews who he hadn't adopted, so no heirs when God called him back to his presence. So, a crisis developed in the capital as to who was to be the next Basileus. My uncle and I had been secretly working on this problem for a year. We knew the sentinels were behind us, as well as the exiled Vitalian, and that would mean the army in Thrace was loyal to us. The Central Army was already with us, as their commander saw the need for a strong and stable leader from the West once again. So, once the death had been announced, we all headed to the Hippodrome to watch who would take their seat in the Imperial box and be proclaimed Basileus by the city, Senate, and most importantly, by the army."

He was silent for a moment to hold the suspense or to wet his drying throat as he then had another large sip of wine. I had a question and saw the moment to ask was now, although I was not quite sure if it were the right kind of question that Justinian would expect of me or if I were to come across as a simpleton.

"But surely there were others after the throne and had been preparing for this day?"

"Good, Belisarius, that's what I like about you. You think around the problem. Yes, the High Chamberlain Amantius had planned to place a puppet by the name of Theocritus on the throne and run everything from behind the scenes. But he was an idiot, as his superior birth right had made him over ambitious and disdainful of those of lower birth, such as my uncle. So, he paid my uncle a large amount of gold to bribe the loyalty of the guards and the commanders of the army. All the officials assembled in the palace in the third entrance hall, and a heated discussion began on who was to be Basileus. Amantius was feeling smug, according to Celer, the master of the offices, who was already with us, and Celer demanded that they recommend a name. At this point, Amantius announced his candidate and looked to my uncle to give his nod of approval. The rest of the officials, including the patriarch, looked aghast at the suggestion. My uncle ignored him and instead offered a friend of his, a fellow officer, John, as his nomination. This was just a ruse to find out if there were any other candidates."

The Caesar went quiet again, pausing, looking around the empty tavern as if suspicious of keen ears, but there was nobody. Then he gave me one of his huge grins before he returned to the tale, clearly proud of his uncle's cunning.

"My Uncle sent a messenger outside to the guard units in the Hippodrome to begin proclaiming John as their candidate. This caused the Blue faction of the mob to shout and throw objects at John and the guardsmen."

He paused again, looking around to see if either Theodora or Antonina were within hearing distance of us. Since both were occupied dealing with clearing up the tavern, he continued, "We knew the Blues weren't in favour of us, as we had supported the Greens, and the late emperor had been a keen supporter of Blue teams in the Hippodrome. It just confirmed who our enemies might be in the future. They were caught completely off guard during the election, as no one had bothered to bribe them, as my uncle was meant to have done! We had already bribed the Greens to support no other candidate but my uncle. So, they shouted down John. Now the guards, with prompting, began to proclaim me as their choice. I, of course, loudly and publicly refuted their offer. And the Greens, of course, booed me loudly. Each time the guards had banged on the doors of the Ivory Gate demanding the Imperial regalia, and they were, of course, refused. We had bribed the palace officials to refuse any choice from the Hippodrome. This left the Senate with little choice, as key members were already with us. So, they demurred at the choices given. Even I was ruled out as being too young and inexperienced, which, of course, pointed to one candidate, my uncle, who was elected by the Senate. The patriarch agreed as he favoured the Chalcedon doctrine, and we already had the army."

With the conspiracy section discussed at last, he returned his voice to his normal level and finished the tale. I was not sure I was impressed by it, or even if I quite understood everything, he had told me, but I accepted that he seemed to think it was something I had to understand. With his new position, he needed to know he could trust people and, in a way, perhaps, it was just another confidence exercise.

"So, the chamberlain and his officials clad my uncle in the Imperial regalia and led him to the Imperial box. The curtain was drawn back, and out stepped my uncle. The guards, the Greens, and most of the crowd, apart from the dyed-in-the-wool Blues, cheered for the new Basileus, as he took the oath and announced a celebration and a bonus to all soldiers. This was partially paid with the bribe money, so saved the treasury excessive expense. The next step was to have his marriage confirmed by the Senate and patriarch. They issued a dispensation — what else could they do?"

He was pausing again to have a drink. With the cup now empty, he waved it above his head as a sign for more wine. Antonina wandered over with a fresh jug, and a secret smile for me, and placed the jug on the table, and quietly withdrew.

"My Uncle was sixty-six years old and we both knew that he would not have enough time to begin our great work. So, the next day he had the Senate proclaim me overall commander of the army, a senator and count of the domestics. In this way, we held all the major levers of government and the remaining offices were controlled by our allies. As for Amantius and Theocritus, they paid the price for lack of planning. Gangs of Greens chased after them till they sort sanctuary in the Church of the Holy Wisdom. We then offered them exile or Holy Orders, and that was the last of them, a rather bloodless change of government."

"So, what happened to Vitalian?" I asked as I hadn't realised, he had been part of the plan, and his murder had been rumoured to be at the hands of my master, the Caesar.

"Oh, he returned to the capital and was made commander of the central field army, and in the third year of my uncle's reign, he was made consul. Marinus was made the Praetorian prefect that year as well. In those first three years, we achieved the impossible. We brought unity to the Church of Christ, for the first time in ages, with the doctrine of Chalcedon, which the West of the Old Empire had always preserved, and we refuted the Alexandrian doctrine. Now, all we had to do was free our people from the deviation of those such as the Goths."

"What is it the Goths follow? I understood they were not like us, followers of Christ," I enquired. My understanding of what the Goths believed was almost zero, which seemed to be the general thought of the populace. All I knew was that they weren't like us, that and being barbarians and basically pagans as everyone else understood.

"Good question and one that deserves a good but difficult and perhaps confusing answer. They follow a deviation or heresy of Christ's teaching. One first formulated by Arius and dealt with at the Nicene Council. One could easily say that the Alexandrians follow a deviation of the understanding of the true nature of Christ, but that is curable. The Goths aren't pagan, though it would be better if they were, as ignorance in belief is better than pure falsely held belief — we could baptise them and bring them into the Church, but they need to be removed as their false belief can easily poison a true believer. Even now, they try to force true believers into following their ways. As I said, we can forgive those who walk in the dark, as they can be shown the light. But those who walk in the false light and force others to follow them have no right to exist. They deny the Trinity and say that our saviour, Jesus Christ, was the firstborn and not equal to the Father or the Holy Spirit as if he was a more Super Angel, neither wholly man nor God. That is the problem. It denies the true nature of Christ, and so the emperor made it an offence to teach this heresy. So, any followers of it are criminals and should be dealt with by the maximum the law allows".

"I am still a little confused. A Super Angel — what does that mean?" I said.

"You see how dangerous it is. I already made a mistake; Super Angel is another esoteric heresy. We believe that Christ is the son of God, unique and equal to the Father. Anything else is wrong. That is why the creed is read out, and we acknowledge its correctness. Does that make it clearer?" Justinian grunted, rolling his eyes as if he'd hadn't made such a mistake before or that it might be the drink talking. However, though, he did not explain what it was to me, I was already itching at my chin in concern at these thoughts and even grimacing over them.

"Yes, I see how easy these heresies are at deceiving one." I thought that was a good enough response to aid his pride as he grumbled and then rubbed at his eyes gently. I could tell he was getting tired, although I knew if Theodora walked past right now, he'd probably perk up, but he gave a shake of his head and then a soft grunt.

"Good, I have had enough for the night. Escort me back to the palace."

We left the tavern; all this intellectual, religious thought had put him off staying overnight with Theodora. I imagined his conscience was pricking him concerning his relationship with the tavern owner. I never did find out why Vitalian had been murdered and by whom, or if the Basileus had been the hand or the one giving the orders. One thing I was sure of, was never to ask him a question on belief as it left me more confused than ever. I just followed orders on those matters. It was much easier than to try and understand the differences or false doctrines.

With the Persians who hated us Christians, it was easy to see the difference. First, they did not believe in Christ, and that made the difference quite clear. Instead, they believed in two gods, the god of light and day, while the other god was of the night and evil. So, our practice of burial was seen by them as a terrible sin as we were giving our dead to the evil one. They instead left their dead in the light to be eaten by the animals. They also worshipped a fire inside their temples, I never saw one, but I knew they were our deadliest enemy. Not only did they want to take our Empire for themselves, but they also wanted to force on us their beliefs. One of their main targets was our churches and monasteries. The Armenians, Georgians and Lazi all followed Christ and were always fighting the Persians to preserve their faith and ours. One of the main causes of conflict in recent times had been Persian persecutions of Christians inside and outside of their Empire; in defiance of treaties, we had made with the Persians. Armenia was split between both Empires for much of the time, and most of our records showed our conflicts with the Persians had been over control of this vital region as it allowed access from Persia into the heart of the Eastern Empire. That kind of difference in religion I could understand, but anything else just seemed too difficult.

Chapter Two

"We, the army of Mesopotamia swear loyalty to our new Basileus, Justinian, by the grace of God, emperor of his chosen people," exclaimed the massed ranks before me.

"The emperor has rewarded you because of his succession, with five golden solidus coins and a day of celebration." I paused, my throat dry from shouting, and in response, the army gave a great cheer. I dismissed them, and within a short time, the place was heaving with drunken bodies as they did their utmost to convert the donation into wine. I was always amazed at how quick the locals appeared to supply the needs of the newly enriched soldiers and quickly provide the means for them to spend it even faster. The party atmosphere continued well into the night.

The next morning, we all returned to duty, and the heat soon made me regret the excess of wine I had enjoyed with my fellow officers. I took a stroll down to the riverbank, to enjoy the coolness of the shade offered by the trees lining the riverside, as well as the peace away from the hustle and bustle of the construction camp. I sat on a fallen beam. I remember watching a wading bird, fishing in the shallows; nature continued no matter what we did around it.

Suddenly, my silence was disturbed by a figure running in my direction. In his right hand, he clutched a Persian sword, which seemed odd as we used the traditional cavalry sword. Then I realized he was wearing a different set of uniform from my men wore. By the time I had grabbed my sword, the Persian had closed the distance between us. I hadn't time to curse my stupor or my failure to comprehend that it was the enemy charging me. His sword raised as we came together, I had just enough time to swing my blade upwards and catch his downward thrust and avoid a deadly blow to my head. I felt the force of his blow as our swords clashed and his blade's tip flashed past my face, as our swords lost contact. His move had left him off balance, with his sword below his chest line, as he moved to regain control of himself, he thrust his sword forward.

I stepped back with my left leg so that he moved beside me, I slipped in behind him, as I continued to spin on my foot. I raised my sword to hip level and thrust forward with its point entering his back just below the ribcage. His sudden scream of pain jarred me. I quickly withdrew the blade, his blood sprayed out and washed my hand and arm. He stopped moving forward as his legs collapsed under him and he dropped to his knees, then fell sideways. His mouth frothed blood as he turned to stare at me vacantly. I finished him off with a blow to a point below the neck; his body went limp. Fully alert now, I swung around, my sword in the ready position. The sound of branches being broken and heavy footsteps caused me to swing in that direction, and I crouched, ready to spring at whatever emerged from the low trees and scrub.

"Belisarius, where are you?" The call came from the bushes, and I recognised the voice as belonging to John, one of my men, and replied in a relieved voice. I was very pleased to hear a familiar voice after such an attack, and then I heard more noise.

"I am down by the river, in front of you." I could hear men speaking in a mixture of Roman and Goth, which assured me that they were my men, accompanied by the sound of undergrowth being shoved violently out of their path. Within a moment, John and several soldiers were by my side, checking the area for more enemy and already looking rather puffed out. John knelt over the corpse beside me and inspected it with the tip of his sword, just in case my blows had not done the job.

"We killed three already but lost the fourth, though I think you accounted for him," John grunted as he finished probing the corpse and straightened himself up. He looked towards me, expecting a reaction, and I had to admit hearing that irritated me greatly.

"How the hell did they slip through our lookouts on the other bank?" I turned and barked at him; John was akin to my second-in-command and generally the one who knew what was happening. But as always, I had to sound stern and under control, which was always difficult when I was feeling rattled, but John was as straightforward and calm as he always was.

"They killed the men at outpost one before they crossed last night and laid up, hoping probably to kill you, if they got the chance."

It was not meant callously, but my position in the group and my growing reputation was starting to make me a prime target for our enemies. But then anyone in our uniform was a target at outpost locations.

"How did you find that out? I thought you said they were all dead."

All the same, there was sometimes a sort of matter-of-fact manner in which John delivered any information to me. In fact, he was smiling as he practically strolled over to me.

"Before one died, we had time to interrogate him. We also learnt that they were not on their own. There should have been two more groups attacking us." He paused again, kneeling as he pointed with his sword to the insignia around the would-be assassin's neck. He stretched out to snatch the item from the corpse and check it over in his hand, with a growl. Then he stood up and turned towards me, the insignia dangling from his left hand. "His weaponry and insignia are worn only by the Immortals, the king's or more correctly the Shah's personal guards."

"Right, take twenty men across the river and collect up all the observation posts. I think we can gather from what has happened that the Persians know we are here and what we are doing. I have no doubt that these men came from a much larger force close by."

We returned to the camp, John crossed the river with his group, and while he was undertaking his mission, I called together all the officers. We sat and discussed how the situation had altered and our next move. I decided we would continue with the construction of our fortress. In the meantime, the perimeter of our camp would need to be patrolled continually until we had dug a defensive ditch and erected a palisade.

In the evening, John returned with his men and eight survivors. He reported to me that all three outposts had been attacked during the night, two had managed to hold, thus accounting for the missing Persians. The dead at the captured post had been cut up badly. Locals had found John and reported to him that a large Persian army was close by. John had followed up the reports and found the Persians, avoiding their scouts, and had watched long enough to estimate that it was Xerces judging by the banners being displayed, the Persian King's most favoured son, leading a force of something over twenty thousand men, considering the dust clouds the columns had kicked up as they marched in our direction. He

47

anticipated we had maybe four days before their army reached our location.

With this information, I wrote several urgent dispatches, one to Libelarius, general of the East in Antioch, informing him of the change in the situation here and the probability of a decisive battle shortly. This would give him time to build up his forces and march to intercept the Persian army, either here if I was successful or closer to him if I was not. The second letter was to my wife, Antonina, in Dara, requesting that she ensure the garrison stayed put and did not surrender the city at any cost. The last letter was to the Basileus informing him of what had occurred and that I expected to hold the site for as long as possible and so delay the Persian advance. If we couldn't, I hoped we would be able to withdraw to Dara and await relief from Antioch. I assigned John the task of ensuring that the dispatches were escorted as far as Dara and from there, the Imperial post would do the rest.

Libelarius would reach us within two months with a relief army if we managed to hold on here or at Dara. If not, he would try and intercept the Persian army before they crossed the Euphrates, as by then the Persian line of advance would be obvious. With that done, I summoned my officers once again for a council of war. I explained what I had just done and what I intended to do. All non-combatants were to leave, as well as our sick and baggage train under a light escort and head for Dara. I then divided up my forces as follows — the rest of the cavalry would remain with me close to the river, half of them would dismount and take up positions on either side of the road thereby blocking the ford. The remainder would tackle any units that tried to force the ford and the infantry I dispersed along our line of retreat towards Dara. They would hold positions along the road and prepare bridges for demolition after we had retreated over them. They would set fire to the bridges, once the arches had been packed with wood, straw, grass, reeds, literally anything that would burn and so weaken the structure and cause it to collapse.

I didn't know how long we could withstand the forthcoming onslaught; it all depended on how quickly the Persians deployed their forces against us. The terrain was on our side and funnelled them into us and protected us from being outflanked. We prepared our positions and waited for them to come.

The light was just beginning to spread its warmth across the horizon, the rising sun lit up the dawn clouds of mist from behind, and as its first rays ran across the plain before us, it glinted off the armour of the advancing Persian cavalry. The first Persian troops entered the water of the river and slowly made their way towards us. The last mists of dawn still draped both banks and the Persian cavalry appeared and disappeared as if they were ghosts as it wrapped itself around them like a death shawl. Mounted on my horse, I watched the graceful advance, every move I made rippled through the chain mail of my armour with a clinking noise — it was a comforting noise as it gave me a sense of protection. With luck, it would stop all sword blows, and most arrows would be deflected. My mount sensed my mood and became anxious under the strain of the combined weight of its frontal armour and myself. I turned to my left. The standard-bearer was close by me with the dragon lying limp atop of the standard, with its long tail waiting to unfurl in the heat of the charge. On my right was the trumpeter — he awaited my signal to blast out the order to seek battle. His eyes were settled on mine and awaited my hand signal, so he could sound the advance and launch us forward. The dismounted archers concealed on the bank, awaited his call as well — two blasts and we would charge, three and we would pull back and one long blast for the archers to rip into the Persians.

The Persians continued across the water. I waited till I could see the end of the formation as it entered the river. The front of the formation was now about to leave the water on our side and had picked up speed in anticipation. I raised and dropped my left arm, my shield dangling as my arm moved. One long blast erupted from the trumpeter, and the lead element of the Persians dropped onto the sandy beach of death. Overhead, a wave of swishing black death flew into the Persian formation, the centre of the of which was trapped, unable to move forward and unable to turn and retreat. The end of the column had entered the water and were themselves confused as to what to do. Our fire gradually raked the almost still formation as horses panicked Trapping already fallen riders as more fell into the water, weighed down by their chain mail suits.

A second column charged into the water, and this time they were prepared for us. They headed at high speed for our side of the bank, oblivious to our fire and the fate of their fallen comrades. As they crossed, they let rip with their arrows, volley after volley, reducing our rate of fire. They reached our side with fewer casualties and still at some speed. Now I waved my shield above my head, and the trumpeter sounded two blasts. We all surged forward, first at a gentle trot to ensure we all kept as one mass and to give the Persians time to emerge out of the water. When our charge hit them, they would be in the correct position, and our archers would strike from their flanks.

The Persians mounted the bank. They looked magnificent — their mounts covered in scale armour, the riders in suits of chain mail glittering in the early light. They wore brightly coloured caps upon their heads. Armed with either lances or maces, as they had dumped their bows on sighting us approaching. We charged into them. The noise was deafening as horses crashed into horses, metal tore into metal and lances pierced skin and broke bones. We quickly became entangled — at this distance, bows were useless — instead, it was swords, axes and maces. I protected my chest with my shield and with my right arm, I slashed away at anything to my front with my axe. With the mail hood still covering my head, the heat was terrific. Sweat quickly formed and flowed down my face, stinging my eyes, clouding my vision in brief flushes. We were lucky there was no wind to blow the dust as it would have stuck to our faces and eyes leaving us blind.

After what felt like hours, my arm ached and demanded to be rested, but I continued. If I had rested, it would be the end of me. I don't know how long the first clash lasted or how many Persians I hit, when quite suddenly they were gone from in front of us. I reattached my axe to my hand, wiped the sweat away with my free hand brought my mount to a halt and looked around. Riderless horses, still covered in armour, ran aimlessly around into and out of the river, over many, many bodies of motionless metal rocks. Other horses kicked aimlessly into the air as they desperately sought to stand again. Under them were many riders who screamed with pain as each time the horses moved, they were crushed a little more. All around, were the sounds of men screaming mixed with horses, in comparable agony, but the battle had ended.

Looking at the far bank, I could see Persian stragglers putting as much distance between themselves and the river as possible. I looked behind me to check my own damage and was saddened; I had lost over half of my force. An eerie calm settled around us all the same as the dismounted archers moved around the dead and finished off the dying and assisted our wounded. Others did their best to catch any loose horses and tie them up with ours, knowing that the mounts would be of use to replace what we had lost. We had only a brief lull, but it was long enough to drink water and for the archers to fill their quills. Then a shout announced the next wave of Persians was approaching.

This clash echoed the first one, our archers slowing them down as they attempted to storm the riverbank. They quickly saw our archers, and they became their prime target, and this time we took losses. We were too close to the riverbank to charge them. Instead, we drew our bows and let loose as they charged out of the water towards us. They hit us hard. It was our turn to take the heavy blow as they charged into us, and again it was hand-to-hand fighting. This time, we began to give ground, pushed back by the pure weight of the Persian formation. I gave my trumpeter the signal to withdraw. We had to stand firm a little longer while the archers mounted and retreated to the first line of infantry.

Suddenly, I felt a pain on my left side. It seemed to hit me so suddenly and profoundly that I almost fell out of the saddle. I looked to my left and saw a Persian close beside me, his mace ready to strike again. I raised my left arm, but the shield or what remained of it dangled from my arm. I couldn't see the face of my opponent, only slits where his eyes were, his face covered in an armoured mask — he was one of the so-called 'bread oven' Persian heavy cavalry. He misjudged his second blow, and it brushed down my left arm as it punched the air next to me, causing him to lean further over. I had one chance and lifted my axe over my head, exposing my left side. I caught the Persian on the back of the neck as he had continued to move downwards, caught by his mace's momentum. I was lucky, thank God, and his neck broke under my blow. He crashed to the ground, dead, his mount standing still, shocked at the sudden lightness on its back.

An unknown arm grabbed my left and pulled my attention away from the dead Persian. To my relief, it was one of my own men, though I was prepared to attack with whatever swings my aching arms could make. Thankfully, it was not needed. My trumpeter gestured to me it was time to move back, I then realised my left arm was completely numb, and I was unable to lift it and reach the reins. He saw this and moved forward and grabbed my reins, turned my mount along with his, and we pulled back. The light about me changed. It darkened till only two tunnels of light were left.

I came to, lying on my back with the infantry officers surrounding me, all looking very tired and dirty. Once I had regained my thoughts, I learnt that as I had called the retreat, the Persians had also begun to regroup. It had given us a breathing space, allowing us a chance to pull out safely. Several of my men had escorted me back to the first blockade. They had taken me down from my mount and protected me, till what remained of the cavalry had regrouped with us and the infantry.

The light was fading fast, and the Persians had not attempted another crossing since our last encounter. Once a count was made, I found I had once more lost just over half of my remaining force. What was left was exhausted and we were low on ammunition, food, and water, not only for the men but the horses. We camped in the dark that night waiting for the dawn, then dressed back in our armour ready for the next onslaught; but it never came. We waited till noon, scouts went out and returned without sight of the enemy on our side of the river or within sight of the east bank. I called together what was left of my officers and decided that we would withdraw back to Dara, collecting up the infantry as we went. The wounded were gathered and put onto mounts and sent on, the rest of us removed our mail coats and used the remaining mounts to carry them. With bows in hand, we marched with the infantry back to Dara. We never saw the Persians again. By the time we reached Dara, my arm was still numb and limp. A surgeon kindly twisted it around till it popped back into my shoulder — a pleasant experience if it wasn't so painful.

There was not much time to discuss the question of what might have happened. I was too exhausted and knew I needed to rest. I ordered John to take command of all the forces in Dara. I was then ordered to bed by Antonina as I had a headache that caused my vision to blur again. I spent several days in bed, and she remained faithfully by my bedside till I was ready to resume command. I had a black eye and grazes running down the left side of my face; I had been even more injured than I had initially thought.

I had only delayed the Persian force by a day or two at most. They continued their advance into Syria; Libelarius, alerted to the advance, could move forces to intercept them on the plains close to the Euphrates. To support this deployment, he moved part of his reserve from Phoenicia, using Diocletian's great military road to block any possible Persian drive towards the old trading city of Palmyra, under the command of Bouzes. The two forces clashed close to the city of Callinicum, our forces were defeated and the commander, Coutzes, was killed in the battle. The Persians also suffered heavy losses but were still able to retire in good order. The reserve forces in Palmyra stayed put, awaiting orders from Libelarius, who was paralysed by the loss of Coutzes and gave no orders. So, therefore, we were unable to follow up and hound the Persian withdrawal. Before re-crossing the river, at the site of our battle, they destroyed all traces of our construction of a new fortress.

The relieving force arrived in the East just as winter broke over the region and took up residence in Antioch. The Basileus appointed Pompeius as the commander of this force under Libelarius, who remained general of the East. I had never met him, but I understood that he was a nephew of the late Emperor Anastasius. Rumour suggested that blood was his only qualification for the post, and his later actions only encouraged this view.

The winter was one of the harshest I ever experienced in the East. We had deep snow, which made movement in and out of Dara almost impossible. It had its compensation as Antonina was with me and the base required very little of my time. We made up for lost time and enjoyed the cold winter evenings together.

Spring came late. When it did, the rivers in the region burst their banks, and wide-scale flooding ensured loss of life and livelihood, many crops that should have been planted couldn't be. I did my best to relieve the situation. I relied on the local population for my supplies, and the last Persian raid had resulted in a loss of part of the harvest. We could have a famine later that year, so I granted a stay on the collection of taxes for the region. I requested extra supplies be brought in from Antioch, as well as cashing in part of my bounty to ensure my men were paid. Antioch coughed up the necessary supplies; they'd had a bountiful harvest and had not been plundered. Once this arrived, I confirmed the cancellation of the tax for this year.

At Easter, another Persian army crossed into our province. My scouts reported a mixed force of Persians and Arabs crossing the river at the same place as our battle of the previous year. I dispatched letters to Antioch and the capital requesting support; if I had ever doubted the importance of a fort at that location, these two years proved the need for it. I sealed up the city, after bringing in the villagers with supplies, and waited for the Persians to arrive.

By some luck, the Persian force bypassed us and headed towards Syria, evading all resistance and plundering as they advanced to Antioch. They scorched the area around Antioch while our brave general of the East sat comfortably behind the long walls of the city. Once the Persians had burnt enough and were weighed down with plunder, they began the march back to the frontier. Only then did our brave commander advance with the field army and followed limply, at a comfortable distance, all the way to the frontier. Then, he camped there for a month before returning to Antioch without any real confrontation.

In August of that dreadful summer, Antonina received a personal message from Empress Theodora. She came and found me enjoying watching the birds, fishing in the river; once fed, they settled on the thick reedbeds scattered along the river's edge. I had a good view of this from the Eastern Gate tower. She rushed up to me, her flowing robes of cotton and silk dancing as a light breeze washed over the walls, catching the material, the whites, blues and greens flashing as the cloth beneath rippled. Her hair, for a change, was not tightly done up, and she wasn't wearing a headscarf, it was hanging loose like a lion's mane. She grabbed hold of me and hugged me tightly for a moment. I looked at her beaming face and understood that she had some good news.

"What's all the fuss for, my darling?"

"Theodora has not forgotten you or me." She emphasised this with a broad smile as she practically sang out in delight, and I found myself dumbstruck. She kissed me on the lips. I returned the kiss, speculating what exactly had been done for us.

"It's wonderful what she has accomplished for us."

"Well, tell me?"

She stood back, took a deep breath and then seemed to nearly hop on the spot.

"You are the new general of the East, my darling." Her eyes looked as if she was going to cry with happiness. She continued, as the shock of the news had stunned me into silence. "The Basileus was furious with the lack of action from the army of the East, and he is sacking Libelarius. Theodora suggested you, he agreed, knowing he could trust you."

For a moment, I remained quiet, blinking slowly and trying to comprehend what she was saying, and indeed, the consequences of this decision. Once the shock had worn off, I looked around us to see that the guards had seen Antonina arrive and had discreetly moved away so we could talk. I felt rather giddy for a moment, relief washing over me as the news finally sank in.

"So, I am to be promoted to general of the East. Oh, well, you better start packing our things, ready to move to our new home in Antioch."

It seemed like a dream; I would now oversee all the military forces in the East. Now it would be me who could decide how to deal with the current Persian military threat. I thought of Timostratus and thanked him for what he had taught me during my time serving with him. This was my chance to prove how good a general I could be, and that his trust in me had been well-founded. I wanted revenge for the deaths, not only of my men last year but for all the defeats we had suffered at the hands of the Persians. I wanted most of all to deliver a resounding defeat on them that would force them to sue for peace on our terms, not on their conditions. The official orders arrived by dispatch a week later, and I called John into my office to discuss the changes with him. He entered my office, and by his cheerful manner, I knew that he might have got wind of what I was going to say, and it was always a relief to see him looking not only confident but even a little cheeky. I stopped reading the documents and looking up from my desk. I tried to remain straightforward and emotionless, precise and wise, but it was hard not to hide my own pleasure on the promotion.

"John, as I am the new general of the East, I can now afford to maintain a personal guard. Since the death of Timostratus, you have been unofficially in my service. How would you like to command my guard?" It sounded so foreign a thing to refer to myself in this rank, but there was a big grin on John's face, and I was a little cautious of it. There was a wicked little flicker in his eyes that made him give me a sudden sceptical look as he cleared his throat with a slight cough and then he lifted a finger.

"Yes, but on one condition."

"Name your condition."

I had not been expecting that, but with the trust I held in this man, the confidence he exuded that gave the men the same kind of reassurance it gave me, I was quite willing to part with more than I should to keep hold of him if it were the case. But, as always, John astounded me with his mindset on the work and his general demeanour that just filled the air with a calm, easy-going air whenever outside of battle, and I had to admit I could have laughed for his response.

"That I be allowed to pick the men under my command." John quickly brought the finger to tap at his chin. Clearly, he had already thought of this possible opportunity and was already trying to decide on the kind of men he needed. Watching that little motion of his finger irked a snort of amusement from me, glad I had not needed to do anything more in order to gain his approval.

"I agree, as long as you train them to be as good as you," I stated, still trying to look unsurprised by his remark, hoping I were giving him a look that said quite plainly that I had faith in him. He hadn't let me down, and I doubted he ever could.

John was as good as his word and had assembled a force of one hundred men by the time we moved to Antioch in the autumn. Antonina loved the city and went mad spending money on clothes, carpets and many other luxury goods. What wasn't needed for our accommodation, she had shipped back to the main house in the capital. We both had hoped to return to there for the winter and to be with our young daughter Johanna and Antonina's older children. We had also planned to bring them back out with us when we returned in the spring, but the new command changed that plan. They would travel, probably in the summer, to join us in Antioch. I needed to concentrate on the business of running an army before family.

My first problem was to replace our losses from the last two years. My staff prepared the papers so I could call a draft in the spring and, in the meantime, letters were sent out to all the main cities and towns in the

East asking for volunteers and recently retired soldiers to return to the ranks. A draft, would at best, bring in a quarter of the men we needed, and they would be of the poorest quality but who else could be spared? The rest would be recruited from our allies and tribes throughout the region, at quite a cost. Unfortunately, this would require a direct money grant from the Praetorian prefect's office, and I would also require assistance from the office of foreign affairs, as they would deal directly with the allied peoples and arrange the transfer of these men to me.

The normal bureaucratic method was to write to all the departments and await their reply, but then nothing would happen until the prefect's office had satisfied itself that there was a requirement for these men. Only then would it authorise the transfer of funds to the other departments. Finally, they would inform me of just how many men they would or could pay for, and my new staff explained that it could take up to two years before I received the men. The situation we were in required that I bypass the normal channels and ask the Basileus directly for the men. This would speed the whole process up, but, of course, it would alienate the civil service, and they would take revenge, no doubt, by delaying the annual grants of money to pay for the army. The Eastern army's pay was always delayed as it saved the exchequer money but caused widespread discontent, and that was dangerous for the security of the Empire. My personal finances had steadily grown and had quadrupled due to my recent promotion, but I could only pay the army for one month if it came to it. With that dealt with, I set my staff to planning a campaign for the spring again in Mesopotamia to relieve the pressure on this front.

The last Persian assault had opened us up like a sheep to slaughter. I was sure that the Persians would try again and may even attempt to sack Antioch. The economic damage this would cause in the region would bring chaos to the Empire's finances. The possibility that the route to Egypt would be open to them for the first time would be more than a dream for the Persians. The Sassanid dynasty saw themselves as the direct inheritors of Darius of old; they wished to regain his old Empire, and only we stood in their way.

Now was my chance to put into practice my strategy of a pro-active defence and keep the Persians on the defence instead of us. Unlike the

Persians, we did not want to expand and would settle for a continuance of the status quo regarding our frontiers. I wrote again directly to the Basileus outlining my intentions and plans for a spring campaign and, of course, the requirement for more men. I would have preferred to have seen him personally, but the needs of preparing the army required my presence in Antioch.

I spent the rest of the autumn touring the frontier fortresses so that the regional commanders knew their new commander and could express their views on the situation and make bids for men and equipment. The general opinion was in line with my strategy and some suggestions merited further study by my staff to see if they could be used. I completed my tour by visiting the Imperial armouries to check on production, quality and quantity. I also pressed them on the need to complete an earlier order so I could refit the army by spring. To meet these costs, each province was required to contribute about ten per cent more than normal, and I would keep the extra to pay for the army while the rest was sent back to the capital. This would hurt the East, but it was better than the Persians stripping the countryside and towns of anything that could be carried, including people. The harvest in Syria, Phoenicia and Palestine had been good this year, so the commutation would not be so severe on the landholders. Moreover, I allowed them to pay in cash rather than rations as gold and silver were easier and quicker to move. Plus, the local markets here had enough to supply the army's needs.

Close to the time of the winter solstice, I had an unexpected visitor who had made the arduous journey from the capital to my headquarters. Hermogenes, a tall thinly-built Greek, scholarly in manner, with a white beard and grey hair arrived. I knew of him and his reputation as an honest man, a word not normally associated with high officials, but he was different and well trusted by the Basileus. He was sent from the Praetorian prefect's office and had been assigned to assist me with civil and financial matters and with him came Rufinus.

Rufinus's family had come from Rome during the time of the Gothic conquest. He was of old Roman senatorial stock, a typical Roman heavily built with thick black hair and no beard. His oratory skills were excellent as well as his mastery of Roman, Greek and most importantly Persian. He personified my idea of a Roman. His mission was to attempt to negotiate a settlement with the Persians and save us the cost of a campaign. They also brought with them sealed orders from the Basileus, which informed me that a mixed force of allies and mercenaries had been raised and would be here in the spring. The pair were complete opposites in attitude and manner. Rufinus was loud and cheerful and good company in the evenings with tales of his ancestors dealing with past emperors. He made the long, dark nights fly by; Antonina, John and I never missed an evening when he was in full flow.

Hermogenes, though, was quiet and efficient during the day, completing all his tasks well ahead of expectations, in the evening, he enjoyed a good drink and was entertaining in a more refined manner. He would suddenly become all philosophic and explain Socrates' ideas or Plato's ideal society. During those winter evenings, I learned a good deal about how others saw themselves and understood the world we occupied.

In late winter, my new secretary arrived. He had originally been hired while I was at Dara, but he had been unable to take up his post till now. He was keen as he had travelled north along the coast during the winter. He entered my office after his arrival and presented himself — a confident man of similar age to me, but certainly a non-military type, bookish and scholarly. To be honest, it was exactly what I expected from a trained legal mind from the schools at Beirut. He spoke with the confidence one expects from a lawyer, and I could hardly guess the importance of the fellow to me in the future.

"Sir, I am Procopius of Caesarea, your new legal advisor." He stood looking down at me for a while after introducing himself. As the moment passed, his expression changed to one of worry, as I had failed to respond to him straightaway. It took me a moment, of course, because I had not really expected someone to introduce themselves with that title.

"Oh, I thought you were to be my new secretary. If you prefer the title of legal advisor, feel free to call yourself by that. If you can undertake the role of secretary as well, I would welcome that greatly."

For a moment, I was a little worried that the one thing I actually needed at that time, a good assistant, had not been offered to me. A relieved expression fell upon the face and he answered swiftly and with a little more keenness as he understood the reason I was startled.

"Yes, sir, I can do what is required of me," he replied, looking very confident with himself, and I found myself looking over him again. I wondered if he would be able to survive the military life beside us. His manner was that of a lawyer, but he still had the look of youthful inquisitiveness concerning the world around him. In fact, even as he spoke, his eyes moved casually around the office as he listened to me, taking everything in. He took some getting used to, but once he had settled in, he proved a valuable source of information. He also proved very adept at writing my dispatches and dealing with civilian and bureaucratic matters. In fact, he was useful for saving me from the headache and pure frustration of meeting landowners with complaints about my soldiers or how much produce they were expected to send us.

In March, Rufinus left us and travelled to Hierapolis to meet with the Persian officials and attempt to settle our differences. He was determined to reach them by the time of the spring equinox, as this marked the spring festivals and the start of the Persian New Year. He reckoned this would be the best time to begin talks as the new year made the Persians, he hoped from previous experience, more amenable. Before he left, we had discussed strategy; I had received a dispatch from the Basileus as the snows had cleared enough in Asia-Minor and Isauria to allow the post to travel without too much hindrance. He informed me that General Sittas was coming east and would take control of matters in Armenia and would be communicating directly with me. I still intended to deploy eastwards at the end of spring, as this would give the army time to assimilate the new recruits and allied troops that could be expected to arrive at any time now the passes through the mountains were more accessible.

Chapter Three

It was the first day of May in the third year of the Basileus's reign; the sun was already powerful enough to deter one from moving about at midday, and the road behind us was thick with dust. The landscape was dry and what grass there was had been either burnt brown or been eaten, along with the thorn bushes. Only the date palms appeared to be thriving in the heat, and the only animals visible were resting in the shade of the palms; they viewed the procession of twenty-five thousand men along the road to Dara with mild contempt. I hated moving during the hottest part of the day, and I knew my men felt the same. But I had little choice but to force the pace and reach Dara as soon as we could.

Rufinus's message to me had arrived and been straightforward and clear, the talks had collapsed, and a Persian army, estimated at forty thousand, was amassing close to Nisibis. Rufinus had told me that they had used the talks to allow time for them to prepare an army and they had caught us out in the process. The message had reached me a week ago in Callinicum — the field army and I had deployed there while the talks were in progress as a sign of goodwill, instead of at Dara as I had wanted. Rufinus had overruled me on that matter, and we had compromised on Callinicum, as it was as close as we could be while appearing friendly to the Persians. Sittas, now the Basileus chief of staff (of the army), had arranged to hold a conference with me back in Callinicum at the end of the month, depending on the situation. He had moved the central field army from the capital to Melitene, marching as fast as they could. We had corresponded with each other concerning the Persian threat. I think we both didn't expect Rufinus to have any luck with the Persians. He had agreed with my proposal to strike into Persian territory close to Dara and draw them into battle, on our terms for a change, and deliver a surprise defeat.

Once I had achieved this, Sittas would be able to re-deploy his army from guarding the passes into Asia-Minor. I knew this was an extremely optimistic course of action, but one I hoped the Persians would not expect after our recent performance. Sittas would then be free to storm into Persian Armenia and destroy as many of their bases as possible. With this twin-track approach, we should be able to force the Persians to accept our terms at a new set of talks led by Rufinus. Of course, we could not attempt this until Rufinus had decided that the time was right for us to strike. Instead, the Persians had been planning the same as us, except they seemed to have been ready well before we were. Now, we were running to save the situation and not be the ones accepting their terms.

John and twenty of my personal guard had gone on ahead to ensure that Dara was secure and to arrange logistic support for our army when it arrived. Once John had completed that task, he would cross the river and set up covert observation posts deep inside the Persian frontier zone. Carefully watching for any movement that might indicate the advance of the Persians so giving us advanced warning of their move towards the river and us.

The closer we came to Dara, the more crowded the road was with all types of people and their belongings. I had noticed that the few fields we passed were deserted and the villages we moved through were empty. The news of the Persian army had reached the population already, and they were seeking safety in the only place they could, the fortress of Dara. I wondered how many times whole villages had uprooted themselves and encamped into the fortress, only to return and rebuild what had been left devastated. I eventually had to move the army off the road and divert across country, entering the fortress by way of the East Gate, which faced towards the city of Nisibis, the expected route of the Persians and the only route free of refugees. The inside of the fortress was flooded with a mass of humanity; whole families huddled under tents squeezed so close together that it was impossible to count the individual tents. The smell pulled at the inside of the nose and refused to leave no matter what I tried to do to avoid it. It hit one, wherever you were in the fort — a mixture of baking bread, boiling water, and waste products of both human and animal origin.

I could barely fit my troops inside the fortress comfortably. Instead, I left the cavalry mounts under guard outside to graze in comfort. My one fear was that the Persians would besiege us. There was enough food to last my troops till autumn, but with the refugees, we had scarcely one and a half months of stock. We could not endure a prolonged siege. Coupled with our inability to protect the refugees from missile attacks coming from outside the walls, so, like it or not, I had only one chance to save the situation, and that was to defeat the Persians outside the city's walls.

The sun was climbing in the early morning sky, after clearing the distant mountain tops and spreading its light along the valley floor, it travelled quickly up and over the city walls. I enjoyed rising early and walking along the parapet in the quiet of the dawn, watching the sunrise, it gave me time to allow my thoughts to prepare for the day ahead. John and his men had returned to the fortress, and this morning, I was to meet them instead of going for my stroll.

He came straight up to my office, where I had assembled my commanders, ready to discuss our tactics. Hermogenes and Procopius had worked hard with my staff the night before and prepared a sand model of the area in front of the East Gate. John walked across to the display and carefully viewed it from several angles. He was still coated in a light film of dust, from his boots upwards to his hair, where his sweat smeared the dust into a lightly streaked muddy stain. Beads of sweat fell down his face and joined others in his beard; he looked utterly worn out. His normal enthusiasm seemed lacking, and the rest of us watched him without saying anything, but the room was charged with an atmosphere of expectation. I broke the uncomfortable silence.

"John, what news have you for us?" I could feel the others breathe a sigh of relief at the words. Clearly, they were expecting the worst just as I was, after all, it was the only safe option to expect, and John remained sweaty and grim in expression as he gestured with his hand.

"They will cross the frontier today and be at Ammodios by nightfall," he stated, as candidly as was to be expected as he pointed to the far end of the display, well east of our location. All eyes focused on the place he had pointed to as he continued, "As we expected, there are about forty thousand, and the majority are drawn from the Imperial army and includes the Immortals."

"How do you know all this? What did you do, sneak into their camp?" Hermogenes said, the tone in his voice rather sceptical and causing a sudden sensation of anxiety about the group. I could not recall a time that anyone, not even I, had ever thought to question John on his knowledge. John looked up at him, his face showed a pained expression, but there was anger flickering within his eyes. I half expected him to split Hermogenes in two for disbelieving his words, but the exhaustion had overcome his confident ability, and he simply replied with an exasperated sigh.

"You are correct. We moved through their camp two nights ago, that's how I know what they are up to. Mind you, I suppose I could have 'knocked' on their general's tent and enquired directly what they were planning for us." Even tired, he'd managed to leave a little quip that had Hermogenes's face coated with embarrassment, and he mumbled an apology. He was quiet for the rest of the meeting, but there was much to discuss, and somehow, the questioning of John did not sit well with the mood along with everything we had learnt.

"In that case, we have to prepare a reception for our guests and with only this day to do it," I said, and there was a general nodding of heads and murmurs of agreement, but no offers of how to greet them. I felt at a loss myself but was drawn towards the still muddied and visibly disquiet form of my trusted companion and turned to him with a soft grunt, so as not to sound like I was making a point that would rub at his now-bruised ego. "John, you better take your men and go down to the cookhouse and eat. I want you to rest so that you can be ready for the morrow."

Even with my attempt at tact, it was clear that John was sore from the request, and he took a moment to give a nod acknowledging my entreaty. Then, he rose slowly, walked out of the room with just as languid a pace as he could manage. I could tell that part of him was trying to check if he was being sent out because I did not trust him or because my request was genuine, but he only had to look over to me to know that my wish was well intentioned. As he passed Hermogenes, he just glared, and Hermogenes visibly shrunk for a moment.

"To continue, gentlemen, I propose that we field our whole force in front of the city close to where the valley is at its narrowest and block the plain." I moved over to the table and pointed at this feature with a small pointer on the sand map, and they were all grim as they considered it. "I know we don't have enough men to form enough formations to achieve this. But to compensate for this we will dig a series of ditches so funnelling the Persians into confined areas from which we can attack them on two or more fronts. The weight of their numbers should force the front units to become compacted, ideal for a cavalry strike. Secondly, I think they are overconfident as we have failed to halt them or even act aggressively. Their overconfidence could be their undoing if we use it properly."

As I spoke, I carefully dug a shallow line in the sand, it extended from the centre of the plain outwards in a parallel line to the fortress, for about a quarter of the width of the plain. From the ends of the first line, I drew a line back towards the city for about half the length of the first and repeated it on the other side. We had a shape resembling a square with only three sides, the open one on our side. From the bottom of this square, I continued two lines running out from it to a point close to the beginning of the hills. The ditches now resembled a poorly drawn Greek letter Omega. My commanders continued listening, their faces locked in concentration.

"We'll place six hundred cavalrymen on each wing in front of the trenches. Two more on each angle, the infantry will protect the flanks by being positioned behind the ditches and securing small gaps across the ditch. These are to be used only for cavalry in the forward positions to retreat through. Hermogenes and I will stay with the remaining cavalry and my personal guard and will secure the centre of the square and support any gaps that form. Your men will engage the enemy with bows when they come in range. I expect you to sort out your fields of fire and ranges and have them well marked. Every missile must strike its target. Any questions, gentlemen?"

"Belisarius, may I suggest that I take a mixed force of the Huns and Alans and conceal ourselves on the hillside to the left of our positions? We could sweep in behind the Persian advance so attacking them from three sides?" The question came from the commander of our Hunnish allies. His suggestion persuaded me to give an encouraging sound of interest and rub my chin. I turned to him, asking if he was quite sure they could achieve it and he gave a snort. There was suddenly a large smile sweeping across his face as he straightened somewhat and then nodded his head confidently. "Without a doubt, they are excellent mounted archers; they will tear a hole right through the rear of the Persians and will cause panic and break up their formations. This making it altogether easier for us."

"Assemble your men on the plain and collect every able-bodied man in the city and set them to work digging the ditches. Thank you, gentlemen." With that, and a little more confidence in what was about to take place, the conference broke up amid animated chatter and banter. They were happy now they had something to be getting on with, and we would have one more meeting to discuss any last-minute changes before we assembled on the battlefield ready to fight, but I felt a little anxious all the same.

The fortress buzzed with excitement and fear as the defences were constructed. I kept an eye on their progress by visiting the gate towers and watching the activity on the plain before me. The plain in front of the fortress was alive with activity as men and animals toiled away at the line of ditches. The colour of the plain changed from dry-looking browns to a deeper, richer colour as the spoil was spread around the plain to dispose of it. There was no vegetation on the plain apart from scrub as the farmers' animals had long ago stripped it of any goodness, and the lack of rain only compounded the condition of the soil. The only green lived on the hillsides where the farmers grew vines and olives in terraces.

The night before the battle, sleep came and took me away in its sweet embrace. Normally I would have paced the room, anxiously awaiting the dawn, but this time was different. Before going to bed, I had composed a letter to Antonina and the children; I had explained what was happening and what I hoped would happen, and if it did not occur, my great sorrow at my demise. I also told her how much I loved her and the children, I missed her presence, and I longed to be reunited with her again. Perhaps that was what had soothed me that evening, if only because I could not recall any other motion or moment of consciousness before the dawn.

The trumpets sounded just before sun up, and the whole fortress awoke to the smell of freshly baked bread and bubbling army porridge. This was to be washed down with a diluted vinegary wine; if nothing else the meal gave you something to be sick on as your fears and worries worked away inside churning up your stomach, while you waited for the enemy to attack. This was the hardest period of the battle, the waiting.

No matter how many times I fought, the fear never got any better, and the only release came when you began fighting. It was a tedious moment because all those recruits not used to any form of combat would be the most ill at ease and the ones that could bolt and ruin everything. Soldiers needed to hold their nerve or at least make a show of it in order to survive the terrible long wait.

The army moved out of the gate, and the cavalry slowly crossed the pathways over the ditches and got into position. Early morning revealed our first sight of the Persian advance. Their first formations kicked up dust as they moved forward, the cloud hung in the air for a time, as there was no breeze to disperse it. It concealed the real size of their formations. Hermogenes and I took up position on a mound so we could view the battlefield behind the first ditch, as did the rest of the command staff and bodyguards. We had specially prepared this position and had used some of the soil to construct the mound. The sun shone along the ranks of our mailed troopers mounted on similarly armoured horses, their reflection rippled back. They almost resembled quicksilver, flowing around in its liquid shininess. The infantry positioned behind them, shields to the front with the first rank deploying spears so protecting the archers behind them. The bows had been strung ready to let their arrows speed on their deadly paths, the spears were held upright to rest the men, and the horses shifted uneasily under the weight of armour.

The Persian army slowly deployed in formation just out of arrow range in front of us. Until the dust settled, it was unclear how large a force they were positioning, and the sun shone behind the Persians throwing a hazy early morning shadow over them, making it difficult to count their formations. As the dust settled and the sun crept higher in the sky, John's figure of forty thousand looked about right. I could feel my stomach tightening into a knot while the gentle trickle of sweat travelled down my face running into my eyes, making them sting. I looked around me. Everyone else seemed calm and steady, waiting for the Persians to move forward. I went over the plan and the orders I had given; did everyone know what to do? Had they listened? Would it work? It all depended on the Persians advancing towards us and parts of our cavalry withdrawing, pulling the Persians to the sides. This should split the Persian cavalry charge in two, allowing my men in the centre to hit them from the sides, as they passed beside them.

A shout went up from our front ranks alerting the rest of the army to movement towards us from the Persian front line. A small group of horsemen were steadily riding for us with large banners hanging limp. These were heralds from the commander of the forward company bringing word that the Persians were unarmed and sought a meeting with me. John and my bodyguard accompanied me as I made my way to the front of our lines, trepidation filling me as we approached the three very colourfully dressed Persian officials waiting. They were escorted by six heavily armed cavalrymen, their eyes covered by fine silk veils; they held aloft standards adorned with magnificent peacocks and winged lions, on top of these were something like winged dragons.

I moved through to the front rank of our cavalry and rode out towards the group and stopped in front of them. Their mission had two purposes: to show how well equipped they were and so ready for a fight and to gauge the morale of our army before even talking to me. We all did it, and it was a sign of confidence on their part, which generally meant talking would achieve little.

I rode up to them and then steadied my mount, eyes locking with the figure slightly ahead of the others. "I am Belisarius, general of the Basileus's forces in the East. You wish to speak to me?" There was a moment, of unspoken judgement, between the pair of us and I had to remain grim-faced and confident as I looked to him. Any sign of anxiety on my part would reflect badly upon the situation. I needed to reflect the utmost certainty as the figure finally responded.

"I am Perozes, the servant of the King of Kings. I order you Romans to make ready for me a bath in your quarters so I may wash the dirt of your defeat off me tonight." Perozes and the two other officials promptly turned their mounts away from us and rode away with their escorts without waiting for me to reply. I was a little confused. I had expected them to offer us terms for the surrender of the city and our withdrawal, not this level of cheek. I turned in my saddle to where John sat on his mount.

"John, what was that all about?" I was more than a little perplexed. For a moment, I had almost accepted that this being was asking to use our bathing facilities, but when I turned to John, his expression remained as grim as my own, though there was a lick of humour twinkling in his eyes to vex me.

"It's sort of a Persian insult, in that he regards us as no better than slaves and expects to destroy us by tonight. Belisarius, you have been insulted by the commander of the Persian army, in person too," John stated as if I should be honoured, and the serious tone of his voice faded as he burst out with laughter. I joined him in the laughter as we slowly returned to our lines. Throwing that insult and then galloping off had seemed childish rather than intimidating. They were indeed overconfident in themselves and were underestimating us. We now had a chance.

Noon arrived, I ordered the men to eat and drink, starting in the rear and working forward so as not to allow the enemy to see us refreshing. All they would see would be the front lines feeding, and if they charged, the rest of the army would be ready.

It was late afternoon, and the sun was now shining down on our backs, making it very unpleasant to stay in our position, but it was now also shining into the eyes of the Persians. A fresh shout erupted from the front ranks, and our attention was directed to our left wing; a formation of Persian cavalry gathered speed as it charged our cavalry. I bit my lip with tension as the seconds flashed by. Would my commander remember what to do? Suddenly, our cavalry reeled around and moved towards the rear. The Persians slowed as they reached our cavalry's last position and finally came to a halt. When they had halted, our cavalry reeled around again and charged straight at them.

As our men closed with them, a cloud of arrows flew towards the Persians, who seemed stunned by the sudden movement, and swiftly, a few Persians fell to the ground. The rest beat a hasty retreat to their lines; thank God, our men stopped at their previous position and did not follow up their attack. A loud cheer went through the army. This first little victory raised morale and cleared the tension from all of us. The heads of the fallen Persians were mounted on the standards of the victorious cavalry company and paraded around the front of our lines, and again the army cheered. I sent a message to the head bearers, to ride through our ranks to the city walls and display to the people our tokens of victory.

A little later, a lone Persian rode up to our front rank and started insulting them and challenging anyone who thought they were brave enough to step forward and fight him. I passed an order forward that no one was to accept the challenge. The Persian continued to ride up and down our front ranks, jeering. As he approached the left wing, someone stepped out in front of him and accepted the challenge. The Persian stopped and looked down at the man standing in front of him, holding only a spear. Before the Persian could make up his mind as to how to react to this inferior challenge, the man moved quickly, and with his spear, jabbed upwards and caught the Persian in the chest, slipping through his armour from below rather than from the front, as it was designed to deflect a blow head-on. The Persian toppled over and hit the ground, his horse started and broke free of the rider before cantering back towards its lines. Our man was swiftly atop of the fallen Persian, and before the rider had any more time to react, he slit his throat.

Hermogenes, in the meantime, had left me and moved to the left wing, as the man returned to the front line to loud cheering. Hermogenes then summoned this fellow to his presence, and ordered the man, who was called Andreas, not to venture forth again. It seemed this fellow was an ex-wrestler and attendant of the left wing's commander, the kind, used to reacting to threats, and though it had been amusing enough, the lack of discipline bothered me more than anything else.

It was around the time of day that one normally has the evening meal, that the Persians again sent forth another lone rider. He rode up to our lines, fully armoured from head to foot, as was his mount. With his right arm, he held a long spear, and in his left hand, he brandished a whip. As he approached our positions, his armour shone in the last rays of the day; he shouted his challenge for combat to our army. He rode up and down, as had his predecessor. Not one of my men moved to challenge him this time. This continued for quite a period, and the irritation it caused to my men was quite apparent by the sound of raised voices, jeering and movements in the ranks.

A rider broke again from my left wing. He came to a halt a short distance from the Persian challenger. For a moment, they watched each other, then together, as if a voice had spoken to each at that instant, they lowered their spears so that the points faced each other. Then, the two galloped towards each other, spears protruding forward, seeking a point on which to strike their opponent. The two mailed-figures rushed head on. Over the short distance, their spears, finding the mark required, struck home. The sound of bone and armour crunching together was more perceived than heard as it echoed across the plain, as both horses collided head-on, throwing their riders to the ground in clouds of dust. Their horses slumped to the ground next to each other, rolled onto their sides, legs kicking for a moment, then nothing. Both riders began stirring, the Roman was up, suddenly crouching on his knees. The Persian slowly lifted his head and turned towards our man. Both reached along their bodies for their swords. Our man was a fraction faster and unsheathed his, he raised it above his head, the metal of the blade catching the last moments of the sunset as he plunged it down onto his opponent's chest.

The whole of our army exploded in a thunderous cheer. A number of men broke ranks and surrounded our champion and lifted him onto one of their mounts and carried him back inside our formation. I looked to the Persian lines, half expecting them to use the opportunity to strike forward and catch us off guard, but nothing moved in our direction. The cheering gradually died down. Again, Hermogenes moved to the location of our newest champion, without the need of orders from me. Instead, he firstly punished the man for breaking ranks, and then before anyone could carry out the punishment, he pardoned him and reward him with a small bounty for his skill and courage. Shortly afterwards, Hermogenes returned to my location, and I learned our champion was none other than Andreas. I dispatched one of my guards to locate Andreas and escort him to the fortress and arrange for a public display of gratitude for his success to be held straightaway before we lost the light. I decided that reward served the morale of everyone. If he had been killed, it would have left us deeply unsettled and the army with a much-diminished level of morale to deal with before the forthcoming battle.

The sun began to fall below the western horizon, and darkness appeared in the east, as we observed the Persians abandon their positions and withdraw to their camp for the night. Once the plain was safe, I ordered a withdrawal back to the fortress. I left scouts out overnight to maintain a watch on the Persians and alert us to any unexpected movement.

The next day, at dawn, I deployed our forces as before, and the

Persians followed suit. We faced each other, this time no champions came forward, instead Hermogenes and I exchanged letters with Perozes requesting him to withdraw and save needless killing. He refused. I also learnt from our scouts that he had received additional forces of perhaps a few thousand. He was now playing a waiting game: to build up his forces till he decided he had enough to commit to battle. If I had more forces, I could have attacked him on the first day and forced him back before he gained reinforcements. At sunset, the Persians withdrew. It was becoming a game of nerves.

The following day, I was awoken well before dawn with the news that the Persian camp was already awake and would soon be deploying onto the plain. As I scrambled into my uniform, and then my armour, the rest of the army was woken and prepared for a rapid deployment. Once dressed, I assembled my commanders as the army shuffled out of the gates to their pre-assigned positions.

"Remember your orders. Do not be drawn out into the plain, even if they are running away. I expect you to lead your men by example and control them. Don't let them become carried away. Use your centurions to maintain discipline in the face of the enemy," I stated firmly, to remind them of my orders and to reassure myself that I had insisted upon tight discipline. I paused as that had been the stern section of my orders, now overlooking the eager faces of the younger commanders and the more prosaic faces of my experienced officers, I continued, encouragement was now needed, and I had to make it brief as time was not on our side this day, "This time, we will defeat them and teach them a lesson in the process. Again, exhort your men to fight well. Tell them that we have twice beaten their champions — that was the best they had. Now let us by the Grace of God and the intercession of Mary, the Mother of God, crush them and inflict on them the bitter taste of defeat. Let the name of Dara haunt them. While for us the name will recall our first great victory of Roman arms under our Basileus over them."

I dismissed them, and they quickly took up their positions. Later, from our scouts, I received word that only half the Persian army was deployed, and the other half was being held in reserve. We maintained our position all that morning, the sun continued to beat down on us, and I was beginning to feel a little more than concerned. This was the third day we had been forced to stand all day in the heat. Obviously, the Persians intended to wear us out before they attacked. Midday came, the men were fed, and water was passed around in the usual manner. But it was not to be a quiet day it seemed.

Suddenly, it happened. Blasts of trumpets thundered across the plain, causing a flock of birds resting on the hillside to take to the wing. The sound of startled birds and trumpets echoed around us. Then the sky was filled with black darts, darkening the sky for a moment as they flew towards us. The sound of their feathers sliding through the air reached us just before the enveloping cloud of arrows did. Several of my guards slid from their mounts, arrows protruding from their chests, necks and legs. The army quickly responded with a coordinating flight of arrows, returning the compliment of sudden flying death.

The Persian right wing began their advance towards my left; they rode steadily picking up speed. The leaders dropped their lances level with their mounts' heads; the sun shone on them, reflecting back in silvery flashes as they rushed onwards. The sound of the charge drowned out every other noise. From the ranks of the charging cavalry, a huge dark swarm of arrows erupted and flew straight into our left wing as the Persian mounted archers sought targets before crashing headlong into my men. Our archers reacted, shooting from their mounts directly into the oncoming armoured mass. As they drew level with my position, I ordered the troops on my left flank to shoot into the side of the advancing Persian column, thus catching them in the crossfire. Our cavalry used bow and spear, and the Persian charge stumbled and simply collapsed under our writhing fire.

The whole momentum of their attack was slowed as they hit head-on with my left wing. The sound of the crunch was tooth-jarring as both lines merged into each other in a noisy flurry of screaming horses and roaring humans. The fighting took on the personal close-quarter match of sheer strength and endurance in the afternoon heat. My left flank had ceased fire, for fear of hitting their comrades as both lines merged, but the Persians continued with their massive bombardment of all our positions. We responded, but they now had the advantage of being able to rotate units back and forth so allowing them to continue with their heavy barrage of us. As they charged up to our lines, letting rip and withdrawing, my left wing began to shift backwards very slowly, and it appeared that the Persians were gaining the upper hand.

I dispatched a messenger to order the Huns to attack the rear of the Persian right wing and cut it off from the rest of their army. Even so, it seemed like an age before the Huns began to sweep down the hillside and onto the rear of the Persians. The Huns clothed in brightly coloured robes of reds and blues, with peaked caps were a truly inspiring sight for us as they flowed across the plain, filling it with wild blood-curdling screams as they let loose their bowstrings and death flew into the backs of the Persians.

The Persian rear was unable to turn and fight back, their formation so tight as it had become squeezed into our lines. They attempted to surge forward to escape the oncoming angels of death that were scything their way into them. I ordered my infantry to cross the prepared gaps over the ditches and attack the now stationary Persian cavalry and relieve the flagging left wing's cavalry, who were bearing the brunt of the assault and dying where they stood as they were gradually forced back to the ditch.

The main standard of the Persians suddenly dropped out of sight, and then it was all over. The remains of the Persian cavalry, those who could pull out of the attack, fled as fast as they could back to their own lines. The stragglers were cut to pieces by the combined forces of our infantry and the Huns.

The air was suddenly filled with silence, and no more arrows flew. The Persian lines stayed motionless; no forays forwarded by archers. My left wing slowly regrouped, and the wounded were removed to the rear where the physicians tended to them before they were moved back inside the fortress. The Huns dispatched the enemy wounded and grabbed as many loose horses as they could, before falling back. The infantry moved as quickly and placed as many of our dead as possible into the ditches — after the battle they would be honoured. We left the Persian dead where they were — they formed a nice set of obstacles to impede another charge.

The peace lasted for a while until the Persians had finished licking their wounds, then they returned to the offensive.

This time, the whole Persian left wing surged forwards, under the usual cover of a prolonged missile assault that caught a few of my men unaware. Now, the front of the charge was led by the Immortals. They were totally coated from head to foot in chain mail with brightly decorated shields strapped to their left sides and sashes of bright ribbons streaming from their helmets. The horses were covered in bronze-coloured lamellar armour, and the horses too had a bright plume attached to its armoured head. Behind the front rank of the Immortals, rode the standard-bearer, he was dressed in a white tunic and a cone-shaped helmet with a leather cap over it. The standard consisted of a long pole, at the top suspended from a cross piece were bulbous shapes and brightly coloured sashes made of silk. It all fluttered in the wind as the rider galloped with his fearsome looking colleagues towards my right wing.

As they sped up, a large dust cloud hid the presence of the Persian army from our sight, only the path of the incoming arrows told of their presence in front of us. I quickly shifted all my troops, including my guard, from inside the forward square to the right flank. I intended to repeat the flank attack against the incoming Persian cavalry. The ground shook as they headed towards us, then swung slightly more to the right as the Immortals led the charge. By now, my cavalry was also charging forward to meet the assault head-on. The air was full of hissing arrows, which were soon replaced by spears, stones and anything that could be lethally thrown at the fast-incoming cavalry as they came within range. The clash of arms was thunderous at that point of impact and seemed to silence all other noises on the battlefield as the contest developed between both cavalry forces. Very quickly they were intermingled, and the fighting grew intense, sounds of metal-on-metal cut through the air, as did the sound of horses roaring in pain and, above these sounds, came the shrill sound of men dying in battle.

My wing buckled quickly and was forced back towards the ditch. There they would have only two choices: stand and die or ride into the ditch and die. I ordered my massed forces on the right flank to cross the ditch and strike deep into the Persian line cutting it in two, then turn right and sweep into the midst of the Immortals. My men slowly filtered across the ditch and smoothly formed up on the outer side and when all assembled, they charged. The distance between the charging right flank force and the Persians was less than a spear throw, and they quickly cut their way through the Persian side. It was made easier for them as the riders had no shield protection on their right side — instead, it was their weapon station side. The Persian right side opened up like a ripe peach does when squeezed too hard. The sound was like that of continuous thunder as my men hacked their way through the Immortals, leaving a trail of dead and wounded.

My right-wing cavalry had stopped retreating and was now able to hold its own, now that the pressure had been released. The Persian standard weaved and bobbed around in the melee, and it became obvious that someone on our side was after it, then it dipped out of sight. The Persians caught on the other side of the thrust noticed the fall of the standard, and their cohesion faltered, as their only reference point vanished. Now it was my chance to break the attack. I ordered all my remaining archers on the left flank to move across and engage the rear and flanks of the Persians. This they did, and within a short time, Persian archer fire had markedly declined.

Then it happened. The Persian attack collapsed, and they broke and fled back towards their lines; they dumped whatever they could to increase their speed as they fled. My archers now had an even easier task as the backs of the Persians were the weakest point — their armour was secured on their backs — leaving the odd gap where the armour met, and they were cut to shreds. The only unit not to break was the Immortals, even without their standard, they stood their ground as gradually my men encircled the almost motionless horsemen. They fought stubbornly but gradually, with no support from the rest of their army, their circle reduced in size as the perimeter was marked with the dead and dying. Then the last fell, and the Immortals were no more.

Their standard was brought to me, by one of the cavalry, who had attacked into their rear. I rewarded the man with a pouch of coins I had on me. The standard was added to the others we had captured, and it was sent back to the fortress and then would later go to the capital.

My right wing regained order, and the centre was refilled as men carefully re-crossed the gaps. The day had been long and hard, water and biscuits were handed out. It would soon be sunset, and yet we were all still roasting in our armour. We looked to the Persian lines for any sign of movement, but they had not moved since the retreat of their last attack.

Dusk approached, and it became hard to see the Persian frontline, but no campfires could be seen either. Then, the first reports reached me, to say they were pulling out and retiring back to Ammodios.

We had won our first victory over them, and they were the ones leaving their dead behind.

We counted eight thousand, of them dead on the field. This helped to celebrate the third year of the Basileus's reign, and I had the standards of the defeated Persians along with a sample of the gold and silver that had been picked from the dead sent back to the capital for a triumph in the Hippodrome to complement the anniversary. We encamped around the fortress, with the Persians on the retreat we no longer needed the safety of the walls — or the smells. The men celebrated the victory, and I cancelled a meeting with my officers and like everyone I partook in the celebrations. Inside the fortress, the population also sang praises to God, then began to pack up ready for the move home the next day. All I needed was a bath to clean myself of the stench of the last three days, and after the celebrations, I returned to my office and fell asleep.

The following day, I summoned Procopius to my quarters and had him write three urgent dispatches. One was to Rufinus, giving him a complete report on our defeat of the Persian army. The second was for Sittas, explaining the current military situation. The third and most important was for the Basileus. I not only gave a full report but also expressed my fears that without a settlement, we would have to permanently maintain two field armies in the region. This would leave Thrace and Illyricum in a permanently defensive posture and leave us vulnerable to incursions. Hermogenes would take this last dispatch to him directly and give his personal view, which I hoped would cast me in a favourable light.

My next need was to equip and replace the losses we had suffered. With a great victory, we should have enough volunteers as the chance of loot and bonuses was a great incentive. My scouts continued to report the dispersal of the Persian army beyond the frontier, yet the campaign season was not over, so I would have to remain here at Dara for the time being.

The following month, I received a dispatch from Sittas, he congratulated me on my first real victory, and informed me that at the same time as we had been fighting, another Persian army had crossed into Armenia. He had caught them encamped three days from Theodosiopolis. He charged through the camp and wiped out most of their army and chased the remaining back across the frontier into Persian Armenia. God had indeed smiled on him, and with the aid of Persian defectors, he had been able to bribe the local Persian commander to change sides. With that, he gained the surrender of two Persian fortresses and was able to secure the frontier of Armenia from any further Persian threats. Now, we had two victories to celebrate.

Rufinus had not remained idle in Hierapolis, and once news of the victory at Dara and Armenia reached him, he contacted the Persian leadership. Shah Kavad then requested his presence in their capital of Ctesiphon. He informed me of this and his intended journey to the Persian capital. He suspected that the terms would revolve around money and he envisioned that in exchange for an annual amount of gold, Kavad would firstly refrain from making territorial claims on the Empire, which should end the incursions. Secondly, he hoped to use the gold to bribe Kavad to guard the vital passes in the north against barbarian incursions as this would not only secure our provinces but also aid Lazi, Colchis and Caucasian Iberia, as well as serving the needs of the Persians themselves. If not, he would likely allow us to invade into Persia and destroy as much as we could. In a sense, it would be a return to the old arrangement of mutual defence to which we made a heavy contribution, but it was better than the cost of war and allowed us to defend the empire as a whole once again.

As winter approached, I used the respite and began strengthening the garrisons of the region, recruiting local troops for the defence of their home. I planned to disperse my forces in such a way, that in the event of a renewal of hostilities in the region, I would be able to deploy my forces more rapidly and be less of a burden on the city of Antioch. John and my staff accompanied me as I returned there to arrange logistical support for my new deployments and just as importantly for me, to spend time with my family.

We entered Antioch on the first day of winter, so far, the weather had been mild and only occasionally had we sought shelter from the heavy pounding cold rain. The sky was clear, and the sun hung low over the horizon as we made our way into the city through the Great East Gate. Across to my left, the walls of Theodosius stretched up the foothills to the Mountain of Saturn, enclosing the first church Saint Peter had built when he first came to the city soon after leaving Jerusalem during the first persecution. It was a place of considerable pilgrimage and respite from the tribulations of the world. The walls then carried on up Mount Silpius and back down to the Southern Gate. Just for the difficulty of the route these walls followed, they were in their own way as impressive as that of the capital's, yet they were not as secure — the greater the length, the more troops that were needed to guard them. When Antioch was first built, the Tyrant's Palace was built on a separate fortified island in the River Orontes alongside the city, so should the city fall or revolt, the rulers of the city would be secure. Antioch had, over time, continued to expand outwards, leaving the older sections with their own walls surrounded by newer sections, which were in turn protected by the city's newer walls.

After Alexandria in Egypt, this was the third-largest city in the Empire. In sections, the city was poor, and the buildings overcrowded and in need of repair. The landlords had no need to pay for repairs as the regular great movements of the earth that plagued this city removed these and state money allowed them to rebuild the tenement blocks as shoddy as before. Even now, after the recent movement of the earth and subsequent fire, they were already rebuilding. The rest of the city reflected its importance as the trading centre of the East; markets and shops of all kinds lined the path of the main route into the centre. They had returned to business soon after the fire and unlike other parts of the city were being rebuilt at their owners' expense. The colonnades were marbled and impressive with their stature and seemingly ageless, even with the cracks from the earth shakes, they still reflected the grandeur of the city. I avoided going directly into the centre and the forum area, here repairs had not even begun. I suspected the money was diverted by the council to their own areas first, then the forum.

I turned right on the inner wall road, which took me to the bridge over the river and then onto the Tyrant's island where my headquarters and residence lay, next to the still damaged basilica and across the road from the stadium, opposite the Hippodrome — one of the first buildings to be repaired enough for races to be held. The Golden House of God and the Bishop's headquarters were under reconstruction, the dome had collapsed in on the church, yet its straight angled walls had held up well, though a few major cracks could be seen in the six faces of the wall of the church. The windows were gone, the marble floor had survived, but many of the mosaics inside had not. Winter rain had also damaged the interior to make matters worse. The island had escaped the fire; otherwise, I would have no headquarters. Since my first visit to the city, it had undergone a remarkable transformation, but this would be put in jeopardy if the Persians sacked the city. It could well be the final straw that broke the camel's back and sunk the city. Deep down I am sure part of the city would be rebuilt due to the city's curious nature of endurance.

The old harbour at Suedia, which served Antioch, was a different matter. The river mouth was now well away from the harbour, and sailing was undertaken only when the tide was at its highest, and even then, there was a risk of ships grounding. Most merchants moved expensive loads in smaller boats along the river to where the larger ships had anchored in the new river mouth. The inner port had dried up, and only sections of the outer port could be used by merchants and the navy. I entered the headquarters and then marched into my apartments, almost forgetting the swarm about to greet me. I was immediately surrounded by servants who almost dragged my clothes from me right then and there. I put up a strong defence, but the tiredness of the journey let me down, and I was hauled off to the bathhouse grumbling about the fuss being made of me.

"Make sure you scrub every bit of him and shave that beard off his face. It makes him look like a clever Greek." I turned my head towards the sound of that voice. There was John standing in his dirty clothes laughing like mad at my predicament. It was just like him to mock me in such a situation. I tried to find something firm enough to grip in the room in my efforts to try and prevent the flood of servants carrying me away.

"Well, just don't stand there, *save* me from these lunatics," I bellowed out at him, looking past the mob to see him wave his hand slightly before he almost rolled onto the floor with laughter as firmer hands grabbed my waist which elicited a rather unmanly sound of shock from me. A louder laugh thundered from him, and wiping the tears from his eyes he slowly staggered after my retreating form. Finally, he stopped laughing and was able at last to reply to my call for help.

"Hang on, sir. I will summon your personal guard to save you from your servants." He burst again into laughter, bending forward, and slapping his knee. I realised just how bloody stupid I must look and after a moment glowering in his direction, I gave a splutter of laughter. As I began to move from the mindset of a soldier to that of a master of a household. I started to fully join in the laughter, realising the absurdity of my actions. Finally, I relented and allowed myself to be guided out of the room and down to the bathhouse.

The water was hot, and I lay in it for what seemed like a week; my skin wrinkled, and the sweat just oozed out of me. The servants yanked me out of the water, then they dropped me first into a cold rinse and then into the hot room. I was finally laid on a still cool slab of marble with my stomach pressed against its smooth surface. The masseur worked away at my back, legs and shoulders. The heavy pressure relaxed me for the first time in months, and a sort of sleep drifted over me. The pattern of the masseur changed, and it became quieter in the room, apart from my heavy breathing, as parts of my body gave way to the practised hands. Gradually the touch became lighter. I could now smell something vaguely familiar in the room, a musk or scent, yes, I was sure I recognised it. I rolled over onto my back and didn't I have a shock. It was Antonina who was massaging me. I had been away too long, and I had forgotten even the smell of my wife.

"Antonina, how long have you been here?" I sighed, sounding almost drunk after being so relaxed after such a long time. She curled an eyebrow at me, almost as if she might be annoyed before she gently flicked a finger at the bottom of my chin with a wry smile.

"Well," she replied with a slightly mocking tone, shifting to push her knuckle to her hip and almost pout at me for not having made a fuss of it earlier. I sat up on the block, shifting to let her join me as she bent forward to stroke my cheek as she settled beside me. "I was beginning to wonder how long it was going to take you to notice my presence."

"It's great to see you again, my love. Forgive me for not realising it was you," I began, but she gave me another pouting expression before she flicked the edge of my nose this time with her long fingers and then her fingers moved slowly over my face.

"I forgive you, you tired old man."

Then she gave a snort of disgust, "Yuck, you can lose that beard straightaway," she replied, giving my whiskers a hard tug while giving me a slightly disgusted look. We both gazed at each other, then she dropped her hands from my face to hold mine; it did seem like ages since we had seen each other. It seemed like an eternity since I'd seen her eyes, stroked her warm skin or gently pinched a lock of her hair between my fingers. I could tell she was thinking the same; her body seemed almost on the edge of trembling as I finally leant in, kissed her on the lips and enveloped her within my embrace.

I awoke the next morning and felt completely refreshed and ready to deal with the mountain of correspondence that I imagined had accumulated during my absence. I entered my office to find Procopius hard at work, with Antonina dictating replies and looking radiant in the sunlight seeping in through the window. She looked up to me as I moved through the room and spoke softly to me as if it was just the two of us in the room. Procopius was quick to ensure his eyes were dropped to the paper and his pen, clearly indicating he was there to work rather than to nose in on our private conversations.

"Good morning, darling. You look like you slept well, did you?" she asked, smiling knowingly, then suddenly straightening up and shifting in front of my desk. I had the curious sensation she was trying to block my access to the desk, and it was not only worrying but curiously amusing to think she'd rather I did not suddenly hurry to work. But then when I stepped forward to pat her shoulder in reassurance on my sleep, her eyes had a curious look of daring to them.

"Yes, I did. You seem to be doing well without me," I teased, and she gave me a curious kind of smile as if to say that I certainly did not need to get involved. However, I had my duties to attend to and was never really one to enjoy being idle when there was work to be done. "Do you mind if I carry on with my work?"

"Yes, I *do* mind. I mind so much that Procopius here is well able to do the whole lot and all you have to do is sign at the bottom," her tone informed me that she was now annoyed with me. I decided to leave my office and allow them to continue; I knew better than to get on her bad side in this situation. I went for a walk around the grounds and was distracted the moment I found the children playing.

Phocas was slowly growing up, and soon the first signs of manhood would appear. He had the look of his mother, but the build of an athlete. Johanna was starting to walk now, and she spoke Greek; she looked more like my mother than Antonina but had the dark hair of her mother. Melissa was now at an age when I dare not let her be around my guards on her own. She was the spitting image of her mother, and I was relatively nervous she might have the same kind of attitude to entice trouble. Zenobia was still a young lady and declined to join them playing — she said she had better things to do, such as study. I settled amongst them, chatted and played till lunchtime, and then we were summoned inside by one of the many servants. As we entered the dining room, I paused to say casually to Melissa as I gazed around the room, which was much larger and grander than our house in the capital.

"Is it my imagination, or have we suddenly grown servants? I don't recall so many here in the spring. Look at the table — it is glowing with gold and silverware." I was rather bemused, and to my great relief, Melissa spoke as candidly as always and with a haughty tone that rather suited the rank we'd developed into.

"Mother has quite taken to the high life. She decided that the general of the east's household should reflect his position. And she is right."

We sat down for lunch, and a delicious feast was laid before us. Small meatballs in a thick garlic sauce, chicken pieces in yoghurt, baskets of fresh bread and salads of chopped vegetables mixed with a soft grain covered in oil and garlic, all washed down with rich red wine. I sat there, looking around at my family. I felt really at home again and comfortable, the thought of battle forgotten by this whole new feeling of luxury. I looked across at my beautiful wife and smiled — she smiled back at me and then spoke.

"I have a surprise for you, my darling. I have arranged a break for just the two of us. Everything is in hand, and your staff will know where we are and can send messages to us if needed," she stated with a firm smile that I was rather startled by, but very quickly it triggered my work mind. I was questioning the idea of being away for any reason.

"I don't think I can spare the time. I still have so much to do.

"Rubbish, and you know it. It's all arranged. We leave this

afternoon," she replied in a triumphant tone, her eyes saying very firmly that I would be offending her if I dared to raise any dispute.

I knew I was beaten, so I just looked at her and mouthed, "I love you."

We rode south out of the city, accompanied by a small detachment of my personal guard that afternoon. After journeying for several days, changing mounts at the many Imperial mail posts, we finally reached the mountains of Phoenicia; the first snows of winter had already coated them. The snow dipped down into the upper valleys petering out before the mountains plunged down towards the coast. We travelled along south along the coastal road with the sea on our right, the mountains on our left, passing through the many towns and cities dotted alongside the sea. Antonina had become an accomplished rider and had no intention of travelling in a coach as women of her station were expected to do.

John, thankfully, after some argument regarding our safety had stayed in Antioch; but he had insisted on personally assigning the best guards, and together with the pack animals, he intended that we looked more like merchants travelling, rather than what we really were. He didn't expect trouble, but he had decided that the mountain parts of our route south required an escort, and the smaller, the faster we could be if we ran into trouble, the better for us to escape unharmed. The other advantage was we didn't attract the attention of every merchant or shop keeper we passed on the journey trying to sell a great man everything from the best wine to the greatest horse since Alexander the Great had passed through. The further south we travelled, the denser the population and wider the coastal plain was in places. The lower foothills were covered with the remains of summer cultivation, still green olive trees, while the vines had died down. We stayed at inns along the way and enjoyed the informal settings and the time on our own. All I knew and really cared about was that we were together once again.

On one stretch the road rose suddenly upward till we eventually crossed the summit of a mountain. It tired the horses, so we stopped there. It was cold, and we shivered in our cloaks while we waited for the horses to recover. It was worth the effort, the sky was clear with a light blue shade to it, the sun weak, offered little warmth, yet its light still made the sea a deep blue colour, with streaks of green. It looked cold and unforgiving, but the land below us was green and fresh-looking in the light. We stayed for a while, enjoying a short walk while the horses rested — the trees here were still lush and some of the tallest I have ever seen, even up here. Walking under their branches was like being under the cover of a colonnade, except the air smelt sweeter. The smell was familiar but more intense — it was then that I realised that these were the fabled cedars of Libani. With such wood as this, Solomon had built his temple, and the wood was still imported to the capital for use in buildings, especially churches, as it was still the finest and strongest.

The sky clouded over, and light snow began falling, it quickly took hold, and the air became cold enough for the horses' breath to look like smoke from a campfire. We didn't wait around much longer; we finally reached our destination — the thriving port of Byblus, and stayed in a large house that Antonina had arranged. The feast of the Nativity of Our Lord was soon upon us, and we entered a small nondescript church close by. The liturgy was celebrated in the local Aramaic language. We followed custom and separated as normal to participate in the ceremony. I stood in the main aisle, and Antonina with the other women in their section. I listened to the haunting chants of praise, and I felt it stir something within me, it was a mystical sensation. We met up at the end of the liturgy and returned to the house escorted by my bodyguard. Afters, at the house we ate freshly caught fish, we both enjoyed the peace and quiet of the house and again made up for lost time. The winter storms curtailed any plans we had to visit the surrounding area.

We stayed about a month — then on a clear late January day, we took a navy vessel that was attempting the risky journey north along the coast. We were lucky and missed the storms that make journeys such as this dangerous. We left the ship at the mouth of the Orontes and rested for the rest of the day. Even without a storm, the journey had been rough, and the short hop to the beach had been quite an experience. Horses were collected the next day, and with our baggage, we returned to Antioch. The rest of the winter was peaceful, and I was able to remain in the city till Easter.

It was a beautiful late spring morning, the sun had barely risen above Mount Silpius, yet the air was rapidly warming as the light dropped into the city. With it, the smell of spring drifted up from the river catching the blossoms and greatly improving the normal smell of the city. I was standing on the walls looking down into the Orontes river; it was already turning brown with the run-off from the fields higher up. The river was still full of melt water, as it twisted and turned assaulting the supports of the bridge as it travelled past the city. I heard the clatter of a speeding rider cross the bridge. I looked down to see a rider in great haste; he looked like an Imperial dispatcher. I expected he carried a message for me, and I turned to make my way down to my office. It was then that I felt a presence beside me and noticed the pleasant smell, it was quite different from that which had drifted up from the river, but I recognised the perfume.

"It's a beautiful morning, is it not, my darling," I stated with a soft smile as I turned to face her, and Antonina stepped to my side. She seemed to peer out at the universe for a while before turning to look at me carefully. I could tell something was up and pondered if perhaps she'd heard the dispatcher and was going to complain at me hurrying off to work.

"Yes, it is, my love," she replied gently as she moved next to me and in doing so, blocking my path to the exit. I guessed that she was going to ask me something important judging by the gentle heavy breaths she was taking in. She looked directly into my eyes. "Darling, I want to go back home to the capital. I miss the city and my friends."

Her eyes peered into mine expecting an answer; I felt something was wrong, but as to what it was, I had no idea. I thought she was happy here and wanted for nothing. Then it occurred to me, who she meant by friends — she meant the Augusta. Well, there wasn't much I could say, I wanted her to stay with me, but if she wanted to go back, then it was better she did. So, I accepted her decision. There was no point in arguing with her. "When do you want to leave?"

Her eyes lit up with relief for a second, as if she really thought that I might have wanted to argue the point, but I did not.

"As soon as the merchants begin sailing again to the capital. The children will come with me. I don't want to be apart from you, but I hate the climate here, the city and the people."

I hadn't realised that she felt this way. I thought that all the servants and expensive goods had made her feel at home here in Antioch. Now I felt lonely at the thought of her and the children returning to the capital; we could be separated for quite a long time, depending on how long my command lasted here. While I was busy fighting, I didn't miss her as I knew she was safe and that reassured and made up for the loneliness. But as soon as everything quietened down, that's when I missed her company, and when I needed her.

"God only knows when I will be released from here and able to join you," I said with a slight sinking feeling. Yet as a soldier, I should be used to the separation. It was normal. "Much as I enjoy the challenge of command, without you it's going to become very lonely."

"I am dreading being on my own in the capital," she replied, which didn't make sense and confused me as to why she was leaving. I was concerned. Indeed, for what was going on? But then she seemed to perk up a little as she spoke, although there was a slightly sad shiver within it. "I will ask the Augusta for one more favour. That you be given a post in the capital so we can be together."

Tears welled in her eyes, slowly running down her cheeks, making her make-up run ever so slightly. I reached out and placed my arms around her, and we embraced. She had the knack of controlling every situation, even when she was upset, but I could never really bring myself to argue with the person I loved. However, the moment was interrupted by a voice calling up from deep within the exit to the wall. I couldn't see the speaker but instantly recognised the voice as that of John.

"Belisarius, I am sorry to disturb you. There is an important dispatch for you." He quickly joined us, standing at a discreet distance as I released Antonina. Both of us regained our composure quickly as John waited silently.

"Thank you, John. I will read it here." I kissed Antonina, and she walked back past John and towards the steps she had walked up. John handed over the dispatch. The news it contained sent a shiver down my spine, and my face must have changed colour given the look I received from John. I carefully re-read the dispatch; there was no doubting its content. The negotiations had failed. A large Persian army under the command of Azarethes and Alamoundara with Lakhmid support had crossed the Euphrates in Assyria. They were thought to be heading for Samosata, once the capital of ancient Commagene, which sat on a vital crossroads, between the East and Asia-Minor.

The dispatch was signed by our client king of the Ghassanids, Arethas. I had not met our Arab ally before but knew of him, and there was no doubting his loyalty to us. So, if they managed to reach that city, they would be able to cut the East off from Armenia and the capital. Then they would have the choice of marching into Armenia from the back door or down to Antioch. I had not thought they would risk moving such a large army through a desert, but this move could well explain why the Lakhmids — the Arab allies of the Persian- were with them, they must be guiding them along the caravan routes. It would allow them to outflank all our fortresses and slip in behind us into Syria.

My options were seemingly few. I could either march north to Samosata and wait for them or remain here and protect the city and region or head directly towards the Euphrates. There I might, with the aid of the Ghassanids, stand a chance of catching them before they did any real damage. My choice now would determine not only my fate but that of the region; sit still and wait here or muster as many men from the south, move north but leave Antioch exposed. In the end I had little choice but to march out and find them. I ordered John to follow, and I rushed down the stairs to my office and summoned all my command staff for an urgent meeting. I laid my plan before them, and we agreed that only an advance to the East was feasible in the time we had left to act.

"John, make your way to Hermogenes with this dispatch and tell him what I intend doing," I said, keeping controlled but there was a speed in my words to emphasise the need of it, and John nodded his head firmly. "Everyone else, prepare your men, collect field rations, we need to move fast, today would have been best. Push the men as fast as possible so we can be on the move by tomorrow."

My men hurried out. Trumpets bellowed out the summons to all the troops and were echoed by other trumpets throughout the city. By the end of the day, the last of the men had made their way back to the headquarters and were busy cleaning kit, drawing weapons from the armoury and sharpening swords. Horses were brought back into the city from their grazing and, a mule train was fitted up with supplies. A wagon train would follow on with more provisions and weapons.

Once the last of my officers had left, I had nothing to do now they were busy, so I returned to my quarters. Here they were busy too, wagons had already been brought in, and the first loads of chests were being assembled ready for the journey to the coast. I found Antonina busy ordering the servants how to pack her clothes and personal effects. She turned as I entered the room.

"Antonina, your timing is excellent. I feel better knowing you and our family will be away from here. You better pack as fast as you can. Once news breaks that we are marching out, it will be hard to find passage to the capital," she smiled at me. But there was a slightly worried look on her face, shrouding the full extent of her anxiety.

"So that was what all the trumpets were for. The servants began mumbling something about the army moving, but I didn't pay much attention. You know how panicky they get as they will be out of work soon," she said, trying to keep the conversation gentle, and perhaps the mood light, rather than the panic I knew was there.

"Procopius will give you special passes to ensure your ship takes you. You will be carrying my dispatches to the capital, so you will be an official messenger. I love you; I love you all, now I must go. I won't have time to see you off as I must call on all the officials of the city. That will take up the rest of the day and evening. Tomorrow I leave, as you should.! We hugged and kissed, and I left swiftly. It was always better that way than lingering to hear a single sob.

We camped outside the city of Chalcis. Hermogenes returned with the requisitioned supplies from the city. Thousands of little fires lit up the dark night, I stood outside my tent and looked around at the ghostly figures moving about the camp. The gently chatter of men mixed with the smell of burnt ash, still burning wood and dung loitered in the air. It helped make the damp mist that had begun to roll in from the river feel less cold. One of King Arethas's scouts had returned just before dark with news that the Persians were retreating towards the frontier. They were close to the city of Gabboulon, and with any luck, we would not have to risk fighting them and still achieve success by chasing them out of the Empire, without them having done any real damage to the region.

"You look troubled, General. May I offer you something to warm you and help sleep?" The voice made me jump. Turning, I saw a tall, lean man, older and no doubt wiser than me. A black beard covered his face, and his dark eyes were protected by equally dark eyebrows. He was wearing dark-coloured clothes with a long wrap that covered his head and draped over his shoulders in the traditional style of his tribe. I hadn't heard him as he came upon me out of the flickering light of the campfires.

I hazarded a guess at who my new guest was; Arethas. I knew he and his men had joined us in the camp, his Roman was clear and precise. He had been educated in the capital. His late father had determined that good relations could only be strengthened by having a thorough knowledge of your ally. I, like everyone else, had heard tales of their tough life living in goat skin tents when they went into the wilderness. Yet they also had towns built around oases and were civilised. They maintained a link between the settled and nomadic existence of their ancestors; their wealth came from guarding and controlling the merchant caravans crossing from Arabia and the East. With nothing to stop me accepting the invite and needing a good sleep, I accepted his offer.

He led me to his encampment, which was less ordered to my eyes in the light of the big fires his men had gathered around. The camels seemed to be wandering around, but as I passed one, I noticed the long tether dangling from one of its legs, the horses were penned close to the tents. My guards followed behind; they were my permanent shadows on campaign. I passed many tents with the men lounging outside, some of them were chatting in their language, while others listened to one of them who was kind of singing and talking to the group gathered around the fires. They appeared far more relaxed than my men were.

I was led into his tent, which was lower than a Roman one, but much longer and made up of sections. Many small oil lamps hanging from the guide poles, lit the inside, yet the tent wasn't filled with sooty smoke. Arethas gestured to me to sit on a fleece, and he reclined next to me. The floor was covered in rich carpets; this felt less like a campaign tent than a home from home. A woman covered from head to foot approached and gave me a hot drink and then gave the same to Arethas. Another similarly clad woman brought us silver dishes filled with dates. Arethas explained their customs, such as hospitality to any traveller who entered their tents and the importance of family and tribe. The need to avenge blood was of utmost importance to them, with some of their feuds lasting for generations. Eventually, these were solved by compromise agreed to by families and entailed gold and marriage; even though they were Christian like us, honour was sacred to each member of the tribe.

So, with their arch enemies so close, his tribesmen wanted and demanded blood to settle feuds. He expected us to attack the Persians and their allies as soon as we could, as this would not only enhance his prestige but also that of the Basileus. Another drink was produced, this one was again hot, but I could clearly smell honey and coriander. I sipped the drink; it tasted as good as it smelt. We talked on for most of the night. I awoke at dawn; I was still inside his tent, covered by a sheepskin. Arethas was already awake and offered me water and something cold to eat. I thanked him for his hospitality and returned to my tent, where my staff were waiting for me.

It was the day before Easter. I ordered the camp to be struck, and we moved on, following the trail of the Persians, our scouts out hunting them. Word came back shortly after we had begun moving that the Persian army was still encamped, opposite the city of Callinicum. They had not made any attempt to move, but their camp was stretched out on the valley floor between the river and high ground and so confined by the terrain. We approached to within two miles of them and halted. The army moved into defensive positions while I held a conference with my commanders and Arethas.

"Gentlemen, as you are aware, the Persian camp is close by. My intentions are to remain here and wait for them to break camp and then allow them to return to Persia. I don't want to risk a battle in the valley as it favours the defender. The Persians are doing exactly what we want them to do. God has granted us a victory, why risk losing it." My statement was simple, and I made sure to speak calmly but with as much authority as possible. There was a moment of silence, a sort of stunned silenced. Then the commander of the infantry was the first to reply, and he was not happy.

"I can't believe this. The enemy is only a short distance away and clearly unready for us. My men need a chance to prove themselves. If you won't fight, then I will. Anyone who wants to follow me can." It was a shocking statement and caused a general murmur of approval that travelled around my commanders. I was not pleased, especially when it was clear the situation could easily come apart if we reacted the wrong way. But Arethas then spoke, and though I had assumed he might be just as unreceptive of my thoughts, he gave a soft snort as he stroked at his long dark beard.

"I see the wisdom of Belisarius's plan, and it would be the easiest route to victory. But the army and my men will not see it this way. If we don't fight, they will brand us cowards and unworthy of being their commanders. We are forced to fight today, Belisarius."

I looked around at the commanders; here I risked a revolt and the destruction of my command. The old days of the commander having total control were gone, each commander was appointed by the Basileus and so directly responsible to him. Even as general of the East, I too was directly responsible to the Basileus, it was like having an invisible presence.

Many of my commanders were older than me and had more experience, and this made Arethas's point all the more obvious. He was right, and I was wrong, sometimes the right choice isn't the correct one for such circumstances. A battle was being forced on me, and I had no way to prevent it without a revolt, unlike Arethas, who was in sole control of his men. If he wanted to fight, he could, and I couldn't stop him. If he went into battle on his own though, we would look like cowards. There was no choice but to accede to the decision of the king and my commanders and go into battle. I took a deep breath before I spoke, the weight of it and the possibility of all that needless death weighed heavy on my mind.

"Gentlemen, prepare your men for battle. Although it is against my better judgement, I will do my utmost to bring us victory. The infantry will form up on my left, closest to the river. The cavalry and I will take the centre and Arethas and his men the right."

They began to disperse quickly towards their men, but I stood there for a moment. I was looking towards the riverbank, the bulrushes rustled in the breeze as the heat of the day gathered, flies buzzed around me, seeking my sweat. I hadn't realised how much I had sweated in the last few moments since finishing my speech; I didn't like the situation one bit. We were going to attack a position similar to the one I held against the Persians and defended so well, and this deeply worried me. But I had changed my mind and followed the majority decision, instead of sticking to my original position; was I about to regret this? The last of the commanders had saluted and departed, and only John was left beside me, he had remained silent throughout the meeting. But I needed to query him as I turned to look directly at him. "John, will you lead my bodyguard in the battle? Feel free to remain with the baggage if you wish to avoid what I consider to be a highly dangerous encounter."

"Belisarius, you worry too much. Have confidence, I will be at your side as always, unto death. I would rather that than live as a coward," John said, appearing to look through me and beyond. Sometimes I thought I understood my Armenian friend, then events like today reminded me that there was much about him that remained closed. He had some secret, dark probably, that he had not shared, for like our Arab allies, the Armenians took honour very seriously, and they too had long-lasting blood feuds. It wasn't my business or would not be till the day he asked for my help.

We both returned to our steeds, and the servants assisted us with mounting and adjusting our armour, ready for battle. They unpacked spare weapons from the packhorses and loaded us up. We would have no more food till Easter morning as the vigil had already started. All we could have was water, and it would be a long day ahead.

We spread out along the valley floor following the road, three columns moving together, the element of surprise long gone with the mists of the dawn. With the time it had taken us to form up, the Persians would have had to have been born deaf and blind not to be aware we were coming. Slowly, we moved forwards, at a pace the infantry was comfortable with and as we rounded a bend in the river, the valley opened wider, and a low hill dominated the right wing's approach. The riverbank was covered with reeds, and several small islands could be clearly seen in the centre of the river. The valley floor was flat, unbroken scrubland; the only trees were close to the river. Just this section was perfect terrain for cavalry to operate on. I hadn't seen this from our camp, and this confirmed my apprehension.

Awaiting us, fully lined up across our path, was the whole of the Persian army in formation. Cavalry with their Arab allies facing our infantry. We slowed as I ordered our wings to close in with the centre, I wanted to remove any gaps between our formations, as well as leaving our allies the freedom to move in the valley. Both sides slowly approached, never yet charging, waiting for the optimal distance. I realised we were handicapped by the infantry; we couldn't charge without exposing them. We were on the defensive. I ordered a halt and all weapons charged ready for the Persian assault.

Then the Persian line surged forward. The thunderous sound of their horses building as they approached in a general charge. The Persians rushed towards our lines, each section shooting arrows into us and reeling around to be replaced by another as they enjoyed the stationary targets. But it also allowed my men to have a better chance of hitting the backs of the moving targets. The breeze behind us gave our shots a little more range. It was our Arab allies who took more of a toll from the bombardment as they lacked the heavy armour our cavalry wore. The infantry was luckier as they escaped most of the bombardment and instead were showered with spears rather than arrows. Holding still was tearing at my men, quite apart from Arethas and his men. The Persians maintained this flowing advance and retreat in an effort to draw us out. We managed to hold firm.

In the afternoon, it all went wrong; the Persian left wing opposite our allies exploded from their positions. Their masked and armoured cavalry moving in unison appeared more like a wall of flashing steel as they charged at full speed. The noise was deafening as the horses advanced, even from the centre, as it was mixed with the screams of the Persians and sounds of their trumpets blasting. The dust trailed behind them as they charged into my allies, a black cloud of arrows shot from the Persians into the Arabs, and they fell like wheat under the blow of the scythe. The massed wall of Persian steel then veered to their right and swung away from my allies crippled front rank. As it moved, it changed formation into that of a huge wedge and then charged again, this time into the small gap between my position and the Arabs.

A cold shiver travelled up, and down my spine; my mouth went dry. It was the moment that I knew the Persians had broken through our lines, and defeat stared us in the face. They continued streaming through the gap, as Arethas and his men broke and fled, totally exposing my flank. The armoured Persian cavalry saw the flight and turned again, but this time took off in pursuit of the fleeing Arabs. I watched in horror as a third of my line disintegrated and, in that moment, the Persian commander saw his chance and launched his next assault on us. I never saw it, as I was still mesmerised by the unfolding disaster.

"Belisarius, they're charging at us," John screamed into my face, rousing me from my shock. I looked around and saw the look of horror on those guards close to me as they prepared themselves for the oncoming crash. John brought my guards into a tight formation surrounding Hermogenes and myself. We did not have time to launch a counter charge. The crash came suddenly as if a giant wave had rolled over us, we all seemed to move backwards under the impact. The Persians charged into the front of my position, shooting arrows up to the last moment, then switching to hand-held weapons as they closed in on us. They mowed down the first rank under sheer pressure and the second row quickly gave way under the enormous power of their impact. Arrows were still being shot into our position, filling shields with spines, making them useless to hold. The company in front of our position gradually gave way as men were unhorsed in the fierce hand-to-hand battle. I attempted to gather the men close to us to form a wall of steel and push back on them in an effort to slow their advance.

I didn't need to be told what had happened. It was clear the Persian left wing had ended their pursuit. They had quickly reformed and turned around and were now charging at the rear of my formation. As stream of deathly tipped arrows flowed into us from behind, striking the rear of our formation, piercing through armour wherever they found gaps. Even horses were struck in their unarmoured rumps.

We were now surrounded on three sides; the weight of Persian fire was quickly disposing of the centre of my formation. We were in danger of being surrounded totally. There was no choice, but to retreat, but the only safe route was to pull back and into the infantry who were in a far better position. They at least had one side protected by the river and an escape. I turned to John and Hermogenes and shouted.

"Breakout, full back on the infantry. If we don't, we're finished."

They nodded their agreement. No sooner had they agreed when we were assailed by the dull thud of Persian arrows landing around us. Hermogenes pulled an arrow out of his shield. Neither John nor I had been caught, but it was far too close. I shouted back to them before turning to the trumpeter and signalling the order to pull back. "Where's Ascan the cavalry commander, find him and use a few of his men to cover us."

"I'll stay. What's left of Ascan's cavalry will secure your withdrawal. Move." John barked back at me, drawing his sword, and signalling my guards to form around him. When they were with him, John pulled away with the rest of the guards and headed over to where Ascan and his men were fighting. Hermogenes had already issued orders, and the main body of cavalry was forming up where it could. Others were attempting to fight their way out of the chaos. Some men couldn't extract themselves without risking their comrades and fought where they stood.

I followed Hermogenes as he began to swing outwards and turn towards the left flank. The air around us still hissed with the deadly shafts. The Persians had spotted our change of tactics and were attempting to break through to my location. As I turned to flee, I saw John for a fleeting moment; he was hacking his way into a heavily armoured Persian cavalryman, who in turn swung his mace at John. I left John to fight his personal battle as I raced towards the river. As we approached, the infantry opened their ranks and allowed us into their position, shooting over us to ward off the pursuing Persians.

What was left of the cavalry reassembled behind the infantry, under the command of Hermogenes, who had made it through, I joined them. I dismounted and made my way to the infantry commander's position. Hermogenes had seen me dismount, so he followed suit and joined me. The three of us stood together. We could still just see what remained of our cavalry being pushed back towards us. Persian arrows were raining on our positions all the same; men held shields over us.

"Hermogenes, dismount the cavalry and let the horses go. We'll fight on foot. There's no room here for horses." He moved away as soon as I gave the instruction, infantrymen covering him as they moved back to the cavalry. I turned to the infantry commander; my face grim.

"How are your men?"

"Not good. The recruits were the first to flee, and I assume the Persians got them," he stretched out his arm and swept it towards the front of our position.

"This is all that we have?"

I could hardly believe it. As I looked upon what was left of my army. I noticed that he looked just as exhausted as the rest of us. All around his position lay the wounded and dying. Men continued to drag their comrades back to this location, collected more arrows then returned to their positions. The sound of the wounded was enough to convince me I would find no help here.

"Commander, deploy the men where you need them. Pass the word, every man to grab a shield and protect the archers while they fire."

He shouted to his chief centurion, who ran forward to his fellow centurions and the orders were passed forward. The cavalry made their way to my position, collecting the larger shields of the infantry where they could, or else using their own ones. They cowed under colleagues while they did their best to quickly break off Persian arrows embedded in their shields. The whole formation began to retract inwards, as each man used his shield to cover his companion to his left. The archers from the cavalry joined the infantry archers and began to fire in volleys at the Persian cavalry as they galloped past, who in turn were hurling spears and shooting arrows into our positions.

No matter how much we shot back at them, they continued to squeeze and compress our position. If we stayed put any longer, we would end up as target practice for the Persian cavalry. I leaned across to the infantry commander and shouted into the side of his helmet.

"We need to slowly withdraw to the riverbank." He signalled his agreement. Gradually, we shifted sideward, we left the dead and wounded behind. The Persian arrow storm never let up, wherever one stepped it was on either a dying or wounded man. The air gradually filled with thick earthy dust that stuck to our blood and sweat, kicked up by the constant charging of the Persian cavalry. Slowly, we began to resemble pigs wallowing in mud, rather than soldiers. The sweet smell of death lingered amongst us. The corpses seemed to almost move on their own, so thickly did they become covered in flies. I was lost in thought as I gazed at our once brave, but dead army.

"Belisarius. Stop talking to the dead and concentrate on the living." The voice sounded familiar but worn and strained. I turned to face the sound of the voice, and there was John, standing with his head covered by one of my guard's shields. His left arm was hanging limply by his side, his chest armour ripped in places, yet the tough figure still lived.

"My God, you're alive! Thanks be to God, I thought I'd lost you, old friend!

"It will take more than a Persian to send me to my Maker." He grinned, leaning against his battered shield, helmet loose upon his head but none of his usual humour lost.

"What happened back there?" I said my expression one of shock but mixed with joy and awe to know I had not lost such an important ally. However, John hesitated for a moment, seemingly catching his breath before he looked down at the ground for a moment as he replied.

"They hacked Ascan to death. His men died at his side. They refused to leave him. Their sacrifice was worth it. You, Belisarius, made it here and you are alive. Now lead us." He looked directly at me. He spoke not just for himself but for all those still alive, and I understood as I grit my teeth at the bitter news.

"You're right, John, this sour taste of defeat has defiled my mouth." I spat on the ground; now was not the time to run or panic, but to try and save the situation. But we haven't lost yet."

I stood up and grabbed John by the shoulder and half dragged him over to the infantry commander who was having arrow wounds on his right arm cleaned. I shook the feeling of defeat out of my body. As we watched the surgeon clean the arm. I took hold of his chief centurion and asked him how the front was doing. He reported that so far, the Persians had not charged his lines; instead, they were trying to wear them down with missile fire. I told him to go forward and directly control the defence and concentrate as many archers as possible on the front ranks of the Persian cavalry. We needed to deplete them faster than they could wear us out.

Once the commander was stitched up, I ordered him to take a few men and scout the riverbank for an escape route. John and I moved to the front positions; we found the chief centurion running the defence with what was left of his centurions effectively controlling our archers' fire. Another Persian charge rolled forward, and a surge of missiles flew at us. This time, the shields were used to counter the shallow angle of their flight to great effect. Then up popped our archers from behind those same shields, they caught the Persians as they were turning just after finishing their attack on us. The strings were pulled back level with their ears, and then they let rip and down fell a good number of the Persians caught from behind. Another row of archers emerged from behind these, who now set about reloading. The second row's fire caused almost as much damage as the first. Another flight whooshed over our heads, then silence as the archers retreated under cover. The Persians failed to return fire as they retired back to their lines.

I realised that we had a slim chance. If the Persians continued with this tactic, we could hold out till dark. If they charged, supported by any infantry they might have, it would be a different story. I moved around in the lull, encouraging as many men as I could reach before John firmly suggested my place was back in the rear. Thank God, we still had infantry. Today they proved their worth. Under a good commander, they could remain firm even under the most furious onslaughts. The light began to fail, and the Persians failed to follow up on their last assault — the loss of light made a cavalry charge dangerous. With dark came the end of the Easter vigil and we could eat again. Through the gathering darkness we could clearly see small fires being lit way past where the Persian lines had been. As the fires grew more numerous, we knew that the Persians had retired for the night. I called all the remaining commanders together, it was a small group compared to this morning, but the faces though tired, were not defeated; we were a sorry bunch, but we were still alive. The Infantry commander reported that a river crossing was feasible from our current location. I looked around at the group, and I think they knew what I was going to say. No one liked the idea of retreating, but it was preferable to dying.

"We can't wait here for them to finish us off," I said, pausing then continuing, "if we retreat up the road, they will cut us up. We have no other choice but to cross the river here. Those not strong enough will have to be left behind if no one is willing to carry them. Any questions?" No one spoke, so I continued, "We will stagger the crossing; first we will move the walking wounded to the island. Those who can swim will continue across and then make for Callinicum and summon help. The rest of us will wait on the island. We need to set a rear-guard up here to cover the last section of the retreat — my guard will undertake that."

There was no answer from them, just a shrug and gentle bobbing of heads. They moved back to their men and prepared them for the crossing. We needed to dump all excess equipment here and carry only what was required across the river. Anything that could not be packed on the remaining animals was discarded, along with our dead. Any weapons that were to be left were damaged beyond use. The first to make the crossing to the island were the men who were good swimmers. They carried ropes which they secured on the island then swam on for the far bank and then on to the city.

Perhaps we might be able to return at a later date and bury our dead, I pondered, as I watched the shadows move down to the riverbank in the darkness. The wounded could not help but make noise as they dragged themselves or were carried to the riverbank. The river current was stronger than expected, the ropes helped guide the men and animals over, but we still lost a number. In the darkness, slippery rocks were hazardous and being knocked over by an animal was a constant danger. The occasional scream for help was the last we heard of these poor men, caught by the current and dragged away.

The infantry, moving in ones and twos, entered the river, they splashed their way through the shallow water, hanging with one free arm from the ropes as the water deepened, closing up to their chests until they reached the island. My guard was the last to follow, those with a mount, forming the rear-guard, before finally entering the water and making a noise as the horses churned through the water, before climbing out onto the island. We had made a great deal of noise, but the Persians failed to investigate; I was one of the last to cross with the rear-guard. On the island, we placed the animals in the centre while we formed an all-round defence. Gradually, the only sound came from the animals and the wounded. Men removed wet clothing and hung them on bushes to dry out a bit, but within reach in case of an alert.

As the last stars started to fade, but before the light of dawn arrived, I was called over by the sentry commander, he pointed to a distant bobbing light approaching upstream We stood together, straining our eyes as we peered into the darkness, trying to make out what it was. After an interval, the light still hadn't faded, I told the commander to wake all the men and prepare them for a fight. As I watched, a few more lights appeared in the same direction, and the sound of water being forced out of the way reached us. The archers loaded their bows and made ready as John arrived next to me.

"You think it's the Persians?" he said, and I murmured agreement as I removed my sword from its scabbard. Following my example, he removed his sword, and we stood ready. Tension began to build in the men around us all. No one was quite prepared for another onslaught, but if necessary, we would face it.

"Greetings! Hello! We're Romans from Callinicum!" a voice shouted out from, close to the source of the bobbing lights. The sentry commander shouted out a call for the password. The unknown voice replied, "There isn't one, as it's not dawn yet."

It was the correct answer. If a password had been given, we knew that they had been compromised; we all stood down, putting away our weapons. The lights came closer, and it was clear enough to see Roman figures wading through the shallows pulling the boats in our direction, and there was great relief in it. The boats were guided in and then tied up; we would use them to cross to the far bank. The river on that side was too strong for the men, but the horses and pack animals could just about make it.

Dawn came, sentries returned to their duties and a mist enveloped the island and banks, and we began the slow process of transporting what was left of the army across the river. The chief centurion took a count as the men were ferried over. By his count, we had left four thousand men on the other bank. By lunchtime, we had finished crossing, and a column was assembled on the riverbank, while the boats were wrecked to ensure the Persians could not use them to come after us.

I had failed as a direct result of changing my mind. If I had enforced my decision, we wouldn't be in the mess we were in now and be a defeated army. We had lost a good number of men and suffered a humiliating defeat. My army was no longer capable of operations, and we were reduced to having to walk back to Callinicum. All I could do now was distribute the able-bodied men to garrison the cities and fortresses of the surrounding region.

We reached Callinicum before dark; our entrance was not celebrated by the inhabitants. They barely batted an eye; they were too busy collecting supplies, ready to sell to us. We were a desperate bunch as we hobbled through the main gate shortly before dark. That evening, I stood on the walls and looked out in the direction of the battle. The air was cold, and a slight breeze was enough to make me shiver. The river moved past us and down to the site of the battle, the light from the lanterns on the walls glittered on the surface of the water. It showed no reaction to the past day's events, its indifference to us was reassuring; at least the world hadn't ended, although deep down that is what it felt like. The cold finally got to me, and I pulled my cloak up round my neck and wriggled inside to gain warmth. I was worn out.

A week passed, the Persians hadn't arrived, and the men cleaned up and began to regain a little confidence. Parades were held, and weapon practise was undertaken outside the walls. Uniforms and equipment were repaired, and the wounded slowly crept back to health.

On the last day of the week, Hermogenes received a dispatch from Rufinus ordering him to contact the Persians and negotiate a settlement at any cost. I heard nothing, which was a sign that I was in disgrace over my defeat. I waited for my orders and my replacement to arrive. Hermogenes had advised me before he left, to couch my reports in light of the fact that the Persians had continued with their "retreat" so that our defeat could be seen as part of an overall campaign to successfully eject the Persians from the Empire.

It was an optimistic approach, and I dithered before having Procopius write it up that way. My official report to Rufinus and the Basileus made out that my tactical defeat had really been a victory. As I had forced the Persians to continue with their "retreat" after inflicting enough casualties on them to deter them from continuing with their offence. But I still laid the blame for the defeat on myself and requested that I be removed from my command over my failure. Procopius said I was being too dramatic but wrote up the dispatch as I requested.

While I awaited their decision, I concentrated on rebuilding the army. The quartermasters put in their requisitions and the army continued to train and rebuild its confidence. We began the process of absorbing new recruits who continued to arrive even though word of the defeat must have spread across the region. Arethas, later that month, sent me a personal dispatch and in it he apologised for his force's retreat, but he emphasised he was still loyal, and he would be sending us fresh horses to make up for our losses.

This was one of our recurring problems. We could only ask our allies to fight with us in battle. We couldn't directly order them how to fight, and if they decided to retreat, there was little we could do. We needed them as they protected our desert flanks and guarded convoys, and for that, the gold they were paid was worth it.

Two months passed before I received a reply from the capital, and I was summoned back; I was no longer in command. I was to appoint a deputy to oversee the army till Sittas arrived later in the summer to take command. Once my deputy was settled in, I said my goodbyes to the army, and together with John and my bodyguards, we began the journey back to Antioch. There, I settled my affairs visited the local dignitaries and made my farewells. I had learnt in my time here, that no matter what you thought of these people and the roles they had, they were part of the administration. Their co-operation was vital to the running of the provinces the collection of taxes, law and replenishment of the army. They may be as corrupt and immoral as it was possible to be, but that was the way things were and would continue to be.

At the end of the month, we rode out of the city through the West Gate over the Orontes River and headed towards Asia-Minor.

Chapter Four

The journey from Antioch had taken longer than I thought it would, even though the weather had stayed fine. The autumn was coming in fast, and the heat of the day grew less intense. The smell of fruit ripening stayed with us for most of the journey. Whenever we stopped, fresh fruit was offered to us, and the apricots were by far the most delicious. As always, the fruit was accompanied by a fermented fruit juice which had quite a kick to it. I am sure this is what slowed us, apart from picking up stomach bugs which added to the delay. It was sapping to be bedridden for days at a time and constantly needing to go outside and then wash.

We reached the capital in the late autumn, and after dismissing my guards, I went straight to the palace. I had hoped for an audience, but the palace refused to allow me access and would only take a written report, even though I waited for nearly a day. In the end, I headed home to wait on a summons. With my guards I took a ferry back over to Chalcedon and collected mounts and rode on to the house.

I finally arrived at my home outside of the town of Rufiniannae just before dark. The main house seemed quiet from the outside. Lamps had been lit, the air was a touch colder, and a breeze blew in from the Propontis. I took my mount to the stables and removed the saddle and blanket. By the time I had completed this, the servants had arrived and led my animal away, as well as dealing with my guards' animals. I dismissed the guards, and they went over to their quarters. John who been at my house since our return, intervened and placed several on sentry duty as he was unhappy with the situation, and I had to admit, I was feeling very unsettled.

We went to the bathhouse, which the servants had fired up. It was bliss to lie back and have servants remove the grime and dirt we had accumulated over the last months journeying back from Antioch. On reflection, it was probably a wise thing that I did not gain an interview with the Basileus that day. We remained in the heat for a good while before heading for the main part of the house. The residence smelt welcoming as we entered it, the smell of herbs and cooking dominated the air. I noted with satisfaction that the sentries were now on duty and congratulated John on restoring discipline. We walked along the central corridor to the main reception room. I swung the door open, and a loud cheer greeted us.

The room was brightly lit. The room was filled with faces I recognised as well as some I did not. Antonina rushed over to me. She was wearing a beautiful silk dress that was brightly decorated in vibrant blue, reds and green colours that swirled and curled around her as she moved. Her face was shining, and her eyes were decorated in the Egyptian with thick, long lines caressing her eyelids. My heart was racing. She looked even more beautiful than I had remembered and I could think of nothing to say but the moment needed no words to express what we felt for each other. We embraced and kissed. Our embrace felt like it lasted forever. When we parted, my daughters rushed to me and hugged me tightly. Finally, Phocas was by my side; I gave him a hug.

"My family and friends and guests, I am glad to be home with you again. Thank you all for this welcome. Please, eat and drink and enjoy," I said, not quite sure what else to say for this unexpected but greatly appreciated welcome. There was a general chorus of thanks that echoed around the room. The guests made their way forward to greet me and formally introduce themselves. Once this was done, they made their way over to the wine and food. As the atmosphere relaxed, the guests began questioning me on the situation in the East, and the news that King Kavad was dead and that Chosroes was the new king of the Persians.

I had heard rumours of the recent events and my guests, some of whom worked in the palace, were able to add to what little knowledge I had of the Basileus's plans for peace. I learnt that Hermogenes was to accompany Rufinus and two other senior officials in the following spring and visit the new King and obtain a fresh "everlasting peace agreement." The general opinion was that the Basileus was prepared to accept most of the Persian demands concerning Dara, as well as paying for the maintenance of Persian troops to secure the Caspian Gates. None of them seemed to know why he was prepared to accept such terms in return for peace. The rumour with the largest following was that he wanted to campaign in the Balkans and needed no distractions in the East. This, apparently, was the reason that Mundus, the commander of the army in Illyricum, was in the capital along with his personal guard force of possibly over a thousand Eurlain warriors.

I only knew Mundus by reputation, he had served the late Emperor Justin well, and since then had commanded the army of Illyricum. He had dealt successfully with continued Gothic incursions; he was the most senior and experienced general currently in the service of the Basileus. I hoped to meet him, but this was tempered by the knowledge that I was no longer in favour, my recent defeat had seen to that, and I wasn't surprised. Results were all that mattered for a commander. My name had not featured in the rumours concerning the new campaign.

The party slowly ended, and my mood was somewhat down, with the sure confirmation of my predicament, by the lack of my name being mentioned in regard to the forthcoming campaign. I was now sure I was in still in Justinian's bad books, the guests gradually disappeared into the bright moonlit night. John had already abandoned the party and found entertainment more of his suiting elsewhere within the house, no doubt with one of the female guests. With the last farewell, I could finally make my way to the bedroom, and as I made my way, I noted the servants were working feverishly to clear up. Once they had done that, then they would be entitled to go to sleep till dawn, when they would start preparing the house ready for us to rise.

I entered my room, dumped my clothes on the floor and told the servant to leave the room and not bother with my clothes. I didn't want to be disturbed any longer, and I dived into the bed. It was soft and warm, the fleeces made for a cosy layer under me, a welcome change from either a blanket or straw. I was safe, at last. The last oil lamp flickered and hissed, then darkness filled the room, and I could close my eyes and enjoy a well-earned rest.

I thought I heard footsteps padding along the tiled floor; it could be a cat out hunting for rats or mice. They were light sounding, so not a man in armour, and with that thought, I paid no more attention, rolled over and attempted to go back to sleep.

The splash of water, however, completely wakened me, and I sat up in the darkness. I shivered from the shock, quickly looked around as a shadow moved into the bed next to me. Before my heart could pump and clear the last of the sleep from me, another sense kicked in. The smell told me who it was as she slipped into the covers next to me; her arms pulled me back down to her level. Antonina felt warm and comfortable.

The smell of burning buildings had been enduring in the air over us for at least four days.

 The dense cloud of thick, black smoke had finally shifted from haunting the Imperial section of the city thanks to a change in the wind and now drifted towards the Asian shore. I stood on the top of my house, on a section of flat roof which was easy to reach, as I had for the last three days, and looked across at the capital. I never thought I would ever see this, an insurrection. The city's prefect had attempted to execute the ringleaders of both the Green and Blue factions after they had fought each other in the streets around the Hippodrome, a number of bystanders had been killed, taverns and shops had been looted and burnt. The mob had quickly turned from the normal fighting among themselves to outright rioting. With the arrest of their leaders, the factions had for once come together and temporarily settled their differences, united they stormed the prison, releasing their leaders and fellow comrades held within. With that, the riot turned into something completely different in nature — an insurrection and all hell broke out.

The Imperial section of the city became their prime target; the Church of the Holy Wisdom was sacked and set alight along with the Baths of Zeusxippus and the main market. The Basileus had retreated into the palace, and only silence emanated from within. The capital was paralysed, and as no orders were issued, the garrison remained surrounding the palace and did nothing to halt the insurrection going on around them.

The leaders of the factions became emboldened as they were no longer being contained by the authorities and they set up their headquarters inside the Hippodrome. Demands were then sent to the palace. One of their first demands was for the head of the Praetorian prefect — he had imprisoned the leaders of the Blues and Greens over an earlier altercation-, John the Cappadocian, who was frequently referred to behind his back as "the Chain". He confined anyone he suspected of avoiding payment and only released them on payment of outstanding taxes and a commission. John had to be the most hated official, as he was responsible for the raising of tax by any means. He, like me, had risen from below, first a clerk and now Praetorian prefect. The Basileus had promoted him as an outsider and a man who got results and more. They also demanded the head of the city prefect, which was just for revenge purposes, as he had been involved in the arrest of their leaders. Lastly, they demanded the sacking of the Quaestor Tribunianus; according to Procopius, he was the most corrupt judge, which was saying something. For a very large fee, he could fix any legal settlement. The poor and less well-off had reason to hate him as the rich used him as an instrument to strengthen their power and wealth at their expense. It was becoming obvious that these demands were just the start, and that they wanted a complete change of government.

The Basileus, along with most of the Senate, remained in the palace, silent except for a message sent to the Hippodrome announcing that he had agreed with their demands. Once the message was announced to the mob within the Hippodrome, a huge shout of the Greek for victory, "Nika, Nika, Nika," echoed throughout the capital. He had just poured oil onto an already large fire; now they began to contemplate a change of Basileus.

Once word of this reached me, I dispatched Procopius with a personal message to Mundus. In it, I proposed that I cross over to the capital with all my guards and whatever soldiers I could collect, secure the port closest to the palace, combine our forces and offer our support to the Basileus. If we lost the Basileus, the Persians principally among our enemies, would surely take advantage in the spring and invade. Secondly, our necks were on the line here. A new regime may well want to dispose of any members of the last regime and start with a clean slate.

Later that day, shouting from the courtyard disturbed lunch. John and I rushed out to see what the cause of the noise was. My guards had already detained a boy when we arrived on the scene. He was dragged over to us, and he looked like a young beggar. A rough brown cloak was tied tightly around his body and head, yet his bearing suggested that he wasn't what he appeared to be. The commander of the guard saluted as we stepped over.

"General, the boy demands to speak to the Lady Antonina." He hit the figure around the head for the perceived cheek of his request and continued, "He has a letter for her, he claims."

The other guards shook the boy hard until he released the letter, which was handed over to John. He looked it over and very quickly handed it to me. He made a quick observation that the letter bore the Augusta's seal and with it, he gave a quizzical expression. I was slightly relieved and slightly anxious. I looked over the seal and nodded in agreement and ordered the guards to bring the boy. John and I proceeded with the boy and the letter towards Antonina's apartments. We arrived at the door, the guards dropped the boy who quickly regained his balance, and I handed him the letter as we awaited Antonina's arrival. The guard commander's sword was just visible behind the boy's back. Should the boy do anything to threaten Antonina, he would drop him like a stone falling into a pond.

The door swung open and out stepped Antonina, accompanied by two of her maids. The guard's sword glittered as it moved a fraction closer to the back of the boy. Antonina looked flustered as she stepped into the anteroom. A red cloak had been hurriedly placed on her shoulders. She looked at me, John and then the boy and spoke.

"I am the Lady Antonina. Well, what have you for me?"

"I have a message from my mistress for you," replied the boy, his voice was strangely weak for a boy of his perceived age.

He then stood erect for the first time, a hand reached up and pulled away the hood. The hair fell still tied slipped out of the hood, and it was now clear it was a young woman, not a boy who had spoken. The guard's sword visibly drooped and then was sheathed quietly, and he stood back. John and I stared at the young woman, at a loss for a moment, then I remembered the letter and its seal. Antonina was slightly bemused for a moment, but the puzzled look was quickly lost, then a faint smile replaced it. She recognised the young woman and then said in a more relaxed tone, "Well, what can I do for the Augusta, my dear?"

"My mistress begs you to ask your husband to come to our aid in the palace. The Augusta does not trust those around them; they advise flight. She wants you and your husband by their side, *now*, my lady." The girl handed the letter over to Antonina, who noted the seal and opened the letter, quickly reading it. Then she handed it to a servant and told her to burn it, straightaway. She had the girl taken into her quarters. Then turning to us, she said, with a very stern expression, "Go to the palace and save them."

I looked at her, and I knew she meant it. There was little I could do to refuse her demand, even if I'd wanted to, or that of the Augusta. I turned, followed by John and the guards. A voice called out as we left the anteroom, just to give me the little boost of confidence I needed.

"Thank you, my darling. You honour me. I know the Augusta will never forget you for this. God protect you all."

I trudged out to the courtyard with a grim determination upon my face as I turned to John and gave my own stern order.

"Send a messenger to Mundus, tell him we are coming now. Get the guards together, we leave for the palace now."

We rode into Chalcedon. I It was empty; the inhabitants had gone inside to wait for news from across the water. We found the barges tied up and the crews sitting around doing nothing. With a few points from my guards' swords, they soon stirred themselves and rowed us across to the Imperial port. We disembarked and led our mounts inside the Great Palace. They were taken to the main stables, and we headed into the complex.

We stood in one of the many ante-halls, helmets held in arms, shields and spears resting with two of our guards. The Palace was in chaos. Servants and officials were running around like headless chickens after a frenzied slaughter gone wrong. The guards at the gateways and corridors had also been sullen, which was a sign that chaos was slowly seeping its way inside the palace. All I knew was that the mob was holding an assembly in the Hippodrome.

A tall, heavy-built man entered the hall. His face had the texture of leather though his eyes were those of a youthful man, bright blue, fiery and lit his face and contrasted with his silver cropped beard and hair. An old-style helmet with a red feathered plume in his left hand, and his right held the hilt of his sword. His armour was also out of fashion. A heavy-looking leather cuirass contoured to his physical features, and a second shorter sword was strung across and down his left side. I took a guess at who this man was.

"General Mundus, I have come at the request of the Augusta. She has also asked for your help. Will you join us?"

"Hold on, son. Why the hell do you think I'm here? You think I wear this for fun?" he grunted, tapping his chest with a slightly amused expression that gave me some relief.

"Just for the fun of it or maybe to have a bath." I responded swiftly, not skipping a beat so allowing the humour a moment to sink into Mundus. This was followed by a deep belly laugh that told me this was a man who was not taken aback by anything, let alone the kind to back down, as his blue eyes bored into mine.

"When you were a boy, I was fighting with your uncle in the East. Did you know that? Who do you think got you your place in the guards? He wrote and recommended you. I owed him, and he was right about you, even then."

I was more than a little surprised to hear this as he marched right to my side. His tone had been almost a little menacing as he'd gripped both of my shoulders and shook me a little. "Right. Let's forget the history lesson. What do you plan to do?"

I'd been thinking about this since word of the riot had reached me. As I learnt more, I had slowly devised a simple plan. I knew that even with Mundus's forces we were still outnumbered by the mob, yet we would have the element of surprise, and while they remained in the Hippodrome, they were surrounded and destroying them inside was the simplest solution.

"First, we march on the forum of Constantine, then divide up and secure the Great Palace. Then we secure the entrances to the Hippodrome. Once we have them sealed inside, we enter and wipe them out," I stated, and Mundus lifted one of his silvery eyebrows in curiosity.

"Why the forum and not go straight to the Hippodrome?"

"Because that's where I would place guards to stop anyone leaving the palace. Secondly, it also works in our favour; it has two main entrances and acts as a bottleneck. Shut it and we have them cornered in the Hippodrome. Leave it open, and they have a major escape route into the rest of the city, and we would have little chance of catching them and finishing this revolt."

"Good, you know the city better. My men are ready and waiting, follow me. We need to secure the Imperial couple from the rioters and remove any threats to them first," he stated, with the seemingly can-do attitude of someone glad they'd not had to come up with the idea. It was refreshing, to say the least, but my mind was focused solely on the situation at hand, ending the insurrection one way or another

I turned and sent one of my guards to bring the rest of the men to where we were. Once they had arrived, Mundus led us off through the complex and to my surprise, he was saluted, and the once sullen guards fell in behind us. His presence seemed to reassure them, and they may well have been awaiting orders, which so far hadn't come. Mundus led us to one of the many large courtyards which was filled with his men standing in formation, ready. We stood in front of his men, my men falling in behind them as Mundus turned to me and gave a firm grunt of approval.

"Good, then let us proceed. We have an Empire to save, young Belisarius," he stated, making a point of my age as if to remind me who the senior figure was, in case I had any ideas of ordering him around. But then he turned from me to look at his men and suddenly gave a great bellow. "Men, this is General Belisarius, obey any order he gives you as if it came from me. You four, follow me, the rest follow General Belisarius. Kill anyone who resists or just gets in your way."

He led us to the main gate, his men turning smartly in formation and falling in behind us as we passed them. The gates swung open, without a word of command being given. Mundus had obviously been preparing for our arrival. Once we stepped out of the palace, Mundus placed his helmet on his head and removed his swords, one in each hand. He began to run. We joined him; his men were arming themselves as they poured out of the gate.

We quickly reached the forum. The only people visible were those moving their goods and family on carts as they headed out of the city. The main noise was of boots hitting the paved stones of the Triumphal Way. I stopped. Mundus carried on with his men, I then led my men into the entrance of the forum; the smell of burnt wood was all prevailing.

"John, take half the men and secure the far side of the forum." Led by John, they moved quickly across the open square, splitting into groups as they reached the far side. I deployed archers to cover the advance; a shout rang out from the far side. My archers let rip as a small group of rioters made an appearance and fell as quickly as they had appeared. I ordered a charge, and we crossed the forum to join John.

As I arrived, I could see that John's men and the archers had killed many of the mob. The rioters were armed with a variety of weapons: clubs, axes and a few swords. They were no match for us. We left the forum and were met by a hail of arrows from the top of the Hippodrome. A man next to me collapsed with an arrow sticking in his face, blood gushing from the wound coating the stones on which he lay motionless. We were met with sporadic fire, each time the mob's archers fired, it was answered by my men, and the rioters rate of fire quickly decreased as well as their accuracy. We reached the space between the Hippodrome and the palace after clearing the Augusteum. Mundus had surrounded the outer perimeter of the Hippodrome and I the inner, we met up again, the mob was now sealed inside the Hippodrome.

We both entered the palace through one of the now-secure gateways, through the entrance hall and directly to where we knew the Basileus, Augusta and senators were holed up. They were now secure from any attempt by the mob to break in; the regular guards had been replaced by a mix of Mundus's and my men. With that complete, we were now ready to deal with the mob without fear of a coup.

We entered the royal apartments and were led through the maze of corridors to a balcony which faced the Hippodrome. Before the curtains were a group of elaborately dressed noblemen, wearing enough gold and silk to pay for the upkeep of the army for years. They panicked on our entry, some flung themselves to the floor and wept for mercy, others grabbed anything they could to use as weapons and moved to protect the balcony.

Two figures stepped out from behind the curtains that screened the balcony., The statuesque build of the Augusta, and the heavier set, short, bearded man. I was still shocked by their appearance. Both lacked colour in their cheeks, their eyes red and sore looking; they were almost ashen in every aspect. Even the well-made clothes seemed faded and worn, neither wore any regalia and they looked ready for the grave.

"Belisarius, Mundus, we are glad to see you, look at the state of us," said the Basileus as they both walked towards us. We both prostrated ourselves on the floor, then rose as they reached our position. Now, the colour had returned to them, and Justinian almost seemed to have his humour back. The Augusta looked angry, and she was now biting her lip, her oval face turning more round as her mood deepened. A sound of cheering and shouts of "hail, hail," came echoing into the room from the balcony. The Basileus looked over his shoulder at the direction of the voices and said, "So, they have elected my successor, Hypatius, the nephew of Anastasius. Well, they're in for a shock."

"Just when they thought they had us on the run, you both came to save us. Now deal with them as traitors." snarled the Augusta, and even the Basileus's face showed he was slightly taken aback by her outburst. But he nodded his agreement. She spoke again, this time much calmer, the anger now gone from her face. "Belisarius, Mundus, can you enter the Hippodrome and grab Hypatius alive?"

"Yes, Augusta, we can try," replied Mundus.

"Trying isn't good enough, I want him alive," she calmly replied.

"I'll take my men through to the Kathisma by way of the tunnel and snatch him before they realise what's happening," I said firmly, though I was still a little startled by her insistence.

"I'll lead my men into the spiral staircase and secure the Snail Gate, which should divert their attention from Belisarius and his men," Mundus said, but I was a little doubtful of his plan and questioned if it would work.

"We can but try," Mundus announced as we both bowed and marched out of the room. As we reached our men, I sought John, who was looking about expectantly. I ordered him to remain with as many men as he needed to secure the apartments and make sure no one entered until I returned. I then instructed him that if the mob got through, to get the pair out of the city to Chalcedon and summon the fleet. John shook both of my arms, then we separated and set about our bloody tasks. Mundus had already gone on ahead with his men. Now I moved my men into position by the tunnel's entrance.

Mundus sent a runner to tell us he was ready to storm the spiral staircase and the Snail Gate and we were to wait till we could hear screams, then we should storm the tunnel. Time passed slowly, and the heat of the afternoon mixed with the persistent acrid odour of burnt wood made me sweat heavily. The mob was still lauding their new man, and they seemed oblivious to us, even though we had them surrounded already. Either they didn't know or assumed we were part of the coup. An almighty set of screams echoed down the tunnel and through the sides of the outer windows of the palace, as Mundus and his men began attacking the mob grouped around the Snail Gate. I signalled the lead men to rush the doors at the far end.

The door was firmly secured. Normally there would be guards on either side, but they were most definitely missing. The doors themselves could only be bolted from inside and so should have opened outwards, but they had been blocked. I reached the door and pummelled on it with the hilt of my sword.

"Open this door in the name of the Basileus." There was no reply to my order, which I repeated while my men did their utmost to force the door. It was not going to give into us, no matter how hard we tried. It occurred to me that it should have been us who had blocked the doorway to prevent them from getting into the palace, and not the other way around. But be that as it may, it wrecked our plans for the seizing of Hypatius. I sent a message to Mundus and, leaving a small detachment to guard the doorway, pulled my men back inside the palace. Mundus joined us shortly afterwards. He looked hot and bothered, his sword was red with blood, and yet he looked cheerful.

"I'm sorry, General. We couldn't force our way in," I said, exasperated and frustrated, but to my surprise, Mundus was rather nonchalant as he just shrugged his shoulders in return.

"For the time being, we have them trapped, my boy," he replied, not seeming in the least concerned by my failure as he clapped a hand to my back. I could still not tell if he was trying to belittle me or was just being himself. However, we both got a shock when a familiar voice called out to us.

"Gentleman, all this gloom and doom, anyone would have thought the world had ended," said Justinian.

We both turned to look at one another for a moment, not quite sure we had heard it right until it sounded again.

"Belisarius, take your men and force your way into the Hippodrome using the public entrances, concentrate on the Bronze Gate. Mundus, you and your men, storm into the arena using the Gate of Death. Kill anyone who resists."

We both bowed, the Basileus had spoken. He was back in command, and the confidence had completely returned to his voice. I didn't think I would reprimand John as he had no choice but to obey an order and allow the Basileus to make his way to us. I could just make out his figure, standing well back from the Basileus, grasping the hilt of his sword, playfully waiting to be let loose on the troublemakers. Mundus led his remaining men down to the Gate of Death. The Basileus, with some of my men, turned and departed back for his apartment as John came over to me.

"I couldn't stop him. He ordered me to follow, so I did," he said, grinning as he raised a hand to prove that he had no control on the matter. For a moment I gave him a slightly sour expression, but he was right, he couldn't have said no even if it was more sensible and anyway, it seemed to have given us all a bit of a boost in our efforts.

"Very well, take half the men and follow on after a short pause, behind me. Once inside, fan out and clear the rows of the mob." John bowed and pointed at several men and signalled them to wait with him. We then marched out of the palace and retraced our route back to the Augusteum then on towards the Triumphal Way; we moved quickly along that part of the route. About a third of the way along, I signalled my men to turn to our left and cut through the arches and along a narrow street to the Bronze Gate. A few rebels attempted to block our way, most just ran for it as they saw a heavily armed force moving in their direction and they knew what was about to happen.

The huge wooden doors with their ornate bronze fitting stood under the archway and blocked our path. My heart pounded in my ears; it was loud enough for the men standing next to me to hear, I was sure. My mouth was dry, and even the sweat had dried up on my face, and only the scarf around my neck was wet with the exertion. The sound of boots clattering on stone behind us alerted me to John's advance on us. I looked again at the doors; they presented a problem, but we had brought enough axes with us to fell a forest. I nodded at the men, and they set to, hacking away at the tough wood.

Splinters flew about, mixed with curses as axes hit the bronze on the door. The first group of axemen were replaced by another. Rocks and bricks began to fall on us from above. The mob had finally realised where we were coming from and set about defending the gates. Shields were raised above heads but the height the lumps of concrete were dropped from killed a number of men. We were forced to pull back from the doors; the defenders were resisting us well.

I was suddenly pushed out of the way by one of my men as a racket came from behind. On turning, I saw John leading many of his men at a run, between them they held horizontally a recently requisitioned cut stone pillar. They charged past us and hit the door at speed. Even the defenders had been caught off guard by this sudden rush, then the rocks and mortar started falling again. My archers responded swiftly, the angle was steep, but they received no return fire, and the defenders' fire reduced markedly.

A large crash sounded from the gateway, followed by an equally large cheer. Part of one side of the doorway had given way, and my men were climbing into the gap. Spears were thrust forward as they entered the space where once the door had stood. What was left of the broken door was opened, and then we were in.

"Forward, take no prisoners," I shouted as I charged through the doorway, into the tunnel, trampling over a good number of lifeless bodies. Ahead was daylight and then I was out into the arena. The track itself was in the shape of an elongated oval with the longest sides parallel to an island in the centre and on the far side stood the Kathisma. The stadium swelled in the opposite direction to my entrance as the mob saw our approach and tried to make for the furthest entrances and exits. I stood on the clean sand of the arena and surveyed the scene, looking towards the central island where I could see a few of the mob had climbed up the obelisk, in a vain attempt to evade my men. It made little difference to my men; they just stood around at the base and waited for their victims to fall as the surface presented little grip. At the other end of the track, I saw Mundus's men emerge from the tunnel entrance and begin spreading out. The part of the mob that had been on the track now desperately attempted to climb into the stadium as Mundus's men moved along the perimeter and killed anyone they could find.

The stands were only partially full, and most of the mob was now situated around the Kathisma. Outside of the Hippodrome, my men reported people leaping from the outer wall in an attempt to flee. Those that weren't killed by the fall onto the stone paving were quickly finished off. Mundus's men now began scaling the stadium's seating. I directed John to do the same from our end. Once they were in the stands, they fanned out along the rows from top to bottom, they then slowly marched towards Mundus and his approaching men. The mob was trapped between the two advancing rows of armed men. On the track, the rest of my men formed up and followed the march in the stands mopping up anyone who tried to leap back onto the track. The noise was horrendous, the sounds of screaming men and boys as they tried to flee in any direction only to be cut down.

As my men swept forward, they left a trail of corpses in their wake, and the more compact the mob became, the more it tried to fight back. All they had was what they could prise off the stadium. Lumps of wood torn from the seating were thrown into the advancing armoured men, making not the slightest difference to their advance. The mob was squeezed between two armoured claws. Looking up at the top of the Hippodrome, we could see men trying to climb over the edge and disappear as they realised, they had nowhere to go but to leap.

Once one side was emptied, we then moved towards the Kathisma from both ends. It took most of the afternoon to reach the Kathisma. The men were becoming exhausted by the constant need to slash and stab their way forward. The more compressed the mob, the harder it became to kill enough of them quick enough to keep the overall pace up. I moved towards the Kathisma, walking among the dead, the stadium seating was now the colour of blood. The sand on the track was already darkened by the mass of dead laying on its once dry surface.

Someone from behind us fired an arrow in my direction. It skimmed past my head as I ducked, following its passage. I turned and looked for the firer, I could see no one, but three of my men slightly to my rear must have, as they rushed towards one of the exits, we had only just passed and disappeared down it. There was shouting, and I rushed over to the exit, sword in hand. A large group of the mob had been surrounded as they tried to force their way out.

I was joined by more of my men who had been attracted by the

118

sudden movement of the three soldiers to the exit. With swords in hands, we entered the exit. I made contact with the mob; my sword thrust forward into the nearest cloak. I withdrew it. My hand was soaking in blood as I pushed the corpse out of my way. I moved forwards again, just stabbing forwards till whatever was in the way ceased to hinder my progress. With my men beside me, we gradually descended over a half-living mass of bodies till we reached the gate at the bottom. There we met up with those of my men who had blocked the entrance from outside, the sound of screaming and groaning echoed inside the exit way. I turned around, my men doing likewise, and we moved among the roiling bodies, slitting throats as we moved, till we reached the start of our odyssey.

Back in the stadium, the only sounds now were of sudden shrieks as those still living now joined the dead, and then it was all over. Nothing apart from our men was moving in the stadium. I ordered my men to search the dead and remove anything of value, and this was piled in one place on the track. Quite a pile loot soon amassed.

Once this was done, I had John divide it out among the troops; the last task had been completed. Mundus and I collected our men together, and once we had accounted for everyone; we departed the Hippodrome. Anyone who wanted to claim their dead was welcome to; they would have until the next morning. Then the prefect would have the unclaimed corpses thrown into the sea, and for the next month, I wouldn't be eating fish.

We led the men back to the palace courtyard and arranged food and drink for them and a place to clean up. They would be useless for the next day at least, as they would need to get drunk as well as have a good wash. They had a lot to clean themselves of, after a day like today.

Mundus, John and I left the men and silently walked back towards the Hippodrome. The city was silent. Those that moved did so in silence, and even their carts and animals maintained a respectful quiet. The Hippodrome though was different. It was filled with the sound of weeping as corpses were found and collected. No one looked at us. Instead, they bowed down and kept their faces looking at the ground as we passed, no comment was made. The realisation of the scale of the punishment silenced anyone from even thinking woe unto the Basileus, let alone his generals. I don't know how many were executed by us, but it must have been in the thousands.

We entered the palace, and the atmosphere had changed completely; fear had been replaced with a sense of victory. The guards were back in place and were supplemented by our men. Palace officials rushed around and in the lobby was a large group of senators, churchmen and other dignitaries, who had come to show loyalty now that it was safe to. When we had left the building earlier, not one of these creatures had come forward to support the Basileus in public or even privately. Now he had violently and utterly suppressed the uprising. He had the city once again under his control. If they ever doubted his control, they no longer did, opposition to him in any form would be silent. Any future plans he had would receive unanimous support from these creatures. We were escorted into the Basileus's private office where he was sitting behind a desk. As we entered, he looked up as we prostrated ourselves before him.

"Mundus, Belisarius. You have completed your bloody task well. You have saved the Empire and ourselves from the rule of tyrants," he said, still sitting at his desk and looking as calm as ever despite how panicked he had been before. I thought to say my thanks, but to my surprise, Mundus spoke first, and I remained silent as he straightened and gave a proud salute.

"Thank you, my emperor. Is there anything else you require from us?" Mundus queried, and I was intrigued. I had never heard anyone address him in the old way, but Mundus did, and could, so it seemed.

"Mundus, stay and talk with me." He directed Mundus to a chair in front of his desk before he looked at me and stated firmly, "Thank you, Belisarius, your loyalty and work here today has removed the stain of your recent defeat. You have been away from your family for too long. Go and rest with them."

I saluted him and turned to leave the office accompanied by John. We both walked quietly out into the main lobby and from there towards the entrance hall and our way out. Just as we approached the entrance hall, a voice called after us, and we both turned back. A young woman was rushing towards us as fast as she could. Considering the ornate nature of her palace clothing, it must be for a pressing reason, and so we waited. Others in the long corridor glanced at us but carried on with their business. The young woman halted in front of us, bowed her covered head, and spoke. "My mistress, the Augusta, requires the presence of you, General Belisarius, you must attend upon her," she said, huffing and puffing, and I looked at John and then at the young woman. She was dressed in the correct manner to be one of the Augusta's personal attendants, so there was no doubt that I had been requested.

"Very well," I said to the attendant and then turned to John, knowing full well he was probably not included in the invite. He looked at me curiously for a moment, almost confused why I might be summoned by the Augusta and not her husband. Then he grinned and said, "If she demands your presence, I guess the Lady Antonina is involved," and he gave a soft grunt as I patted his shoulder. "John, await my return here in the lobby."

"Yes, but don't be too long. I can't stand being among all these arse-lickers. If one comes over and bothers me, I swear, I'll rip their tongue out," John grunted, his eyes darting about to catch anyone who was trying to listen in on us and ensuring the threat was passed on. He waved his right arm in the general direction of the mingling palace staff, moving about their work or stopping to gossip. He then stomped over to an alcove and made himself as comfy as he could, he pulled his hood up and covered his head.

"Lead the way," I said, turning back to the attendant. I followed as she led me back in the general direction of the Imperial apartments. I was then led off to a section I had rarely visited and not normally on my own. Then, I was outside the Augusta's office within her private apartments. The lobby was well decorated in several different types of marble and lit by numerous oil lamps, which cast a yellow light over the rose Egyptian marble columns. All the stone gave the lobby a cold feel, but it was the cold of pure luxury. The window frames were draped with thick woven material dyed purple. The curtains covering the entrance to her office were of finer material, and both parts were decorated with gold threads making up images of flowers. The curtain opened, and the attendant directed me to enter. I entered, she left closing the curtains behind her, and I felt oddly scared.

"Belisarius. Come in and sit down here," the Augusta ordered, as she pointed to a gilded wooden chair which was close to where she was relaxing on a sofa, draped with a purple woollen cover. Her face, even in the light of the oil lamps, reflected the strain of recent events. Her eyes were sunken and worn, her complexion was paler than normal, and she looked ill. I sat down in the chair. She remained in her relaxed pose until her hand reached over and lifted a golden goblet, and she had a sip from it. Replacing the goblet, she looked up at me, making eye contact. She had a very strong stare, it dug deep into me, and I became quickly uncomfortable the longer she maintained it. The only thing to break it was the regal tone of her voice as she seemed almost to relax into a more friendly manner. "I wanted to thank you, personally for coming to our aid."

"It was my duty to protect your persons," I replied. There was not really much else I could say. A person could not really ignore the request of the Augusta, especially when it had been such an urgent one, but suddenly an intrigued expression had appeared on her face that startled me.

"You realise that if you were ambitious, you could easily be the new Basileus. But I always knew you to be honest, and once you had given your word, you would keep it, come what may." She paused, looking again directly at me, her eyes again boring deep into my soul, looking to see what lay within. The pause seemed to last an eternity. The more I thought about what she had said, the more discomfort I felt. I wondered where this conversation was going.

That day was the best chance I would ever have of taking the purple for myself, but I did not, and I have never wished to. I proved myself loyal, and I am still loyal. I must return to my story.

"Here, take, drink with me and let us wash the terrible taste of today away." The Augusta took another sip and dropped her gaze to the small table upon which rested another goblet. She pointed to the small table. I reached over and picked up the goblet and drank it down. It was a good rough red wine, and she was right. It did clear the throat of any taste, as well as warming my empty stomach.

"If you ever require anything that is in my power to grant, ask, and you shall receive. If you need anything of the Basileus, ask me first. Be careful, we all have enemies, as you have seen. It would be wise to entrust such messages to your wife, Antonina. She knows how best to communicate with me."

"Thank you, my Augusta."

She then clapped her hands, and the attendant re-entered through the curtains, bowed and awaited her orders. I stood up and knowing the interview was over, I bowed deeply. She directed the servant to escort me back to the lobby, and as I turned to leave, she spoke once more.

"One more thing. Be very careful of success — it breeds more enemies than friends. Even your closest friend may despise you for it." She then stood up and walked towards me; her right hand raised roughly in line with her hips. I turned, bowed, and kissed her hand. Then she waved me away. I left the room and followed the attendant back to the lobby. I was glad of the escort. The palace really was a maze of corridors, discreet rooms and passageways, leading everywhere and nowhere.

I had known her for a while, but this was the first real hint that she had real enemies and the Basileus as well, within the palace. I suppose being a soldier, swearing loyalty to them, it never occurred to me that *real* enemies could lurk not only in the capital but here. She had also warned me that I had enemies, no names, but it was a warning. I understood why John hated the palace. So many faces, but which was the real face of the people you met here? In the field, the enemy was the enemy, and it was that simple. I knew officials got in the way, but I hadn't quite understood that it was more than just plain ignorance or arrogance — I was becoming their enemy.

The attendant led me back to where John was curled up in the alcove, and he stirred on our approach. The attendant left us in silence. John shook himself as he got up, and we both walked out of the palace to where some of our guards were waiting. The rest had gone into the taverns and brothels to lose themselves till the morning. We walked back towards the harbour in the dark, even the few lamps just cast dim shadows in the darkness. The night reflected our mood; the sky was dark grey, no clouds or moon to light the route. The air was very cold. We both wrapped our cloaks tighter around our bodies as we felt the chill, then snow began to fall, melting as it landed on my face, turning into water and then running as cold drops down my neck. I didn't have the energy to shiver from the experience. The streets were completely empty now, except for patrols of guards. They were there to ensure that no mobs were allowed to form, and the dead were buried discreetly by their families, no processions.

The ferry was rough and took longer than normal as the wind churned up the channel between the capital and Chalcedon. We had left the horses behind; it was too dark to safely bring them across. In the morning the main force of my guards would embark on the barges and cross, bringing all the mounts with them. The only group of people we passed after landing carried a body wrapped in a bloody cloth on a litter.

We heard weeping as we approached them from behind. They heard our approach, and they glanced at us, they halted, heads bowed, silence replaced the weeping. We continued by; they were heading for the burial plots outside of the city's walls. There was no priest with them or children. It was going to be a quick burial before the city awoke and noted who the mourners were. I suspected that there were many burials like this that night; Darkness hiding the mourners, the deceased were beyond caring.

It was dawn before we reached my house, and we were both very cold and wet. John's cloak had a mound of snow on it, and mine probably looked the same. We entered my courtyard; John directed the guards at the entrance to be replaced, and those guards who had accompanied us were sent to their quarters to clean up and take over from those left at the entrance. John left me before I entered the house, a brief handshake, and he was gone into the growing light as snow continued to fall as a grey dawn began. On entering the house, the servants quickly surrounded me and removed my wet cloak, my blood-soaked wet boots and tarnished armour and sword. Somewhere in the city I had lost my helmet, and only now did I realised it was gone. I would buy a new one.

I was led out to the bathhouse, stripped of my underclothes and scraped down with oil. Then I took a hot plunge and finally I ran out into the snow and rolled around till it hurt. I ran quickly back into the bathhouse, warmed up and then dressed. Back in the house, a hot meal had been prepared for me, accompanied by hot wine. Once finished, I made my way to my bedroom and entered. Antonina was asleep in the bed, and she looked peaceful. Her hair lay loosely around her and gave the appearance of a dark halo. I tried to slip into the bed without disturbing her.

"Thank God, you're home safe, darling," she murmured, half-awake and proving my attempt had failed.

"Go back to sleep, my love, everything is fine," I whispered, but instead of going back to sleep, she suddenly sat up, her hair forming an additional nightgown around her.

"We heard rumours of what had happened at the Hippodrome. Are you alright? They say thirty thousand are dead," She paused, making herself more comfortable, then continued with a morbid expression upon her face. All she queried was whether we had indeed taken no prisoners and there was such anxiety in her face I almost questioned what had happened myself. But with a soft sigh I lowered my head and nodded, there was no point in making the situation out to be any lighter than it was — grim as it was, I was never dishonest with her.

"Yes, we killed everyone we found. I don't know how many there were. We just kept on till there were none left alive." It almost choked me to say it, but my expression remained grim as I spoke. I had not relished the work, and I don't think any being truly could. However, Antonina was quick to share her opinion as she scoffed in disgust.

"Who ordered the killing? Mundus? He's a barbarian, you know." There was anger in the words, and I had to admit, from what I had seen, he probably was the one person I could claim did not seem to regret the murder of any deemed an enemy. Perhaps it was just from his old-fashioned schooling on things, but her distaste made me grimace, as she was quite wrong in her assumptions.

"No, the Basileus did. He had recovered enough by the time we reached him to deal with the situation. I am sorry I had to do this, but these people would have destroyed the Empire."

"I know you would have preferred not to have killed citizens, but they left you no choice. I am sorry it had to be you, my darling. But Theodora needed us," she replied in a much calmer voice than before. Indeed, her tone seemed to shift immediately, and for some reason, it did not sit well with me as I sat on the bed and looked at her. But she was quick to assume I was displeased with what had happened and so she reached over and hugged me. She was still warm from the bed, and it warmed me too. After a short pause, I spoke again.

"Well, the good news is that my actions today have redeemed me. I suppose that is more important for us. I am on leave now for the moment, thanks to the Basileus."

"That is good news. I was waiting for a message from Theodora on what was going to happen, but now I need not worry. We have time for each other." With that, she pulled me closer and down into the bed, the covers were pulled over us, and I fell asleep in her arms.

Later that day, word reached us that Hypatius and his brother had been executed that morning for treason, following their betrayal and capture by the Imperial guard. Their shredded bodies had been thrown into the channel. Both the Green and Blue factions were banned from attending any games in the capital and were not allowed to elect leaders till the following new year.

I enjoyed my leave, the capital returned to calm, and Chalcedon prepared for spring, as a sudden thaw unblocked the major roads into the city. News came that Rufinus had left the capital and was heading to Persia to begin talks. Around Easter, they sent word that a settlement had been achieved as the new King Chosroes had little interest in a new conflict while he consolidated his throne. So, a new "perpetual peace" between the Persians and us was in the offing. The Basileus would be pleased, and it would give him cause to celebrate after the terrible January we had experienced.

Summer arrived, and my leave continued. I wasn't called back to the palace. Instead, we listened to the rumours that the Basileus had fermented the riots as a means to be rid of his reliance on the factions of the city. These and other rumours floated across from the capital, but we put little store in them. I had witnessed the events at first-hand and knew they were untrue. It sounded more like a reference to the pagan anti-Christ, Nero and his burning of Rome, than the Justinian, I knew. The reason the rumours began, I suspect, is because in the summer, the Basileus announced a massive set of rebuilding programmes for the capital. We learnt this first hand from the Augusta who was now directly communicating with Antonina. Part of the plan was to build a completely new Church of the Holy Wisdom, replacing the original, now sadly damaged, with one more suited to the grandeur of his reign, as well as other new public buildings to replace those damaged or deemed in need of repair.

By late summer, the roads had a continuous stream of countryside labourers looking for work in the capital. Even Chalcedon lost a good deal of its beggars as they crossed over for the work on offer. The upside of what some began calling in private the Nika riot was work and food for the poor, for a good, many years. The cost would be borne by taxpayers across the Empire, and this would, of course, bite into monies available for the army. Then John received word from Armenia that family matters required his presence. He begged leave to go; I granted it, of course. He didn't know how long he would be gone but hoped to be back in the new year. Phocas, who had developed into a man, was set to replace John's presence at my side. John had become like an elder brother to him and helped him develop his military skills, and he'd become quite a proficient rider, so I was confident in this choice.

The autumn came and with it cooler and wetter weather. I was becoming bored being at home for so long, even hunting for game could only bring a short bout of activity. At least it served to keep my riding skills and archery up to date and brought variety to the meal; otherwise, I would have taken up fishing, casting a net from the shore of the Bosporus and seeing what came up. I tried once and was bored with the continual repetition and lack of a decent catch. It was a good thing the family wasn't relying on me for food.

One evening, I sat in my office reading a copy of Livy's *History of Rome*; I found the Roman hard at times, some expressions were no longer in use, so I had to make copies of the sentences, take them down to one of the schools in the city and have a Roman teacher of law explain the exact meaning. Anyway, a servant entered the room and said that the mistress required my presence in the reception room, which meant we had guests, and I had probably forgotten about it. It was a short walk under the colonnades which linked the wings of the house with the central area. The air was cool, and the moon had just begun to rise in an almost cloudless night; the stars were already on show. It would be a bright night, and if it had been warmer, I could have sat in the garden and read in the moonlight.

As I entered the main building, I could hear chatter and occasional laughter coming from the reception room. I entered, and the room went mysteriously silent; every face turned to watch my entry. The silence continued as I walked over to Antonina and the children who were standing at the far end of the room. I recognised a few of the guests who stood politely on either side of the room, those who had been seating stood up and straightened their clothes. There, next to Antonina, was a young man of medium height, clothed in the current style of the senatorial class, which he was far too young to be a member of. I recalled I had seen his face around the house during the summer but had thought nothing of it. Antonina grabbed my arm, squeezing it a bit, and I could tell something was up, and I was being warned to behave. She was wearing some of her best clothes and jewels, which she only wore on important occasions.

"I see you have forgotten that we had a reception tonight," she whispered into my ear, almost a little harshly to tell me I was in serious trouble.

"Looks like it, what's the occasion?" I whispered back, looking around and noting that the children were also wearing their finest clothes. Antonina hid her annoyance, and she led me over to the young man, who had a slightly embarrassed look on his young face, and she said in a less hushed tone, "Darling, I have a surprise for you. You remember young Ildiger?" She almost purred, trying to sound polite and in charge of a situation I was obviously making very awkward. But at the mention of the name, I was unable to stop my tongue from leaping ahead of my brain.

"No, I don't recall the name. Should I?"

"The young man, standing here, you fool," she hissed while pointing very gracefully at the now very pale looking man. Memory filled in the gaps and the face and name became one.

"Oh, yes, I remember. Why is he standing with our family?" Playing the fool was always a defence in family matters. She appeared to take no notice of my last comment and instead took Ildiger by the hand, turned and reached with her free hand and took Melissa's, then joined the young couple's hands together. Melissa had grown, and she looked even more like her mother, she even wore a dress of a similar design. Antonina turned to me and eased the couple in between us, so not only presenting the couple to me, but also to the assembled guests. Agh, I had that sinking feeling, as I guessed where this was going to end. Ildiger released Melissa's hand and turned to me and bowed. He addressed me in an overly polite manner, loud enough for even the deafest guest hiding in the entrance of the room to hear clearly.

"Belisarius of Germania, I, Ildiger son of Asper, make a request of you," in a hesitant voice, he continued, "Sir, I wish to marry your daughter, Melissa."

I was right about what I suspected the gathering was for. I could think of no, good reason, why they couldn't be married. It had all been arranged. I looked around at the guests and then at the couple. All were waiting for my approval, especially the couple before me. Antonina just waited, knowing full well that I wouldn't disapprove of the match that she obviously had taken a great deal of time and effort to arrange.

"Yes, I approve of the marriage."

Melissa rushed over to me and gave me a great big hug and whispered to me, "Thank you Father. Thank you."

The room erupted into applause, and the servants started serving wine and sweetmeats as a party began. It continued well into the night. It was agreed between the families that the marriage would happen in the new year.

Winter passed over us, with still no word from the Basileus regarding my future. Antonina was happy as it meant I would be around now till spring at the earliest. We often wondered about John. We had received no word from him, and we asked any visitor who had come from Armenia if they had any knowledge of him, but no one had anything to report. The marriage took place in much splendour, and the celebrations continued for two days. For a wedding present, I reluctantly gave Ildiger a position in my guard. I also allocated them a section of our house to live in together.

Spring arrived, and with it, I really began to feel restless. I started making plans to return to my family's home and see who still lived. Since my parents had both died, I hadn't stayed in touch with the remains of the family? So it would be interesting to see what had become of the old home.

Then, with the first sailing of ships in the Mediterranean, news arrived from Rome concerning recent events in the West. There had been a recent coup in Carthage, in the Palace of Hilderic, king of the barbarian Vandals and our ally. A duke by the name of Gelimer had replaced him as king. He was expected to send a delegation in the summer to demand recognition and payment of fees for the continued alliance. The Basileus was publicly furious, and a dispatch had been sent to Carthage, demanding the return of Hilderic as King. Privately, I learned via the Augusta, that he was, in fact, overjoyed as it gave him an excuse to think about flexing his military might in the West, for the first time, especially given the peace between us and Persia.

Chapter Five

One day in the sixth year of his reign, Antonina and I were sitting in the shade of the portico on one side of the garden. The warm air drifted across from the garden, gently stirring the blossoms of the spring flowers and scenting the air with their perfume. The lemon trees would blossom soon, and the scent of lemon would soon engulf the garden, bringing with it the clear promise of summer. The gentle atmosphere was broken by the sound of a visitor being escorted to us. We stirred from our daydreams to notice the figure's raiment and so recognise his importance. The servants brought the palace official to us. He bowed, handed over his letter of appointment and spoke.

"Sir, would you accept an invitation to have lunch with the Praetorian prefect today at his office?" The letter held the seal of the prefect's office, so there was no doubting this was an official invitation to see the second most powerful official in the capital. An invitation from him couldn't be refused out of hand. But with this figure, I knew very well that this was just a polite way to summon me to his office because he wanted something. Otherwise, of course, you would simply have been arrested if it was anything unlawful.

"Yes, of course, I will attend. I will be ready in a short time. So, you can go and tell your master," I stated with a soft yawn as I looked towards Antonina for a moment, but before I could say anything to her on the matter, the messenger gave a suddenly stern response that made me grimace. It meant only one thing, the need for me to hurry up.

"Sir, I am to escort you when you are ready. I will wait in the main hall for you." With that, the official turned and was led back the way he had come by the servants. Antonina, who had remained quiet till the official had gone, spoke and her tone was curiously insulted.

"What does he want with you, husband? You know, the Augusta says he is always scheming." She was looking particularly beautiful in the Persian silks she was wearing. The sunlight shimmered over them as she stood up and came over to me. She looked quite concerned, which was unusual, and I took it to mean she'd had no word from the Augusta that this might happen. This was intriguing. I had no time for John the Chain, but I was unaware that I was important enough to warrant a personal audience with him. He'd do nothing without the Basileus's knowledge, so something was afoot in the palace and I was involved. Finally, I might have a role to play since my enforced leave from duty. Rather suddenly, I felt a rise of excitement that something good might indeed be on its way, and I turned about and hugged Antonina as she gave a startled cough.

"You know as well as I do that if John wants to see me, it must be important. And anyway, I have no intention of getting into the quartermaster's bad graces. You never know where that could lead, and it's better to have the devil on your side." I made a comical gesture of being hung as I spoke to stress the danger John as an enemy posed. She was not amused, giving a slightly sour look before she hugged me tight, then released me.

"Take some of your bodyguards. You know how that intimidates palace officials and makes the Basileus laugh to see his chamberlain flutter at the sight of all those big strong men," she said with mirth, and a suddenly cruel flicker in her eyes to say she would be very unhappy if I did not. I kissed her and went into the house.

As I walked through the house, Procopius ran to catch me, and I halted to allow him to catch up. Once he had caught his breath, he spoke as I kept the official waiting. "Sir, do you require me to accompany you to the palace?" The news of the visitor and his comments had quickly travelled among the servants and through the house. Procopius had been busy since our return; he had completed my accounts and that of the army I had commanded. He'd submitted these already to the Praetorian prefect's office months ago, but he also dealt with the legal side of the marriage of my stepdaughter, as well as the household accounts and any legal matters. When he wasn't busy, he continued his legal studies, and for relaxation, he told me, he studied Thucydides. He didn't seem to be bored or understand what it meant to be inactive, but he did not like the thought of being left out of official situations either.

"No, I will just take a handful of bodyguards for show. I won't need a record kept. He will have that under control. If he sees how smart you are, he might poach you," I said with a snort of humour to try and lighten the rejection, but he still appeared crestfallen. He'd never been in the office of the prefect, and I imagine he'd like to see the centre of bureaucracy in action, but he turned and left. Servants met me in the main hall. There I changed into a fresh tunic and a toga befitting my rank. Lastly, I hung my sheathed sword across my shoulder. I summoned the deputy commander of my guards and ordered him to pick six of the most imposing men ready to accompany me. We left my house and headed for the port in nearby Chalcedon.

The official guided us to an Imperial navy barge; the crew were awaiting his return. We were going to cross in style to the palace, as well as landing on one of the Imperial quays close to the prefect's office. We had the horses tied close to the quay, and then we boarded the barge. It was brightly painted, with small shields placed alongside the rowers, more for show than protection. An Imperial pennant hung from the only mast, which had no sail attached to it. The barge was far too small to fight in as it only had room for twenty soldiers, so there was plenty of room for us on the planked seats. The rowers were skilled, and we crossed quickly, all other shipping getting out of the way of our passage once they caught sight of the Imperial pennant.

Along with my guards, I was escorted by the official through the tall, light coloured marbled entrance hall, straight up the main stairs to the office of the prefect. Like the rest of the palace, there was no shortage of marble in the décor. The office lay at the end of a short corridor, which was airy as many windows resided high up close to the flat roof. Light pierced through the windows, and where it didn't reach the floor, it left small pools of golden light on the walls and columns. Where it caught the mosaics on the floor, different colours glittered in the bright light. Along both sides of the hall were benches filled with applicants waiting for an audience with the prefect. I had heard that one could wait days just to get a seat on a bench up here. They looked up at our approach and watched silently as we approached the entrance doors to the office. They remained quiet. Imperial etiquette demanded silence at the approach of any official inside the palace. Once we had entered the office, they would begin chattering again.

The servant opened the doors and motioned for my guards to wait by the doorway. I nodded to the guards to wait, and I walked through the open doors, which were closed firmly behind me. The only clear space in the room was by the windows with a small doorway, which led to his private apartments; otherwise, the walls were hidden behind shelves full of documents, meticulously categorised. John was busy at his desk, going through scrolls and books with many officials moving them around so he could better see something on them. One official or servant stood ready with wax and a lamp, ready to prepare a document for his seal, but he looked up and beckoned me over to his desk while ordering his officials to leave the room.

"Belisarius, come and make yourself comfortable. Some wine? I have a particularly fine one from Syria." The tone of his voice was pleasant, but still heavily underlined with his native Cappadocian accent. I indicated my agreement, and he signalled that we move over to the windows before he joined me; he poured two glasses of red wine and brought them over.

"Thank you, Prefect, looks good." I took the proffered wine and sniffed it before taking a sip. Then I gave a soft smile of amusement before speaking calmly. "Yes, that really tastes like Syria."

John turned, and we both looked out of the window. The window gave us a good view of a small part of the city. The fire-damaged Church of the Holy Wisdom was already covered in workers as they dismantled it. Restoration work had also begun on other fire damaged buildings. The capital was busy, and soon, the damage from the riot would be invisible to the eye. John looked tired, and his clothing was plainer than I expected, it was still well cut, and his badge of office hung around his neck. His dark hair was cut shorter than the normal style for the palace, and his beard showed flecks of white among its dark curls. His brown eyes still shone with energy, and he had obviously recovered from his impetuous sacking during the riot. But I wondered if his confidence had been shaken by the events. We sipped our wine in silence. Once the glasses were empty, he took my glass and beckoned me to follow him through the doorway to his private apartments. They were luxurious; they lacked for nothing — gold and silver plates, cups, vases and cutlery, silk curtains were draped across a balcony entrance, fine wool carpets on the floor covered the polished marble surface. Paintings of mythical scenes covered the walls, centaurs, and the like, you mostly saw these in taverns and not in the palace, as these were pagan in origin. In the palace, the wall painting was either religious or the standard Imperial design. There was a certain decadence about these apartments and the man who lived here. There were plenty of servants, but I didn't see any men in here, only young women.

One of these quite beautiful servants beckoned us through the silk drapes and out into a covered balcony, with an even better view of the Imperial quarters of the palace. A small table had been laid with grilled mullet, by the look of it, fresh bread and salad and, of course, wine and water jugs. There were just two chairs. I sat in one and John, the other, the servant poured wine and mixed water into the glasses. Then she stood behind John, waiting for any orders.

"To old comrades in arms, no longer with us," John said as he raised his glass, and I followed suit. The wine was excellent, and the food suited the mood. I didn't refuse the fish, as it would have been rude, but swallowed it quicker than I normally would have. John instead seemed to enjoy taking his time chewing every bite thoroughly. He looked over at me, grinning and said in a rather unsavoury sort of tone, "I heard you gave up eating fish after the riot. I have been eating nothing but fish since then. It tastes like victory to me, as the fish has a meatier flavour to it." Then, he laughed loudly at this very distasteful reference, and I felt like spitting it out, as we both clearly understood what he meant by "meaty flavour." But I had eaten worse and wasn't going to give him the pleasure of my discomfort. So, I ate heartily, and we both cleared away the food, and the servant removed the empty plates. She then carefully refilled our glasses and went back behind the curtains. With lunch over, it was time for the real purpose of my visit, and John began the conversation.

"How is Antonina, your most beautiful wife?"

"She is well and sends her greetings to you, Prefect," I stated, keeping polite but very quickly John dismissed the need for such with a curious kind of grin that could only be referred to as sly. Antonina had mentioned he was always scheming, and I could not help but feel she was right in that.

"Let's not be so formal, Belisarius, call me John as I have no wish to refer to you as General Belisarius every time we speak."

I was not sure I liked that, but I could do nothing more than agree to this before asking why he had called me. As we were being so forward with one another, I thought it only fair to ask upfront, but I was not sure of the answer.

"We have both known Justin, son of Justin, for a long time. I'm worried. Do you know why you were called back from the East?"

"I fucked up," I said, putting it bluntly, but I was sure this conversation was going to take an unusual turn. I was still slightly shocked by John using the familiar address for the Basileus as if they were just comrades, not emperor and servant, and it just made this whole situation feel all the more disquieting.

"No, I will explain. We both know that Justin, son of Justin, has the potential to be the greatest emperor since Augustus. What drives him is the thought that one day soon, he can reclaim the western half of the Empire and so unite us once again. Well, that's the reason you were called back here and why I am so dammed tired."

He paused for a moment, looking at me and waiting for a question I might have. I was still a bit shocked. Where was this leading to? I knew a campaign was being planned, I had assumed it would be Thrace or Illyricum, but as I asked no questions, he continued, "The situation in the Vandal Kingdom in Africa has allowed him to feel that the time is right to begin the reconquest. The recent coup and the failure of Hilderic to regain his throne has essentially null and voided the treaty, as we have refused to recognise the new leader, Gelimer. He has kindly presented us with a pretext for war by his demands and failure to recognise the sovereignty of the emperor."

"I heard about events in Africa, but we can't spare a large army to invade again. Even with peace with Persia, we still need to keep a large army in the region. That leaves very little spare," I interjected, leaning over the table towards John as he gave a look of exasperation, as if I'd just said exactly what he thought I would and yet still not quite understanding the situation.

"I am in favour of the expedition in principle, but it's the cost that troubles me. Look at the repairs we're having to undertake; taxes have already been raised to pay for them. We can borrow to pay for the campaign while slowing down the repairs. But we must be victorious and with the treasure we know the Vandals took from Rome, it should be able to pay for itself. But it will have to be a small force." John announced.

"So, who is to command it?"

"You, of course, that's why you were recalled. He had wanted to launch it last year, but the political situation wasn't right. He wanted a pretext so as not to alarm the Goths, for example, or the Persians. It must seem like we are going to the aid of a fallen ally," he said, looking directly at me, a sly grin covering his face once more and making his nose look slightly hooked.

"I am delighted, but how long have I got?" There was not much I could say, and I had to admit, I was itching to get off my backside and back to work after such a long respite.

"Not long," he said and clapped his hands thrice. The curtains moved after a moment, and two servant girls appeared carrying rolled scrolls, which they laid on the table. John opened the scrolls; several were maps, the others were official documents. "This will help you organise yourself. It's the latest list of army and navy numbers, along with maps of the old African provinces. We found these in the Imperial archives. See, no expense spared for you, Belisarius."

I looked over the maps and documents, but before I had time to speak, John spoke once more, and it made me feel curiously uncomfortable again.

"I'll see you tomorrow in the council chambers." He chuckled as I collected up the scrolls and the servants assisted me. I was then led off the balcony, through his apartments and through the empty office. My guards took hold of the scrolls, and we were then guided out of the palace, back to the waiting barge.

Already my mind was racing as we crossed back to Chalcedon, the journey back to the house was a blur as my mind was elsewhere. I went straight to my office and laid out the maps and weighed the edges down on the floor, placing the army and navy details on my desk. I knew from my reading and military training that Africa had been the focus of several previous retake attempts. The boldest had been a large army marching from Egypt, which had failed, so we needed a different approach and to keep the Vandals in the dark for as long as possible.

The door to my office opened, and in walked Antonina. She was carrying a tray with a cloth over it. I looked up from staring at the maps and smiled at her arrival. I hadn't realised it was dark outside as my office was in the shade in the afternoon, so the lamps were lit already. Though I was so focused at the time the servants could have entered and lit them — if they had, I hadn't noticed.

"It's started then, the planning for the Vandal campaign?" she stated, always seemingly one step ahead as she stepped over to the desk. She placed the tray on the it, poured wine into two glasses and offered one to me as she took the other. I queried if she had a message whilst I was out, and as I looked at her, I felt a smile cross my face. I felt even more in love with her if that was even possible. She was better than all my guards as she continually watched after our interests and always knew what was heading our way. As I queried the state of the Augusta, she gave a soft chuckle. "She is as lovely as ever, and she wondered if I would like a verbatim copy of your conversation with John."

She chuckled, and I grinned. I was slowly becoming used to the intrigue within the palace; everyone knew or had to know everyone else's business. But I always preferred it coming from Antonina's mouth as she knew what was necessary for me to hear and what was just plain gossip. She then continued gleefully after sipping more of the wine, "Well, you know she likes to keep a close eye on her enemies. Anyway, she and the Basileus had already discussed the idea of the campaign, and they agreed that you should be the commander. Of that, she only told me today."

"Well, it's great to know where I fit in the chain of command, at the bottom," I laughed, trying to sound indignant. It was amusing though to know that Antonina always seemed to be the second point of contact for the Augusta, and yet I was always out of their little loop unless it was something concerning me, but perhaps things were better that way. I certainly had no ear for politics. I was a soldier.

"I knew you'd be working hard on the task already. Here, eat these and then rest. I'll see you later. Goodnight." With a soft expression, she turned and left the room, closing the door behind her. Once I had eaten the cheese and bread, I returned to the maps. How would we reach Africa without alerting the Vandals? I decided to put off that question for a while and instead looked over the lists. John was right. We had very few men to spare, and I was glad I had taken the other John's advice on our return from the East and recruited a thousand new guards so that my own resources would supplement the size of the expedition. With that thought, and the wine making me feel drowsy, I went over to the couch and laid down on it.

I must have fallen asleep and been dreaming as it came to me, the solution.

I sat up and went over to the desk and looked at the navy figures, then took a rough guess at the size of the army and yes, we had enough transports. The only way to reach Africa was the same way the old Romans had done when fighting the Punic Wars — by ship from Sicily. The Vandal fleet, if still close to Carthage, would take too long to intercept a fleet departing from Sicily to Africa. The currents favoured them, but they had to know when we left and where from if they were to reach us in time. A message from Sicily could not go directly to Carthage. It had to travel slightly north before cutting back to Carthage, taking almost as long as it would for us to reach Africa. Hence the strategic importance of Sicily to both the Romans and the Punic Kingdom — it controlled access from the eastern half of the Great Middle Sea to the western half.

If we could sail west from the capital, down past Greece, hop across to Gothic Southern Italy and then Sicily, we could reach Africa before they knew we were coming. What would really help us, would be if the Vandal army was west of Carthage when we landed. But that would be unknown until we reached Sicily and our spies reported to us. We would also need the support of the Goths in allowing our invasion fleet to enter their waters and use their ports in Sicily otherwise we would have to fight our way to Sicily before even trying to attack Africa.

With a basic plan in place, a few notes scribbled down, I made my way to the still darkened bedrooms and hoped I would feel refreshed enough for the council meeting, as it promised to be a long day.

The council chambers were on the opposite side of the palace to that of John's office. The chambers were lit by sunlight entering through the many apertures below the ceiling. Although the chambers felt airy, there still lingered the smell of burnt oil from the lamps, hinting at many a late-night session. In the centre of the room rested a large table surrounded by chairs. Present in the chamber, apart from John and me, was the Basileus and Peter the Patrician who was the foreign affairs advisor. Peter was of noble appearance, quiet but menacing in his silence. He was renowned for his oratory skills, and that was only excelled by the grace of his performance. So skilled was he that it was rumoured that he could persuade a two-legged blind mule to run in the Hippodrome and then have it thank him for the experience afterwards. He was well-dressed as suited his station, and like the majority of the Basileus's advisors, he was conservative in his dress code. The Basileus wore the Imperial purple mantle over his normal clothes — it was secured with a large golden bejewelled clasp. He had aged. Six years of reign had taken its toll on him. His beard had hints of grey, and his hair wasn't as luxurious as it had been when he acceded to the throne.

Situated in each corner of the room were his Imperial shield-bearers; they were all dressed in multicoloured robes, and each held a long spear by their side and rested a long oval shield beside it. On each shield was the Chi-Rho symbol, with the shield boss marking the centre of the cross. Moving around the table were palace officials and sitting within earshot of the table were a group of scribes. Yet, the room still had an air of informality as I walked towards the table, and only the Basileus turned at my approach. I went to prostrate myself, but he signalled it wasn't necessary. Then he spoke in a calm and relaxed manner; his old form had returned.

"Well, old friend, do you think you can do it? If not, I can find someone else to make a mess of it for me?" he said in a light-hearted manner, but there was clearly an air of confidence in the tone. He knew I was the man for this job, and his confidence gave me more confidence in my own ideas as I bobbed my head stiffly.

"Yes, I can take Africa, but it will depend on the size of the force I will have as to how successful I will be," I stated firmly, knowing that I needed to speak confidently in order to gain the ears of the other men present. I joined the group at the table who were studying a cluster of maps that showed Africa, Sicily and Southern Italy. The Basileus looked to the maps and then turned to me expectantly, questioning softly what plan I had in mind, and I began to motion with my hand. "I propose we sail the army to Sicily then land south of Carthage—"

"I can give you as many ships as you require to move your army. As you well know, manpower is the one thing we don't have in vast numbers, quite apart from the extra cost, don't you agree John?" The Basileus cut me short before I could explain any further and I was both relieved to hear I could have as many ships, but I was also a little disquieted as my emperor had broken my concentration and jolted my confidence just slightly, as he'd turned quickly towards the beard-thumbing and rather startled expression of John the Chain.

"Yes, Basileus, that's what I want to discuss," replied John, caught off guard by the Basileus's remark, but quick, all the same, to make a point of his own. When the Basileus turned to look at him for a moment, his voice became more serious and perhaps even subtly more displeased as he beckoned John to speak. John was swift to check himself before he stood up and addressed the others. "We can't afford the cost of the operation to recover the West. The recent rampaging of the Persians through Syria has cost us dear. I don't expect these provinces to be able to supply the grain and taxes as normal. If we are only undertaking a limited operation of say, no longer than a year, then we can borrow against victory. It will mean reducing the capital costs of rebuilding for a year." He paused looking at us, we at him, then he continued, "Then we can just about manage, but of course, if Belisarius and his army become bogged down, then we will be in trouble. If the campaign does become extended, we may have to devalue the coin, by reducing its gold content, which might well cause a repeat of last January. But if Belisarius succeeds and grabs the treasure, we know the Vandals have amassed, then none of the above will be a problem. We will make a profit on the campaign and Belisarius can still have his bonus. Africa, once under our control, could easily make up for our losses in Syria in just one year. I looked at the returns of the provinces before they were lost."

The room was quiet while the others digested what he had said. I looked at him, puzzled. He hadn't mentioned his opposition to the operation in these terms, in fact, I had thought he was encouraging me. I looked at him, and he looked back at me, his face a mirror like in its smoothness. The Basileus, after a while, spoke only to then turn back towards John and almost mutter a query on what else might be giving him cause for worry.

"Yes, I have sought advice from military commanders on this subject. Their collective opinion is that the Vandals are too strong for us to challenge. Apart from having the most active fleet, they haven't suffered a defeat on home ground yet."

"Well, it's about time they were smashed. It will be a lesson to all that the Roman Empire is not an old woman waiting to die. Belisarius, I can spare you fourteen thousand men, we can hire a force of Huns and Heruli to supplement them. With your guards, that gives you a force of sixteen thousand men." The Basileus looked directly at me, almost completely dismissing John's last comments, and it was clear that he did not want excuses not to get involved in this campaign. The rest turned to look at me, and John had a smile on his face. Court politics I would never understand, I could hardly tell if this was good or bad as the Basileus turned to me and gave a stern expression.

"Well, Belisarius?"

"Yes, Basileus, I can do it. I have considered the problems this operation presents. We will have to move by ship, as the land route is too long and would give the Vandals ample time to prepare for us." I pointed to the maps laid out on the table and traced the route. I pointed towards Carthage on the map and then moved my hand southwards, following the coastline as I outlined my plan. "If we land directly in the area of Carthage, we may well leave ourselves open to be cut off by their fleet. The bay is a bottleneck, and I have no wish to be trapped in it. Also, they could intercept us at sea before we even land. I prefer to launch the fleet from the Syracuse side of Sicily and land south in this region and secure our position while we scout for the Vandals. Then, depending on where they are, we either wait for them to come to us or we go after them, destroy them first, somewhere outside of Carthage. Then we seize their capital before they have time to call in any allies or regroup. Once their capital is ours, we will have a safe harbour, and the Vandal fleet will have lost its base. Then we can, at leisure, subdue those who continue to resist."

I paused and surveyed those around the table. They were in deep thought, contemplating my last statement. I gave them a few minutes to make sure they were quite aware of my suggestions and to accept any kind of query that was likely to happen. I had assumed there might be one or two, as usually, someone had an alternating opinion with regards to any attempt on Carthage and yet with no questions. I continued, "But we have two problems. First, the only route we can use means entering Gothic territory in Sicily. The island is well situated to be the final navigation point for the African coast, as well as the last chance to replenish the supplies."

"May I interrupt, Belisarius?" asked Peter. We all turned and looked at him; he continued, "I anticipated that the expedition would require assistance from the Goths. I have, in your name, Basileus, met with Amalasuntha and secured permission to enter Gothic territory so we can land and purchase supplies from them. The regent Amalasuntha was only too happy to assist us in dealing with the Vandals. They have already caused much suffering along the Italian coastline."

"Thank you, Peter. Will your sources be able to supply the latest information to Belisarius when he reaches Sicily?" enquired the Basileus. I was stunned as to how quick others had been to anticipate my thoughts and concerns.

"Yes, I have agents in the region and in Carthage, who hopefully will have returned before the fleet sails. So, Belisarius, you will have the best intelligence we can provide." Peter finished speaking and returned to studying the map. The Basileus then gave a sound of approval before turning toward me and ushering for me to continue.

"Yes, that settles that problem, but it still leaves the Vandal fleet to contend with. If they are active in the area when we arrive, it would mean our fleet having to counter them, leaving the army without support, should anything go wrong. If we marched from Egypt, they could use the current and move the Vandal army to intercept us, landing either in front or behind us at a place of their choosing. Their fleet is problematic." I paused and looked around at my audience. If we had surprise on our side, the Vandal fleet would be a minor problem, and if we seized Carthage, it would totally neutralise their fleet.

"Well, Belisarius, I think we should let you into a few of our secrets. Don't you think so, Peter?" The Basileus's voice echoed with a cheerful tone. Peter nodded in agreement as he continued, "Well, my friend, we have been planning a little something to keep Gelimer occupied and hopefully his fleet as well. The Vandal governor of Sardinia has fallen out of favour with Gelimer, and with a little extra gold and a promise of support, he will rebel against Gelimer before you reach Sicily. Secondly, the city of Tripoli in Libya is also ready to come over to us. This should stretch Gelimer rather nicely."

"Well, if that can be made to happen, it will certainly reduce the odds. A small force has many advantages. It will be easier to control and supply as well as being more manoeuvrable. Quite apart from our tactics having been honed fighting the Persians, we should be far superior to anything the Vandals have encountered," I replied emphatically, my confidence fully regained by this information.

"Well, it's agreed. We invade Vandal Africa. All of you here present will support any requests that Belisarius makes. Belisarius, if anyone should be slow in helping, come to me directly. Now, I expect you to be ready to sail before summer. I have already ordered sections of the army to assemble here as well as the fleet. John has calculated the amount of supplies you will need. I have also selected your officers to assist your own staff. Lastly, you will be granted the power of imperium, your decisions will be my decisions, and you will be Military Master of the West." The Basileus snapped his fingers twice, and a servant came towards him, holding a scroll. He pointed to me, and the servant presented me with my written orders and promotion. I bowed and then saluted the Basileus and spoke.

"Thank you, my Basileus. I will conquer Africa, with the grace of God, for the Senate and the Empire."

"Thank you, for attending. We will meet again before the fleet sails," the Basileus replied, then he stood up, turned, and everyone bowed, as he began to make his way out of the chamber, his guards immediately moved in to surround him. With the escort, he left the chamber and headed back towards his apartments. The meeting broke up, Peter and John left separately. I remained in deep thought, looking at the maps on the table. With the Vandal fleet occupied, the landing in Africa would be more straightforward. If Tripoli revolted before we reached Africa, Gelimer may be forced to send part of his army to Libya. Then I would be placed comfortably close to the capital with only part of the Vandal army left to defend it.

I left the palace still in deep thought and only really emerged from it on entering my office. Antonina was there resting on the couch. She sat up on my entry. She said, "Well how did it go,", an eagerness in her voice, and I gave smile.

"Well, he confirmed my command of the invasion. We have till the summer before I leave for Africa," I replied.

"I have been thinking about the campaign. I am coming with you. If it fails, I do not want to be left here on my own. If you die in Africa, I will die with you, my love."

I was startled by her words, but she was gazing deeply into my eyes, her face glowed in the lamplight. There would be no telling her, "No". She had made up her mind, and that was that. In a way, I was glad she was coming. She noticed my face relax, and she knew that I had accepted her presence on the campaign. She rose from the sofa and took my hand and led me out into the garden. We walked together in silence in the bright moonlight. The cool breeze reminded one that spring was still present, as it nipped against the skin.

By the end of spring, the Golden Horn was filled with my ships, and outside the city walls, my army was encamped. The city was buzzing with excitement as the merchants and publicans blessed their luck at having us stationed there. I spent most of my days training the new army. The mercenaries had arrived and set up a separate camp. They preferred to spend their first instalment of pay in the city, then train. Rumours were running wild as to where we were to campaign. I hadn't informed the men and didn't intend to till I judged it was the correct moment to tell them.

It was the afternoon, and the heat was intense even though it was only the end of spring. The sun was not yet at its height, but its heat and light still filled the courtyard, making it uncomfortable to linger. A large group of men dismounted, and as their horses were led away, they entered my home. The servants guided the group through the anteroom and into the main reception room. Inside another group of servants stood behind a row of tables placed against an interior wall. On these tables was a selection of meats, fish, salads and bread. Other servants stood ready to serve wine when required. In the centre of the room was a table covered in a sheet. The room had been scented with rosewater to cover the aroma of those having to travel from the capital in the heat of the day.

The guests were ushered to the refreshments and allowed to indulge themselves. They soon relaxed as old acquaintances were renewed and new ones forged.

Once the atmosphere was comfortable, I entered, accompanied by my deputy guard commander, Solomon. He was a tough heavy-built man that John had recruited in Antioch; he was part Persian, part Arab. Till John returned, he would command my guard in Africa, and Procopius was also with me. The room went silent. All the men stood to attention and saluted as I made my way to the centre table. They followed us over to the table and formed an outer ring.

"Thank you for attending at such short notice. What I have to say is for your ears only, you're not to discuss any of this outside of this group," I said as I removed the sheet from the table, revealing the collection of maps John the Prefect had given me. Solomon looked at the servants and nodded his head, and they quickly made their exit, closing the doors behind them. I waited till they had left, then continued, "I can now tell you the real reason for your presence in the capital. I know that you have been under the impression of a campaign in Illyricum — that was one of a number of false rumours spread to ensure that our enemies would not learn of our true target. The target for us is Vandal Africa. The fleet will convey us to the shores of Africa, and there we will defeat the Vandal army as soon as we can. Then we shall take Carthage."

Where there had been a murmur of confusion over the rumours before, there was suddenly silence as they drank in the situation. Then, the audience became excited. They wanted to ask questions or query why Africa, but I had not finished speaking. I paused, allowing them to chatter, then I raised my hand and silence returned.

"The fleet will be commanded by Admiral Calonymus." I pointed to the admiral and his staff. They formed their own group, dressed in naval fashion, amongst the others. "He will move us through the Peloponnese, then to Southern Italy and finally to the port of Catania in Sicily. From there, we'll sail for Africa, bypassing Malta, landing as close to Syllectum as we can. There will be several disembarkations en route. As usual for this part of the campaign, the weather will be the main cause of any delays."

I looked at the admiral, he was a well-rounded Greek from Egypt, and he looked relaxed. He reminded me more of a merchant than an admiral, but he knew his stuff and had already planned the route. He smiled as he also began to fully understand the campaign. The other guests were my military commanders, and they had been given tasks to plan for, but like the admiral, not details of the overall mission. They looked at each other, nods and smiles and quick, quiet comments were shared. The blinds had been removed from the group, and now they understood better how their assignments fitted. The need for secrecy had been important, and it ensured that Gelimer would be unaware of us. Now, even if word reached him, we would be but a few days behind the messenger.

"Now that you know your objective, we sail in four days on the summer solstice, weather permitting." The audience grinned. Now they knew when and where. All they needed was the how, so I continued, "Admiral Calonymus, now that you understand the mission is there anything you wish to add?"

"Yes. What about the Vandal fleet and the use of Gothic ports? I specifically mentioned that we would need to use these to be able to land in Africa," he asked.

"Well, Admiral, the ports are open to us. As for the Vandal fleet, I received news this morning from the office of Peter the Patrician. The Vandal fleet is in Carthage and is preparing to embark troops under the command of Gelimer's brother to suppress a revolt in Sardinia," I replied.

"Um, I would expect part of the Vandal fleet to be deployed to the eastern approaches to Carthage. Because that is what I would do if I were them," replied Calonymus with a soft chuckle of amusement.

"That's a good point, and we have no intelligence on that. Will it affect us reaching Africa or Sicily?"

"No, our route will hug the north shore of the sea, and we will be approaching Sicily from Southern Italy. Our approach to Africa will be well to the east of where I suspect they might be," he replied.

"Good, that settles one problem. I have been promised up-to-date intelligence when we reach Sicily. With luck, Gelimer will be concentrating on Sardinia and not us." I paused, turning to Cyril, one of the ablest commanders the Basileus had assigned me. He was from

Illyricum, built like the Basileus, same dark hair, a mix of local and Roman blood and older by a few years. He was capable of working on his own, was reliable and would complete the task and more — he had initiative. "Cyril, I know that you enjoy working on your own, so I have a special task for you. You are to sail tomorrow with five hundred of your men. Your final objective will be Sardinia. You are to support the rebels there. If you are victorious, take over the island. If the revolt fails, retreat to Sicily, then join up with us. But before reaching your objective, you, with Admiral Calonymus's deputy, will secure supplies along the route to Sicily. He will know where to land, and the prefect, John, will supply the needs and the means. Once you're finished in Catania, you will then make for Sardinia."

"Sir, a pleasure, and I will have the island for you before you reach Africa," he said, his face beaming with pride, his olive complexion lightened as the broad smile crossed his weathered face.

"Solomon will now issue you with your written orders. The cavalry is to embark first and get their mounts settled, and then the infantry will board. You will ensure that each of your captains check that their men are fully equipped before they board. If you have any deficiencies, I am very pleased to say that the prefect, John, has been persuaded to open the coffers and pay for it, not yourselves, which makes a change." I had the feeling that they wanted to cheer, but that might provoke the prefect. Solomon, with the help of Procopius, distributed the orders and the commanders read over them. Then we began discussing and asking questions over any misunderstanding they had with the orders as I wanted to ensure they knew exactly what they had to do. Once they were all happy, I dispersed them back to the capital with the following message. "I will see most of you during the coming days in the harbour. Good luck to you all and we will convene our next conference at the first port call en route to victory," I paused. "Victory, by the grace of God, for the Basileus and us," I shouted, and they responded with a great cheer, and then, with purpose, they left the room and went back to their men to prepare.

The next morning, I was standing at the entrance to my office, deciding whether to go in or take a walk around the guards' barracks, just to check how their preparations were going. I was already packed, but I hadn't dared ask Antonina how ready she was to leave. Procopius approached me, with a happy look upon his normally serious face. He bowed and then spoke.

"Sir, I had the most startling dream last night. In this dream, we were all in a tent, and your guards entered carrying clods of earth and golden treasure. A voice announced that Our Saviour would aid in our victory over the Vandals. I think the earth meant the conquest of the Vandal Kingdom and the gold that the treasure of the kingdom would be ours." Procopius looked at me with shining eyes, feeling that he had indeed been granted a special vision. I thought for a moment about his dream, and for Procopius, it was very unusual for him to talk like this, especially of dreams. He must be excited at the forthcoming campaign, but, of course, he wasn't the only one.

"I have had no dream yet. But it is reassuring that you have," I stated, putting a hand to his shoulder to inform him I believed his dream, then I was suddenly distracted. A disturbance came from the main entrance to the house. I heard the sound of raised voices followed by heavy footsteps swiftly moving along the marbled floor as they hurried towards the sound of the disturbance. It could only mean that the guards were dealing with an intruder, and suddenly, Solomon appeared next to me, his sword drawn. I unsheathed mine, and we made our way cautiously to the main entrance, leaving Procopius behind. As we approached the entrance, we were joined by four more guards, spears at the ready, shields across the line of march.

We reached the main entrance and were greeted by a scene of utter chaos; loud shouting and swearing in what I took to be Armenian, Greek and Roman came from a large group clustered around the entrance. A group of guards with spears had surrounded a tall, thin, ragged-looking man, with long flowing black hair and beard. He had one of my servants in an armlock, and with his other hand, he held a drawn dagger against the servant's throat. I stared at the scene for a moment, and then a faint smile crossed my face. I relaxed and sheathed my sword. I recognised the figure — it was John the Armenian. He'd finally returned; he must have completed his personal business at home. Solomon and the guards alongside me had also relaxed their weapons.

"John, what do you mean by entering my house in such a manner?

Would you mind releasing my servant. You know how long it takes to train a new one," I said with a chuckle of amusement, the scene slowly unfolding. The remaining guards relaxed and put away their weapons and the servant had stopped resembling a mountain top covered in snow, as the colour slowly returned to his face as John released him.

"The next time this idiot refuses to allow me to enter and has the cheek to call me a beggar and threaten to have me whipped, I'll slice his stomach open and pull out his entrails and hang him by them," John cackled with glee. The servant fled towards the kitchen area and safety.

"Well, you have to admit, John, that you look and smell like one. Or are you wearing the latest fashion from Theodosiopolis," I laughed and added, "I am glad you are back. You made it just in time."

"Well, I expect you wish to wash and clean up, John?" Solomon asked with an equally bemused expression.

"Since I am here, why not?" John replied in amusement.

"How did it go at home, John?" I asked as we walked over to the bathhouse.

"The matter is settled," he replied, the tone of his voice ended any further discussion or enquiry on the subject.

"When you are ready, come and see me in the dining room for supper, and we will discuss the forthcoming campaign. You as well, Solomon." We all paused for a moment then John continued to the bathhouse, we both turned and returned to the house. Solomon commented, more to himself than to me.

"Knowing his people, I expect blood was spilt."

"I expect so," I replied.

Solomon changed his mind and went back to John, probably to make sure the servants looked after him properly. I went into the office and found Procopius sorting out documents on my desk. In one pile, he had assigned those that needed to be signed by me. In the other, those that I needed to read first, before signing. We all met up again for supper with the meal eaten in silence. No one, it seemed, wanted to ask any questions of John. Once the meal was done with, I decided it was time to speak to him.

"Well, John, I need your services yet again."

John looked up from his plate, a smile crossed his now clean-shaven face. He now had his hair slightly shorter than when I had last seen him. He looked like his old self once again, and he replied swiftly. "So, what have you got for me, sir?"

"The forthcoming campaign is to be against the Vandal Kingdom. I need your scouting skills and your leadership of my guards. I can always trust you to do more than I ask. You also inspire the men."

"Thanks for your praise, but what do you really want me to do? After all, Solomon here is quite capable of leading the guards," he stated.

"Well, I want you to pick a small squad from my guards, those you think most capable of tracking and scouting. I need you to be my eyes and ears in Africa. Which means for most of the time, you will be on your own, and they need to be as good as you to survive. Will you do it?"

John rose to his feet and walked over to the windows and looked out into the darkness of the night. Both Solomon and I remained quiet, awaiting John's decision. John slowly turned and faced us, his arms now resting on his hips and a big grin on his face. I knew that face and the answer he would give.

"Yes, I'll do it," he replied with a curiously sly twinkle within his eyes, and I had to give a soft chuckle of amusement at it.

"Solomon will assist with anything you require; I am sorry you only have two days to get ready." I paused, then continued with a sly expression of my own, "John, I am glad you're back, Solomon here was dearly missing you."

"That's not what I said," Solomon said, sounding mildly indignant before he decided to correct the matter. "I just said, I never knew how much work he actually did, he always made it look easy, that's what I meant."

"I am only teasing, Solomon. It's good to have the old team back," I mused. Solomon agreed, and he and John took quick swings at each other, and any tension between them was gone. John was back in charge, and Solomon was once again his deputy.

"Right then, Solomon, let's get to work. There's no time like the present. We'll have plenty of time to rest on the transports," said John.

I turned to walk out of the room. John called after me, "Thanks, my general, I'll enjoy the challenge, and we won't let you down, will we, Solomon?"

Solomon nodded his agreement. I headed back to my office, I still had a lot to read, and the oil lamps were not the best light to read by at night. There was still much to think about — the voyage would be the easiest part. The hard work would start once we landed and, in the morning, I would read over Livy and Polybius's accounts of the fighting in Africa. It would at least give me an idea of what I faced, except luckily for us it was the Vandals we faced, not a Punic army.

On the night before we sailed, Antonina and I entered the Imperial Grand Hall. I wore my best uniform — made of white material with a cloak secured to my right shoulder and silk socks. I never felt comfortable in this gear as it was for ceremonies, not fighting. Antonina wore perfection; a gold-embossed silk dress, a small plain silver cross hung around her neck, gold bracelets on each wrist and a small, unadorned tiara to keep her hair in place. She held the trail of her dress in her left hand. It had been quite a journey, and she had refused to dress till we reached the palace. Her handmaidens had to carry the dress carefully to the palace, then help her to dress. I had hung around with nothing to do till she was ready. Palace servants along with the chamberlain were also forced to wait before escorting us to the hall.

The grand hall was exquisitely decorated with exhibits from all parts of the Empire, with arches dividing the hall on either side, supporting the central roof. On the walls of the arches were some of the most beautiful mosaics I had ever seen, each depicting a previous emperor and his visions for the future, gold and silver contrasted with jade and jasper tiles. On each pillar lay a depiction of an animal surrounded by flora and the rest of the walls were painted in white, to enhance the mosaics. Even the floor had dressed marble cut into varying patterns.

We were led to the far end of the hall, in front of us on a raised platform were the three Imperial thrones, one for the Basileus and next to his was the Augusta's. These were made of wood and lightly decorated so as not to distract from the Imperial personages. But the third sat behind them on its own platform; it was the plainest of the three thrones. It was empty, as it awaited the return of Christ, where he would assume his rightful place on that throne. Behind them on the rear wall rose a magnificent Chi-Rho symbol in gold mosaic, surrounded by a circle of cobalt blue, above this was the most haunting image of all, that of Christ the Lawgiver. The image looked down onto the court below, and it seemed to suggest that the person of the Basileus was his to command, whilst also stating that the Basileus was the sole representative of his here on earth.

The air was laced with the deep scent of frankincense mixed with myrrh and sandalwood. The whole hall was lit by huge candelabras hanging from sturdy chains from the ceiling. Although as one entered the hall, it appeared dark. It developed a sense of space the further one progressed into it. The hall itself was almost empty. The court, with its slow and beautiful ceremonies, had departed for the day. The Imperial thrones were empty. We continued our journey under guidance, and we turned right in front of the thrones. I felt the need to prostrate myself in front of them, but our guide kept moving, so there was no need. There in front of us was a massive set of doors, made from the same cedars we had seen growing on the mountainside in Phoenicia. They were imposing and even more so as they were swung open on our arrival; though little effort was required to move them, even though they were as thick as my chest and far more solid.

We entered the private reception area of the Imperial couple. The room's walls had frescoes depicting wild animal hunts and other Imperial pastimes gloriously painted upon them. Tapestries hung between the artworks covering up the bare brickwork and reflected a more private atmosphere. I imagined each new arrival to the throne could choose to replace the décor here with whatever they liked. The Basileus and Augusta stood in the centre of the room. They both wore Imperial purple-dyed clothing with detailed gold and silver stitching showing Imperial symbols such as the eagle. Each wore a diadem of exquisite workmanship; his of plain gold, hers of jewels with a long row of hanging pearls. These pearls almost formed a veil as they reached down to her shoulders. They stood in silence, holding hands. Behind them lay a small feast surrounded by couches, accompanied by a crowd of servants who continually flustered over the table's contents, as we approached the couple. We both performed obeisance to them, while the chamberlain bowed deeply, then he spoke.

"Oh, Basileus, I present the Military Master of the West, Belisarius and his wife, the Lady Antonina. They wish to pay homage to your

153

exalted selves." We stood still, awaiting the next step in Imperial etiquette.

"You may approach," said the Basileus, in a stylised ceremonial tone. I then moved forward, with Antonina behind me. A foot distance from the Basileus, I knelt and reached forward. Gently, with both hands, I took hold of the hem of his purple robe and lifting it to my lips, I kissed it, then gently released it back to where it had rested before. Antonina positioned herself three feet behind me, kneeled and performed a low bow, with her eyes just gazing at his footwear. I then stood, and she followed suit. The court officials, along with the chamberlain who had accompanied us, bowed towards the emperor and shuffled back out of the room, still facing the Imperial couple.

"Belisarius and Antonina, please come and join us for supper. We wanted to spend some time with you before you left. I know Theodora is going to miss your company, Antonina." The Basileus's voice had returned to its normal tone of informality, with his accent more noticeable once again. All the requirements of Imperial ceremony were complete; this was to be a private meeting. The Basileus motioned towards the servants, they came forward and with great skill, removed the diadems and the Imperial outer garments. Now they looked more relaxed.

"Antonina, come this side and talk with me, while the men discuss war," said the Augusta as she gestured to two of the couches, which were comfortably placed close together. The Basileus pointed to the other pair, and we moved over to them. Once settled, the servants began offering us fruit and wine. The conversation was light, to begin with, as we ate and drunk our way through the lavish supper.

"Belisarius, please stop referring to me as Basileus here in private, we go back too far for formalities like that. Call me Justinian. It reminds me of times when life was easier," he said and continued with a soft chuckle, "My old friend, I know that I have given you a very difficult task to undertake."

"The task at first seemed almost impossible, but with careful study and with the assistance of Peter and his network, I think we can pull it off. If we know where the Vandal fleet is, we stand a very good chance," I replied as Justinian nodded his head in understanding.

"I knew you were the man I could trust to undertake this campaign. You're honest enough to tell me if it were possible, that's why I trust you now, as I did before."

"Unlike John the Chain. I don't know why you trust that man. He only plans to make himself rich at your expense. You should kill him now and be done with it," injected Theodora, her voice dripping with venom. Justinian began laughing. He reminded me of what he had been like before his uncle died.

He turned to Theodora and with a smirk said, "If I want to upset her, I only have to say I am going to invite the Praetorian prefect to join us for supper. Then she blows her top. You should hear her, shouting and bellowing at me, like a customer who can't pay for all his drinks."

"I hate that man. He spies on me, his men follow me everywhere, trying to dishonour my name with you," she replied in a hurtful tone.

"Talking of spying, my love, how is your network these days?" He mockingly laughed, continuing with the teasing.

"Without it, we would have lost our heads by now," she said, her voice calm once again.

"You know, Belisarius, in this room, are gathered two of the greatest scheming minds in the Empire," he said, grinning and looking directly at Antonina. She returned his glance with a knowing look.

"Antonina, I think we should leave these two old crows together," announced Theodora. As she began rising to her feet, Antonina did the same. The two women, accompanied by servants, left us. "We are going to talk elsewhere, dear."

They both comfortably reclined on couches in Theodora's private rooms. The servants had been dismissed, and the curtains were closed over the windows and entrance Antonina later relayed to me her discussion with the Augusta.

"Antonina, if there is anything you need or your husband needs, you write directly to me. I will have Justinian do his best," Theodora said quietly.

"You have already, thank you. I am going to miss your company; the campaign isn't going to be easy. It's hard to trust anyone, as most seem to be on the lookout for themselves at your expense. I can do more for him there than here. I know that you will help us as much as you can."

155

replied Antonina in equally hushed tones.

"I would prefer you were both here. In that way, I would know we were totally safe. But your husband is not suited to the Imperial court and its clandestine ways; he is too honest and would easily become trapped. On your return, we might consider moving you into the palace," she replied.

"Thank you again. You are right, of course. I'll watch his back and push his cause through you. Otherwise, we would still be stuck in a little fort in the wilderness of Armenia," replied Antonina.

"At least we both know that he will not exploit his power and chance his luck in a coup," she stated. She rose from the couch, as did Antonina. They both then left the rooms.

Once the ladies had departed from the hall, I turned to Justinian and spoke to him with a low tone but a curious expression.

"This campaign is only the first step in the recovery of the West, isn't it?"

"Yes, I have waited a long time to be in this position. When my uncle was emperor, I realised, as he did, that we would never be complete until we had rescued our western lands. I then promised myself that I would try to attain this. It's part of my duty to God and the Empire," replied Justinian.

"Well, I thought as much. You often talked about the need to return the city of Rome back to us and the western half of the Church. It makes sense. So, the overall objective must be Italy, as Carthage makes the perfect base from which to supply an army there. It also controls all the sea routes back to us. So logically, the next step is Sicily?"

"Yes, Italy is my main objective. John said as much to me in private, when he tried to dissuade me from this campaign." He paused. "The time is now ripe to begin. Persia is quiet for the moment. The Church has been pleading with me to save our people from the Arian ways of the barbarians. Even the merchants have been petitioning me to deal with the Vandal Government's decision to increase export taxes and mooring fees. Now there is enough public support for the operation. I know you can do it for me."

"Well, I am ready for the challenge. It will be a good chance to test the army in combat and give us the confidence to mount the main

156

challenge of invading Italy," I replied.

"I am full and a little sleepy from the wine; tomorrow will be a long enough day. I must now retire and save your charming wife from one of Theodora's schemes," Justinian said, yawning.

"Yes, it's going to be a long day."

Justinian got up, and I followed suit. I bowed, and he strolled out of the room. I stood and waited for Antonina to return as the servants rushed around, cleaning up. After a while, I saw her walking towards me. She looked as elegant and beautiful as ever. I was a fortunate man to have such a wife. She smiled as she saw me waiting for her. Once together, we hugged, and as we did, she whispered to me.

"Theodora has warned me that we must be careful. Your new command has aroused a great deal of jealousy in the palace. People may be after you. She has promised to help us in any way she can."

We were then escorted out by a side entrance and made our way home, crossing the channel in a lamp-lit boat. The sea was lit by small fishing boats working hard to complete their catch before dawn and the opening of the markets.

The procession slowly moved out of the soldiers' Church of St. Sergius and Bacchus, close to the new building of the Church of the Holy Wisdom. The church was a short distance from the harbour of Contoscalium on the southern side of the city. Already several ships of the fleet had moved to that location. At the front of the procession were the junior officers in my command, minus body armour. Following them were the unit commanders and their attendants, in full uniform and following behind them senior palace officials headed towards the Hippodrome, as it flanked the Great Palace. The Patriarch, in the presence of the Imperial couple, had celebrated the Divine Liturgy. We had accompanied them, along with senior court members and my staff, while outside, the rest of the procession had waited for us. The procession consisted of all the palace officials in their finest attire. The whole Imperial Guard lined the route, facing inwards, their shields reflected the strong light, giving an impression of a silver snake weaving its way through the streets. The populace had turned out to watch the departure of the fleet. Many a sweetheart was wondering if their new-found loves would return to them.

I followed them with some of my personal guard. I wore my full uniform, with an old-style leather cuirass. I had borrowed it as I thought it suited the occasion and my new rank. I don't think I would have been out of place marching with the legions of old. Escorting me was Solomon and John the Armenian, also in full battle gear. Behind us was a contingent of the Schola's senior officers, shields and spears carried on either side, in their white uniforms. Finally, Justinian was accompanied by Theodora, both in full Imperial regalia. Behind came the patriarch still in his clerical robes attended by his archpriests and monks. Lastly, the lesser court officials filled the rear of the procession. From start to finish we almost stretched half the distance from the church to the Hippodrome. We moved at a slow, steady pace, and as the Imperial couple passed the crowds, loud cheers went up praising the Basileus.

The sun was already approaching its zenith by the time the front of the column reached the harbour. I was sweltering in the heat and looking forward to boarding the ship and removing the armour, which had proved to be quite uncomfortable compared to the slightly more flexible chainmail cuirass I normally wore. The fleet stretched out from the harbour with the anchor chains stretched as they just about held their ships captive in the strong current. The transports, with their single masts hanging from the central post at an angle when the sails were unfurled, would form a huge triangle with their base parallel to the ship's deck. They had brightly coloured sides, painted with stripes, each slightly different from the other.

Their oars were raised waiting to be used to guide them out of the harbour. Others that were already fully loaded had their oars in the water, and the oarsman strained to keep them from heading south. The warships with their twin masts, sails still unfurled, were also kept in place with ease by their crew, while the twin banks of oars remained steady and under control. The red tips of their sails could be clearly seen, even tied up. They each had a row of shields protruding over the side protecting the rowers. A long, single deck ran down the centre of these ships with a castle at the rear. They were painted in many shades of differing colour. Only the flagship and a transport were tied up in the harbour waiting for us.

We weaved our way through the gateway out of the walls and into the harbour. Admiral Calonymus and his staff stood at the boarding plank of the flagship waiting for me. Antonina, with Procopius, stayed in the aftercastle, as the procession divided up between those boarding the ship and those watching us leave. As the Imperial party entered the harbour, trumpets blasted, and their sound echoed off the walls, announcing their arrival. They made their way towards the jetty on which we stood ready for them. The Imperial guards lined up along the jetty, forming a corridor for the Imperial couple to proceed through. We came swiftly to attention as they approached. They halted a few feet from us, and we all bowed low. Here, slight formality was allowed as we were outside of the palace and wearing armour. The patriarch moved forward of the couple, who deeply bowed as he passed them, we also again bowed. The patriarch stood in front of us, the archpriests gathered around him. One held the holy water, while two others held the ends of his mantiya, ensuring it didn't touch the ground. The patriarch raised his arms and blessed us, then showered us with holy water and said, "May our Lord Jesus Christ, through the intercession of all the saints grant you victory against the heretical Vandals and bring back to us our brothers and sisters in Christ. This campaign is a sacred mission to restore to the majesty of Christ what the evil one has removed." He blessed us again and with his retinue, retired back towards the city. The Imperial couple then advanced forward, halted where the patriarch had just stood and the Basileus spoke.

"I wish you success, in the name of the Senate and the people of Rome. May God grant you victory."

I, along with John and Solomon, saluted again. We turned and walked up the gangplank and boarded the ship.

Admiral Calonymus, once we were all aboard, launched the campaign. "Cast off, Captain," he shouted. He led me to the aftercastle, and we joined Antonina and Procopius. The crew set to work quickly; the rowers began powering the ship out of the dock. We stood and watched the dockyard, and slowly the people who were watching us became smaller. I turned and looked out to sea. It was covered in transports already moving away with their sails unfurled catching the southerly breeze, and oars raised as they weren't required. As we joined the already moving fleet, the transports formed a long centre line, the warships were formed in the front and the rear — they only used one sail, as they were lighter than the transports. I have never seen so many ships in one place at one time; we were a mighty fleet.

By sunset, we were heading steadily south from the capital, the sea was calm, and we were gently rocked from side to side. I went down to our cabin, below the aftercastle, close to the admiral's. It wasn't that big, but there was a bedroom for us and bunks next door for my staff. It was dark as only a few lamps were allowed below deck, for fear of fire. By tomorrow we would be opposite Troy on the Hellespont. By the end of the day, we would make our first venture out into the open sea, heading for the first of the Greek islands which would guide us along the Greek coast.

Chapter Six

"By God. I will not stand for murder by anyone in my army. We are all subject to God's justice and here on Earth, that is the law of Rome. You are not amateurs. You have seen death before. There will be no indiscipline in my army. Any soldier who disobeys will receive the same punishment," I shouted to the assembled soldiers.

A section of the army stood to attention on the beach. Behind them, several transports were drawn up on the shore, gangways hanging from their bows. The rest of the fleet had heaved to in and around the bay. To the south of us was the port of Abydos on the Hellespont sleeping peacefully in the midday sun, completely oblivious to the performance unfolding before us. I stood with a small group of my officers facing the army, between us and the army, lay two naked men, spread-eagled on their backs, hands and feet tied to stakes, and through their chests protruded two bloodied sharpened stakes. No sound came from the dying Huns, even in the slow process of death, they made little noise. Their fellows having executed them in the standard Hunnish fashion for the murder of their comrades, following brief investigation by their commander. We remained standing for some time before Solomon and John walked over to the bodies, poked them with their boots and shouted back that they were dead before they came back over to me. Satisfied that the punishment was complete, I ordered Procopius to write dispatches for all the ships. These were to be read out aloud, informing them of the events and the punishment.

"Solomon, embark the troops," I said.

"Yes, General," replied Solomon. He set about the task of having the commanders instruct their trumpeters to summon the army back to the ships. It had taken most of the morning to disembark, and it would take the rest of the day to embark and reform the fleet. We had been at sea less than two days, and already we had lost a day. Hopefully, the terror of the punishment would deter any hotheads from losing their tempers too freely in the confined space of the transports. Procopius had been reading to me, various texts on sailing, over the past two days when he came across an idea for leading a large fleet. I thought it worthy of discussion with the admiral, so I turned to him as we made our way back to the small boat which would take us out to the flagship.

"I have been considering the problem of keeping the fleet in formation. One of my staff has a suggestion," I said, wondering how he would take a advice from a soldier on how to do his job.

"I am open to anything that would assist us. The fleet is entering rougher waters, and we will be sailing at night and in fog," he replied.

"I suggest that the lead ship and its escorts, have the lanterns from the stern moved to the sides and placed on the end of poles. We could also perhaps paint the rear sail in red. The lanterns could be lit at night, and in fog."

"Um, I like the idea of red sails for the lead ships. The lanterns, I suppose, could be seen better at night. But fog, until you've seen a sea fog, you'll understand why the lanterns at the rear of a ship are important. It would take a day to paint the sails, and we could have the lead ships make port in Abydos while we form up, and then we can sail and meet up with them. It's a valid idea. I'll give it a try." He left me at the small boat and made his way to speak to two of his captains to discuss how to implement the idea. I decided not to board the boat yet, and with my senior staff, walked up the nearest hill, I wanted to see the fleet as a whole and this offered me my one chance.

Once there, we looked over the bay; it resembled a dead carcass covered in flies. The water was filled with our fleet, and all the ships appeared to be moving in one way or another. I was amazed we had got this far without loss of any ships or any becoming separated. After a while of gazing at the scene, I led my staff back down to the beach, and we were rowed back to the flagship.

The sun cast long shadows across the bay where it caught the waves, and they turned a golden colour. The sound of trumpets echoed through the fleet as, at last, we were ready to continue with the voyage. By now, the local crows would have begun eating the executed pair. We headed for Abydos.

The ship creaked as it rocked and the sound of the constant breaking of waves on the bow rumbled continually through the ship. Antonina bent over the bunk containing Procopius.

"Are you an angel?" said a feverish voice from the folds of blankets on the bunk.

"No, it's me, Antonina. Belisarius's wife," she gently replied. She helped the semi-limp body to sit up in the bunk and passed him a cup of water. He could not reach it, so she very tenderly held it to his lips while he managed to slowly sip, one drop at a time. The cool liquid refreshed him, and weakly smiling, he lay back on his bunk. He gazed up at Antonina, a look of thanks and interest crossed his face as well as slight confusion.

"You look much better now. At one point last night, we thought you were going to die. Belisarius insisted that I keep a careful eye on you. Who else would there be to keep our affairs in order?" she said with a broad smile, as she mopped his sweaty brow with a cool cloth. Procopius, now conscious of his environment, looked around the cabin and then back at Antonina, a quizzical look now on his face, "What happened? the last thing I can clearly remember was being ashore at Methone for a few days."

Antonina gave a scowl. "It was the biscuits that the Prefect John supplied us with. They were diseased. We lost a lot of men and a good many more are sick, like you," she said, pausing to allow him time to understand what had been said. She continued, "All because he decided to cut corners and only have the biscuits baked once, instead of twice. Belisarius is livid with him."

She got up from the side of the bunk and moved over to a small opening and forced open the cover. To let air to circulate in the dank and sickly atmosphere, as well as letting in some welcome light. The light caught the figure of Antonina, making it seem like she was daubed in gold. Procopius shivered at the sight of her semi-angelic look. His breathing increased, and he slumped back into the bunk. She reached over to him. "Are you all right?" she said, as she shook his limp body, and he came to.

"Yes, it must be the effects of the illness. I'll be fine," he murmured, sounding better already.

"You've been like this for a week. Tomorrow we reach Sicily," She paused. "If you feel better tomorrow, you can help me buy extra amphorae to hold water for the crossing to Africa."

"Yes, I'll be happy to," he said.

Antonina then turned to me, nodded, and we left the cabin. Procopius's condition had vexed me; the rotten biscuits had caused many casualties. By the time they had been noticed, too many had been consumed before they were thrown over the side. We'd been hungry for four days now, at least we'd be getting fresh supplies tomorrow. We went up to the aftercastle and basked in the hot Sicilian sunshine. The sun wasn't yet fully overhead, so we could see the white, smoky peak of Etna already.

Below it, a bank of clouds covered the Sicilian shoreline which was invisible in the haze, and out to the right, another bank of cloud showed where Italy ended. Otherwise, the sea was a perfect pale blue. A light breeze slowly moved us towards the island, but we needed a strong wind. Calonymus had already received a message not to dock at Catania but instead to sail on to Caucana. The men were too weak to row in the heat, and Calonymus had advised against pushing them. He was unsure of the conditions on the other ships, but judging by ours, it wouldn't be good. We desperately needed supplies, and a rest was required before making the next jump to Africa.

It had been fifteen days since we had last stood on land. The leg to Sicily, avoiding Southern Italy, should have speeded us up, making up for lost time. We had thought we had enough rations and water for the crossing, except we hadn't appreciated just how bloody mean the Prefect John was, and none of us expected him to cut corners like this. Baking the biscuits only once, left moisture behind and they rotted slowly from the centre outwards. If they had been baked twice, they would have been dry, like a desert, and lasted till winter. No one liked dried biscuits, but with wine and water, they provided enough food to keep going. Now we would have to restock completely in Sicily, and that would delay us.

We reached the small port at first light, a light summer rain greeted us. Only the front section of the fleet docked. The transports waited to come into the port; it could handle about thirty at a time. The men would be allowed to disembark, and there they would assist in loading their stores onto the ships. Once loaded, each ship would embark its men and anchor in the bay while the next group entered. It would be a drawn-out process. I sat in my cabin, reading over the reports that had been sent to me by my commanders scattered across the fleet. There was a knock on the door, as Solomon entered.

"General, there is a Gothic official to see you on deck," he said.

"I'll be up in a moment. I want Calonymus to attend as well, Solomon." I tidied up my desk quickly, folding away the documents, then placing them in a trunk to keep them safe. I buckled on my sword and arranged myself. First impressions were very important when it came to dealing with barbarians. Before I left the room, I picked up a sealed scroll and tucked it into a fold of my tunic and went on deck.

The sun was still hidden behind clouds, the rain had stopped a little while ago, and the air had that fresh feel to it as the rainwater quickly evaporated in the heat of the Sicilian summer. On deck, the first smell that greeted me was the odour of fish, but it was mediated by the sweet and fresh smell of citron that filled the air surrounding the small port of Caucana. The Gothic official was waiting for me with several of his counsellors. They were all dressed in a similar manner to those of our court, he even wore a toga in the Roman style, except his bearing and build was that of a stocky Goth. His eyes were blue, and his hair was similar to the colour of straw. He didn't bother to bow or show any form of respect, and he spoke in a brutal form of Roman, just like that of our Gothic mercenaries.

"My lord, Belisarius, I am the governor of Caucana. You are welcome in the name of our regent Amalasuntha and the Gothic Kingdom of Italy."

"Thank you, in the name of our emperor," I replied. My officials had formed up beside me, and judging by their faces, they didn't think much of this dressed barbarian either. The governor walked over to the gangplank and looked to my other ships which were disgorging men. He looked mightily unhappy as he watched them swarm all over his port area. Turning, he looked at me and spoke again with that rough tone.

"I suppose you expect me to supply you with *my* supplies?" There was almost an aggressive threat within his words, and I was not quite sure how to react at first, if only because I was not sure if he was challenging me or testing me.

"Yes, I do. You were told to expect me, and my men had already paid in advance for the supplies." This Goth was brave. He was trying to fleece me of my own supplies and then try and double charge for supplying us with what was rightfully ours.

"Well, I know nothing of this," he exclaimed.

I had had a feeling in the back of my mind, ever since the biscuit problem, that officialdom would be more of a problem than the actual fighting. But this was why I had brought up the scroll Peter had given me before we had left. I reached inside my tunic and handed it to him.

"Read this. It is a letter of authority from your regent. It orders you to cooperate with me."

He looked slightly bemused and opened it, glanced at the writing, and then handed it over to one of his hangers-on. It suddenly occurred to me that he probably couldn't read. He was now deeply embarrassed at being handed a letter which he couldn't understand and was too high and mighty to ask of this minion what it actually said. I decided to leave him to squirm, and we all stood there in silence while he decided what he was going to do. Judging by his face, he was trying to extricate himself from his own mess without losing face. We could be here all day. Then one of the minions spoke in fluent Roman to him, and I had the feeling that the man was rather enjoying the moment.

"My lord, it is from the regent, and it *asks* you to assist the Romans here." There was a short pause, then the Gothic official regained his authority and mumbled something at us.

"Please give me a list of the supplies, and I will arrange for them to be brought over to your ships. You need not land any more of your men. We will load the ships."

"Admiral Calonymus here will accompany you and arrange the sorting and collection. On behalf of the emperor, I thank you for your kind assistance."

The Goth turned and walked down the gangplank accompanied by his advisors and the admiral and his assistant. I decided that we would stay on board. We had humiliated him enough for today, and we didn't need any incidents to mar our departure. I was sure one of the first things he would do would be to send word to the Vandals that we were coming. But I reckoned we could be ashore before his warning reached Carthage.

We returned to my cabin. Procopius was up and about, looking far better than when I had last seen him. He had already sorted my desk and retrieved the documents and checked over them. Solomon and I sat down, and we both looked at Procopius, then I spoke. "Good, I am very pleased to you're up and about. How are you feeling?"

"Well, sir, much better, thanks to the kind support from her ladyship," he replied. Even his voice sounded stronger.

"Are you feeling well enough to undertake a special mission for me?" I questioned, and he gave me a sudden surprising expression of excitement, his voice filled with enthusiasm. "Yes, what would you like me to do?"

"I need you to go ashore, travel to Syracuse and go into the merchant area and find a Greek merchant named Timothy of Chios. Once you have found him, tell him who you are. He will give you a verbal report, do not write anything down. If anyone asks, you are arranging a shipment of wine for me back to our capital."

He looked a bit confused, as well as concerned. "Why me and not one of Solomon's men or Solomon?" he asked.

"It's because it's you and not them. If I send one of them, the Goths will become interested and ask questions. You look like what you are, a lawyer, not a soldier. Should they ask questions of you or Timothy, it will seem reasonable. Do you understand?"

He nodded, then a thought came to his mind, and he asked a question. "What about the Lady Antonina and her shopping."

"Change of plan due to the unhelpful nature of the Goths. We will be staying on board. The admiral is ashore dealing with the logistics, and I am sure he will deal with the water problem if he feels it needs dealing with. You must go now."

He nodded. I gave him a purse of coins, plenty to pay for a carriage or whatever they used to travel here, as well as enough for food, accommodation and to put a down payment on wine. He took the purse and placed it within his tunic and left the cabin.

Solomon looked at me and grinned and said quietly to me, "I don't think he needs to know that Timothy is one of Peter's agents. Once he has the message, he should guess."

"Yes, you are right. No need to fluster him and make him more anxious than he is. He should be back within two days if he rushes, and he can always hire a boat back if he is clever."

Procopius left soon after we had spoken and on the fourth day, late in the afternoon, he returned. He rushed up the gangway, and I ushered him, together with Solomon and Calonymus into my cabin. I ordered a guard outside with instruction that no one was to enter or wait outside. Procopius quickly described his journey. I thought it was better to allow him to speak rather than question him. He might have seen something of interest to us. He spoke in a rush.

"I reached Syracuse on the second day of travelling by horse. The roads aren't maintained here. There's no rest house along the road or a postal service. I found Timothy after much searching in the port. The city still has impressive walls, and they go down and around the harbour, you know. Timothy has a splendid house inside the city, but he wasn't interested in your wine order. But instead, he told me this and ordered me to rush back to you." He stopped, looking around at us to make sure we were indeed listening to him completely. Solomon looked at him and barely containing himself barked at him to spit it out.

"Procopius, here, drink some water," I said, handing him a cup, which he swallowed down in almost one gulp. He passed it back to me just as quickly, I refilled it, and he drank, this time more calmly. He waited a few moments after he had refreshed his palate before he spoke, although Solomon was still looking quite frustrated by his lack of speed.

"He, Timothy, told me that one of his servants had only just returned from Carthage. While he was there, he learnt that the whole Vandal fleet was away with an army of at least five thousand men in Sardinia. Also, they were not expected to return till late autumn. Secondly, King Gelimer was not present and has taken what is left of his army out of the capital and into Numidia. No one in Carthage is alarmed, and no one has heard of any Roman fleet." He stood, smiling, and handed over to me the half-empty purse. I gave it back to him as a reward for his excellent work.

"Well done, Procopius, go and rest."

He smiled and bowed and left the room. I looked around the room. We were smiling broadly, not least Calonymus. This was perhaps the best news we could have, our delay made up for perhaps by this knowledge.

"Are we ready to sail, Admiral?"

"The wind is poor here, but we can row till we find a better one, and by then the current should help. We are almost loaded. Tonight, with a good moon, they should be able to sail. The rest of the fleet, already in the bay, can start to leave now," he said, as he began to leave the room, already thinking ahead and eager to get moving.

Most of the fleet set sail. We were delayed till the following morning as the moon was hidden by cloud, but we more than made up for our delay, as a strong tide gathered us up outside of the port and the light wind improved. We were now at the rear of the fleet, headed for Cape Passero, and from there onto Malta. The combined tide and wind forced a slight change in the route. Once in sight of Malta, the fleet would turn towards the setting sun and head west. We aimed to land south of Cape Mercury and Carthage. My main thought was to get the men and animals ashore as soon as we could since we had all been at sea too long with weeks of being cramped up. We needed a shakedown before we even thought about fighting.

As night fell, we lost sight of the clouds above where Sicily should be. Now the stars would guide the fleet and we were lucky as it was a clear star-filled night, the moon would set long before dawn. I went below deck, where the rocking of the boat was less intense, and I entered our cabin. Antonina was waiting for me, and the table was filled with food. Fresh fruit, bread, ham, and fresh wine. I had got used to the good food that Sicily provided.

"Darling, you have hardly said anything since you joined me for supper? Are you all right?" she asked, dangling a bunch of grapes over her pretty mouth, nipping one or two off while awaiting my reply.

"I am just worried. This time we are crossing more ocean than before, and I am worried about the campaign. Have I planned for everything?"

"Dear, you will succeed. Look how far we have come. The Vandals are unaware of us, their fleet is away, and their king is out of the capital. What more could you want?" she said.

"I am sorry, you're right. Will you excuse me, I think the wine was too good, and I need to rest." I stood up and moved over to the bunk and lay down on it. Antonina stayed and finished her wine. The bunk was comfortable and quickly drifted off to sleep.

The next morning, I was woken by Antonina. It was almost midday, and she had a light lunch ready for me. I ate slowly, this time enjoying the food and the wine. I realised that I could now rest. It was up to God and the admiral if we reached Africa. So, I had nothing much to do till we landed. I spent the next couple of days in enforced rest.

We had our first conference on the flagship with my senior officers shortly after we left the coast of Malta and had changed course. We had caught up with the fleet and had now assumed the lead once again. Calonymus informed me that we should be landing in a large bay, close to Caput Vada in Byzacena. He had recruited a local fishing crew to pilot us to the coast, and this would place us about one hundred and twenty miles south of Carthage. The location of the remaining Vandal army would be the great unknown. We discussed my plans for the campaign. We all agreed that the best outcome was for Gelimer to seek battle with us before we reached Carthage. We could besiege the capital from land and sea, but the Vandal fleet would at some point return, and that could be a catastrophe for our fleet. We should reach Africa within two days or so.

During the day, the warships moved to form a circle around the transports in case the Vandal fleet should suddenly appear. The greatest danger would be when we came close to shore. The transports lacked manoeuvrability compared to the warships, and would-be sitting ducks, for the Vandal warships. This was my main fear, the Vandal fleet catching us offshore before we had time to land the army. This is of course, what had happened the last time we had attempted to destroy the Vandals, sixty-three years ago during the reign of Leo.

Calonymus had informed me it would take over four days to land the transports, set up a base camp, allocate supplies and personnel to each unit, but it could take even longer depending on the order the transports disembarked the men. For the army, this would be the most dangerous time. Disorganised, we would be easy meat for the Vandals. Before noon, on the second day, I was called to the bow of the ship by Calonymus, and we both took in our first glimpse of Africa. I wondered what Scipio had felt upon seeing the shore for the first time at the head of his army. I was in a far better position than he, he faced Hannibal a worthy opponent, I faced an enemy of unknown quality.

The coast appeared green in colour and flat, the opening of the bay a visible gap of blue in the flat terrain. The cool breeze that had been with us the past days was abruptly replaced by a much warmer one that drifted across the bow. It reminded me of Syria, and the conditions were supposed to be like those around Antioch — the best land lay between the sea and the mountains of the interior. I remained on the bow as we headed towards the shore. By the afternoon, the captain reported that we had reached the headland and the gap was the bay we wanted. We headed into this, and the warships heaved to off the cape. The transports began following us in, sails stowed and the rowers taking the strain. We entered the bay, heading for what looked like a sandy beach, using the tide and rowers to push us as far up the beach as possible.

The bow shuddered as it rolled into the beach and came to a slow halt. The bow was just out of the water, and the ship was steady, the waves rolled by. Sailors jumped overboard carrying thick ropes, large stakes, and hammers. They made their way up the beach stretching the ropes out till they became taut and the stakes were hammered in and the rope tied up. The ship was secure from rolling back out to sea. We had landed in Africa, would this be the easiest part of the campaign?

Chapter Seven

On that first day of the July, I assembled my staff and the admiral on the aftercastle. They, like me, were looking at the shoreline, the crew of the ship was now busy preparing to unload us. A gangway had been lowered from the side of the bow, down to just where the waves were breaking on the beach. A second one was being prepared on the other side.

"Solomon, has John got ashore yet?"

"Yes, my general. As we agreed, he took his scouts ashore as soon as his transport reached the mouth of the bay. John will scout the bay and if he sees anything, will light a fire to warn us," he replied.

So, with John out scouting, we could begin unloading all the transports. I turned to look at Calonymus, who had a big smile on his face. "Admiral, thank you for getting us here. Now let's unload as soon as possible."

"Yes, General. If you would like to go ashore with your staff, we will bring in as many transports as we can. Then the warships will drag them back out into the bay. So, allowing the next group to land," he replied, signalling to his staff to relay the orders to the fleet.

This was the last part of Calonymus's mission, and I left him to it. Followed by my staff, I walked to the bow and carefully made my way down the steep incline, and I walked on land for what seemed like the first time in months. Now I was back in my element. We walked up the beach till we reached the beginning of the plain. Here I decided we would make camp and directed my staff to begin laying out the markers for the campsite. Each unit would be assigned a different section of the camp, and there they could organise themselves. The first unit of my guard would have the task of setting up the defence of the campsite and begin patrolling the area.

While my staff got to work, I stood and watched as the first group of transports rolled up the beach and came to a shuddering halt; it seemed more difficult for them, unlike the flagship. Once the sailors had tied the

172

ships up, the gangways were assembled and dropped on either side; they were wider than ours in order to allow horses to use them. Horses were blindfolded before being led down the ramps, their riders leading them down one at a time. The infantry, boots hanging from their spears, trooped down the ramps and made their way up the shore to my position. They halted, formed up and waited for their officers to join them, who then they were assigned positions and marched off to them.

The cavalry was different. The horses were led up the beach and then tied up, while fodder was brought to them. Water had already been located in land and divided between the men and animals. Once fed and watered, the horses were corralled. The cavalrymen's equipment was brought ashore by heavily laden pack animals, who went back and forth collecting equipment and stockpiling it. Once a transport was empty, this could be seen as the vessel would begin to rock in the waves. The crew removed the gangways and untied the ship. The oars then came down into the water, and they attempted to break free of the shore. When they couldn't move, a slow operation began to have a warship manoeuvre in close to them, throw lines to it and slowly turn and begin pulling the transport out into the bay. Some remained tightly secured to the beach, waiting for the tide to change to float them off. It was a long and slow process, but gradually the army began to appear out of the sea, and the camp gradually filled.

At dusk, I returned to the flagship just as the tide changed and I could clearly feel the ship lift and fall as the waves crept onshore. I went into my cabin and began collecting enough equipment to enable me to stay ashore. My household and Antonina were to be unloaded last. They were safe on board and would not interfere with the main task of landing the army. I had just managed to fill a sack when the door opened and in walked Antonina. She was looking as beautiful as ever and seemed quite happy with the situation as she spoke.

"Darling, why are you packing? I thought we would land tomorrow."

"Oh, you and the household will, but I'm needed in the camp. We must be ready as soon as we can. Just in case the Vandals show up unannounced."

"But I thought we could enjoy our last night of luxury on board together." She paused, her face looked disappointed, while her eyes twinkled at me with that message that only she could give with them. I felt a tremor flow through my body; I sighed at the thought of missing her delightful company for yet another night.

"I am sorry to disappoint you, but needs must, and you wouldn't be comfortable sleeping on the ground. We will have tents ready for you and a real bed once we take Carthage." I reached over and gripped her shoulders gently with both of my arms, then kissed her. She responded, and we embraced for what seemed like an eternity. How did she manage it? I always left her presence feeling guilty for doing my duty, but at least it would be only for another night. I was still glad she had decided to join me on the campaign. "I'll see you in the morning, when you come ashore, my love."

"Yes, until tomorrow."

We kissed again, and as I began to make my way out of the quarters, she spoke softly. She laid back on the bunk and sighed deeply. I did not have the time to say much more, as the moment I stepped out the admiral was there waiting for me.

"General, tomorrow we will move back into the bay, the last of the transports should finish unloading. We will then wait for you here in the bay, till you have further orders for us. At dawn, a squadron of warships will begin patrolling the coast towards Carthage."

"Thank you, Admiral. Please come ashore with me. I am holding a conference for all my staff tonight."

He agreed and followed me down the gangway and onto the beach, Solomon was waiting for us. We walked back together to the camp, which was clearly visible now with all the fires and lit torches that cast a flickering presence over the low wooden palisade that had been quickly constructed. As we approached the camp, Calonymus spoke.

"General, may I be the first to congratulate you on commanding a Roman army in Africa for the first time in over sixty years. May God grant us victory, and the holy saints watch over us and grant us victory in our righteous war."

I stopped, and we both shook hands. He now thought of me as an equal, him the old sea dog and me the young Scipio.

"We couldn't have got this far without you and your fleet, Admiral."

We entered the camp through the guarded entrance; no gate had been assembled. The route to my headquarters, which should have been by now an unpaved near-straight road, was missing. Most of my staff had already come ashore, and we met for the first time together. It was a short meeting; the camp was unfinished the outer trench hadn't even been started, and the supplies were still piled up outside of the camp. The good news was that the horses were now all ashore, watered and fed. The workshops would be ready by tomorrow evening when the farriers and armourers would have all their equipment and furnaces up and running. We were also promised our first hot meal next evening. Yet, the engineers who should have been landed first were not yet ashore.

"We need those engineers to set up the camp properly," Solomon growled.

"I know. Why wasn't I told during the day they were missing?"

"I am sorry, I was busy dealing with your guards, as John is still out patrolling," he replied.

"Admiral, any idea where they are?" I turned to face the man, and he groaned.

"No, General. I assumed all was going well as you hadn't queried the unloading, till now," he replied, pondering over it, yet clearly too tired to want to consider it any more tonight.

"Can we find them now?"

"No, it's too dark, and we won't be able to find the transports with them in till dawn. Meet me at my ship then, and we will find them," he replied.

I nodded my agreement, then added. "You'll have to tell my wife and her party that they will have to wait to come ashore, as the camp isn't ready enough for her."

"I will, General. I am sure she will be pleased by that," he replied, then he left my tent.

He didn't know my wife that well, and I was sure he'd soon see a side of her he wasn't going to forget in a hurry. Rather him than me to bring her bad news. I dismissed the remaining officers apart from Solomon.

"Chaos isn't it, all the planning for the landing, useless," I groaned in dismay. It had all been going so well till now.

"It was to be expected. We have never done this before. I thank God that we reached here at all," Solomon said, his words suddenly rather reassuring and reminding me of the luck we'd been granted thus far.

"Yes, you are right, but tomorrow we will have to sort this out. While I am hunting the engineers, have all the supplies brought into the camp and send out more patrols. If you notice anything amiss, send a message to me." I dismissed him and made myself comfy on the floor of the tent.

I awoke just after dawn and made my way down to the beach. The flagship was already afloat offshore, a small boat was tied up, but the crew was missing. I looked around; there was no sign of them. So, I waited impatiently by the boat. It couldn't have been for long as the heat of the sun only slowly began penetrating through my clothing, warming my skin. From the direction of the camp came a small group of figures running towards me. It was the boat crew; they had been here since before dawn, but after I hadn't appeared, they'd gone into the camp to inform me of their presence, but they had become lost and only found the cookhouse it had seemed. After stuffing their faces with fresh bread, they had started back when they caught sight of me, hence the running. They quickly rowed me over to the flagship. It was much rougher in a small boat fighting the waves than it had been in a large warship.

As we approached the flagship, I quickly became aware of two things. Firstly, the warship, although anchored, was rolling in the waves. Secondly, so was the little boat I was in. As we approached, I stood up and was nearly thrown into the sea; one of the crew caught my arm and steadied me. He explained that my best chance of boarding was to wait till we were almost next to each other. Then, when both boats reached the bottom of a roll, I should jump for the gangway, as both ships would be at their closest. They wouldn't come any closer as the oars were still in the way. A crew member of the flagship had already descended the gangway; other crew members had secured him by rope. He shouted to me as we dipped. I just froze. I hated the thought of drowning here in the bay.

Both crews shouted encouragement as the next roll began, the crafts almost seemed to touch, and the shouting became wild. The gap was no more than a large step in length. I flew through the air and crashed into the sailor on the gangway, and we both then crashed into the side of the ship. The small ship pulled away, just missing the oars and made its way to the port side. A rope was thrown, and they connected themselves to the flagship and drifted along the port side, just out of range of the oars. I regained my dignity and thanked the sailor for his help and clambered up the ramp and onto the deck. Calonymus and Antonina were waiting for me, she spoke first.

"I thought I was going to be a widow for a moment there. Thank God you are safe." She walked over to me and gave me a big hug and a kiss. The others on deck looked on with mild interest. Antonina reassured, released herself from me.

"Admiral, sorry for my delay. Any word on the engineers?"

"Yes, General, they are in the process of landing now. Since you weren't here, I found the ships and have instructed their captains to land as soon as they can," he replied, looking at me in a sympathetic way. I didn't appreciate his look or tone. The fact that I had wasted time in coming out here on that dangerous little boat and I would now have to get back on and be rowed ashore, making it more bitter news to swallow. Was it worth an argument with him? No, he could simply pull out when I went back ashore and leave us in the lurch if things went horrible wrong. Instead, I decided to order Solomon and several of my guards to come aboard. I would have Solomon keep an eye on the admiral and ensure he did what I ordered when I ordered it. Turning to Antonina, I said, "The admiral will bring you ashore as soon as he can." I then turned to him. "Isn't that right, Admiral?"

"Of course, I will beach again once everything is ashore and deliver your lady and her party safely to you," he replied, and I nodded in appreciation.

"Well, it seems I have wasted a journey. I'll get back ashore, Admiral."

He nodded and shouted orders to his crew. The smaller boat was summoned back and, using the rope, it was guided in. I went back down the gangway and waited at the bottom for it. It was much easier this time, as the rocking of the flagship was less noticeable. Once aboard, they rowed quickly for the shore, and the waves carried us in. As I landed, Solomon rode over to me, dismounted and I walked over to him.

"Solomon, everything all right here?"

"Yes, General. Over there, the engineers are landing. We should be up and running by nightfall," he said.

"Good, there is something about our Egyptian admiral, I don't trust. So, I want you to take several guards and board his ship when he beaches. I want you to command the fleet, discreetly. I will send orders to the admiral, and you will have a copy. Make sure he does what I say. Any problems assume command and deal with him. He has been useful so far, but without any battle at sea neither he nor his men will gain a chance for monetary reward."

"Yes, General. You can rely on me to fulfil your orders," he replied, mounting his horse and riding off to the camp. A group of riders approached me as I walked up to the camp. It was John and his scouts. He halted close to me, the rest of his group slowing down and forming up behind him.

"John, no need to dismount. Any news?"

"Nothing, Belisarius, just peaceful countryside." He removed his helmet as he spoke. He looked tired and dirty, but I was glad to see him.

"First, go and clean up, look after your men and horses. When you are ready, I want you to organise the cavalry and deploy them at a distance from the camp, in roughly a wide crescent. While you do that, I am going to get the camp built properly. It's a mess. The engineers have only just landed."

"Right, I've already found some suitable defensive positions for us. I'll deploy the cavalry to give us the best chance of stopping an attack reaching you," he replied, fastening his helmet back on.

"I want you back by sunset. Leave one of your officers in charge."

He saluted with his right hand and moved off, followed by the remaining guards, and headed to the camp. I stopped and looked around at the beach and then at the camp. It was a bloody mess. I walked back to the beach and headed to where a number of transports were unloading. I found the senior engineer on the beach shouting orders to his men as he did his best to organise them. He was wearing his armour, and his helmet was strapped well on his head. I noticed that all of his men were similarly well turned out, odd considering they had been sitting in the bay for a number of days. His grey hair poked out of the sides of his helmet and matched his beard; he carried a short, thick stick. On seeing me, he stopped what he was doing, rushed over to me, saluted, and I returned the salute.

"Thank you. You see the camp; can you sort it out for me? It needs a ditch and ramparts as it will be our main camp here in Africa. I want the cavalry camped on either side of the main axis, the infantry on the perimeter. My guards will be next to my headquarters with the stores also close to me. This will be the first of many as we march on Carthage. I intend to have proper marching camps built each night. That will be your job. Use as many men as you need. We need to be secure at night," I said.

"Just like the old manuals recommend, sir?" he asked, a gleam in his eyes.

"Yes, they knew the value of building marching camps in hostile lands, and keeping good order among the men, no matter what conditions were like," I responded, pleased to see a hint of excitement and perhaps eagerness from this man.

"Leave it with me, sir. The camp will be ready by last light, or there will be hell to pay among this rabble," he said, pointing to his men with a wide grin of satisfaction. I left him to it. I was sure he'd beat any man not pulling his weight. I headed back to my headquarters, my stomach rumbling, reminding me I hadn't eaten since last night.

By early evening, the camp had already taken shape; the outer ditch and perimeter wall were complete. Tents had been erected, and the supplies were neatly stacked close to my headquarters. I decided to postpone the evening conference until tomorrow afternoon as my officers were still busy organising their units. The camp and the army began to look professional. The delay in the construction of the campsite had only slightly put back my timetable by two days. I had underestimated the difficulty of landing on a beach as compared to a harbour and with dark quickly rushing in, I returned to my headquarters. As I approached the newly constructed south gate, the sentries patrolling saluted as soon as they recognised me.

The torches, which hung from the palisade, cast a yellow-orange light over the barriers as they were moved to allow me to enter the camp. I followed the now correctly laid road to my headquarters, past a mass of tents and horses corralled securely. The camp was filled with a mixture of smells, mostly animal crossed with cooked fish. Apart from the sounds of men chattering, wood crackling on fires and animals resting, it was as peaceful as any army camp can be. My command tents were well lit from the outside, and I was glad to enter them again. The air was much cooler now, and the moon was rising, casting a light silvery coating over the scene. Putting down my cloak, I was greeted by the servants and shown into the dining area. Chairs and tables had been set up, and an area behind was curtained off to act as a bedroom, a bed had even been assembled. Wine and hot food was shortly placed on the table, and the servants waited while I ate my supper. Once the table was cleared, I sat down and tried to rest, but I felt stale, and the smell and feel of sweat made me uncomfortable, as it dissolved the sea salt encrusted on my skin. I decided to bathe before going to sleep.

Accompanied by the servants, I went over to the far corner of the fort to where a small stream entered. There, a temporary washing area had been erected. Downstream, at the other end of the camp, the latrines had been sited. Drinking water was drawn just before it entered the bathing area. A small wooden area had been built over the stream, and the stream's banks built up and narrowed to allow the water to gain strength. I leant over the wooden floor and washed my upper body in the stream, then quickly dropped into the stream and rinsed my lower half. With the salt washed off, I dried myself, and the servants handed me fresh clothing. Eventually, a better sized bathhouse would be constructed, with a steam room, which would allow us to clean properly. Back in my tent, I took a quick look over the papers stacked neatly on my desk, nothing stood out, so I went to bed and slept properly for the first time since landing.

The remainder of the transports landed in the morning, along with the flagship, and Antonina and her household arrived at my tents after lunch. Procopius had arrived earlier, having been rowed ashore at dawn. Since then, he had set up the office and got to work, checking on the number of men and horses that had come ashore against the number of stores we had, and calculated how long these would last before we needed to find supplies locally. While Antonina was settling in, he gave me the figures; four days' supply of dry fodder and seven days of rations for the men, enough wine for a week and water wasn't a problem. We had enough empty amphorae already to hold two days' worth of water for a marching army. The longer we remained in camp, the more amphorae there would be available, so the next day would see foraging parties sent out to collect more supplies, ready for our advance. The main task would be to scout a day ahead and spot a suitable site for a camp, with plenty of grazing and fresh water. We had no wagons and needed the pack animals to carry equipment, not food, and with that information, I called a conference.

The officers assembled in my main command tent in the afternoon. Calonymus and some of his staff also attended. With everyone seated, I stood and congratulated them on our success so far. I then asked John to make a report on what he had learnt. He stood up next to me and spoke.

"I moved inland in a wide circle for a distance of about twelve miles and found no evidence of any Vandal force in the area. The locals, who are mostly Roman, are friendly to us and willing to supply us if we pay. They also report that there has been no Vandal army in the local district since the early summer." He paused, looking at his audience. "Which leads me to conclude that the Vandals are as yet unaware of our presence. And when they do know, we will have the advantage as they will have to come to us."

I had the table moved and with a stick drew a very rough outline of the coast to Carthage, including the bay. I pointed to the bottom of the sand map to indicate where we were located, "Gentlemen we are here," I said, then I pointed to a general area inland and due north west of us, "This was where we assume Gelimer to be, and unless we gain other information, this was what we have to go on, and I was hopeful the information is indeed correct." I added.

"We are simply going to march along the old coast road towards Cape Mercury. Admiral, the fleet will shadow our movements and protect us from any flanking movements by the Vandal navy. Before the bay, the road sweeps inland heading towards Carthage. At that point, Admiral, stay outside of the bay, till we call you in and then head directly for Carthage. If all goes well, you will be docking there." I followed the route on the sand map, so we all had a general idea of the plan; simple and direct.

I continued the conference and explained the individual tasks I required of each commander. John was to continue scouting ahead with three hundred men, the Huns, under a Roman commander, would move inland and protect our left flank, keeping a good distance between us so that the plains were covered up to the first of the hills. This should stop any sudden attack by the Vandals catching us stretched out on the road. The infantry and baggage train would move along the road, baggage in the centre. The cavalry would form a barrier around the road, staying as close as the terrain allowed. I would follow behind in the rear with my guards, covering the rear of the column. Calonymus was most aggrieved when I informed him that Solomon would be accompanying him. I felt this was a sensible move, as I needed the fleet close by and reliable.

"Lastly, I intend to fight Gelimer at some point between where we our and Carthage. As we advance, we will put ourselves between his capital and his army. If he waits too long, he will be cut off. I suspect he will be very confident of being able to defeat us, Vandal history, has been one long list of victories against us, which means is has to be confident of victory. So, he will attack us before we reach Carthage. Barbarian arrogance will be our greatest weapon. The formation I have outlined allows us to react fast and deploy the cavalry in front of the infantry. Nevertheless, the infantry has the vital role of securing the road and holding it come what may. Thank you, gentlemen, we leave at dawn. May God grant the emperor his first victory." I finished the conference, and the officers slowly filed out, chatting away to each other, and discussing what they had heard. Solomon remained behind and asked to speak to me privately.

"General, I have a number of men outside under guard who have been caught looting a local farmhouse. What would you like done with them?" he asked, stern as always, but I was immediately frustrated by the theft.

"Great. Now we have upset the local Roman population, the very people we have come to save. First, have the victims compensated. Then, have the thieves flogged in front of their units before we march tomorrow. After that, have each commander lay down the law again and tell them they must treat the civilians like Romans, not barbarians."

Solomon listened quietly to what I said and then left the tent. I heard him outside give instructions to the guards to have the men tied up on stakes now, then be flogged before their units marched out tomorrow morning. Solomon would be with the admiral by then and tomorrow would be a long day again, but, at last, we were finally ashore, and there was still no sign of the Vandals. I entered the private part of the headquarters tent and relaxed on a comfortable fur which had been laid on the floor.

I must have slept for a few hours. I felt a soft toe gently forcing its way into my left ear, then a toe pushing my nose upwards. I opened my eyes and recognised the owner of the feet as Antonina. I looked up at her face. She was thoroughly enjoying waking me up in this manner, standing barefoot next to me. There was a huge smile covering her face as she looked down at me. She laughed.

"Well, you are the strangest rug I have ever seen."

I said nothing in reply. Instead, I grabbed both of her ankles and pulled them towards me sharply. She swiftly lost balance and collapsed in a heap on top of me. I rapidly released her ankles and moved to her waist and pulled her closer to me.

"This rug can do other things as well."

I was awoken at dawn by the sounds of movement outside. Antonina lay asleep next to me. I dressed and left the tent, ready to brief John and his men. The air was cold and fresh; light was already developing on the horizon. This was still the best time of day, fresh and full of potential; John and his men were tightly wrapped in their cloaks. They had been up longer than me, and the chill of the night was still in their bones.

"John, I want you to deploy a unit of your men well ahead of even yourself. Use your best leader to command it. If you can, keep them as far forward of us as you can, at a minimum a day's march. Overall, I want you to watch all the towns that lie in front of us and anything else of interest. Send a rider back at noon and at dark to keep me informed. When you find the Vandals, let me know, but don't engage them, shadow them. Good luck."

"I'll do my best. See you in Carthage," John saluted and with the rest of his men he mounted up. They made their way out of the camp, past the punishment area, with the half-frozen defendants still tied to the stakes. They looked impressive as they left the camp, John at the head of his small column, his men's shields strapped to their left shoulders, quivers and swords hanging from their belts and spears resting in their pouches on the side of their mounts. Lastly, came the servants with the pack animals carrying their supplies as well as the spare mounts.

The sound of the horses leaving was quickly drowned out by the blast of trumpets sounding reveille. The camp was speedily filled with the sound of an army waking and the smell of bread being removed from hot ovens. The horses stirred at the sounds of familiar movement close by and anticipated activity once they were fed and watered. The army ate breakfast quickly. Everyone knew that today was special, and that extra effort was required. The tents were swiftly collapsed and packed, mules were brought over, and they were loaded. The army moved from being a stationery force to a mobile one. Wagon trains were assembled, units formed up in place of their tents, officers rushed around checking their men and equipment. In my tent, Antonina took charge of the movement and issued orders to the household to pack fast, and her horse was prepared for her.

The floggings were finished, the army stood to attention during the punishment before I ordered them to begin the march to Carthage. I gave a short speech to those of the army close enough to hear me; the message would be passed along during the march.

"Soldiers of Rome. We have come not to conquer this land, but to return it to its rightful owner, our Lord God, who on Earth is represented by the person of the emperor. We must treat all the population as if we were still inside the Empire, as we are. We need the co-operation of these people, not only to supply food, which we will pay for, but also to provide guides and intelligence on the Vandals. Once we have destroyed the Vandal Kingdom, these people will be free again as Romans, and they will expect us to protect them. If you treat them badly, they will never trust the emperor or us, and they will not willingly assist in the cost of protecting this province. Some of you may even be posted here in the future or decide to retire here once you have finished your service. Would you not prefer to live among friends, than enemies? Anyone from now on caught looting Roman property will be hanged. Vandal property is ours for the taking, and you will all receive your fair share of the spoils." I paused. The army began a loud cheer that developed into a massive roar of excitement at the prospect of victory and gold. They were now rested from the voyage and motivated to march and fight the Vandals.

"Today, we march on Carthage. We have one hundred and twenty miles to go. Somewhere out there, along our route, we will meet and obliterate the Vandal army. Then Carthage will be ours for the taking. Good luck, I will see you at the next camp tonight, God willing."

The first column of cavalry rode out, followed by the Huns, then the infantry and finally the baggage train. It took time, but it was orderly and looked impressive. The column hurriedly joined the coastal road and slowly snaked out of the camp northwards. We left the camp in the control of a small number of men with the sick to guard. I assembled my command staff and ensured that the Huns were on our left flank. I sent messengers out to the front to check on the lead elements progress and to report back. The first day would be the hardest as we had not yet developed a routine for each day — this would come quick enough.

The infantry set the pace of the whole column, which allowed the forward cavalry to practise manoeuvring in and out of each other, advancing forward and then being relieved, as well as allowing the mounts to be changed regularly. For infantry, there was nothing but marching from one halt to the next. At first, the column resembled a caterpillar moving, a ripple travelling along its length every time a new order was given. Gradually over the day, a natural rhythm formed and spacing increased between units and the baggage train so allowing each to halt without colliding. The speed of the column increased once it was using the road.

At the rear, we could take a more leisurely approach riding for an hour, then walking and resting the mounts then catching up with the column. We could also practise manoeuvres. The majority of halts that first day were caused by caution on reaching a settlement alongside the road. They presented no threat, but I wanted to ensure that the inhabitants were alert to our arrival and could clear a path for us, or just be ready to sell items to the army as it moved through. By late afternoon, I had sent word to the column that at the next natural obstacle I wanted them to practise taking up defensive positions. So, at the base of the next hill, the column moved off the road and formed an elongated square, with the infantry surrounding the baggage train, the cavalry forming up on each of the four sides. With practise, this would improve and become a natural reaction. It also had a secondary effect as it broke up the monotony of the march and allowed the infantry and baggage handlers to rest.

After I had ordered the column to advance again, I realised that we had been making better time than I expected. At the current rate of marching, we would reach Carthage in less than ten days. The condition of the road improved the closer we moved towards the city, and the milestones were also being maintained. We were also producing less dust than I expected, again the condition of the road was chiefly the reason for this. On the left flank, there was no sign of the Huns even though I was kept regularly informed of their movements, which meant anyone watching for us would be in for a surprise.

Then one of John's men came riding down the column to find me, he brought word that John had reached the first city on our path, Syllectus, and they were awaiting my orders. I sent the rider back with orders that John should send in scouts during the night and ascertain if it was garrisoned or not. Depending on the size of the garrison, John was free to capture the city before we reached his location.

That evening, the engineers selected a suitable site for the marching camp and with the aid of the infantry, assembled the camp. It was up and running before dark. A picket of cavalry was dispatched up and down the road to watch for the Vandal army. The Huns would be guarding our left flank during the night. The fleet, which we could see all day, anchored as close to the campsite as they could, and formed a night-time defence around the transports. Once the food and drink had been shared with my fellow officers, Antonina and I retired for the night.

The next day arrived sooner than expected, I awoke with a start from a good deep sleep. The camp was promptly filled with an air of expectation. Even Antonina was up and dressed and taking charge of the packing of the headquarters. Breakfast was dished out rapidly, and the camp was collapsed and ready to move by mid-morning. The quartermaster and his men were dispatched towards Syllectus to buy the provisions we now required. We followed on behind them. We halted at midday, and dry rations were eaten by the army, while I waited for a message from John. Just as the army was reforming back on the road, it arrived. The city of Syllectus was ours. The scouts had found the city ungarrisoned, and John had taken control that morning. The population was overjoyed, and he expected no problems from them or any difficulty in purchasing supplies. The returning messenger also carried orders for John that I wanted to meet the city council when I entered the city. I wanted to discuss their situation and how they would be assisting us.

The signs were good. The condition of the roads indicated that the old Roman city councils may still be functioning well enough to be incorporated straight back into the provincial system of government, which would be installed following our victory. This would also mean that taxation would start flowing quicker than expected, as well as supplies for my army. It occurred to me that the Vandals may not have been as destructive as we thought and instead had treated the provinces similar to how we once had when conquering new land. We took control of the central administration, allowing local laws and customs to continue as they were gradually Romanised. We had always been too small to overwhelm the conquered population and preferred to co-exist and absorb the tribal towns and countryside's leadership so that they wanted to be like us. My father had explained this to me when I was a youth when I questioned why the population was made up of different looking peoples who did not always speak Roman. Even Thrace, a thoroughly Latinised province, still attracted peaceful barbarians who wanted to be Roman.

I sent two of my guards to inform the commander of the Huns that the city was ours and they could resupply from it.

Late in the afternoon of the fifth day of July, we entered the city of Syllectus. The population turned out to welcome us. They lined the main road as we marched into their city; this was the first proper welcome we'd had so far. The pace of the infantry picked up at the sound of cheering as they didn't want to miss out on anything on offer. The city was a fair-sized one and again was in good condition. I felt that this was a good omen or blessing for the campaign, as it pointed clearly to the continuance of civic pride and responsibility for the maintenance of cities. If this was true of this city, then the rest of Africa could be in a good condition and ready to re-join the Empire.

Antonina and I were greeted by the civic leaders with honour, and we were wined and dined at their expense. We were given suitable accommodation for the night as we would have been in any other city of the Empire. The army was easily billeted in the city, the one thing that was clearly noticeable was the smaller sized population. The council leader expressed his pride at being once more under the emperor. He also said how pleased he was that his city should be the first in Byzacena to be released from the evil of the heretical Vandals. The local bishop, who blessed the whole army the next day as we marched out of the city, echoed the sentiment. He implored God to grant us a great victory over the disciples of the devil, meaning the Vandals.

For the next couple of days, the routine was the same, each town and city we passed through surrendered and welcomed us and provided billets. The mood of the army continued to rise as they slept less outside and had filled bellies; they were ready for anything. On the ninth day as we approached the city of Grasse, John sent back a message that his men had captured one of Gelimer's royal estates, which lay outside of the city. He recommended that we camp there that night.

The estate of Gelimer was luxurious. The main palace lay in the centre of a large park that contained animals suitable for hunting. The palace even had a small purpose-built lake. The palace had only recently been vacated by the Vandals before John's force entered the complex. The palace itself resembled a much smaller scale version of one of the emperor's palaces, so lavish was the décor inside, no expense had been spared in building and decorating it. The reports of the wealth of the Vandals, I had assumed to have been inflated, might actually be true. What would we find in Carthage? The emperor hoped the fabled treasure of the temple of Jerusalem, brought back to Rome by Titus might still be in one piece. It had been looted from Rome, during the great sacking by Gaiseric the Vandal.

I allowed the army to loot the palace. We managed to find a number of wagons and fill them with moveable loot, which I left under guard with orders to head back to Syllectus. This would be sent back to the capital and sold on my behalf and shared then with my officers. The estate now reverted to Imperial control and a small guard was left to secure it. Once it was up and running, all its revenues would go straight to the Imperial treasury.

John and his men joined me that night at the palace. He looked tired and flustered when he entered the reception room, in which I had gathered my staff. He came straight over to me and spoke firmly.

"Belisarius, we have just had our first contact with Vandal scouts. We beat them off with no trouble. But you know what this means, don't you?" He paused.

"Yes. Gelimer and his army are close by, and it looks likely that they intend as I hoped, to attack us before we reach Carthage." I gripped his outstretched arms, and we both smiled in agreement. We were finally going to come to battle with the Vandals, and, in the manner, I had hoped for. "Thanks, John, go rest your men. Good work."

I ordered a conference after we had eaten; there was no need to rush. The meal was wonderful, our cooks did a great job, finally having a proper kitchen to use. Antonina retired to her rooms after the meal, leaving me to get to work. My officers assembled, including John, who had in the meantime, washed and changed his uniform. I stood in front and looked around at them, they all seemed well pleased and excited by the news of the Vandal army, as well as the good food and accommodation. I explained that we were now halfway to Carthage. It had taken longer than I expected, dealing with newly liberated people for one, had slowed us. The Vandal army had finally begun to show itself, as we had clashed with their scouts.

So, they now had a good idea of where we were, but we still had no idea of where they were. But where they intended to attack was still an unknown, and so the scouts would move further out, giving us more time to prepare for battle. I wanted the Huns to move further inland and cross the hills running parallel to us. They would continue shadowing us, and they should see the Vandals first if they came from the west. I gave their commander permission to attack them without reference to me. We would lose sight of the fleet in about two days when the road turned inland. At that point, we would be on our own. My officers asked questions, and I could answer most in general terms, and to those I couldn't answer, I admitted ignorance. We finished, knowing in some way what lay ahead, but not when. They departed for their rooms and I for mine.

The bedroom Antonina had chosen could best be described as Imperial. We were lost in the room, so large was it the bed seemed minute compared to the vastness of the cavernous space. The main material used for the room was marble; even the floor was made of it. It was cold to touch with bare feet, but all that marble kept the room a comfortable temperature during the warm night.

The next day passed without incident. The following evening, the Huns on their way back to us thought they caught sight of campfires on the horizon as they crossed the foothills to our southwest. John arrived in the camp that evening with reports from his scouts. They had reached a major defile which the road entered, so avoiding Cape Mercury and cutting inland. They had followed the route as far as a village called Decimum, as it lay close to the tenth-mile marker from Carthage, and they had found no sign of the Vandals. The road to Carthage was open, but John remained cautious.

"Belisarius, I would like to take all of my men and charge through the defile, and on to Carthage and secure the city for us. It looks like the Vandals are behind us and won't catch up till we are at the city gates. We don't want to be caught between the city walls and the Vandal army."

"I was thinking along those lines as well, John. So far, the only signs we have all point to the Vandals being behind us." I paused as I listened to his queries and then thought it through myself. It was the best bet we had in such a matter, but it was also a big risk to take. I pondered a little longer before I said t. "Let's take a risk, tomorrow your men storm the defile. If the Vandals have managed to overtake us, then you'll spring the trap. If not, you will be in Carthage by noon. Signal the fleet to join you. We will reach you there by late evening. I will force the pace; if I hear nothing from you by noon, I will send a squadron of cavalry to support you in the city."

"Thanks, Belisarius, I will have the city ready for you. This campaign has been easy so far, let's take full advantage while we can," he said, saluting and then leaving my tent, humming some cheerful sounding Armenian ditty.

John was as good as his word, and his force departed well before dawn on the thirteenth day of July I summoned my officers to my headquarters tents and explained to them what I hoped John could achieve this day. I decided to alter the plan and ordered the front section of cavalry to break off from the column and head to the entrance of the defile and secure it, following on behind John and his men. I just had a feeling that this defile was the only place that the Vandals could use to their advantage. They did, after all, know the ground and so far, hadn't shown themselves, apart from scouts. I doubted Gelimer would risk allowing us to reach Carthage. Could he trust the population not to come over to us and bring the city with them? So far, they had dropped any allegiance they had to him in our favour.

It was John's comment last night, regarding the ease of the campaign, it must have sunk into my thoughts during the night. I decided that the infantry and baggage train would halt this side of the defile, and the engineers would reinforce the camp. The Vandals were a cavalry people, and if they attacked us from the rear, they could easily tear up the column, hitting the infantry and cavalry as it traversed the defile, especially at either end. I decided that I would rely on cavalry to secure the route to Carthage before the rest of the column moved. So, a fortified camp was constructed, much to the dismay of the infantry commanders who were looking forward to reaching Carthage. I also had the surgeons set up in the camp, and all spare mounts were corralled inside it.

To the commander of the Huns, I gave a special task. Using a local guide, they would take control of the hills behind the village as well as the only track through the salt marshes. There they would conceal themselves and wait. This, I hoped, would secure the left flank better and surprise any Vandals trying to flank us. Lastly, one more squadron of cavalry was to travel through the defile and take control of the exit. It was going to be a very long day. If I were wrong, we would still take the capital rapidly, and the column would be delayed by at most two days.

The day wore on, and still there was no message from John or the lead units of cavalry. At noon, I ordered lunch to be taken and had the water ration doubled. Just waiting around in battle gear was draining. By late afternoon, my patience was wearing thin. I called my remaining commanders into my headquarters. I ordered them to prepare to advance through the defile and onto Carthage. I dismissed them, went into the rear of the headquarters and found Antonina, busy packing. I asked her to take charge of the camp in case anything should happen. She should hold here for as long as she could and then make a fighting retreat to the coast and join up with the fleet. I left her and went outside. My horse was ready for me, my weapons were held by servants, waiting till I was steady in the saddle before they passed them up to me.

The trumpets sounded the alarm, and a dust cloud raced into the camp from the direction of the defile. The infantry manned their defensive positions, archers loaded and made ready. My guards formed up around me, ready to fight. Then a call announced it was one of our men. He wasn't being chased, so the camp stood down. My guards remained tense around me. The man was led up to me, and I dismounted, as did my officers. He was one of my cavalry commanders. He had taken two squadrons into the defile, and he was covered in dust and sweat — a gash bled through the grime on his face. He was given wine first before he cleared his mouth with it and then took a deep gulp, before speaking, his voice full of excitement.

"Sir, sir,"

"Calm yourself, tell me, what has happened?"

He took several deep breaths, but this did little to ease the pitch of his voice. "General, we entered the defile, and I left one squadron there as you commanded. We then advanced through it. We saw no sign of the Vandals or John." He paused, his voice gradually becoming calmer. "It was as we approached the village of Decimum that we realised something was wrong. Scattered across our path were a good number of dead Vandals, and riderless horses. We moved with caution and found twelve of our own, dead. I recognised their clothing as being part of your guard. The men with John — they were laid out as if ready for burial. There was no sign of John and his men or the Vandals."

He stopped speaking and looked around at us. We all stood there, with bated breath, waiting for him to continue. He took more wine. Once that was down his throat, he wiped his sweat encrusted face, which mixed with the wine, dust and blood to form a reddish mud before he continued, "Many cavalrymen trotted towards us from deep within the defile. I realised that they were Vandals and not our men. We tried to stop them, but they quickly overwhelmed us, and we retreated. I left what was left of my men to hold the entrance, while I came back and reported to you. I don't know how long they can hold them." He paused again, gulping air. "I assumed that John had destroyed the Vandal force and continued on to Carthage, expecting us to bury his men as we came through behind him. I sent the remaining squadron forward to take control of the end of the defile and support our men there. We moved up and passed into the defile. Then we saw dust clouds approaching us at speed. I, at first, thought it was the Huns, but the direction was wrong. By the time I realised it was the Vandals, they were already in range and had let rip a volley into the cavalry. They retired back onto the high ground while forcing us back to the entrance. We fought them. They were stronger than us, eight hundred versus over two thousand and more were coming. I have no idea what has happened to John or my other squadron."

"Get back to your men. We are coming to their aid," I said, then turning to those surrounding me. "Rather than us ambush the Vandals, they have ambushed us. We can either stay here and let the rest of those men die or launch an assault on the defile. Get your men up to the defile as quick as you can."

I was sure it was not the whole Vandal army, but enough to cause a problem. Had the Huns and John been similarly attacked? I decided to assume the worst. But we had one advantage, the Vandals must have split up to attack my forces, which meant that I could charge into the defile with all my cavalry, punch a hole through the smaller force and reach the other side before they had time to link up. Antonina came out of the tent and up to me.

"What have you decided upon, my darling. I heard the conversation. Is John all right?" she said with an anxious expression that I tried hard not to copy myself.

"I don't know. I have a choice, sit here in ignorance and wait for them to mass or do the unexpected and charge straight at them."

She looked at me and smiled calmly. She must have been the only one in the camp who seemed calm. "I remember you telling me about Hannibal and his battles and how the unexpected was his preferred choice," she mused curiously, and I was pleased she'd confirmed what I had decided.

"Yes, you're right. Thanks, my love, for your words of wisdom," I stated in appreciation as my orderly secured my armoured jerkin. My mount was brought over to me. I stood on a small stool, grabbed the reins and heaved myself up into the saddle in a well-practised move. My guards were already mounted and ready for combat. My officers were also finishing putting on their armour. The orderly reached up to me and handed me first my sword, which I slipped over my head, so it dangled in its sheath on my left side and next, my shield, which I slipped onto my left arm, below the elbow. Finally, he passed up a spear, which I clasped in my right hand, resting its butt on a pouch on the bottom of my saddle. Looking around, I could see that everyone visible was ready. The other officers got to their mounts, their men following suit.

"All cavalry with me, we go to battle the Vandals," I shouted and signalled the trumpeter close to me to blow the signal for the advance. We began to move towards the defile, the lead standard-bearer beside me, acting as the focal point for the army. The smell of sweat mixed with leather quickly filled my lungs, and it was a reassuring smell of past battles. I ordered the cavalry to form a wedge shape; the order was passed using trumpets. The infantry was left to guard the camp. I needed only those who could ride as we needed to strike fast. Beside me, my guards formed up, covering my sides and rear from attack. We had a force of around four thousand cavalry, as we rode into the sun, its light changed us from a silvery coated formation of cavalry to that of golden ones. It looked like God was blessing us in our endeavour. My confidence rose, we looked magnificent, how could we lose. I quickly stopped noticing any smells. Instead, I concentrated on two things, controlling my mount and the enemy.

We approached the defile at a trot. My heart began to pump quicker as the anticipation of battle welled up within me. I wanted to charge into the defile, but training and experience had taught me to approach the unknown with just a little caution. Secondly, once we charged, the formation would slowly break up as it crossed the terrain, and the effect of a solid mass would be lost. Thirdly, we needed all the reserves of energy we had for when we saw the enemy. Gradually, we passed through the entrance, and the defile widened. The road streaked ahead of us towards the low building of the village of Decimum. With our direction relative to the sun altered as we followed the road, the sun slipped to the side, so we were no longer facing directly into its bright light. The ground ahead was flat and on either side were low hills with a slightly larger row on the right side of Decimum.

As we advanced and turned again, following the road, there ahead of us spread across the plain, and the road was a line of dark figures mounted on horses. To their left, a large group of men were positioned, we advanced towards them at a steady trot. It was their infantry, spread out in a line in front of us, like waves in a puddle when a drop of rain hits it squarely in the centre. The Vandals didn't use infantry like this. It could only mean that part of their cavalry had been ordered to dismount; God was indeed smiling on us. Why they were doing this, I didn't question as I had more important things to deal with. I looked around me, the faces I could see were intense in their concentration on the enemy before us, some even smiling. I looked at my trumpeter, the only man close to me who was trained to watch me continually through the battle and stay as close as he could. I looked to him, saying as loud as I could, "Charge."

He repeated the order, then blew the order for the charge. There was a momentary delay as the troops around me, almost in unison, removed their spears from their holders and tilted them slightly forward, as they swung up their left arms to allow the shield to cover their chests. Then we surged forward, the trumpet calls for advance being repeated throughout the army. The lead men swiftly moved their mounts to the charging pace, quickly checking behind to ensure the rest of the cavalry was with them and adjusting speed to ensure we stayed as one group. The noise of the horses over the ground drowned out any other sound — even though I was screaming at the enemy as I imagined others were — even the trumpets were silenced by the thunderous pace of the charge.

I tightened my thighs around the horse and felt the rear of the saddle in my lower back, bracing me as we pushed forward. I concentrated on the area directly in front of me, my spear now level with me, its point dangling in front, seeking a target. The ground raced under me, and I felt as if I were alone, the only one present, shadows formed quickly in front of me. The noise of the hooves battering the ground around me like thunder even took on a distinct distant sound. Some of the shadows began moving, others stood still, waiting for me. Faces suddenly became clearer as I charged towards the front line of the Vandals who stood waiting for us. Then arrows from beside me knocked two or three over. In return, spears travelled past me as well as one or two arrows. Then, suddenly, all there was before me, was a Vandal, standing, his shield raised and spear pointing forward in my direction. I steered my horse directly at him, my spear aligning with his chest, then I veered slightly to the right as my actions became automatic.

I saw his face for a second, and a look of sheer terror covered it, hatred poured out of his bright eyes. My right hand felt the contact with him, and I dropped my grip on the spear, as it continued at its own pace through the chest of the Vandal, forcing him to fall backwards. Then I was past him, with my free hand I had gripped my sword. It was now curving up and over my head, as I saw the next Vandal and with a quick motion, I struck him on the helmet. He dropped like a stone. Now was the point of maximum danger for me. My speed had decreased as we crossed into the Vandal lines. I needed enough speed to ensure that I could burst through and out the other side without coming to a halt. Then I saw another Vandal, instead of standing and waiting for me, he was charging at me, a large two-handed sword held high swinging left to right as he ran towards me.

I aimed directly for him this time. I held my sword, point aiming for him. His sword reached back over his head and behind him as he prepared to take a swing at me. His face was tightened with the force he was putting into his swing. The sword started its arc back up, but then I was upon him faster than he expected. My sword went almost straight down his throat. I loosened my grip as I rode beside him. The force of my blow and movement, combined with his attack, spun him in my direction, my sword still slightly embedded in his face. I yanked on it, and it came free from his head; my right arm felt the release. I swung back to face forward. I now became aware of the battle around me, my guards, still charging, overtook me, I had slowed quite considerably to almost a trot. The shadows were running ahead of us, and my guards were mowing them down, like farmers cutting wheat. I halted, the danger to me had passed, we had broken those here. I sheathed my sword and pulled out my bow and dropped my shield to the ground. With my now free left hand, I took a grip on the bow and loaded it with an arrow from the quiver on my saddle. I looked around for targets, here and there Vandals were running, I took aim at one man and let fly; he crumpled forward and was out of the battle. I found another mark and let rip. By the time my arrow hit him, two other arrows had struck him. My guards formed around me, and there were no more targets. The trumpeter came up to me, and I ordered, "Reform on me." I looked around; those close to me looked in good shape.

Outside of the group, I realised we had reached the village outskirts. I led my guards back onto the road and towards the far end of the defile, looking for Vandals to slaughter. During the heat of the battle, my force had split up, and those that had cleared the Vandal lines had quickly reformed and charged back into them. Now, they too were looking for survivors to slay.

As we moved along the road, more of the men formed up with us. All that was left was the scattered remains of the Vandal army. Dead and dying men and horses lay around. On top of the largest hill, a group of my cavalry stood guard while others could be seen sweeping the hillsides for stragglers. I halted my guard, and I caught my breath. Others around me were silent for the moment. It would take a little time for the body to realise it was safe from death and injury.

The fact that we sat there meant only one thing — we had won. I sent two men back to the camp to inform Antonina that I was alive and that we had won. The day was now late. I ordered the trumpeter to sound "recall" which quickly echoed across the battlefield. I led my men to the town, dismounted and ordered a camp to be made there, while we awaited the return of the officers after they had checked their men. As the men gradually returned to the temporary camp, an eerie silence prevailed over them, each no doubt engulfed in their own private thoughts about what they had done or seen that day. Fires lit the area, and soon the silence was overtaken with the chatter of the men, as they recounted their exploits to each other. Pickets patrolled the area and a slow collection of prisoners were placed in a hastily constructed stockade.

Tomorrow we would bury the dead and discover what had really happened here. I didn't bother resting and walked with several of my guards through the camp and back on to the road. The light was bright enough to see the road and its surrounding shadows. I sent a messenger back to Antonina with orders to break camp and march through the defile at first light.

My silent reflection was broken by a sudden outburst of cheering from the direction of the camp. I turned, as did my guards, and we watched a contingent of cavalry emerge from the cheering camp and make their way cautiously towards us. My guards halted the cavalry a little distance from me, and a couple of words were exchanged, then one of the horsemen was led over to me. The figure dismounted and walked the remaining few paces over to me, unescorted by any of my guards. He spoke once he was close enough for both of us to recognise each other.

"Belisarius, Carthage is ours for the taking. Nothing now lies between us and the city."

"John, thank God you are alive. You missed our little encounter. Don't tell me — you've been to Carthage already?" I questioned, relieved that he had not been killed running into the Vandals. He grinned though, and rubbed his hands together as if to warm them and replied with a wicked grin.

"The city's garrison is no more. We met them yesterday afternoon outside the city. When you reach the city, you'll see what's left of them," John laughed in amusement, but then I asked about his losses, and he gave a gentle shrug. "No, about twenty in all. We killed the garrison commander, one Ammatus. He was one of Gelimer's brothers, I understand. They had no idea we were there. They rode out, as if on parade, and we left them as a parade of the dead."

"Excellent work. Well, together with the number we think we killed, Gelimer's position looks bleak. Looks like he gambled on destroying us here and instead we destroyed him. Tomorrow we march on Carthage and deprive Gelimer of his throne."

Later that night, the Huns arrived in camp, and their commander came to see me. First, he apologised for being so late in reporting to me. They had spent the day and evening engrossed in hunting down what remained of a two thousand-strong Vandal force, which they had caught and brought to battle close to the settlement of Pedion Halon. I grabbed him by the shoulders and shook him with joy. He looked shocked at first, then realised he wasn't in trouble but being congratulated. I thanked him profusely and told him to ensure his Huns were well rewarded for their valour that day. Gradually, I was able to piece together an idea of what Gelimer had attempted to do. He had allowed John and the first section of the cavalry to exit the defile, then with us thinking it was safe, we would enter the defile unaware of his presence. At a certain point, with us well inside the defile, he would attack us from three sides along with the garrison from Carthage after they had defeated John; he would have closed the trap on us. His plan failed, and it was we who won.

It would take a while for us to learn just how badly damaged Gelimer and his forces were, but in the meantime, he had retreated from the area and left his capital open to us. This meant our fleet would command the bay and the sea between Africa and Sicily. His fleet was now essentially useless to him, as they were now blockaded within their port. Tomorrow, at last the city John would enter, while the army camped outside, I didn't want the city sacked. Instead, I needed a peaceful handover by whoever was in charge. The army would enter the city in an orderly manner, like any other Roman army entering a Roman city.

Chapter Eight

Dawn spread her warmth over us; a cool mist gently began to rise as it was slowly heated. We had risen before first light; I deployed the cavalry in a wide semi-circle outward from the village just in case of any sudden Vandal counterattack on the column. It was better to take precautions, and it was also good practice. The sun rose steadily higher in the east as the first column of infantry emerged from the defile, then another until the road from the battlefield was one long column of men. The dead were buried alongside the road, and those who still lived after the first night were collected and carried by the baggage column. The Huns were no longer required to flank us, and instead, I placed them behind John's men at the front of the column as we headed on to Carthage.

I waited for the end of the baggage train to leave the defile before falling in behind and acting as rear guard. The column snaked up the low hills, and we followed at a walking pace. I imagined that by now John and company were already in the city and by late afternoon we would also be outside the walls. As we topped the last of the hills, below us snaked the column and beside it was the sea once again. Out of sight, across the bay, I imagined the great walls and palaces of Carthage lay. It was the great prize of the campaign, defeating Gelimer was now a secondary consideration, for the moment. With the city, we had a secure link with the Empire and a base for the winter, as well as warm beds and food.

A lone rider came back along the road to my location, as I walked beside my mount. I recognised the rider as none other than my wife, Antonina. Even now she managed to look elegant, even while wearing a light cloak, and trousers to protect her legs. She leant over to speak to me. "I gave up waiting for you to come and say, 'good morning' or 'how are you?' So, I decided to come and find you."

"I am sorry, I've had many things to think and do since yesterday. Forgive me for forgetting about you," I stated in a pathetic kind of apology.

She nodded and cheerfully waved her arm over me, making a mock sign of forgiveness, then she said, "I am looking forward to entering the city today. I need a decent bath."

"Sorry to disappoint you. I don't intend to enter the city today. Instead, we will camp outside the city walls tonight. It will give any remaining Vandals time to run or surrender, as well as allowing the city's elders to take control and hand over the city to us, and then we can enter in style."

She looked very disappointed, then she looked down at me and said, with a soft pout, "Do you promise that tonight will be the last under canvas?"

"Yes, I promise that tonight will be the last time you sleep in a tent in Africa."

Carthage was the only city that the Vandals had kept walled; the others had their walls torn down soon after the conquest. Presumably so that if a city revolted against the Vandals, it would be defenceless. Therefore, it had a deterrent effect on the Roman population and made conquest so much easier for the much smaller numbers of Vandals. From our campsite, the city walls still looked impressive, even though there were now gaps where the Vandals had not troubled to repair the structure; obviously, they felt secure enough in Africa. It was a single high wall with square towers distributed evenly along the circumference, jutting outwards in standard Roman defensive design. This would not have been easy to take, even with the gaps and the rubbish-filled dry ditch running in front of the walls.

Even with no defenders, I would be greatly relieved when we entered the city through those walls. The camp echoed with the sound of cheerful, drunk soldiers, finally releasing their excess energy, before entering the city tomorrow. I thought it a good idea and had released what remained of our wine supplies to the troops that night so they could celebrate without endangering the population of the city. Tomorrow, they would be a little worse for wear and less likely to run riot once we entered the city.

I made my rounds of the camp with John and found nothing to worry about. A few fights had broken out, but they had quickly been settled without any need for officers to become involved. I wished John a goodnight and entered my tent. Antonina was still awake and waiting for me. We talked for a while, then retired to bed, and I had a restless sleep. I had much to think about.

We broke camp for the last time after dawn, and the army formed up in formation with my guards, with John and I at the head of the column. Behind us would follow the cavalry, then the Huns, and finally the infantry. The baggage train would remain in the camp — the tents were to be left up as the army might well still be using them for another couple of days while billeting was sorted out. Several corrals would be assembled to keep the horses from wandering. I had already dispatched a message to Solomon and the fleet telling them of my plans and that they could now enter the port.

I gave a signal from the front of the column, and a triumphant Roman army surged forward along the last section of the road before entering the through the already opened city gates. As we approached the city gates, the lushness of the region was clearly apparent with orchards reaching down to the shoreline, a mix of date palms, apples and pomegranates. Small huts were situated among the trees; a few villas were also visible. The sea shone in the autumn sun as we entered the city, the gates were still impressive even though they showed little sign of maintenance. No guards watched our entrance. Instead, part of the population lined the walls and towers. Others stood silently, lining our route, watching us as we pulled out of the gateway onto the main road to the forum.

After walking a short distance, we reached the forum, the city so far looked in good repair. Some shops had been closed, as well as empty looking townhouses, but even these looked in good repair. The colonnade arches were standing, still holding statues which were in a decent condition too. Apart from the sound of the horses, the city was silent, clearly apprehensive.

A group of well-dressed men stood awaiting us in the forum, with them was John and a few of my guards, all on foot. We halted in front of them, we dismounted, and some of my guards led off our horses. We stood facing five senior men dressed in the Roman style, except for one, who was obviously a bishop, carrying a cross and wearing vestments.

One of the group stepped forward, and spoke.

"General Belisarius, this day, the fifteenth of July, we the elders of the city of Carthage, welcome you and your army as our liberators from the tyranny of the Vandals."

It occurred to me as he spoke that they had actually never seen a Roman army, let alone a general. As for tyranny, well, some always seem to do well, no matter what and make a comfortable bed with the devil. Yet, I was being slightly uncharitable. Not for several generations had we ruled here, and they knew no other way than what the Vandals had allowed.

"I thank you, in the name of your emperor, Justin son of Justin, master of the Roman world, who welcomes you back to the fold."

There was silence from the man. He turned and looked at the rest of the group, several nodded to him, and he turned to face me again and said, "General, the Vandal garrison has fled, their fleet is away, and we humbly offer you and your officers' accommodation. And we will organise the same for your men, as well as food and water." He signalled behind him, and one of the group approached, and offered an object in his outstretched hand, and he said, "General, I offer you keys to the city of Carthage. You are now the governor of the province, and we are yours to command."

The man walked over to me and placed the metal object into my hand. The silence around us ended abruptly as the population realised their worst fears were unfounded, and they now cheered us.

"Thank you in the name of the emperor. Would you be kind enough to escort us to the palace?" I said.

He smiled, turned and said, as he walked towards his fellow dignitaries, "Certainly, please follow me. It is only a short distance to Gelimer's palace or should I say, ex-palace."

I walked alongside them, with John and a few of my guards. He chattered away to us, informing us that two days ago, Ammatus, on the orders of Gelimer, had slaughtered Hilderic and his family in the prison before he rode off to his death at the hands of John. This was unfortunate as Hilderic was an ally of ours and deep down I had hoped he might survive so he could be used as client king and control his people for us. Several Roman merchants had been luckier and bribed their way out of the prison before any revenge could be metered out to them. We walked towards the palace and the décor of the city vastly improved as we entered the Vandal area. The bishop interrupted our conversation.

"General, may I have your permission to cleanse the churches of the heretical symbols and books? Some of the Vandal priests have run away, and those remaining are already in the prison awaiting your decision."

Back to church politics and matters of faith, we had only been in the city less than half a day, and already matters of faith were of top priority.

"Yes, Bishop, you may remove all traces of the Vandal sacrilege from our churches. As this was one of the reasons for the emperor ordering our return to save you from this heresy."

He smiled as he blessed the air around us and finished by saying, "May God the Father, through his Son, our Lord Jesus Christ protect the emperor and his servants in their God-given task." Then he bowed to us and walked away, blessing any soldiers he met on his way.

"You must forgive the bishop," said the leader of the elders. He smiled and continued, "The persecution was clever in the way it forced the better off to convert or face exclusion from all official and business contacts. These were the men, like us, who paid for the upkeep of the church. The bishop could not ask the poor for any more money. We were forced to live a double life. The Vandals, of course, offered government money to run the church, as long as he denounced the condemnation of Arius."

"I understood the Vandals were persecuting the Church. I didn't expect them to be so subtle. I expected to find churches burnt and priests and monks, dead, or in prison," I said.

In front of us, surrounded by a well-built wall, lay the royal palace of Gelimer. It had once been the vicar, -the senior civilian administrator- of Africa's residence and basilica. Inside this complex was Gelimer's royal accommodation, a prison and, of course, the treasury. The gates were shut, and a number of tough-looking men guarded the entrance. I could just make out the shape of swords beneath their tunics.

"We put guards at the entrances to stop looting and to guard the prisoners," said one of the other elders. He went forward, waving his arm out to the guards, who saluted him.

"Where did you find them? They look like they can use their

weapons," I said, a little concerned and yet also intrigued.

"They are gladiators from the arena over there," he replied, pointing towards an amphitheatre close by. "With the Vandals gone, they have nothing to do. So rather than let them roam about looking for trouble, we have paid them to guard the palace."

"Good use of your money. I'll keep them on and supplement them with my own guards. Then I'll recruit them into my army. I always need trained men. I'll make this building my headquarters while I am here. I am sure the emperor will send his representative in the near future to govern you," I stated, feeling rather amused by the cleverness these elders had shown.

He then smiled a knowing look, and with his three other colleagues, they bowed to me, and he said, "We thought you might. Whatever we can do to help you, we will."

"Good, I have one last request of you all. I need you to form a city council and begin running Carthage as a Roman city. Roman law will be reintroduced, we have had some changes and the new law codes, I expect, will arrive in the spring. Thank you once again. Goodbye."

They bowed again, and walked away, chattering to each other, no doubt deciding among themselves the senior posts. Then, thinking about who they wanted to be elected to *their* council would keep them busy and out of my way. In the meantime, I would impose military law in the province till the spring and the expected arrival of the emperor's representative.

John, standing next to me, waited for my next order as we both returned our gaze to the closed gates before us.

"John, follow me into the palace. If those guards offer any resistance, disarm and imprison them till we know who they are loyal to."

"My pleasure."

Turning to the guards, he passed on my orders. I walked forward, and the sound of heavy boots crunching on the stoned road informed me that the guards were moving in behind me with John. John moved beside me, his sword clearly on display. As we approached, these former gladiators looked a lot less fierce up close. One of them turned and banged several times on the doors. The doors were opened inwards. I heard the sound of metal sliding through metal as my guards drew their weapons. I slowed my pace, the gladiators drew their weapons, and my hand dropped to the hilt of my sword. Out of the corner of my eyes, I saw John's face tighten ready for trouble, then quite suddenly the gladiators moved to either side of the entrance and then presented arms in salute. I clearly heard my breath leave my body; my shoulders shrugged as I relaxed, no fight today. John also exhaled loudly, more dramatically than me and said, "Thank God for that. I thought for a moment there that we were going to have to fight our way in."

"So did I John."

We entered the courtyard of the palace. It was a typical piazza, common throughout the Empire, a central clear area of paved stone and a pedestal with a statue faced us. It looked Roman but could easily be a model Vandal wanting to look Roman. We walked past it; I didn't bother to read the inscription as it would be replaced with one of our Basileus. The remaining guards had formed up in a loose formation to one side of the entranceway to the palace and basilica. A grey-headed man approached us from the group of guards, he was wearing some armour, and his sword was sheathed. His bearing, even at his age, was military and he appeared to be in command of the gladiator guards. He halted in front of me, saluted and then spoke in good Roman.

"General of the army of the Romans. I, Vegetius, had the honour of serving as a chief centurion in the late emperor's field army. I hand control of the palace to you; the prisoners are secure, as is the treasury. With your permission, I will disarm and disband my men, sir?"

I returned the salute. "May I congratulate you, Chief Centurion, on the excellent performance of your men. No need to disband them yet, unless you think they are unsuitable to assist in guarding the palace?"

"No, sir, they will continue to guard the palace with your men, if that is suitable?" he said.

"Good, tell me, how did you end up here, Vegetius?"

"Slave, sir. Pirates raided my village, and I ended up here, helping to train the gladiators for the Vandal overlords. It was better than working the fields," he replied. There was no embarrassment in his voice; years of slavery had knocked that out of him.

"Well, Chief Centurion, I grant you your freedom and work in my guard, looking after this complex. What do you say?"

"Thank you, sir, it's good to be free," his voice crackled with emotion as he saluted and marched back to his men. He gave his men orders, and they took up positions guarding the entrances and exits to the building. Once this was done, he returned to us and escorted us through the palace. I was surprised to find tables still laid with food, and the kitchens still had food ready to be served on those tables. Vegetius explained that when word had reached the Vandals in the city that we had defeated their army, they at first confined themselves in the palace. Then, when we camped outside the city, they fled on mass, carrying nothing but the clothes on their backs. The servants, with no new instructions, continued to prepare meals in case their masters should return.

I sent word to my guards that they could eat what they wanted from the tables, rather than let it go to waste. I was sure Antonina would soon sort out the household into some order once she arrived in the palace. He showed us the prison, which was situated in the cellars and held very few prisoners at present. He expected that as the city realised it was free, those Vandals still hiding would be dragged in.

Lastly, he took us to the treasury, it was unbelievable. The rooms were stacked with a century and more worth of loot taken from us since they had marched over the River Rhine and into the Empire. In the grandest room was what the emperor had hoped to find, the treasure from the Temple of Jerusalem. Massive candelabras, tabernacles of gold, golden incense burners, gold and silver dishes, just about anything you could imagine made by man for the glory of God. I instructed John to seal these rooms till we were ready to load them onto transports ready for the voyage back to the capital and to ensure that only my guards were used here.

On coming back to the piazza, we heard the cheers from outside as the main column came to a halt outside of the palace. We both went outside to view the army, well as much as we could see of it, as it filled the city streets around the palace. I decided a quick speech was in order as it would take the rest of the day to disperse the army around the city and back to the camp. I mounted my horse. I trotted along the ranks of cavalry and infantry, conducting a brief review, handing out praise to the men. Then I returned to where John waited. I gave my speech to the assembled officers and my guard. The officers would pass on my words to their men.

"We have achieved a remarkable victory over the Vandals, we have defeated them and taken their capital within a month of landing on these shores. I congratulate you. But we cannot rest yet and enjoy the fruits of victory. The city defences need urgent repair as does your equipment. Our last task is to seek out and destroy Gelimer and what is left of his army. Once he is dead or in chains, then we can relax. You will assign tasks to the men, beginning tomorrow, I don't want them becoming idle and a nuisance to the population."

My speech was greeted by total silence. They had expected to be given leave to enjoy themselves. Not one of them dared to voice dissent as they had not yet received their share of the spoils. The bounty was one of my tools for keeping the men in order. I had no intention of paying them till my mission was finished here. I sent orders for the baggage train to enter the city and for the quartermaster to rebuild our supplies, find suitable areas to have them stored in the city, as well as to source merchants to supply all we needed. The fleet had entered the bay and was in the process of docking, and then it would resupply and allow its men ashore. To John, I assigned the usual scouting role, and he was also to use the Huns. I wanted to know where the Vandals were and in what strength they were in.

The flagship had tied up, and its two escorts were alongside, several of the transports had already berthed. The remainder had dropped anchor in the bay, except for a patrol of warships dispatched to keep an eye open for the Vandal fleet. I made my way down to the port and harbour area and onto the flagship. I greeted Solomon. We had a long chat about the conduct of the campaign and how the fleet had performed. He was concerned that Calonymus and several of his officers had come ashore last night before the fleet had docked. They hadn't returned till after the ships docked and they had all been very reticent. I decided it was Calonymus sulking about his demotion and left it at that. I invited Solomon to return with me to the palace. I wanted him to oversee the complex. He agreed and commented that he was glad to be back on land.

Antonina had already arrived and begun settling into the palace. She had by now bagged the royal apartments. I was taken to view my apartment, and they were indeed regal in every way, much more splendid to me than the first palace we had captured. That night, Antonina and I enjoyed our first night in real comfort since we had left the capital months ago.

As military commander of the West, I was now the governor of all that we had captured, and that meant incorporating the old Roman-Vandal administration into our current system. In Carthage, and the other cities, this had already started, and once this was up and running again, then the countryside could be brought under administrative control. I gave the overall command of this to Solomon and Procopius as they had a flair for this type of work. Whatever we achieved would only be of a temporary nature. All we really needed from the province was money, in the form of taxes, and logistics to rebuild the army and defence of the province, quite apart from paying for the operation. Jointly, we decided that we would commute the tax for this year and instead concentrate on rebuilding the province. It would present some problems, but giving it a year, I hoped would allow the system to be ready and efficient when it came time to collect the tax. We also needed a census of the province, but that would have to wait till we had defeated the Vandals completely. The census would inform us of who to tax and how much we could expect. I did not trust the Vandal records, as they had excluded themselves.

We needed the courts up and running, and within a short time, as I was acting as the lead magistrate. Every morning I held court, the public regularly attended to present grievances and petitions regarding this and that, or mostly complaints against my soldiers. One case comes to mind, a merchant brought his complaint to me, he had been robbed and his house ransacked by one of my commanders. This officer, he had welcomed into his house and offered rooms to him, and he had been repaid, he claimed, in this manner. I asked why he had taken so long to come forward with his complaint, and he explained that under Vandal rule, he had no recourse to justice. He had waited and watched to see how I would govern and deal with complaints until he felt confident that if he came to court, he would receive a fair hearing. I was stunned by his complaint. A soldier, yes, that was to be expected, but an officer. I almost threw out the complaint out of hand, but further questioning revealed the man was from the navy, and I handed over the investigation to Solomon. He had responsibility for the navy at the time of the incident. He found the man and had him thrown in jail, to await trial. Justice had been seen to be done.

John returned from one of his patrols with the news that he had received reports that the Vandals were advancing towards us here in Carthage, in strength. Shortly after he had returned, more reports came in to confirm his observations. This was followed by the cutting of the main aqueduct into the city and the failure of the repair crew to return. That evening, I summoned John to discuss the change in events. I had become too confident and had expected Gelimer to use the autumn and winter to rebuild his forces before taking to the field again. This meant that either he was confident of his chances of defeating us, or he was in a desperate situation and only by attacking us, could he claim leadership of his people. With that in mind, I spoke to John.

"With your report and the cutting of the main aqueduct, I am certain Gelimer intends to attack us, either directly besieging us or just starving us out. I need you to scout the hinterland thoroughly and confirm exactly where he is. Then keep your men watching him."

"With winter coming, I can't see him being able to maintain a siege for long," John replied.

"You may well be right, but I would prefer to defeat him again, rather than risk a siege on the city. We can drive him inland away from the agricultural lands and good sources of food. He can starve instead."

"I would prefer to let him starve outside the walls, as they have no siege ability. But the population is too fragile to handle a siege. Anyway, another good defeat and that should finish off his supporters," summarised John, with good humour, even though he was required to take the biggest risks, while I waited safely behind stout walls. But he was right, in the best of worlds, allowing Gelimer to mount a siege would be the best outcome and save us from the risk of direct combat. But the real world determined choices and outcomes and only a direct battle with Gelimer would sort the issue and bring the war to a quick conclusion and thereby fully settling the minds of the population that we were here to stay. We had wine together and avoided further discussion on the campaign. Instead, we discussed the trial of the officer the next morning and how I should deal with it. It wasn't a military matter. It had become political, as the outcome of the trial would set the tone for relations between the population and us.

John departed the next morning. The weather had already changed as the sky was cloudier and the locals expected a storm, which would suit us, as the Vandal army lacked a base. Unfortunately, John and his men would have to brave the weather and the unpaved tracks, which would quickly turn into a quagmire.

So, to the trial. Solomon had already given me a preliminary report of his investigation. The accusations were well founded, and it wasn't just one officer, several other men had been identified and arrested. The guilty and the victim were brought before me in the audience hall of the palace. Word had got around, and the hall was filled with the local population, and the group of elders were conspicuous by their presence. The bishop stood with them.

I entered the hall, and silence greeted my arrival, either a sign of respect or anticipation. I took my seat on the raised dais, and the bound guilty were brought in and positioned in front and to the left of me. The accuser, or rather victim, was summoned before me. A buzz followed through the hall, as the audience briefly chattered about the situation, quiet enough not to be directly heard, but enough to make a point. Nervously, the victim approached me, and he bowed deeply. Once he was settled standing in front of me, less than a few feet from the guilty, I spoke. As this was a military court, he needed no arbiter, nor would the guilty be represented. If this was a civil court, a man of his social standing would have a legal counsel to represent his arguments and show the magistrate the innocence of the victim and the validity of his charges.

"Are these the ones who robbed you?" I pointed to the guilty party, they kept their eyes on the victim, hoping against hope that he would drop the case and save them.

The merchant looked up at me. "Yes, my lord, that is the man, in the centre, who I offered accommodation to, and those with him, helped him rob my home and beat me."

"Thank you," I replied. I looked at the guilty, and then at those assembled. I did not need to do anything else but pass sentence, but the ranking of the senior accused determined that I should offer him at least a chance to explain and ask for forgiveness of the victim and the audience. His guilt, and that of his colleagues, had already been determined once the victim had identified them in public. "Admiral Calonymus, what have you to say by way of mitigation of yourself and your fellow officers?"

He made no reply, and none of his officers wished to make an excuse either. With that out of the way, I said, "I, therefore, find all of you guilty of the crime."

The hall went from silence to a cheer. The merchant still looked a little shocked by the verdict but was sensible enough to refrain from making any outburst in public, and simply bowed and retired from the hall. Now they all awaited the sentence.

"Calonymus, you are dismissed, and you lose all rights and privileges that your previous rank entitled you to. You will pay compensation to the victim. You are exiled, and no one is to give you food, water, transport or shelter, on pain of death. Your fellow officers will also suffer the same fate."

Silence gripped the hall. Calonymus's face had dropped, and his tanned complexion had gone completely white. He and the audience knew exactly what the sentence meant; a slow, painful death unless he managed to reach the border of the Empire. Because of his station, execution for the crime was unacceptable, but exile wasn't, and because it was a military court, he had no right of appeal to the emperor. Now he was branded as a common thief, so suffered public humiliation and a loss of his social position, which he had spent a lifetime accumulating. I expected that he and his fellow criminals would make it out of the Empire; he had enough money to bribe his way out and might even reach the interior tribes alive. But he couldn't return to the Empire without the permission of the emperor. For the time being, the soonest that could happen would be with the last ship sailing from the capital in the autumn. He was now, no longer my concern. The population had seen Roman justice served on a senior military person, and this, I hoped, would serve as an example to them and encourage support for us.

In the middle of November, a Vandal warship arrived in port following a storm. The crew were arrested, and its senior officer was brought to my office, along with several documents. I expected that we would have to torture the officer to reveal any intelligence, but I was surprised on meeting the senior officer to discover the opposite was true. He admitted to his identity, and he then informed us that he was carrying a verbal message from Tzazo on Sardinia, to his brother Gelimer. The message was simple and direct. Tzazo, on learning of our invasion and march on Carthage, was sending back the fleet with five thousand men as soon as he could. He had come here not knowing that we had taken the city already, and part of the fleet was also heading here. He then went on and relayed how Gelimer, on learning of our invasion, had sought an alliance with the Visigoths of Spain. So far, they had not heard back from Spain. If he had been a Persian, I would have suspected a ploy, but a Vandal wasn't sophisticated enough to have developed such a scheme on the spur of the moment.

So, I rewarded him with gold and placed him on the next ship sailing south. I made no secret of this. Once word reached the barbarians, that coming over to us was rewarding, I hoped we could gain senior defectors from Gelimer's camp, so further undermining him. With this news, I summoned my officers together for a conference that afternoon. We gathered in my office in the palace. John was in attendance as he had also arrived back that morning. He had also brought news of Gelimer.

"Gentlemen, I have called you here to discuss our next move. I have two pieces of information which I think you will find most interesting." I paused, looking around me. They were all quiet, but impatient to hear what I had to say. "First, the remaining Vandals are about to receive five thousand men from Sardinia. Second, Gelimer is abandoning his siege of us. The time has come for us to meet the Vandals for the last time. I want the army ready to move at a day's notice, with enough food and water for five days in the field. John is to continue shadowing Gelimer. I also want scouts along the coastline watching for the Vandal fleet and the reinforcements. Solomon, as you now command the fleet, can it put to sea and move towards Sardinia?"

Solomon looked up. He had a full load on his plate, not only running the palace but also since Calonymus's trial, keeping a watch on the fleet.

"No, General. The weather is now too unpredictable to risk them losing sight of land, let alone Carthage. The warships also need to be landed and work done on their hulls during the winter. The transports can ride out storms in the bay better. But till the spring, the navy is essentially useless to you."

"That's a pity. I hoped we might have been able to intercept them at sea before they could land. Anyone have any points they wish to raise?" I said, and then one of the cavalry commanders spoke.

"General, from what I have learnt already from the locals, the weather becomes cold during the winter with a chance of snow on the higher ground. I think this means either we fight now or wait till spring."

"Yes, you're right. The elements at this moment are in our favour. Gelimer looks like he is already suffering. With five thousand extra mouths to feed, it will be harder, but not impossible. Possibly his own men will kill him during the winter and seek terms of surrender. But the only sure way to end the campaign quickly is to find him and kill him. I would like to be finished here before winter sets in and enjoy a well-earned rest; till we are recalled in the spring."

There was a general round of agreement that now was the time to seek battle — any longer, and the weather would hinder us as much as the Vandals. They filed out, work to do and an army to prepare for war. I was left on my own to consider what had been said and if I was doing the right thing. Should I cancel if the weather got any worse? Wait till spring, and then campaign till I had destroyed all the Vandal presence in Africa? The problem was where and when we would attack them. I was sure we could win. I decided to take a leaf out of Scipio's campaigns against Carthage. I needed to make alliances with the Berber tribes of the interior.

The chieftains of the Berbers arrived unexpectedly in Carthage, and before the conference began, one of the city elders approached me and told me a tale that had been passed down by his family. Once, they had been part of the vicar of Africa's administration, and that the Berbers had been regularly paid as allies to guard the desert frontier against raiders (other Berber tribes). Also, the vicar and later governors of the African provinces had acted as intermediaries in tribal disputes, as well as recognising new tribal leaders. It also ensured they didn't raid into the provinces, as in effect they were paid not to. It was a system that had worked well in Thrace and other provinces as well as in the East.

Bringing the tribes back into alliance with Rome would ensure that the Vandals had nowhere left to retreat, and we would then control all the trade routes from the interior.

The tribal leaders entered the palace and were escorted to the audience hall. Here I had a large contingent of my guards assembled with uniforms and weapons spotless, as were my officers. I needed to impress them with a show of Roman power. On their entry, my officers formed a semi-circle behind me. The Berber leaders were dark-skinned, tall, and all wore robes that covered their bodies and head, no jewels were displayed outside of their robes. They seemed amicable to me, but also confident, as they had left their weapons with their grooms. They did not fear me. Taking earlier advice, I presented each of the leaders with ornate gifts and symbols of office in recognition of their importance, as well as part of the new subsidy in silver. We laid on a meal and entertainment for them.

There were no formal negotiations with them. My officers and representatives of the city had already conducted talks. With interpreters, I learnt that the Vandals had tried to recruit them, but they hadn't been willing to pay them to protect the frontiers, so they had refused and instead extracted extra payments from caravans entering or leaving Vandal-controlled land. They offered me some of their best men, at a price, once Gelimer was out of the way. For the time being, I wanted the Vandals to believe the Berbers were our allies, but all I really needed was for them to stay neutral.

Two weeks later, one of our patrols returned with news that the Vandal reinforcements had landed on the coast. The patrol had tracked them for two days from the coast into the plain. They broke contact once they were sure the reinforcements had joined the main Vandal army. The other news they brought was that Tzazo and his men were on foot, they had no horses, which was good news, as we already knew they made poor infantry, as they could only carry light weapons and hardly any armour. Gelimer's reinforcements were going to be more of a burden than a blessing and would reduce the speed of his movements compared to that of the infantry. Further reports now placed Gelimer in the plain of Boulla, no more than a day's march for the cavalry. Now all I needed was their exact location and a couple of days of good weather.

It was already the first week of December, and the weather was becoming colder by the day, the rain had stopped, but the tracks were still muddy. The days were slightly shorter; the sun still shone but lacked the heat to dry the ground quickly. With all this news, I was able to send my last report back to the capital. A merchant was going to chance the calm and sail along the African coast and try to reach at least Alexandria. Then it might try to reach the capital. But at least in Alexandria, the Imperial courier system could transfer the report back to the capital.

So, I sent my report. I explained I hoped to destroy Gelimer by the end of the month, and I also mentioned alliances with the Berbers and the Vandal attempt to form an alliance with the Visigoths. I added my concerns that, come spring, the Visigoths might seek to take advantage and invade Africa themselves. I asked for reinforcements as soon as possible. I hoped the early news of the capture of the Vandal treasury might release funds to pay for more troops. But not being in the capital, I had no idea of what was happening there or in the rest of the Empire.

Chapter Nine

The report arrived on the afternoon of the ides of December. A patrol had found the Vandal army camped close to the village of Tricamarum. This was the opportunity I had been waiting for, and I summoned a meeting in my office. My officers filed in quickly as word spread that the Vandal camp and army had finally been located. Once all the officers were in the room, I addressed them.

"Gentlemen, the moment of triumph awaits us. We have located the Vandal camp outside of the village of Tricamarum on the plain of Boulia. They estimate an army of about ten thousand, judging by the number of tents and the size of the campsite. It's On the opposite side of the river to us, which means we will have an opposed river crossing to deal with before we come to battle." I turned and pointed to the wall behind me. A sketch map had been drawn by Procopius, with the aid of the scouts. "I had this drawn from the information the scouts supplied. This is them; this is the river, and this is the route we will take to reach them. I intend to use every able man for this battle." I paused as I used the tip of my sword to point to the relevant section of the map close to the Vandal camp. I then pointed to other locations on the map, then looking straight towards John and keeping an assertive tone.

"John, you will take five hundred of the cavalry, and move to here," I said pointing at the map, then continued, "secure it, and lay out a marching camp. You'll leave at dawn, don't let them cross the river. The rest of the cavalry will be with you as soon as they can, the infantry, with the baggage train in the rear, by the end of tomorrow. I don't want anything slowing us down," I paused; the faces told me they understood my orders so far. "The rest of the cavalry will follow as and when they are ready and will meet up with John. You will support him and ensure the Vandals stay on their side of the river. None of you will cross that river till I give the order, understand."

There was a general nodding of heads. If anyone crossed the river, the Vandals would attack them, thus pulling more of my troops in to save them, and we would end up fighting in the river at a grave disadvantage.

"The infantry and the remainder of my guards will leave as one column, and we should be there by the end of the day. You may be asking why we are not all travelling together. Two reasons: one, the slow build-up of our troops will stop our men from becoming worn out before the battle. Two, the Vandals will be watching, and at first, they will see a small force, this shouldn't panic them, we don't want them fleeing before we are ready. The gradual build-up should catch them out, and by the evening when the whole of our army is assembled, it will be too late for them to flee. The following day, before dawn, we will attack. The infantry will cross the river and secure the Vandal side for us. Then the cavalry will storm through the infantry, up onto the far bank, and hit the Vandal camp before they can respond. The infantry will support the attack. It is a simple plan, so it is straightforward; everyone happy with what's expected of them tomorrow and the next day?" No one asked any questions. "Good, you have until dawn tomorrow to prepare your men and collect whatever stores you need for two days. Solomon and his staff will assist with that. Lastly, I am sealing the city. No one is to leave for the next two days. That way, we should stop word of our preparations leaking out. Gentlemen, to work, and may God grant us a victory."

They filed out of the room in silence. They had much to digest and their own plans to prepare. They all seemed cheerful at the prospect of the war coming to an end in less than four days. I stayed in the room, looking at the map on the wall. I prayed silently that God would favour us and grant us a victory. I remained in the office till it was dark, then I walked out into the courtyard of the palace. Around the area, the sounds of an army preparing for war echoed over the city. The flames lit up the farrieries, as blacksmiths worked hard preparing the horses for combat, as well as ensuring that armour was up to standard. Around the workshops, men were sharpening swords as others were collecting freshly made arrows. The stables were a hive of activity as troopers checked their mounts were fit, watered and fed before they went to bed. The lamps in Solomon's office still blazed away, figures came and went like ghostly shadows. The warehouse next to his office was still open as a long line of men stood outside, waiting to draw rations and extra weapons.

I continued with my walk, enjoying the darkness and, more importantly, the shadows as it allowed me to watch without being watched. I strolled over to the closest section of the walls, climbed up the parapet, passing the patrolling sentries and walked along the walkway to the nearest tower. I entered and stood on the top fighting deck and looked back, over the city. The city was mostly dark, only the areas where my men were based were lit as well as the main roads from the palace to the gates, which had lamps lit to ensure that men could move easily through the city. Lamps also shone from the lower sections of the guard towers. I walked back to the palace and to my rooms, the activity had shown no sign of easing since I had first watched. I, at least, was going to have some sleep before dawn.

John's force left well before dawn, they clattered out of the palace compound and into the city, heading for the west gate and then out into the countryside. The air was fresh with a slight chill as dawn broke in the east. The first detachment of cavalry was preparing themselves, all well wrapped in cloaks, just their faces peeking through the hoods. Steam rose from the horses as they were led out of the stables. The first rays of light attempted to force their way through the grey banks of cloud, and out over the bay, as a sea fog fought a battle with what little warmth there was. The day was beginning gloomily, but hopefully, the sun would prevail, and the clouds disperse, the last thing we needed was rain. The first troop of cavalry had formed up and begun to leave the palace. The lead company paraded past me and saluted; their standard dipped slightly in my direction. Lastly, on a small wagon, followed their own mobile blacksmith. Then they were through the palace gates and quickly all that was left was the sound of the horses trotting along the paved road of the city.

Already the next detachment of cavalry was stirring out onto the piazza, the officer ensuring that all his men were present before they entered the stables and removed their mounts. This would continue until the last unit of cavalry had formed up. In other parts of the city, the infantry was already parading. By Solomon's headquarters, a wagon train was being formed up. It would carry all the stores, tents and weapons the army needed for the battle and along with it would come the surgeons' wagons. They would wait till the infantry had left the city, before following on.

For me, the rest of the day was filled with dealing with civil affairs. I aimed to leave in the late afternoon, overtake the baggage train and infantry and reach the camp before dark. I returned to my quarters after lunch. It was much quieter. The only sound came from my guards as they patrolled the building. I was as nervous as if I was on my first campaign. To reassure myself, I went back to the piazza and looked around. Only my guards remained, and they were already preparing to leave with me. I went back inside and washed and put on some fresh clothing.

Antonina entered the room while I was dressing; we hadn't seen much of each other since the news reached us. There wasn't much to say, and I was keen to get going. She wanted me to stay and avoid the battle and take credit for the victory, but she knew trying to persuade me was pointless. So, we said our goodbyes and I left the room. My servants were waiting for me and had my armour ready. They helped me into my armour, and then I was out into the piazza. The smell of charcoal greeted me, the last of the fires had been quenched, and their smoke lay around the square. My guards were ready to move, the infantry had already marched off, and the baggage train was ready to form up once we had left the piazza. My mount was brought over to me, and I climbed up. I looked around once and then signalled to the trumpeter to sound the advance. I then led my guards out of the piazza and into the city. I didn't bother with a speech; these were my personal men, loyal only to me.

Once through the gate, it was a slow trot through the deserted streets — the population had stayed away for whatever reason, perhaps fear or just the cold. Also, they weren't allowed to leave the city, so they were also a little angry, and this could be the reason they failed to wish us luck. The commander of the Western Gate was waiting for us, and he and his guards paraded and saluted us as we rode through.

The road ahead was still covered with a mist, and the surrounding countryside was also draped with the grey cloud. The road was literally swallowed up by the mist. As we rode into it, the city swiftly disappeared, and only the olives, bushes and palms close to the road were visible. Those further back formed a ghostly shadow as we passed them, the mist moving in and out of their branches. The air was cold and wet, the breath of the horses steamed out of their nostrils in great clouds. My cloak grew heavier as the damp clung to it, any longer in this and we would soon be soaked through.

The sun gently warmed the air as the ground rose, as we left the flat coastal strip and with it the mist. The landscape came into focus. It was relatively flat, coated with bushes, trees, and fresh grass had grown following the rains and cold air. The main aqueduct also followed the route we took. I hadn't noticed the massive structure as the earlier mist had shadowed it completely. The first part of the route would have made an excellent ambush for a prepared enemy. Now the elegant beauty of the aqueduct was clear to see as the sun shone on the brickwork making the bricks and stone turn a golden hue of brown. Its arches allowed the sunlight to break the shadow it cast on the ground beside it. By mid-afternoon, I called a halt at one of the watering holes, as the rear column of infantry was clearly visible. We were in no rush, we had made good time, and the horses deserved a rest, and it gave us a chance to remove the damp cloaks. The horses were fed and watered, and then the men had a snack of biscuits with water or wine.

We remounted and, moving from a single column, we divided into two files, one on either side of the road, overtaking slowly the long column of infantry. We would all be in place before nightfall. The infantry was moving at a good, steady pace and wasn't resting yet; they had covered twelve miles already. I spoke to their commander, and he decided to allow a break at the next watering place up ahead before the aqueduct left the road and headed towards the hills.

We continued on along the road. We passed the fourteen-mile marker in the early afternoon. A of line of foothills stretched ahead, and we were now heading in a westerly direction. The sun was also low enough to temporarily blind you if you looked directly at the hill line. The odd cloud provided a welcome relief from the brightness of the sun, and it was because of this that I failed to notice the rising cloud of dust approaching us along the road. One of my guards shouted that he recognised the riders as some of my fellow guards who had left with John. I halted the column and waited for the now clearly visible riders to reach my position. They almost flew up the road towards us. They halted in front, their mounts almost sliding on the stone facing of the road. The horses were bathed in sweat, as were the riders, clouds of steam rose from them. The lead rider wiped his dirt-encrusted face and spoke so quickly that I couldn't understand a word he said. It didn't help that the few words I could grasp were in Greek.

"Guardsman, slow down, think about what you have to say to me, then continue," I stated with a grimace.

Then he took a deep breath, cleared his throat and spat a mess over his shoulder, which landed on the road silently. "General, I have a message from Commander John." He paused, regained his breath again and then continued, at a slower pace, "The Vandal army has formed up on the opposite bank of the river. They look like they are preparing to cross and attack us before you or the infantry reach us. Commander John requests your orders and your presence."

"Thank you. You and your colleagues have done well. Grab some water and keep going down the road. You will find the infantry a few miles behind us. Tell the commander that I order him to force the pace and get his men to the Vandal camp as fast as he can. Tell him that I am racing with my guards to assist John. Then carry on till you find the baggage train, find Commander Solomon, and tell him what is happening. Go."

The riders were passed water, which they grabbed and drank quickly. Then they charged down along the column, and on back down the road that we had just travelled.

We were less than five miles from the battle. I turned to my trumpeter and ordered the charge. We were going to have to race there to save John and collect up any cavalry that may not have reached him yet. It would mean we reached John, in a less than an ideal condition, but we would be fired up and ready for battle.

"Follow me," I shouted, as I urged my mount to speed up, the trumpeter finished passing the order and caught up with me as the rest of my men quickly followed suit. We charged down the road. The messengers had only left John a short time ago so we could still reach him in time. My main worry was John. If the Vandals stormed across the river, he could be cut down before we reached him, my orders were to hold the crossing, and he would do this to his last breath. The worst worry was that John might take the initiative and attack first and get caught in the river. There, he would be wiped out by the Vandal archers and spearmen without having a chance to fully cross the river. Panic gripped me again, no matter how much you planned, the enemy always had a habit of doing the unexpected. I had underestimated Gelimer's willingness to strike first. I had hoped that he was still in awe of us and that we could use this to our advantage.

The road went uphill for a short time, and then we crossed the ridgeline. Then, the road slowly dipped down into the plain across the river and into Tricamarum. There below, on one side of the river, the Vandal camp could be clearly seen as well as their army forming up into three distinct blocks, slightly back from the river. John's forces were in a similar layout. We continued the charge down to the battlefield, the first units I could clearly see were of cavalry to my right and to my left as I approached the battleground. Directly ahead on the road, there should have been a bridge, but it was missing. Either the Vandals had destroyed it, or we had, either way, it stopped both of us from moving swiftly across the river and outflanking each other. I signalled my men to slow to a trot as we reached our lines. The horses were in need of a break; they had been carrying fully armoured men at speed. I detached myself from my guardsmen and made my way to the centre formation. That's where I expected to find John. I looked for my standards which my guardsmen, accompanying John, would be displaying. As I approached, John saw me and rode back to greet me.

"Belisarius, they caught us out. We were having lunch after we had laid out the camp when they suddenly began forming up. I used all the men here and formed three blocks. So far, they haven't moved," he said in a calm, quiet voice.

"You've done well, John. How many do you estimate the Vandals have?"

"About ten thousand. Only the centre appears to be cavalry; the two wings are on foot," he replied.

I was eager to see the situation, and so we both rode forward and passed the front rank of the centre block. I had, at the same time, signalled my guards to form up behind them. John and I continued our lonely advance, we moved from left to right, as I wanted to check the conditions of our units as well as that of the enemy. Our men on the left wing were neatly lined up; its centre was formed of archers and its wings of lancers. The centre and right blocks were also deployed in a similar fashion. The distance to the riverbank was only about three hundred paces, and we rode up to the bank.

We could clearly see the Vandal army from our position. Their infantry was dressed in banded trousers, a tunic of green or blue and a cloak, like our men. Their weapons appeared like ours — they must have kept the old arsenal working after they had captured the region. But their helmets were different, more conical than ours, lacking a plume and it looked like they wore no armour. The cavalry was similarly dressed, the horses lacked armour, and the cavalry appeared principally armed with spears; I could see no sign of archers.

I noticed the condition of both riverbanks; they were not steep and appeared to have more of a slope. The river itself appeared to be shallow, as banks of sand were still visible close to the bends. I had expected the rains to have turned the river into a torrent, maybe it would, but it hadn't yet. We continued trotting along close to the riverbank, no Vandals had yet challenged us, let alone fired anything at us. I turned to John and smiled.

"John, I reckon we can cross at this point without much trouble."

"I was thinking the same, the ground is soft, you can see by the depth of our horses' tread, so the banks will quickly collapse on this side making it easier to enter the water. It's the other bank that could cause trouble if it doesn't collapse, it will be hard getting up and out," he said, being careful not to stare too long at the riverbanks.

"If we can cause it to collapse before we cross, it should make it easier for us, what do you think?" I stated, and John looked at me for a moment as if I were being a little too optimistic, and he gave a sudden scoff.

"How are we going to achieve that? The Vandals aren't going to let us stroll across and knock down the bank without attacking us," he said with a clear expression that he had nothing to suggest, and I had to think quickly.

"I have an idea. What if we send a small force across the river to stir up the Vandals? When they reach the far bank, they can try and cause it to collapse before they climb out or the Vandals may give chase before and do the job for us. What do you think?"

He looked back at the river and then back at me and said in a careful voice, "It's worth a try. I'll select a couple of hundred of your guardsmen, mostly archers, they can fire once they enter the river, it might start the Vandals off, it's worth a chance."

"Organise that, then issue orders for the three formations to be prepared to move forward, at first to provide covering fire. Then, if the Vandals move en-masse, they can charge them in the river. If the bank is broken up, then I think we will charge the Vandal camp. I want you to stay in the centre. I'll have overall command from behind you and use the guards as and when they are needed. We haven't much time. Let's be about it," I turned my horse back towards our lines, and John followed, and as I passed the front rank, I shouted to them, "May God grant us a victory today."

They cheered in response, and the cheer was taken up by the whole army. John separated from me and took control of the centre, and I returned to the rear. By then, John had got things started. We didn't have to wait long; a short blast on the trumpet and all three blocks surged slowly forward. The small group had already been dispatched forward by John, and another cheer rose from the formation in front of me, as word was sent back to me by John. By then, my heart was pounding as I waited to know how the diversion had gone. They had entered the river, and as they entered, so a section of the Vandals had charged at them. In a hurry, my men had charged up to the far bank doing some damage.

More cheers erupted, and the formations in front surged forward, followed by the sound of archers letting rip and the excited screams of horses and men. Another messenger arrived with news that my diversionary men had retreated; the Vandals hadn't entered the river. Instead, they had retired back after being hit by several volleys of arrows fired from our side of the bank. I sent orders to John to send a bigger force into the river to lure them in.

Shortly afterwards, the skirmish was repeated with a similar result; the Vandals refused to cross the river. Gelimer was keeping his men under control this time. He had decided not to attack yet, so he must have considered that his position gave him a tactical advantage in that I would have to cross the river to fight him. Doing so would slow down my cavalry and reduce their effectiveness, and Gelimer was proving to be a better commander than I had given him credit for. He knew he lacked cavalry, so to make up for it, he was going to force mine to move slower, giving his infantry a better chance. But in doing so, he had also shown his major weakness, and I decided that the linchpin of his army was his cavalry; destroy them, and the rest of his army would fold up and collapse.

I rode up to John's position close to the river and summoned my commanders to meet us. I then explained my plan for the rest of the battle. My formation would fall in behind John's, doubling the size of the centre and its weight. The centre would then advance first and cross the river and pause. The wings would follow on behind and form up on either side, forming an arrowhead; then we would charge as one. I intended John's formation to hit the centre first, forcing a gap which I and the following units would expand as we drove through. This should force the Vandal's centre back, opening up the flanks of the Vandal's wings. This would also force the infantry to compact themselves as they strove to avoid the oncoming cavalry. My aim was to break through the Vandal line, and my wings would peel off and strike the infantry from the side and roll them up. The river would now act for us, blocking their escape. If this worked, we would destroy them utterly. John agreed with the plan, and the orders were passed by my commanders to their junior officers. The Vandals waiting on the far bank gave us ample opportunity to set up our attack. Once that was completed, I returned to my formation and readied myself for the advance.

I pulled up the mail hood of my jacket, tightened the hood's string to draw it closer to my face. It felt strange — I hadn't used a full mail suit before, normally I used a helmet and a jerkin of mail. But one of the discoveries in the palace had been a collection of mailed suits, well-greased and wrapped in leather and still packed in chests. It seemed a waste to leave them there, and I had issued them to my commanders, and the spares went to my guards. The metal felt cold on my head and neck. It took a little getting used to the way it constrained your ability to turn your head from side to side, but I felt a lot safer wearing this armour, my head, neck and shoulders were for the first time well protected.

The trumpets sounded the advance, and we moved gently forward.

It would take a little time for the front units to create a path up the far bank, then we would be able to move at a faster pace. John's men picked up the pace as they reached the far bank and began collapsing it. A gradual ramp had been created down to the water, which was still shallow and allowed the horses to trot through. The far bank again was a little steeper as the bank hadn't yet fully collapsed. Then we were up on the far bank and moving in behind John's formation. Looking to either side, I noted that the wings hadn't yet crossed. When the first sound of the charge came from in front of us, John's formation speeded away from us. I signalled to my trumpeter to sound the charge, and we rode after them, lances and spears lowered as archers let loose at any target they could see, anything not on horseback.

Then we crashed hard into the back of John's formation as it had been slowed on hitting the Vandal cavalry. Until John's force regained the initiative, we were stuck behind them, unable to do anything. Suddenly, the left wing appeared and charged ahead — their commander must have seen the log jam we were in and altered the plan. They slotted in beside my unit and opened fire on the infantry to their front as well as any Vandal cavalry they could see. Gradually, we began to move forward again, we moved over our dead and dying and then the Vandal dead. Spears and other missiles flew overhead, but at this range, they had lost a lot of their strength and glanced off our shields and armour, they would still give a nasty graze, but lacked the strength to penetrate. The noise around me was deafening, with screams and shouts and horses braying in anger or pain.

Then, John's formation was back moving at the charge; we followed. On either side, we could see the Vandal infantry starting to give way as we moved past them. The Vandal cavalry had put up a strong fight, but our weight of numbers had forced them backwards till they broke and fled. My wings now turned right and left and drove straight into the shifting infantry formations from the side and rear.

Then, like a bolt of lightning out of a clear blue sky, the Vandal army broke and ran for it; most of the infantry tried to make it back to their camp but were blocked and forced into the river. Those who stood their ground were mown down, either killed by arrows or smashed into the ground by a cavalryman's mount. Those who ran into the river became target practice for the archers; there was no need for lancers or spearmen to enter the water. The archers grouped on the bank were ample for the task of slaughtering the stranded infantry. What was left of the Vandal cavalry was chased off the battlefield by John's men.

A messenger found me and relayed that the infantry had arrived and formed up along our side of the river to stop any stragglers from escaping in that direction. The battle was over, it felt like a lifetime, but it was a remarkably short affair once we had closed with the Vandal lines. Now the task was to clear the battlefield. First, we needed to collect our wounded and take them back to our camp for the surgeons to try and save. The next task was collecting up all the loose horses and corralling them. Finally, everybody's favourite task, looting the corpses of any valuables.

The Vandal wounded were quickly dispatched. During the search, the body of Gelimer's brother, Tzazo, was found. I had the head removed and pickled. In the spring, I planned to take Sardinia, and it would be prominently displayed by the first ship reaching land there. Hopefully, this would persuade the inhabitants to come over to us, knowing that their last Vandal oppressor was dead.

To the infantry, I now assigned the task of clearing up the Vandal camp. Solomon led them across the river and on towards the camp which was filled with the remnants of the Vandal nation. We had two types of infantry; the first was drawn from the central field army, which was better equipped with chain mail jerkins, helmets and shields and a variety of weapons. The second was the allied troops and mercenaries, who wore a mix of uniforms and armour. The only thing they had in common was the shield, which was uniform in size, but each formation was distinguished by their unit emblem embossed on the shields. Most had no headgear or just wore felt caps. When it came to the fight, both fought as well as each other.

Solomon, on horseback, led the advance, the infantry moved at a steady pace in formation. Solomon halted them outside of spear range of the camp, he then had them form up into five blocks, three forward and two at the rear. Once in position, Solomon gave the order to charge, trumpets bellowed, and a large angry scream came from the ranks as they ran forward into the Vandal camp. I expected many of them to be felled by a Vandal onslaught of missiles, yet none came. Then they were into the camp, the rear formations were swallowed by the size of the camp, and there was now little sound coming from that direction. John joined me, and we both peered expectantly in the direction of the Vandal camp. We both wondered, silently, what was happening there. Then Solomon, on his horse, appeared out of the camp and made his way at a trot over to us.

"Solomon, what happened to the Vandals?" we both queried together at the grim look upon his face.

"It was a hard battle. Nothing worse than fighting women and children. The men had run away before we reached the camp," he replied cheerfully, throwing off his previous grimace.

"Any sign of Gelimer and his household?" I asked, choosing to be indifferent to his statement as the household of the Vandal king was of more importance.

"We have his wife and children; they say he ran once the battle was lost," Solomon replied, practically scoffing at his own statement and the thought of such a cowardly decision.

"Right, collect up all the prisoners and valuables, and in the morning, you march back to Carthage with them," I stated firmly, but Solomon gave me a grimace and shook his head as he looked downwards.

"I am sorry, General, but the camp is a mess, the men ransacked it looking for a fight. Then they found loot. The Vandal men had left everything behind as they fled. Luckily, they are taking out their frustration on the camp, not the prisoners. I need to leave them for a while to calm down. The fast pace and lack of a battle hasn't done their morale well. They need to let off steam. I'll parade them in the evening, and in the morning, we'll empty their pockets and collect up the loot," he said in a disappointed manner, his face showed the frustration he felt towards his men. John nodded in agreement. Both had a lot of experience handling mixed units, and discipline was always an issue.

"It's the same with the cavalry, there is so much loot lying around and wine, that they won't be in any shape to move till the morning. I am sorry," John said gently, turning to me with a similar expression of frustration.

"Blast, I had hoped to chase after Gelimer while the trail is still fresh. Well, the men have now succeeded twice in defeating the Vandals, each time we were outnumbered, but they fought well. The Vandal Kingdom is no more. Let the men celebrate, after all, we have won an outstanding victory." I hid my disappointment as best as I could. I often wondered if the Roman armies of old had suffered such ill-discipline after a victory or was it that the writers failed to mention these incidents as it cast the Roman army in a poor light, removing some of the shine from their glory and that of their commanders.

"One day isn't going to make much difference. Anyway, we need to plan where we suspect he has flown. Men on foot can't get far. The cavalry will be fresh in the morning, then we can start the merry hunt," replied John, slightly more cheerful now. He probably sensed my disappointment at not continuing.

"Well, Solomon and John, tomorrow we hunt down the ex-king. Solomon, on your return to Carthage, I need you to draw up a list of the loot and the division of it. Then deal with the prisoners; those we need to keep and those that can be sold off. I'll leave it to you to decide. The more we can make, the more we all earn and the more money we have to recruit more men with."

Together, we then rode slowly around the battlefield and viewed the state of devastation. Naked corpses announced Vandals, while small mounds showed where our men lay. I later learnt we killed eight hundred of them for the loss of fifty of ours, a great victory. We were cheered whenever we passed any of our men, and shouts of congratulations were quickly followed by the age-old question of a soldier, "When will we go home?" To this, I smiled and gave encouragement. Until we had Gelimer in chains, or dead, there was no question of leaving, but no need to tell them the truth. As to when that was not my call, the Basileus would decide the fate of the army. I was certain of one thing — many of the men here would be staying in Africa to garrison the province and would never see home again.

I spent the night with my commanders in Tricamarum. We discussed the campaign and battles and how to proceed with what remained to be done. We drank a lot. The Vandals actually had rather good taste in wine, and the wine taken from Gelimer's tent was particularly good. In the relaxed atmosphere, we made several decisions; Solomon, once he was done at Carthage, would then use the fleet and majority of the infantry to capture the remaining coastal cities and then garrison them, weather permitting, and in the spring, he would continue with this. John would take a squadron of cavalry in the morning and begin the hunt. Once the weather became too bad, he was to return to Carthage. I would take the remaining cavalry with my guards and head for Hippo Regius, the next largest city not in our hands. The last thing we needed was for the fleeing Vandals to take control of any of the cities and find money and supplies. We had to keep them on the move, and in the countryside, the winter would do most of our work for us.

Dawn arrived, and so did the wind and rain. The campsite turned into a quagmire. John chased around the camp, rounding up the men he wanted and had them on their saddles before they thought to complain. A local hunter had come forward and offered to track for us, so John got the help he needed, a local with skills. He was off before the rest of the camp had properly begun stirring. I had my guards and cavalry chased up and saddled by late morning, we then headed towards Hippo Regius. Solomon had the worst job of clearing up our campsite, collecting the prisoners and loot together and then marching back to Carthage. He made one decision, the engineers would rebuild the bridge before they left for Carthage, as the Vandals had left a good number of wagons in their camp, which made the movement of our equipment and loot a lot easier for him. He would escort the prisoners with most of the infantry and baggage train. The remainder would stay behind, assist with rebuilding the bridge and then escort the wagons back to Carthage. As the bridge was going to be a temporary wooden structure, it would take only a couple of days, but it would open up the interior for us and reconnect the road network. In the spring, a stone structure would be built to make the bridge permanent.

The wind continued to blow and combined with the rain, it quickly forced its way through my heavy cloak and onto my clothing. I felt cold and damp, my enthusiasm for travelling quickly waned. I called a halt in the late afternoon, and we constructed a marching camp and set up the tents within it. It was a good choice, the weather got worse that evening, and the leather tents were lashed by strong winds. It was hard work trying to keep warm and sleep with the constant sound of rain thumping the sides of the tent. I yearned for a warm fire and comfy bed, campaigning in the winter was not my idea of fun. My clothes refused to dry next to the small fire and instead produced a damp rancid smell that refused to go away. After checking the camp in the morning, I found that everyone was suffering the same effects of sudden cold and rain. I decided we would wait in the camp till the weather improved.

We remained in the camp for three days, and during that time, we collected over one hundred Vandal prisoners who surrendered themselves. The same weather was having its effect on them. I spoke to a few of them and learnt that they had followed Gelimer on foot but had quickly lost sight of him, as he was on horseback and they were left wandering, lost until they found us. They had dumped their weapons soon after the battle and after becoming lost, decided to find us and surrender, counting on our mercy rather than that of the weather or the locals, who now had no love for them. Once we were ready to move, I assigned a squad to escort the prisoners back to Carthage.

Five days after the battle, the rain ceased, and the wind too had died down enough for us to break camp and we continued along the road to Hippo Regius. I took the lead, accompanied by my guards, with the main force of cavalry following on behind. The sky remained grey and foreboding, the smell of damp cloth continued to haunt my nose, and I deeply wished I had sent someone else on this mission. The road continued in a reasonably straight line as it followed the course of the river valley, heading towards the coast. To our left, the foothills quickly gave way to the looming height of the interior, which was still coated in green even though it was winter. The rain had at least done some good, the air had improved and was fresh, even if it had a bite of cold in it, it was refreshing in its coldness.

A shout travelled up the column from the rear till it reached my ears, I halted all to wait for the riders to traverse the column. Word was that they were some of the men who had gone with John, which could mean he had located Gelimer. My mood lifted at the thought of this, and I waited for the men to reach me. They were with me shortly; they and their mounts were covered in steam as they had ridden hard to catch us. The senior of them, who I recognised as one of John's deputy guard commanders, greeted me and saluted. I looked at him. Something was very wrong. No one in the group was smiling — instead, they were glum. He spoke in a quiet tone.

"General, I have bad news."

"What is it?" I asked, dreading the reply.

"Um, um, I am sorry, sir. It's commander John. He is dead," he said, bowing his head.

The words entered my ears and pounded into my brain, like a hammer blow, it left me momentarily speechless. Nothing ever really touched John, he was a survivor.

"Oh, God, what happened?"

"It was a stupid accident. Last night, while we were camping, he went to check on the sentries before retiring, as he always did. As he walked back through a grove, one of the sentries, he must have been asleep, heard movement in front of him. He saw a shape, panicked and shot an arrow into the shape. He killed the commander outright. I am sorry, sir." He was then silent, not knowing what my reaction would be.

"Where is his body?"

"We wrapped him up, and he is under guard at our camp, along with the sentry, sir," he replied.

I sat on my horse and silently thought about my friend, everyone who had heard was quiet too. Word travelled along the column discreetly. I was torn between duty and friendship and decided that friendship and honour were more important than duty. Turning back to the messenger, I stated glumly, "You'd better guide us to your camp. Lead the way." I sent messages along the column for it to turn around and follow us to the camp. With my personal guards in tow, I peeled away from the head of the column, and we trotted after the messenger on the earth beside the road. The column followed suit, peeling onto either side of the verge as we passed them. Later that day, we left the road and followed a track up into the foothills and traversed along the escarpment for what remained of the day.

Just before nightfall, we sighted the small camp next to a grove, the column halted where it was, and we all dismounted. I ordered the men to sleep close to the track and put out sentries and tie up their horses, so they didn't wander. The messenger and his small group escorted us on foot to the tent where John's body lay. A small guard of honour had been placed outside its entrance. They saluted me as I entered the tent, a small lantern had been left to light the body. He lay on a camp bed, the cloth tightly wrapped around him, his sword, helmet and shield lay atop of his motionless body. A stain in the wrapping close to the neck revealed where the fatal arrow had entered his body. I moved over to where his head lay, and I touched the head. I said a silent plea for God's mercy to be laid on one who had shone as a brave and honest man.

I hadn't felt like this since I was a child when my grandfather passed. We had been taken to his room, and he lay there, on his bed, tightly bound in linen, only his face uncovered, still and quiet, empty of emotion. John had become one of my family, and only now did I realise how much he was part of my life. He was gone, like my grandfather; no more. I recalled our first meeting in Antioch; it felt like a thousand years ago. A mood of darkness descended on me. I had seen violent death before, but his was the closest it had come to me in a very long time. I felt a little bit of me die in that tent.

The next morning, we broke camp and John's body was carried down the track by my men, taking turns to carry him. We found a village and with it a church. We laid John to rest after a quick service by a monk who tended to the village. We placed him beside the church walls in a bit of foreign soil, far from his homeland. In fact, he couldn't have died any further from the land of his birth, of which he had always been expressly proud. In his honour, I arranged for a chapel to be built and dedicated to St. Gregory the Illuminator, patron saint of his homeland. I left enough money with the monk to ensure that the chapel flourished long after I was dead.

We followed the track down from the village to the road and then found a large open space on which to form up for a parade. They all lined up in their ranks facing me and my officers. The guilty sentry was brought out in front of everyone; the air was filled with tension as to what would be the man's fate. He stood still, apart from his legs, which could clearly be seen to shiver even in the warmth of the day. His face was heavily bruised, and his hands were tied behind his back. He looked down at the ground and awaited my decision. If I had dealt with this first, before dealing with John, I would have had him stoned to death, but after dealing with John, I felt we had seen enough death over the last few days, so I decided to deal with him more leniently. I cleared my throat and spat in his direction.

"You are guilty of sleeping on duty. Because of that, you accidentally killed John the Armenian, your commander, but I have decided to spare your life."

A murmur of dissatisfaction travelled through the ranks, I raised my hand to silence it and then continued, "You are dismissed, your kit will be shared among your company. You are then to be driven into the mountains and exiled. Should any of my men see you, they can kill you on the spot."

His company commander walked forward and dragged the man away from the parade and led him to the road. There, he cut his bindings, and the man ran for it. Once that was done, I spoke again.

"Parade dismissed. You are to collect your kit and mounts and be prepared to march at a moment's notice."

The parade ended, and the men readied their equipment for a march. I had the officers form around me, and I spoke to them. "Gentlemen, I need volunteers to continue the hunt. It's going to be tough up there in the mountains. You will need to keep up the hunt, searching every crack in the ground, under every stone, till travel becomes impossible, then you will return to Carthage. The rest will follow me back toward Hippo Regius. Once I have garrisoned the city, I will then return to Carthage and spend the winter there."

They were all quiet for a moment, then the commander of the Heruli smiled at me and spoke.

"My men will happily volunteer to hunt Gelimer. They are mountain men and more able to cope with the conditions here."

"Good, the guide thinks he has a trail, although a few days old. It's fresh enough to follow. If you find Gelimer, you can offer him a reward to surrender. If not, kill him and remember there is a nice bounty on his head. Good hunting."

"Thank you, General. I will bring him back dead or alive," he replied, saluting as he turned and made his way to his men. They were on their way within a short time, and shortly afterwards we headed back down the road.

It took a further five days before we reached Hippo Regius, my mood hadn't lifted. The city was ours even before we entered it, and the city elders greeted us. As in Carthage, I ordered them to form a council and left a force of cavalry to garrison the city. I stayed overnight, long enough to rest the horses, feed and water them. The men also enjoyed a night undercover with warm food and wine. The next morning, we headed back towards Carthage.

The walls of Carthage appeared out of the mist, up until then the road had been our only guide. The fog in the morning had been heavy, but by mid-morning, it was sunny and warmer, and we left behind the cold and damp of the highlands. A gentle breeze blew in from the sea with a strong smell of salt attached to it. In places, a light mist still clung to the plain, the sun moved in and out of the clouds, and the air chilled with the shadows and the breeze felt colder, yet when the sun shone it was the opposite. The West Gate was open, and guards patrolled the entrance. Upon seeing us, their commander, in a slight panic, rounded up his men to form a guard of honour and saluted us into the city. I noted with satisfaction that the ditch in front of the walls had been cleared here. The spoil piled up on the far bank, making the ditch deeper and extending the killing ground before the walls.

My guards and I halted after we had passed through the gates. I dismissed the cavalry. They headed into the city and their barrack areas. Once the last of the cavalry had dispersed, I led my guards into the city, the smell of burning wood and charcoal greeted us, it felt homely. We continued to the palace and trotted onto the piazza. There I halted, and my guards formed up, parade-style in front of me, with the officers positioned in front of each unit. I dismissed them and granted them all five days leave from duty.

I dismounted and led my horse over to the stable and gave instructions for its care; there was no need, the grooms and other workers knew what was to be done. My thoughts were elsewhere. My orderlies followed me with the spare mounts and equipment-laden animals. Once back in the piazza, I pulled off the chain mail suit and dropped it to the ground. I felt as light as a feather, but it couldn't rest there, so I gently kneeled and dragged it up onto my shoulder, ready to carry it into the palace. Before I could rise, one of the orderlies lifted it off my back. He

236

bowed and headed away with it to the palace for some careful maintenance before it was stowed away.

The air had grown cold and the sky a deep grey before I could reach the entrance to the palace, the rain started bouncing off the piazza surface, forming up to flow into the sewers. Inside the palace, it was slightly warmer than outside and busy with servants moving around. I stood for a moment and felt the warmth of the floor drive through my boots. The Vandals, like us, liked being warm, so the heating system had been maintained.

I passed through a long corridor and headed towards my rooms. I heard a shout behind me, and I stopped and turned in the direction of the voices. Two figures rushed over to me. I recognised them as Solomon and Procopius. Solomon was the first to speak.

"General, we have only just heard that you were back. Is it true the rumours we heard about John?"

Bad news travels faster than good news. I had hoped to be the one to break it to my staff. Antonina would be most upset to hear of John's demise as he was one of the family. She would miss him as much as I would.

"I am afraid he was killed in an accident a number of days ago. We buried him appropriately. It was a clean blow so he wouldn't have felt much pain," I said in a matter-of-fact way.

"I am sorry. He was a good soldier and friend. We will all miss him. I am sorry to bother you at a time like this, but another matter needs your attention. Can we both see you first thing in the morning? It concerns the general administration and the division of the spoils." Procopius nodded in agreement and was about to speak when Solomon touched his arm in a gesture of silence, and he remained quiet.

"Yes, you both better come to my quarters, and we will deal with the matters then. Thank you. See you in the morning."

The pair departed heading in direction they had come. I continued to my quarters, and sat down at my desk. The steward came over to me as soon as I was seated. I hadn't noticed him or the other servants waiting for me in the room. My thoughts were elsewhere — with my old friend laying in the cold ground far from home — but he stood by the desk, patiently waiting for me to issue a directive for him to carry out.

"Where is the Lady Antonina?" I asked him.

"Sir, she is in her rooms. Sir, she has heard the news."

He had read my mood better than I had, and like all the trained staff, anticipated my needs before I needed to state them.

"Thank you. Please arrange for an early meal for us and the baths to be readied for me."

"Yes, sir. You looked chilled, sir. May I arrange for some hot wine to be brought to you?" he said, waving to one of the other servants.

I nodded, and the servant rushed out of the room. It didn't take long for a goblet of wine to be heated with a fire iron. The steaming drink was placed in front of me. I allowed it a moment to cool, and then I drank a steady draft of it down. It warmed my insides as it travelled down, and a sudden rush filled my body, and I felt very weary. I waited a few moments and then rose with some effort from the chair and made my way to her rooms. I noticed the slight changes to the area, brighter colours and more servants again.

The rooms were as elegant as she was, fit for a queen. The air in the rooms was sweet and scented with a wonderful mix of herbs, spices and roses. The air made me feel relaxed and even more worn out. She wasn't in the main rooms. Instead, I could hear crying and sobbing coming from the bedroom. I entered and went across to the bed. There, lying on the bed fully dressed in what appeared to be an exotic set of clothing and face down in her pillow, was Antonina. She must have heard me enter as she turned over, wiping her tears from her smudged face, and gently sat up. She spoke in a faint voice.

"It's not true, is it? He's not dead?"

"I am so sorry. I wanted to tell you myself," I said.

We remained silent for a while, then servants entered the room and announced that the baths were ready for me. Another brought a goblet of heavily scented wine for Antonina, she drank most of it down quickly and asked for more. I said to the senior maid, "We will eat here tonight. Please see to it."

She replied in the affirmative and we were left alone as the door was closed from the outside. Antonina seemed a little calmer for my presence. I picked up the goblet she had left by the bed and handed it to her. The contents had a rich smell of herbs and strong red wine.

"Drink this. It will make you feel better." I paused while she sipped. "How are you feeling, my love? I am sorry the news was such a shock. I thought John would outlive all of us. The children, I know, will deeply miss him. I will write to them and explain how honourably he served."

We sat again in silence for a while, then the door was gently opened, and a maid came over to us. She reminded me again that the bathhouse was ready for me, in case I had forgotten. Before leaving, I gave Antonina a loving kiss.

"Darling, will you excuse me? I haven't washed since we were last together and I feel rancid."

"Go and have your bath, I'll be awaiting your return," she said, reaching up to me with both arms. We gently embraced and kissed. I felt I needed that bath more than ever.

Chapter Ten

The weather was more severe than anyone in Carthage could remember. I had considered trying to send dispatches along the African coast to Egypt, but Solomon pointed out that without an organised postal system, the messengers would become stranded long before they reached Tripoli. Even if they took several mounts, it was doubtful if they could cross the barren Libyan coastline, let alone survive the bandits. Instead, I continued to have Procopius prepare weekly reports for the Basileus, ready for dispatch on the first boat reaching us in the spring. Together with Solomon and Procopius, we discussed setting up a postal system. It gave me something else to think about, apart from acting as civil governor of Africa, which had become quite monotonous.

Every morning there were more merchants coming forward with complaints about this farmer or another merchant who had dishonoured a contract. The sooner the new governor was appointed, the happier I would be. The army had settled into its winter quarters, and the men had quietened down as they became semi-civilians again, spending time in taverns drinking away their wages. Like me, they craved action. Winter here was warmer than Thrace but still wet and muddy, and not the conditions in which to campaign.

Word finally reached me from the commander of the Heruli's. They had picked up Gelimer's trail and laid ambushes, but he continually evaded them. They suspected he had local help in the form of guides from Medeus in Numidia close to the Aures mountains, but until they caught him, they wouldn't know for sure. But best of all was the last piece of news he sent me. He believed they had him trapped on a mountain called Papua. With the liberal use of cash in the town, they had learnt that he had been spirited away up the mountain on their approach. They had climbed part of the way and blocked all the exits the local shepherds had shown them. He now awaited my orders.

I replied that they should maintain the siege over the winter, and I sent them extra supplies of food, wine and cash to ensure the loyalty of the locals. I decided that starving him out was a better strategy than trying to climb up the mountain and find him. I promised them a large bonus on the successful outcome of their siege. Apart from that good news, winter was slow in moving on. At least Antonina and I had time to reacquaint ourselves with each other.

Just before spring officially arrived, the Heruli arrived back in Carthage with a most important prisoner — Gelimer. The campaign was complete. The Vandal Kingdom was no more, and the lands they had taken from us were now back in the family of Rome. They brought with them the last of the Vandal army, and they were a pitiful sight to behold, bones covered in rags for the most part. They looked like poorly kept slaves of some careless mine owner, rather than a once all-conquering force of barbarians. I was sure many of them would end their lives in the mines dotted around the Empire. We now, however, had an accommodation problem. With these additional prisoners, we had run out of space in the stockade and prisons of the city. So, I had the new city council organise billets for my guards as we turned their barracks into a temporary prison. Once the first ships arrived, I could ship these men back to the capital as part of the Basileus's spoil and for the government to deal with.

Once Gelimer had been cleaned up and given some soup, I had him brought up to my office, his old throne room. I even decided to allow him to wear some of his old clothes, from the days when he had been a king, just to ensure he understood his new position in the Empire. He was informed of the location of his new quarters, the same dungeon he had placed Hilderic in. I had watched his arrival, he resembled an ascetic hermit more than a barbarian king, lashed to a horse. Starving him out had worked. Unlike his ancestors, he wasn't used to living off the land and preferred hot food, a warm bed and a bath. Civilisation had ruined the once-proud race of the Vandals. I wondered if the Goths and Visigoths had also lost their barbarian strengths in the same way Gelimer and the Vandals had.

Gelimer stood in front of my desk, he looked slightly better for a bath and food, but he was weak, so I had a chair brought over to him and allowed him to sit. I ordered that some food and wine be brought in and

I had his chains removed for the time being. The guards then moved to the rear of the room and stood silently watching us. During this, he remained silent, and all he did was carefully examine his wrists; they looked sore from their recent tight contact with iron. He carefully massaged the injuries, and a slight smile came to his face as he noticed I was watching his actions. So, this was the last king of the Vandals. He was tall, about six feet, he was around forty years old, but looked older, living on his wits had aged him. He had the bright straw-coloured hair of those barbarians who had invaded from the lands beyond the River Rhine. He wore his hair long in plaits, had a large bushy reddish-grey-coloured beard and brownish-grey eyes, so unusual that I kept returning my gaze to ponder the strange origin of them. An orderly entered with wine and some food. He placed them on the desk between us. I offered Gelimer the wine and the meat.

"Would you care for some meat and some wine, Gelimer?" I asked gently, and he looked directly at me, and I found it hard to tell what he was thinking. He showed no expression, and his eyes were unfeeling and looked directly at me. The silence continued, and I waited for him to respond. Eventually, he spoke in a decent Roman accent.

"General Belisarius, thank you, I will have some of that and wine would be good. So, why have you brought me into your presence? Is this the condemned man's last meal?"

"Certainly not. I thought you may like to know what is to become of you, your family and your people, now that the Emperor Justinian has regained control of Africa."

"What is to become of the Vandal people?" he asked, between bites of food and sips of wine, though it was obvious he was still hungry.

"You and your family will be sent back to the capital as privileged prisoners of war. There, the emperor will personally decide you and your family's fate. The senior of your people will be sent back as ordinary prisoners. As to your ultimate fate, I have no knowledge. It would be cruel of me to give you false hope. Those of your soldiers who are fit will be offered service in the army and sent to the East. Those not fit enough for military service or who decline, will be sent to the capital, as and when transport is available, to be auctioned. The money raised will be divided up between the treasury, the army and myself. As for the women and children, they will remain here, already some have become attached to my men, the rest will be sold off here in Carthage, and the money raised will be used to pay my army."

He looked glum. His people were to be no more, his fate and that of his family awaited him in the capital. I decided not to mention the fate of captive kings and tribal leaders before the Empire became Christian, a victory parade followed by ritual strangulation in public. We were not like the barbarians or Persians; he would probably be exiled with his family. After a few moments considering what I had said, he spoke.

"To the victor, the spoils and the fate of the vanquished."

We finished the wine and food in silence. Then Gelimer spoke again, a glint in his eye. "If our roles had been reversed, your head would be on its way to the emperor, and your men would be cast into slavery. As for your wife, I hear she is beautiful. I think I would have made her one of my mistresses."

He laughed. I was silent for a moment as I had never considered the fate of my wife if I had failed. We were very different, not only was he a usurper but for all the polished accent, he was still a barbarian.

"I must congratulate you on your planning for our first encounter. That tactical plan of yours was masterful, Gelimer. If only your men had been up to it, then indeed my head would be going home without my body."

"Yes, I planned to destroy your force as it passed the village. We would have hit you from three sides, catching your column stretched out along the road. Then we would have carefully picked you off, one by one." He began laughing at the thought he might have won our first encounter. Then he recovered himself and continued, "But it is you who deserves the credit, for being the better general on the day. I would never have split my forces up so widely as you did. For one thing, I could not always trust my officers to do exactly what I ordered, especially when family is involved, they always want to steal some credit for themselves. Your cavalry's discipline in battle and ability to use many types of weapons, quite apart from being fully armoured, made a major difference at our final encounter. The sheer weight of your firepower and our inability to come in close and fight hand-to-hand, not only undermined the morale of my men but killed them before they had a chance to kill your men."

He seemed to be revelling in the words, talking to me more as if I had bested him in a simple bet rather than in such a battle. It startled me to hear him seem so calm and collected as he spoke, like any other general grumbling about the troubles of command, and it was almost surreal. But then he paused as he considered his next statement. This time he was more serious and spoke more like a barbarian leader.

"To begin with, I never expected Justinian to invade us. Your timing was unbelievable; my brother had only recently taken five thousand men and the fleet to Sardinia. Even when I learnt that you had landed, I could not believe that you were an invasion force, so small was your army. That threw me, and I lost time in making a decision as to what I should do. By the time I realised that you were leading an invasion, a number of cities had already surrendered to you. I lost time and space to you, and I was never able to make up for that. Again, my congratulations on a brilliantly executed strategy."

"Thank you, Gelimer. I wish we could talk more on the battles. It's interesting to learn your opponent's views on how he saw the battle. Now you will be taken back to your cell, and later we will move you to more pleasant surroundings. I will tell you when you are to be shipped back to the capitol."

He stood up, his eyes flashed with emotion for the first time since we had met, and he furiously announced, "My great grandfather helped sack Rome. My grandfather helped defeat the last Roman garrison here. My great grandfather was the last of my family born a Vandal outside of the Empire, who crossed the Rhine with many other peoples and crushed your empire in the West. Now all they have fought for has gone, and Rome is back. My star, and that of my people, is fading. Yours is rising. Belisarius remember what has happened to me. Your star will fade one day, just like mine has," He finished his statement to me. Standing up and turning to his escort, he placed his hands out together, waiting for the chains to be returned. I was stunned for a moment by his outburst. He had been calm up until now. I suppose reality had finally sunk in. He really was the last leader of the Vandals, and they were no more.

"No, there is no need for them now. Your escort will remain with you till you reach the capital. Goodbye, Gelimer, last king of the

Vandals," I stated, shaking my hand indicating to my guards not to use chains, feeling as if there really was no need and that Gelimer had accepted his fate completely.

He turned at those words and looked at me with those strange-coloured eyes. His face exploded into a huge grin, and he laughed a deep roaring bellow that travelled up from the pit of his stomach. He turned away from me and was escorted out of my office without saying another word.

I remained seated in my office, Gelimer's last words to me continued to echo through my mind, strangely enough, I knew his words had some truth in them and I wonder just how long my star would keep shining? Then dismissed the thought, as they were from a bitter defeated enemy.

The sun had nearly reached its midday position. The air was thankfully warm and pleasing as it had warmed the ground I was walking barefooted on. The palace's gardens had been wonderfully set out. The roses were the centre of the attraction, surrounded by many other freshly blooming flowers. The air hung heavy with their scent, and the sound of bees filled the background to this majestic scene. There were many fountains dotted around, and they all sprayed a fine mist into the air as they worked away, washing the stone surrounding them while filling the ponds.

When we first arrived, I hadn't noticed the gardens, but during the winter, I had visited them and often wondered how they would look when the sun began to pump its heat back into the ground. I found a warm patch of earth with my feet and sat down. It was a pleasant place in which to relax. I put down the dispatches I had carried from my office. I wanted to read them here, alone and in peace. The first merchant ship had arrived this morning from the capital, with the dispatches, and on board was a delegation made up of lawyers and merchants, already demanding an audience with me. The lawyers wished to discuss property and land that the Vandals had confiscated from their clients' families. They had brought with them the title deeds dating from when the Vandals had invaded Africa. They could wait. The merchants just wanted warehouses and tax exemptions granted, Procopius would deal with them.

I looked down at the dispatches on the ground before me; they were sealed, and I recognised some of the seals. One was of the Basileus and the other that of the Praetorian prefect, the others I didn't recognise, so they were the first to be opened. The first one was from the Patriarch, and he congratulated me on returning to the fold the lost Catholic souls from the menace of heretical thought. Well, that was good, but I wondered if that was all, those here in the West had always been under the guidance of old Rome. I wondered what they felt about the conquest and if a war over who was to appoint the new bishops would begin. The other I found, on opening, was from my son-in-law Ildiger and he congratulated me on my great victory over the Vandals. Then he requested, in the nicest possible terms, if I could see my way to appointing him to a nice cosy post on my staff at Carthage. Well, that settled it. I already didn't like my son-in-law much. Now I knew I had been right. He had only joined the family to help himself rise in social position and wealth. I would find him a post, but miles from me and without any real responsibility here in Africa. I wouldn't inform Antonina of this letter; she liked the boy and was happy that our daughter was married and provided for and had a name. Anyway, if he didn't get a post, she would write to her mother on his behalf and then I would never hear the end of it. The higher I rose in the government, the more the clingers-on and want-to-be clients would appear, trying to grab scraps from my table. I never liked the patronage system, which was a bit cynical of me as I rose thanks to the patronage of Justin and now the Basileus. But because we were military men, we had skills and abilities and could give back more than we were given, which is probably exactly what Ildiger would say in response. Rome was and still was, being run on the patronage client system. It would never change, even the Church was plagued by it.

I had dealt with the minor correspondence, and now it was time to deal with the important stuff. Taking a deep breath, I opened the letter from the Prefect's office. John had actually written this himself, which meant it was personal as well as being very important. No one else in his office would know its contents. I was even more intrigued by this letter, and more importantly, what was he up to and how was I involved. To begin with, he congratulated me on my campaign, and he relayed that the Basileus was overjoyed at the news of the victory. Then came the crunch, the yearly tax was to be collected straightaway, and all Vandal properties were to be auctioned as soon as possible with all the profits being sent directly to him and the treasury. This would pay for the cost of the campaign and assist with the cost of reconstruction of the capital. Those properties where ownership was unclear were to be seized by the state and rented out to Roman citizens only. All Vandal claims to land and property were null and void. This was typical of John the Cappadocian; his only task was to fill our master's coffers at any price. I knew that Africa needed relief from tax to allow it to recover from the way the Vandals had allowed it to run down. The next year was going to be a difficult and embarrassing one for me. I had liberated the people from Vandal tyranny only to hand them over to the tyranny of John's tax system. The army's morale was liable to slide, a number of men were approaching the end of their service and had already married either Vandal or local women. They expected to be given a plot of Vandal land on retirement, so they could settle and raise a family. Now, this was going to be difficult, and I would probably have to use the land seized already and divide it up among them. Procopius was going to be very busy, and I expected he would need to expand his office to cope with all the extra legal and tax work he would now have to oversee.

Finally, I opened the letter from the Basileus. It was full of congratulations and conveyed just a simple message. I was to return to the capital as soon as I could. No explanation was given or needed to be. Also, Gelimer and the treasury was to be brought back at the same time. It was a straightforward order, but Gelimer's words returned to my mind. I had expected to remain here for some time. Antonina and I had settled in here. What was my reward to be? Had I done something wrong? My earlier cheerfulness left me abruptly. I rose quickly holding all the documents and stormed out of the garden and back to my office in the palace. I charged into the office, Procopius and Solomon were working, and they both jumped to their feet in alarm. Both had turned white as snow and Solomon spoke first.

"General, what is wrong?"

"Good news," I bellowed, then thought better and calmed myself a little. "I've been recalled to the capital. I am ordered by the Basileus, no explanation. But while I am still military master of the West, I appoint you, Solomon, as my successor here as governor of Africa. Procopius, you will stay and assist Solomon. If I'm in trouble, you will be safer here, rather than with me."

"Thank you, General. I am sorry. You achieved everything you were asked to do. Now your reward is to be called back to the capital. Are you sure you are in trouble?" Solomon asked with a quizzical expression upon his face.

"I don't really know. Look, I am sorry for bursting in here like that. It's not only the letter from the Basileus but also one from John the Cappadocian that has angered me. He has appropriated all the Vandal land for the treasury, leaving us with nothing to use as pensions for the soldiers. Here, Solomon, you better read this, as you will now have to enforce it. It means the soldiers' retirement land is being taken by the state." I paused and then said, "Procopius do your best and keep Solomon fully informed of his legal position at all times. If I fall, there will be no one to protect you. They will look for any discrepancies in the administration and then they will have you. So be careful."

Procopius nodded his head in agreement and indicated that he wished to speak. I sensed he was unsure of my mood and did not want to upset me any further. He was always a careful man in his actions, but I nodded my approval, and he spoke.

"General, as to the matter you have just spoken about, I have an answer for you."

I curled an eyebrow in curiosity, just what might Procopius be thinking. I beckoned him to speak, and he nodded his head firmly.

"It's not Solomon's problem. The titles of all Vandal land can be treated as booty and therefore become the emperor's, and because you are the representative of the emperor and have the right to pass laws that he will automatically support, it's up to you how you deal with the land. You can hand out the land to the soldiers, or you can leave it for the emperor's direct decision. This also applies to what happens to any of the old claims. So, the delegations can be sent back to the capital and appeal directly to the emperor and not you."

I laughed, Solomon and Procopius grinned and waited for me to finish. I smiled and thanked Procopius for his excellent legal advice; it made me feel a little better. I explained to the pair that I was now going to enjoy my last public engagement and tell those bloodsuckers that they'd had wasted a journey to see me. Instead, they would have to petition the emperor, and that would take a long time and mean a lot of greasing of palms in the prefect's office and no doubt, John's most of all, if they really wanted their land and goods refunded. I wished them both well and told them that if anyone wanted me, I was indisposed till I sailed for the capital. I left them both working in my ex-office and headed for my apartments on the far side of the palace.

The day was still beautiful, and the scents from the garden still lingered in the corridors. A little sense of calm returned to me, as the smells brought back a brief memory of the peace and order of the gardens from earlier on. The feelings would last till I reached Antonina and told her of my orders. I entered the final corridor, which led to our apartments, and it was then that I noticed how quiet this corridor was. Normally servants would be busy moving through, but none were in sight.

On entering our apartments, I was greeted by servants who took my cloak and asked if I needed refreshments. I declined and instead asked where her ladyship was. I was informed that she was in her rooms and waiting for me. I was to enter as soon as I was ready. I needed no second bidding, better to grab the bull by the horns, than wait for it to come looking for me.

I entered her room, and she was in a semi-reclined position on one of the couches, reading a letter. The doors to the balcony were open, and sunlight was filling the room and steadily warming it at the same time. A shaft of sunlight briefly stretched across the floor as the breeze caught one side of the curtains and moved them slightly. The light hit Antonina's hair, causing it to glow, while the white dress she wore turned slightly silver as the sunlight caught it at an angle. Over her legs, a lamb's fleece rested. She looked up as I entered the room, and she smiled. My mood changed abruptly, and my heart skipped a beat. She could turn me into a quivering lump with one of her beautiful sensual smiles; then she said in a caring tone, "Darling, would you care for some wine?"

"No. I am afraid I have bad news. I have received a letter from Justinian. I have been summoned back."

Her smile didn't change for one second. Instead, she sat up and signalled for me to join her on the couch, and she spoke in the same calm tone.

"Yes, I know about the recall. So, what's the gloomy face for?"

"How did you know about the recall?" I stated, but then, if there was one thing I had learnt in all our years of marriage, it was that my wife was just as aware of the happenings of the Empire as myself, if not more so.

"I also received a letter this morning," she said triumphantly. "Except mine was from Theodora."

"Ah, so while I have been panicking, not knowing what I have done to upset the Basileus and how I was going to tell you, you have been calmly sitting here. So, what do you know that I don't?" I was lost for words for a moment, and in my panic, I had forgotten the strong connection between the two of them. But I was glad that I was not about to have my ear chewed off for doing something —I had no idea what — to upset the Basileus.

I sat down next to her, and she reached over with one arm and draped it around my stiff neck and with the other showed me the contents of the letter.

She continued with a firm smirk, "According to Theodora, you have been too successful. Your victory has only gained you envy and hatred amongst those who seek power and influence over the emperor. They now see you as a threat because you achieved more than what was asked of you. Justinian trusts you. To them, you have the potential to be a Caesar, if he should ever decide to choose a successor."

She paused while I inwardly digested what she had just relayed to me. If I had his trust, why was I being recalled? The last thing I wanted was to be a Caesar. Just being a governor here for a short while had put me off forever from that type of role.

She went on. "Our new enemies in court had no mud to throw at us, till Calonymus's allies heard about his disgrace and arranged for his sentence to be commuted and recalled back to the capital. It seems he had a lot of friends, clients and patrons in the palace who, having secured for him the position, expected to be rewarded with a percentage of his booty. His allies quickly began spreading rumours that you had exceeded your powers and sacked him out of envy and greed. All this so you could claim all the credit and his share for yourself. The next rumour was that you had come to an agreement with Gelimer to take control of Africa.

Even to be proclaimed the Western Emperor."

It just got worse. I had no real experience of court, and it showed. Why you needed clients and allies in the court, just to protect you, I had not really understood, but in knowing that they were supposed to keep you safe from such rumours when you weren't present made me groan. I voiced my concerns to my wife.

"My God, why would they do that? I have never had any ambitions except to serve the Basileus. He knows that."

Antonina waited till I had calmed a little and continued, knowing she had more understanding in this matter than me, "Theodora also believes this was a veiled attack on her, to see who her allies in court are. We were just a lamp light to shine in the darkness of the court. Of course, she defended you to Justinian and, of course, revealed you and me as being part of her and his supporters. Justinian at first believed the rumours. And was at one point planning your removal." She paused.

I had been listening intently. I wondered how much of this was related to the riot of the Blues and Greens. Their supporters were everywhere, and I doubted if they had forgiven me for my role in killing so many of them. They couldn't go for the emperor directly, but they could instead chip away at his supporters.

Antonina continued, "Theodora was able to calm him and he just as quickly forgot the rumours. The reason you are being recalled is that Justinian wants to reward you in public, he felt a bit guilty for doubting you. Theodora says she will continue to remind him of your loyalty and his lack of faith in you."

"Thank God for Theodora's friendship and her continued wise counsel to the Basileus. She doesn't forget her friends," I said, just as relieved that Antonina was my wife.

I felt a heavy weight lift from my chest. I also felt a little guilty at doubting Justinian. Antonina rose from the couch and pulled me up with her and spoke gently to me. "My love, shall we walk in the garden, we have much more pleasant things to discuss. It's been nearly a year since we have been home, and I do miss the children."

"Yes, the garden is delightful at the moment. You are right, it seems like ages since we saw the children," I replied with a sigh of relief, especially glad she was my wife as she understood exactly how to calm me. We strolled back through the palace to the gardens, arm in arm, and out into the bright sunshine-lit garden.

My last day in Carthage was tinged with sadness. I was leaving behind three good friends. Two I would meet again and the third not in this life. I said my goodbyes to all my soldiers and officers and had part of the bounty paid to them, for two reasons. The first, they had done a good job and needed rewarding. The second, I needed to ensure their loyalty while after I'd gone. On the return voyage with the fleet, I was only taking back with me, my guards, minus a contingent to protect Solomon. The Huns and Heruli would also accompany us, along with senior Vandal prisoners, the treasure and "volunteers" for the army.

In the afternoon, we boarded the flagship in the harbour. The sky was clear, and a warm wind was blowing in the right direction to speed us on our way home. Solomon and Procopius had accompanied us to the quay, and they both stood watching as we slowly moved out of the harbour. We had also been escorted by the new city council and senior merchants, who thanked me for returning them to the Empire as well as wishing us a speedy journey. Even the bishop attended, blessing the fleet before it left.

We both stood in the rear castle and watched Carthage slowly sink away from sight. All we had to accompany our departure, apart from a massive fleet, was a squawking band of seagulls, diving behind each ship as scraps were thrown overboard by the crew. We sailed out into the unknown; only the captain knew where we were headed.

Before we lost sight of land completely, another ship's sails came into sight. The captain heaved to, the sails were Roman, and a signal had been flashed using a mirror to catch the sunlight. We stayed on deck as the other ship approached the convoy. One couldn't let go of the handrail, as the ship wallowed back and forth as the sailors used the oars in an effort to keep us in one place. The other ship came within hailing distance of us, its captain shouted across to ours, enquiring where we were bound for and who was on board. Our ship's captain replied, and the other ship came closer to us. By now it was clear that it was a warship using both sails and oars. Its captain then requested permission to address me. I was asked to come to the side of our captain. Once I was in position, our captain shouted to the other that I was present.

"General Belisarius? I have a message for you from Sardinia," he shouted to me.

"What's your message, Captain?" I shouted back.

"General, Sardinia is ours," he paused then shouted again. "The men you sent to support the uprising were betrayed and murdered, I am sorry, sir. Those guilty have paid the price."

"Thank you for your news. Solomon is in command, report to him when you land. Good luck."

Our captain waved his acknowledgement and his goodbyes to the other ship. The crew got to work raising the sails and the rowers set to work pushing our ship to catch up with the rest of the fleet. The other ship veered away and gently turned and headed in the direction we had just taken. I thought about Cyril and his men; he knew the mission would be risky. So far, the destruction of the Vandals had cost me two irreplaceable officers and a small number of men. In the balance of things, our losses had been minute and the gains vast. But it still hurt losing friends. Antonina and I made our way down to our cabin.

The rest of the voyage was uneventful, and we reached the coastlines of Europe and Asia at the end of May. Eleven months ago, we had passed the very same place. Looking at the coastline, nothing appeared to have changed, except I was a year older and, I hoped, a wiser person. Antonina joined me on deck, and we both watched in silence. The sun dipped down to the west and behind us, as it gently sunk behind the cliffs of Europe while casting a deep red light onto the waters reaching across to the distant coast of Asia. Somewhere to the east, below the horizon, stood brown cliffs with white beaches. Across this very stretch of water, the heroes of Greece had passed as they headed for the citadel of Troy. Were the ancient heroes looking down at us? What would they make of us? Were they pleased, or didn't they care what we mortals did or didn't do in a war?

"Darling, are you daydreaming? I've been talking to you, and you haven't replied once," Antonina said, seemingly from nowhere.

"I am sorry, my love, I was dreaming. Was it important what you were saying?" I asked, though really, I was sticking my foot in my mouth as nothing Antonina said could be disregarded. Indeed, she gave me a sharp expression before gently tapping my chest and softly inhaling.

"No, it wasn't, lucky for you. The scenery is beautiful and the breeze hints of the capital, and can you smell fish, is all I was saying," Antonia stated, gently pushing her hip against mine to get a reaction, but I found myself feeling confused by her words. I started to sniff heavily at the air.

"I can smell something," I said, allowing the comment to linger with the smell and then I added. "I think it's cook, preparing another variation of his favourite theme. Fish."

"Sounds good to me," she replied, tugging my arm and pulling me towards the steps down to our cabin. She began to lead me below, and I put my arm around her and allowed her to lead the way. Before we entered the stairwell, I paused, and she looked at me curiously. "Shall we retire down below and have supper?"

"Or we could stay out here and watch the moon and stars rise and perhaps fall," I stated softly, looking at her lovingly, she just shrugged. She smiled but continued with her mission. I leaned forward and kissed her, and she returned the kiss. I lifted her off her little feet, hugged her tight and carried her down to our cabin.

The walls surrounding the palace rose out of the dawn fog — it was going to be a hot day. There, next to the palace, where the burnt Church of the Holy Wisdom had once stood, was a new structure slowly rising out of the ashes surrounded by a huge wooden structure. This would be the largest church in the capital, let alone the Empire when it was completed. Antonina stood next to me; behind us, the rest of the fleet had heaved to. The privilege of landing first would be ours, and it would be at the same port from which we had left. The closer we approached the dock, the louder the noise grew. Once we were past the outer harbour, the noise was recognisable as crowds cheering us. They packed the harbour area. A number of smaller boats made their way towards us, so we slowed our approach.

The captain lowered a gangway so that one of the boats could come aside and drop off its passengers. Once it was close to the ship, the captain ordered all rowing to cease and that the sails be brought down and tied away. Then the anchor was dropped into the harbour, and we came to an abrupt halt as it bit into the sea floor. The rest of the fleet was now blocked by us from entering the harbour. We were still some distance from the quay. Antonina and I both looked down at the small boat as it gently came to a halt at the bottom of the gangway.

Inside the harbour, the water was reasonably calm, so the passengers would have little trouble reaching the gangway and coming aboard. The sound of voices came from the small boat, and we both watched as a team of Excubitors in full dress armour made their way up the gangway. Once on deck, they formed a corridor between the top of the gangway and the aft castle, where we both stood. Then they presented arms and Antonina turned and whispered in my ear, as she had a better view of the gangway than I did. "It's the emperor."

I nodded in agreement, and the whole ship went silent. Sailors who had been busy stopped work and turned to face where the passenger would stand on the deck. The captain and his officers quickly assembled themselves behind us in as much silence as they could. There was the sound of footsteps moving up the gangway, and the first figure emerged onto the deck. I immediately recognised the dignified figure of the Augusta and behind followed her ladies-in-waiting. She walked up the steps of the castle to where we stood. We prostrated ourselves as she stepped into the castle. She stood between two ranks of guards and smiled broadly at us. She was wearing the Imperial diadem and clothed in elegant silks, mostly of purple. The ladies-in-waiting correctly positioned themselves beside her and waited.

"Augusta, you are very welcome aboard," I stood up and said.

She walked towards us and halted directly in front of us. I introduced the captain and his fellow officers, and she dismissed them. With the formalities complete, she moved quickly over to Antonina with both her arms outstretched. She hugged Antonina warmly, like a long-lost sister, and then they began chatting to each other. The guards remained motionless during this encounter, and the ladies-in-waiting almost remained expressionless. Ah, the wonders of court etiquette. I remained still and patiently waited for them to finish. Then, as one, they both turned to me with smiles on their faces, and the Augusta said, "My dear Belisarius, it is good to see you back with us once more. Please excuse the hold up. I wanted this chance to speak to both of you before we land."

I bowed at her praise. "My thanks for your staunch support of me to the Basileus."

"That's one of the reasons for my seeing you now. You must be careful. You are now seen in court circles as supporting me against the likes of John and others. Your recent success has ensured that they are out of favour, but your position is precarious. The more you succeed, the more our enemies will attempt to poison the Basileus's mind. Ever since the riot, he has become more paranoid about threats to his person. Our enemies know this, and they try to exploit this for their own end," she said, in a much-lowered tone.

"Thank you, my Augusta. You know my wife and I are loyal to you both."

She grinned, and her smile beamed even more. Her voice returned to its normal level, and she said, "Tonight, you will both dine with us in the palace and tomorrow, you, Belisarius, will lead a triumphant parade to the forum and then onto the Hippodrome. There, the Vandal prisoners and treasure will be displayed for all the people to see." She paused and then leaning towards Antonina with a mischievous grin said, "Antonina, I have a surprise for you."

Antonina looked very intrigued and replied, "What is it my Augusta?"

Theodora signalled to her ladies-in-waiting, one of them descended back down the gangway. We waited for a few moments, then Theodora led us back towards the gangway. Antonina was excited. She almost skipped after Theodora, then remembered her position and walked instead behind me. As we reached the head of the gangway, we could clearly hear the sound of feet running up the gangway, and there was a young girl at the top of the gangway about to step onto the deck. She looked up at us with delight and shouted with glee.

"Mamma, Papa," she ran straight to us and shot past me with her arms out as she collided with her mother. Antonina picked her up and gave her a great big hug. I was slightly shocked. In a year she had grown and was looking fine and happy. Antonina walked on, still carrying Johanna over to where Theodora stood, smiling.

"You were right, Aunt. They were on this boat, thank you," Johanna said.

Theodora smiled back at her and Johanna's smile in return reflected her love for her adopted Imperial aunt, the same was true of her. Two more ladies-in-waiting stepped onto the deck. We both recognised them at once, Melissa and Zenobia. They had new roles. They walked elegantly over to us, bowing as they passed Theodora. When they reached us, they kissed me first and then welcomed us home. Then they joined their mother, and they began chattering together.

I turned to Theodora. "Thank you again, Augusta."

"It was my pleasure to watch over her. Melissa is making a worthy lady-in-waiting, but Zenobia, well, she is a very intelligent young lady. She still has a lot to learn about court life, my dear Belisarius. I must be going. I am sure they will have a lot to talk about. Until tonight," Theodora replied. She turned and led the remaining ladies-in-waiting back down the gangway, and the guards followed suit. Once loaded, the small boat cast off and made its way to the quay. The gangway was raised, and the captain ordered the rowers to make ready to push us into the quay. At the same time, a few smaller rowing boats attached lines and began assisting in moving us forward towards the quay.

It didn't take long for the warship to begin manoeuvring once again. I watched as the captain and his crew carefully aligned the ship with the quay. As we neared the dock, the captain ordered the rowers to stop, then row in the opposite direction. The ship now seemed to drift into contact with the quay. Then, with a very gentle shudder, we were back in the capital. Lines were thrown by workers on the dock to the ship and quickly secured. The oars had already been raised on the landward side, and on the other, they were kept out of the water.

Shortly afterwards, the gangway was repositioned, and the family and I were able to walk ashore. A small Imperial coach was waiting for us. This was a grand honour — normally only the Imperial couple used such a vehicle to move through the city. We were, indeed, being honoured. My guard disembarked, and I gave them orders to guard the prisoners and treasure once they were unloaded. They were then to stay with these items until they were released into Imperial custody.

Then we climbed aboard. It was a very comfortable four-wheeled coach with a light, almost flimsy, cover that served as a sunshade. The seats were covered in soft cushions. This was the first time I had ever sat in one of these coaches. The journey was steady, but even with the cushions, we felt every bump in the road. Before we entered the city, through the gates, I turned and watched the fleet as it slowly began entering the harbour, the warships had already departed to sail into the Golden Horn and moored there. Only the cargo and transport ships would unload at this harbour. Once through the gate, we were forced to pull over as a large convoy of empty wagons and Imperial guards marched past us, heading towards the harbour. Someone in the palace was ensuring that the loot of Carthage would be inside the palace as soon as possible.

We were accommodated in the guest quarters of the palace. I left the family to chat and went to the Imperial baths. I spent the rest of the day there relaxing, away from everyone. I returned in time to witness the chaos of women panicking over what they should be wearing for the official reception, which was being held in our honour. It was simple for me — I would wear my dress uniform, minus armour and weapons. We would be led to the main reception hall past all the invited guests and palace officials to the high tables where we would sit close to the Imperial couple.

The high chamberlain arrived in the rooms, and it was time for us to head for the reception. He announced that, as the honoured guests, we were to attend the Imperial couple's table. The high chamberlain led us out of the rooms. I headed our family group, and we were conducted, at the agonising slow Imperial court pace, towards the reception, in hushed silence. Antonina and the girls were dressed in exotic Persian robes favoured by the court at that time. The chamberlain led us down a route I had never encountered in the palace before. At the pace we walked at, it seemed to take all night to go nowhere. Suddenly, we stood in front of a pair of tall solid wooden doors which barred our way. The chamberlain approached the doors and knocked several times. The doors were opened by Imperial guards in full regalia. We entered behind the chamberlain. The hall was packed with officials, both civil and military, dignitaries and foreign ambassadors. I recognised very few faces in the room. The chamberlain continued till we reached the Imperial couple's table. He halted and waited for us to join him, then in unison, we all prostrated ourselves before the couple. The couple were wearing purple robes and full Imperial regalia — they looked impressive. We were then given permission to rise and stand in front of the imperial couple, then Justinian stood up and spoke in a loud and clear voice.

"Belisarius, in gratitude for your success, I reward you with the right of a military triumph. You will parade through the city to the forum and then to the Hippodrome. You will be the first I have granted this ancient privilege to. Let it be recorded that you are the hero of the Vandal War and entitled to be addressed as such in all official documents." He paused graciously to let the words sink in, then continued, "Honoured guests of my court, I give you, Belisarius, Military Master of the West and hero of the Vandal War."

I bowed towards him as he said this. The Imperial couple, as one, now moved over to us and then guided us back to their table. The couple sat at the head of the table, me at the other end, the grown children sat between Justinian and me, while Antonina sat beside Theodora. The feast commenced. The Imperial kitchens produced a wonderful fare. The conversation began formally, but by the third course, we were back to how it was before he became Basileus. The ladies-in-waiting came to the table and escorted the 'children' away, back to the guest apartments. The reception continued well into the night, once the food was finished, talk became the main meal. The atmosphere between Justinian and me had become more cordial, and we both reminisced about our lost youth. Theodora and Antonina were by now deeply engrossed in chatter and took no notice of anything going on around them. But suddenly Justinian became serious as he leant into me and spoke firmly.

"I would like you to assume command of the central field army here in the capital. It will give you time to recover from the African campaign and time again with your family. Nothing much has changed regarding the present peace with Persia — hopefully, it will continue — if it does, I have a number of schemes we will discuss together later."

"Thank you, Basileus. I will be honoured to take command of the central field army."

"Now, tell me in depth, how would you assess your performance and that of the army against the Vandals? What were they like as fighters?" he asked.

I remained with Justinian, talking through the night. The other guests were forced to remain due to court etiquette, and could not leave till the Imperial couple had. Then, with all discussed, he stood up, and Theodora followed suit. Antonina and I quickly stood, and we bowed, the reception was now at an end. They turned again, as one, and were led out through the Imperial doors situated at the rear of the hall, escorted by the remaining guards.

Servants arrived and escorted us back to the apartments. We entered the room. The lamps had been lit earlier, and they cast a flickering golden shadow. The room itself smelt of a mixture of burning oil and flower scent. We both noticed that since we had left the rooms, they had been adorned with the most wonderfully coloured and mildly pungent spring flowers. Even the bedroom was filled, and the bed itself was surrounded by flowers and looked like a ship becalmed in a sea of flora. I jumped over the flowers and onto the soft bed. It was wonderfully warm. I rolled around on it and beckoned Antonina to join me. She laughed and refused. She, instead, remained beside the bed and inspected the flowers and gently caressed the buds and smelt their essence. The lamplight cast delicate shadows across her body as she moved gently between the flowers. Tiredness slowly began to overtake me, and I settled more comfortably on the bed, and gently my eyelids became heavier. I shook myself awake. I felt a hand stroking my head, and a slight movement of the bed told me that Antonina had finally joined me.

The morning was bright and clear. The air was fresh as a breeze blew across the city from the direction of the Golden Horn. The procession had started forming up outside the city's walls well before the sun had gained much height. I personally checked the column to reassure myself that the city's population would be impressed by the parade. I would lead the column standing on a chariot of sorts. Today, I would be wearing my full military uniform, including mail armour, minus the hood — instead, my head would be bare. My old heavy cloak was gone, replaced by a newly woven one that Antonina had purchased. By noon, we were ready to begin the march. All that was required was for the military gates to be opened, and that would be the signal to move off.

A volley of trumpets sounded from the walls closest to us and the gates swung open. I raised my right arm and signalled the advance. The chariot jerked forward. I felt a little unsteady on it and kept both hands on the guide rail of the vehicle. I found it hard to believe that men had once fought, standing on these. We moved off at a steady marching pace, over the bridges and through the gates and into the city. We marched first through the exclusive suburbs, where most of the rich resided when not busy in the Imperial quarter of the city.

Our path along the main road was lined with all sorts of people — young and old —cheering, and by their dress, they were the common people of the city. I wondered how many were there for the victory or whether it was the free food and wine that was on offer today, as part of the procession, which attracted them. The larger buildings had balconies. These were filled by wealthy residents who watched and cheered us. Then, along with the mob below, they booed at the Vandal prisoners. Even through the garden sections of the city, people had turned out to watch, and I think every section of the road had a crowd attached to it.

We finally reached the centre of the capital. The street was now broad, shops, merchants' residences and churches lined each side. Several more streets filtered onto our route and they conveyed more crowds surging forward to join onto the tail of the procession. So thick was the crowd with waving arms that they resembled fields of wheat caught in a gust of wind. In front of us lay the great circle that was the forum of Constantine, the founder of the city. Around its wide perimeter stretched a colonnade, said to be greater and grander in size than anything seen in Rome. Many citizens had climbed onto it to gain a better view, while others stood between the arches. We swung to the left side of the forum as its centre was dominated by the column on which sat a great statue of Emperor Constantine himself.

Behind me came a troop of my guards, wearing ceremonial armour, their heavy cloaks replaced with silk capes. Their spears were pointing upwards, each with a small colourful pendant, fluttering, as they were caught in the combination of a slight breeze and the movement of the rider. Then, behind them was a solitary figure, wearing what the palace officials must have believed to be the barbarian clothing of a king. His wrists were bound with a gold chain. He was a solitary, abandoned figure. Rotten fruit had been thrown at him, and their marks stained his face and clothes. Behind him, followed the first wagon with the treasures of his kingdom, set out so all could see it, as the gold and silver shivered with the reflected light of the noon sun.

We trooped in a slow half-circle around the inner perimeter of the forum and then followed the street towards the Milion, which marked the first mile stone on which all distances were based on leading out from the Capital. We marched under the marbled arch of the Milion, through the covered space, which marked the point that every Roman mile marked on every road started from. On the other side of the Milion, across a wide piazza, was the vast Imperial Palace complex, occupying what was left of the city from here to the sea. To our left, was the Church of Hagia Sophia, still under construction, her red bricks clearly visible peering out of the complex wooden structure that surrounded her. This was going to be a church like no other and would attest to the grandeur and outlook of Justinian.

We turned right and marched abreast of the palace complex. It was the same route we had followed during the riot. This time celebrations filled the atmosphere of the city. No one feared our approach, and there in front of us was the blunt end of the towering complex of the Hippodrome. With the sun striking its stone surface, shadows were created, clearly showing the multiple arches, which in turn supported other terraced rows of further arches. Glancing behind, I could see the Vandal prisoners emerging from the Milion. The column snaked back behind me as we followed the outline of the Hippodrome to the main entrance. The gateway showed no signs of having been stormed by us. Now I, as a victor, was about to enter the Hippodrome. The crowds had also joined us and walked alongside the column. It seemed like the whole city was following us to our destination.

In ancient times, a palace slave would have stood beside me, dangling a laurel wreath over my head, and continually whispering, something like, "Remember you are but a man," for today, we were the heroes of the Empire. Every woman would want to be with a hero. Tomorrow we would be just a nuisance and the reason for extra taxes. Such is fame, I suppose.

Finally, we reached those main doors of the Hippodrome. I had not been here since the riot and the suppression of the colours. The damage that had been done was no longer visible on the building, but that was not true of men's hearts, I thought.

The main doors swung open, and in through the dark archway, I went. Ahead, was a pool of light hitting the sand of the interior track of the Hippodrome. No sooner had I entered, then I found myself starting my first circuit of the track. The stadium was already partially full — the rich and connected had already secured their seats for the afternoon show. I continued my circuit, followed by the column. I would keep circuiting till the whole column had filled the track. The seats quickly filled up, and as I traversed the circuit, I was cheered, and a few moments later, the booing started as Gelimer paraded past them. The Imperial box was still empty on my first time around, but on my second it was filled. I halted in front of the box and saluted. Justinian stood and received my salute, then he sat, I remained in situ. Once the column had all passed the Imperial box, I would present myself again. Sitting on her throne next to Justinian was Theodora, they chattered with each other and the guests. My family sat on her side and gossiped with fellow dignities. John and his fellow ministers were seated on the side of Justinian.

The last troop of cavalry filed past me and joined the now-stationary column which was jammed onto the track. The prisoners were forced to stand closest to the audience who still had an ample supply of objects to throw at them. I then dismounted the chariot and was glad to be off that hideous device. I walked steadily towards the Imperial box and halted below it. The soldiers and cavalrymen in the column stood to attention in silence. I saluted again and shouted. "Hail, Basileus of the Romans, your lost lands in Africa are yours once again. I give you the last Vandal ruler, his treasure and his people as your prize."

The crowd roared with their approval as Gelimer was brought to a position close to me, in front of the Imperial box. Justinian stood again, raised his right arm and the crowd settled down as the message travelled round the seats that he had ordered silence. Then, he too shouted his response. "Gelimer, I give you your life. You and your family will be granted a pension and a small estate as befitting your station." He paused as the words travelled around. The crowd roared their acceptance of his divinely inspired mercy. "Senators, people of Rome, the barbarian Vandal invaders of our land in Africa are no more. Thanks be to God."

"Victory for our emperor, by the grace of God." The crowd, on cue, bellowed their response, the stadium exploding in unison as they chanted. The sound thundered about until the hand lifted again. Once silence returned to the stadium, he continued, "Senators and people of

Rome, God has granted us a victory over the Vandals. As a sign of thanks, I give you the games for today and tomorrow."

The crowd, knowing full well that this was on the cards, cheered heartily and seemed to do so with a little more enthusiasm, as there was something in it for them. Finally, the parade was over, and I returned to the chariot and led the column out of the Hippodrome. The prisoners were escorted to a holding area, and the treasure was taken into the palace. My men were dismissed for the next two days and then on the third day they were due back on duty. They would be there, as this was when they would receive their share of the bounty.

I dismounted the chariot and was escorted into the palace and through the labyrinth back through the tunnel and into the royal box to join my family and the Imperial couple, and from there we would enjoy the games. The games were then opened by Justinian. I had arranged for four teams of eight chariots to race; each rider would use teams of four horses. It promised to be exciting, as these were not part of any of the original colour teams and the discreet betting promised to repay some of my costs.

The blue team were the favourites this afternoon, while the greens were expected to take the individual event with their Alexandrine-born champion. The teams paraded around the circuit, colours clearly visible, apart from my team. They all received massive applause from the audience. This was what they had really come for, the excitement of both watching and betting on the events. Once the teams had milked the applause of the crowd and especially of their supporters, they retired back into the bowels of the stadium, and the betting began in earnest.

A single trumpet sounded, summoning the first competitors to the starting position below the Imperial box. The five charioteers came roaring out of the tunnel that led from the bowels of the stadium. They raced out onto the circuit and vied with each other to reach the starting line first. The first race was to be five laps, and for the winner, the right to compete in the later semi-finals.

The five teams eventually lined up below the box. They all turned and bowed before the emperor and geared themselves for the starting signal from the Imperial box. Justinian and Theodora both stood up. The riders could clearly see them and waited for either of them to start the race. Justinian turned and with a gentle nod from Theodora said, "My dear, Antonina, would you please us by starting the first race?"

"Basileus, Augusta, it would be a great honour, thank you," she said, standing and stepping forward to the edge of the box, as Theodora passed her a purple cloth with which to signal the start of the race. The crowd noticed the change and cried as one for the race to start. Antonina looked around at the crowd, and she beamed a brilliant smile and then waved the purple cloth.

The roar of the audience as they screamed and stood at the same time was deafening. It drowned out the noise of the teams charging forward, each rider forcing his team to accelerate as fast as they could before having to slow to take the first bend. No sooner had they charged around the first corner and dropped out of sight due to the central mound, then they seemed to come out of the second bend and back into sight.

The crowd kept up their roar as the green team reached the Imperial box first, closely followed by the red and the blue and my team. Then, they were shooting off down the straight, slowing slightly as they reared around the left bend. The jostling for position could be only guessed at, as the volume of the audience changed as the different sections of the crowd — matching the coloured teams — became quieter as their team fell back, or louder if their team was moving forward and overtaking or had the lead.

Back they came, this time the blue had the lead, barely, as they roared again past us and headed to the bend again. The blue continued to hold the lead up until the final lap. As they came around the final bend, the blue led them out with the red trailing. Suddenly, the green team saw their opening and moved up alongside the blue team, on the inside. Just as the distance was running out, the blue team's horses inched forward of the green's and just enough at the finishing line for the team of judges to make a call.

By then the audience was silent waiting with bated breath for the decision of the judges, which would be announced by the raising of the winning team's colours on one of the masts attached to the central island. The teams had already slowed and made their way off the track and back inside the stadium without knowing the decision. So, when the green flag was raised, a section of the crowd went mad with delight, while the other sections booed and howled their disgust with the outcome and their team's poor showing.

Once the track had been cleared of any detritus, the next race was ready, and the teams assembled once again. The racing continued at the same frantic pace. In the last race, the green team clinched first place in the individual as well as the team races, beating everyone else. They made a clean sweep that day and, surprisingly, we had no fatalities.

The next afternoon we also attended the races, and this time it was horseback and no chariots. The blues had their revenge by sweeping first place in every event. I won nothing, which was quite normal for anyone trying to take on the colours, but at least it added an extra team and gave the crowd extra fun. After all, as a champion, I was expected to contribute to the entertainment of the masses. The games closed, and everyone seemed to have enjoyed themselves. The cost of the event equalled a quarter of my profit from the Vandal campaign. However, this was offset by Antonina placing very rewarding bets. She and Theodora had a good eye for the teams and years of experience of the games from many different angles.

From the winnings, we managed to recuperate half of the costs. I think I understood why she had insisted on choosing the team riders for me. She had made sure that none were better than those she knew were the best and worthy of a sure bet. It also deterred anyone from noticing her betting on the colours. She had more talents than I could name. I wondered how much Theodora must have enjoyed the games now, as she was the principal lead of the events, and now all had to look up to her and not down on her as they once had. I doubted anyone would comment in public about those times, without fear of Imperial retribution, which would serve them right.

With the games over and the reception and "rights" of the champion over, we both returned to our house and family. We, or rather I, was going to enjoy a rest away from the army, and especially government business and politics.

With the spring almost giving way to the summer, I fancied a restful time in the gardens watching the flocks of birds that flew from Asia to Europe at this time of the year. We both enjoyed the peace and quiet of the estate. The spring ended, and the hot and dry summer arrived. I, for one, was pleased to be here and not in the sweltering capital during the day. With no summons from the palace, I was free to relax and found some reading materials on the Punic Wars. I wanted to see how the likes of Hannibal and his forefathers had attacked Rome, as well as how Rome had dealt with these attacks. I had read over it before, but now I had a fresh insight into the conflict and was interested to see how I would conjure images of the war in my mind's eye.

Chapter Eleven

The breeze had a cooling effect as it drifted through the vineyard, the heat of the summer had dried the soil of its moisture, and the slowly swelling grapes were in part to blame. I rested in the corner of the field, under an old olive, which was developing dark olives. Being alone on a day like this was the nearest I could come to heaven, everything was right. Antonina was becoming bored with not being in the capital and was asking about us taking a house there. The older children were already in the capital, hence her bending of my ear. We had been here a month, and tomorrow I planned a long horse ride to the interior, which I hoped would clear any cobwebs out of my head. In the house, I had become restless, and my constant fidgeting was driving her mad, or so she said.

The longer I rested, the more smells drifted over me. I thought I could smell the olives growing above me, but more pronounced was the smell of onions and garlic drifting in from other parts of the gardens. I sat more comfortably and reached for the document I had brought outside with me. But I couldn't concentrate, it was too peaceful. So, I put it back down and placed a small stone on it, so it wouldn't blow away if the wind picked up. I lay down and closed my eyes and thought about where I had been in the last years.

"Belisarius, Belisarius, where are you?" The voice seemed very familiar, but out of place in the middle of the Syrian desert. I began to shake violently, the desert scene disappeared and was abruptly replaced by an image of Antonina leaning over me, looking very annoyed and shouting at me. "Wake up. There is someone here to see you."

"What's the matter, my love? I thought if I stayed out here, I wouldn't annoy you," I replied. Slowly the real world was intruding into my personal world, and my mind began to focus on what she was trying to tell me.

She continued on in an annoyed voice, "When you've quite finished dreaming, there is an Imperial courier waiting for you in the house."

That sunk in quickly and I sat up and turned to her. In the house, for me? Why didn't you tell me?"

Those were the wrong choice of words to use when she was annoyed. So, I stood up and gave her a kiss. She took a playful swipe at me in a pretence of anger, so I gently pulled her to me and gave her an affectionate hug. We both walked back to the house at a swift pace, arm in arm, and entered. She led me through to where the courier stood, waiting patiently for me. He was a young man, covered in sweat and dust, and his clothes looked messed enough to prove he had raced here from the capital. Two of my guards stood watch over him. Once he saw me and recognised me, he stood to attention. He saluted and passed a letter to me and at the same time, spoke.

"General Belisarius, I have a message for you from the Basileus. You are to return with me at once to the palace. Here is a written copy of this order, if you care to read it, sir." The figure gasped, seemingly excited by the fact he'd seen me and was therefore fulfilling his orders.

But I declined the letter and said at once, "Thank you. Your word is good enough for me. You must be hungry and thirsty after such a rushed trip out to me. I will have a servant take you to the kitchen. By the time you are ready, I will be too."

A servant stepped forward to escort him to the kitchens. I turned to Antonina and attempted to speak. She interrupted me before I could say anything. "Don't even try and say you're sorry. You've been waiting for something like this since the first day we arrived," she paused, the anger in her face slowly faded and was replaced by her beautiful smile, and she spoke again. "You'd better have something to eat yourself. I'll pack some clothes for you while you are eating."

Her mood had changed in a moment. Was I now in the wrong? When she was like this, it was hard to fathom what she was really feeling, let alone thinking. I thanked her all the same, stretching my hand out to hold hers as I reminded her of how much I loved her. Then I promised that I would return as soon as I could, but for this, she gave me an odd look and then gave a casual remark.

"You know, if we had a house in the capital, this wouldn't be a problem. Would it?"

So, while I was there, I was to enquire after a suitable house for us, if I had the time, or rather, I should make the time. I placed my arms on her shoulders and kissed her gently on the lips, and she returned the affection. Then she wriggled loose and headed off towards the bedrooms. I turned to my bodyguards and ordered them to go and make ready to leave, as well as bringing four guards back with them when they returned.

I had a light snack with some wine mixed with water, and I collected my thoughts while I ate and drank. Antonina came into the room and joined me at the table, she picked at the food and didn't bother with the drink. She was preoccupied with her thoughts, and when I was finished, she followed me out through the house to the courtyard. The courier and my guards were mounted and waiting for me, my horse, held by a servant, had a clothing bag attached to the saddle. My orderly came over to me and handed me my sword and cloak.

When I was ready, I turned to Antonina and gave her a quick kiss on the cheek. I went to speak, and she simply put two fingers to my lips and nodded, there was nothing to say. She removed her fingers and gave me a caring hug. I then mounted the horse. I looked down at her, and she smiled back up at me. I raised my arm, signalling the advance, and we moved gently out of the courtyard. Once on the track leading to the road, we picked up the pace, the sun was already over towards the capital, I wanted to be in the palace before it dipped any further.

We rode hard and were soon at the ferry port that served Chalcedon, and there waiting for us was an Imperial barge. We led the horses down and onto the barge. Once we were settled, it pulled out into the channel, and then the rowers set a good pace as we ploughed through the strong current heading directly for the palace. There was a swell, and it became quite strong. Before sailing to Africa, this would have made me feel slightly sick, but after that journey, sailing the short distance presented no terrors, and I hardly felt it. The courier, on the other hand, went a slight shade of green and spent the journey leaning over the side, much to the amusement of the crew.

We landed at the Imperial port on the south side of the palace. We led our horses through the gated wall, where this time the Imperial guards were awaiting us. They escorted my guards and our horses to the stables. My guards would be taken to the mess and fed while waiting for me. The courier and I continued on foot, and we entered the Imperial Palace complex. I hadn't been this way since before the Vandal campaign, and I was surprised to see part of the old palace had been demolished and was being replaced by a new section. This looked to be on a much grander scale than before. Each time I visited the capital, there was something new being built. This was unquestionably a reflection of the newly found confidence of Justinian in his Empire and people.

I was led to the chamber where we had first planned the Vandal campaign. The sun had crossed over to the west, and the lamps were lit as we were now in the shade. The courier knocked on the chamber's doors. I waited a short distance away. The door was opened by one of the senior Imperial guardsmen. He looked in my direction — he looked familiar — he nodded at me and muttered something to the courier, who bowed and left me. The guard beckoned for me to enter, so I followed him into the chamber.

Again, the large table dominated the room, and around it stood a number of familiar faces. At the centre there was Justinian, looking directly at me. He waved a casual salute towards me, and before he could speak, I prostrated myself. It felt like I was in this position for a long time, kissing the cold marbled floor. I was being impatient, then he spoke.

"Belisarius, good, come over."

As I approached the table, I said to myself, Well, this looks interesting, the administrative and military elite all in one place and Justinian personally conducting the 'service'. Something big was being planned, and I was going to be part of it. Justinian looked pleased with himself, and the faces around him looked reasonably cheerful too — a good sign, I thought.

Then Justinian's face changed, a severe look came over him, and he said, "Come on. We haven't all day."

I felt a chill travel through my body and had a slightly sick feeling in my stomach. Had I misread the situation, should I have been more cautious in my approach? Theodora, after all, had warned me about the others.

He looked at me quizzically and said, "My dear Belisarius, you have gone as white as a sheet, is something wrong with you? Shall I summon my personal physician?"

Caught off guard, by the sudden fluxing of his mood, I slightly stammered my reply. "Thank you, Basileus-I am well-to be honest, have I done something to offend you?"

Justinian burst into a fit of laughter at my response, and those around him also laughed. I felt really uncomfortable and unsure of what was happening, though I had an inkling that Justinian had regained a little of his old humour from his pre-emperor days.

"Come, stand next to me and cheer up. I was playing with you. I said to the others that you were an easy target. A glare and you'd think I was after you," he laughed again. Yes, he was more like his old self, which was good to see. Since the riots, his humour had died, and he took everything far too seriously. I stood next to him. He patted me friendly on the shoulder and then turned to Peter the Patrician before he continued, "Belisarius, I am sorry for calling you back from your well-earned leave. But this will be of great interest to you. Peter, please sum up for Belisarius and then continue with your report."

I hadn't seen Peter since our last meeting a year ago when we planned the Vandal campaign. He looked his casual Patrician self — I knew he was still conducting all the Imperial foreign relations. He picked up his notes, glanced at them and explained that the current situation in Gothic Italy had taken a turn for the worse. Relations between ourselves and the Goths were at their gravest since Justinian's uncle had been emperor.

I hadn't heard anything about this, even though I had been closer to them when I was in Africa. Peter was better informed here in the capital. He went on and said, "The regent, our ally, Amalasuntha, was removed in a coup, and later murdered, sometime last April. We had expected something along these lines to happen. Her continued support for us may well have been the final straw for the Gothic nobility. Her role as regent had always been precarious, and the Gothic nobility were desperate to take her son under their aegis.

We had hoped she would have stayed regent longer as she played a vital role in bringing Italy closer to us, as well as allowing the pope or western Patriarch in Rome better communications with us. She relied on us to keep her in power, and we bribed a good number of the nobility to stay on her side. We hoped that her son would, like his mother, become pro-Roman, but that hasn't worked out.

Now the anti-Roman party is in the vanguard in Ravenna, and that presents us with all sorts of problems. The main reason for the coup was a failure on our part to trust her. We thought that Amalasuntha was switching sides in an effort to keep power. So, we decided to act. We bribed a Gothic noble who we thought was sympathetic to us and in need of money. This, Theodatus, was a member of the royal family and had recently fallen out with the regent over an illegal purchase of Roman-owned land around his estate. Petty, I know, but this is how the barbarians are."

He paused and took a sip of water from a cup on the table. "Well, Theodatus, we thought, had no interest in becoming king. So, he agreed to sell us Italy, south of Rome, and in exchange, we offered him a grand villa in Bithynia and a huge pension when the deed was done. He was to marry the regent and so become the male regent. He had a ship permanently based at Otranto, ready to whisk him away to exile once the act was done. I visited Ravenna to witness the wedding of the couple. Amalasuntha seemed pleased with the choice, and the marriage was agreed upon. She would still rule but through him. Or so she thought, but he was to remove her from power and rule in his own right. This would appease the nobility as a woman wasn't running the show. On the night before the wedding, the regent attended a party with Theodatus, where the heir, her son, apparently drank himself to death. With what happened later, I believe he was poisoned."

He paused and had more water. None of us had any questions. This was becoming quite a story. "Even with the death, the marriage took place. Amalasuntha had told me she was in love with him, and the nobility agreed. The nobility, following the death of the heir, decided that Theodatus would indeed become king in his own right."

Peter turned to Justinian and grimaced as he continued, "So, it seemed we would gain half of Italy for much less than the price of a military campaign. The Basileus sent a message of recognition to Theodatus, giving him the title of Patrician of the Romans. Gothic Italy had a new king, and it looked stable. I headed to Rome before coming back here. Before I reached Rome, I received word that Theodatus, far from being uninterested in the throne, had thrown his new wife into a dungeon on an island in Lake Bolsena. I was told I was forbidden to enter Rome and that I should come back to Ravenna to see him. He told me of his actions and said it was done in the interests of the Goths, not the Romans. He then tore up our agreement and threw it in my face. He said no Goth would ever give land willingly to the Romans. News of the invasion of Africa seemed to have hardened their position. We had been hoodwinked by the man. We had placed him in power, recognised him, and now he removed our real ally and murdered any hope of an agreement."

Peter stopped talking and had a goblet of wine brought to him. He drank it slowly as he checked through his notes. The room remained hushed. I assumed all of us, apart from Peter and the Basileus, were unaware of the real nature of the events that had unfolded in Italy. When he was ready, he started speaking again.

"I crossed back to Illyricum and sent word to the Basileus and waited for a response. When it came, I headed back to Ravenna and had an audience with Theodatus. I had hoped to persuade him to at least exile Amalasuntha, and we offered to take her in while maintaining an alliance with him. Instead, I learnt that she was dead already, and at the end of the meeting, he handed me a present for the Basileus. It was a gold plate, and it was covered with a purple cloth. Theodatus, I remember, had a huge smirk on his face when I was given the present. He then commanded me to remove the cloth and view the gift he had made for the 'Great Emperor of the Romans'. I was almost physically sick at what I found lying on that platter. It was the head of Amalasuntha. The court around me exploded in laughter and taunts. With the platter, I left the court, boarded the ship, and I buried the head at sea. That was the last contact with Theodatus."

Peter finished speaking, and an eerie silence gripped the chamber, broken only by Peter finishing off the goblet of wine. Justinian was the first to speak, and he turned from watching Peter and looked around at us, still gathered around the table in stony silence.

"Well, Belisarius, now you have a better idea of why you are here."

I was silent for a moment. During Peter's speech, I had an inkling that the events in Italy had pushed us towards war. The double insult to the emperor could not go unrewarded, lest any of our allies feared that we would not support them or at least revenge them.

"I presume that you are planning some form of military response to Theodatus's insults, Basileus?" I stated cautiously, and Justinian grinned.

"Yes, that's why I left you to enjoy your leave. If you had stayed in the palace, you'd have been seen attending my nightly conferences, and it would have alerted our enemies to a possible military response." Justinian pointed at Peter and continued, "Peter and I have been planning our response since he returned and even more so since word reached us of your great success. We have a few ideas that I want you and Mundus here to work on."

He pointed over to Mundus who smiled, his beard now as white as snow. I was startled to see him again, my mind racing back swiftly to the riots and the rather impressive if not brutal manner Mundus had conducted himself. He seemed as pleased as always to be noted, and he gave a soft chuckle of amusement as he grunted in response.

"Well, Belisarius, it has been a long time since we have worked together. Your success in Africa has greatly impressed us all, and I look forward to working with you."

"General Mundus, it will be my pleasure," I responded. How else could I respond when I knew that Mundus and I would be working together.

Justinian looked around at those assembled. No one wished to speak, so he said, "Gentlemen, I propose a carrot and stick approach. Our objective is now to regain complete control of Italy. The land south of Rome isn't enough, as we once sought with our pact with Theodatus. The Goths have proven themselves untrustworthy, and they need to be dealt with as a whole. But, for the short term, I will accept control of Rome and the lands of the south, as well as a very pliant Gothic leader in Ravenna. So, a diplomatic solution would be the cheapest and swiftest option. To achieve this, I want a limited campaign launched on Italy from two fronts. A tight squeeze and they will demand the return of Peter, till then we squeeze them hard. Now, the two of you will plan a strategy that will achieve this. I want to launch this in the spring. Everything must be planned in secret; the ships and armies can't be moved till late autumn at the earliest. The cost will be met by me." Justinian paused and arranged his cloak over his shoulders, and as he turned to leave, said, "Goodnight, gentlemen, we will meet in one month's time."

We all bowed as he left the chamber and entered his apartments, and we were left to discuss among ourselves his decision. Chairs were brought over to the table, and wine was as well, as we discussed the ideas and plans well into the night, it was pre-dawn before we departed the chamber. I left with Mundus, and I learnt that he had a second house in the capital, that he agreed to sell to me. This would allow us to meet and discuss the plans without drawing attention to ourselves and thankfully killed two birds with one stone.

I was very tired as I made my way back to my house, my guards were all fresh and cheerful, they had enjoyed good food, entertainment and a good sleep. We reached home at noon, and Antonina must have heard us enter the courtyard as she appeared at the entrance and waited for me to come over to her. She looked worried as I approached her, but her face lightened up, and a broad smile crossed it as she read my face and understood that all was well. We grabbed each other in relief and hugged and kissed as we walked into the house and out to the garden. I sat down in a patch of warm shadow where the ground was pleasantly warm. I carefully explained as much as I could without really telling her. Then I told her of the house I had just bought from Mundus and that for the rest of the year we would be living in the capital.

Once I had bathed and eaten, I would make arrangements for part of my guard to be based at the Imperial guards' barracks and provide us with a rotation of guards at the new house. Antonina would, of course, be in charge of two households now and she looked forward to living in the capital again. In the evening, my adopted children and my young son came together for the meal of the day, and we sat around in the now-cool garden. I explained that the emperor required my presence in the capital to discuss the Eastern frontier and the siting of a new fortress, as well as other matters of military concern. So, it was easier to move into the capital rather than travel in and out.

There followed an intense discussion among the family over the move and the possibility that I might be sent back to the East. Some thought that returning to Antioch would be bearable given the textiles that flowed through its markets. This appealed to my daughters, the cheapness of silk and other exotic items compared to the cost here in the capital certainly had its appeal. My son-in-law, Ildiger, asked quite openly for a post in the East if I was to receive the command. I stupidly and unthinkingly agreed to grant him a post if one should become vacant, as I had already let him down concerning Africa. Melissa gave me a wonderful smile of thanks for my kindness in offering her husband a post. I had been caught out, and now I would have to find him a position.

My other daughter, Zenobia, looked directly at me and gave me a look that said, you have been caught out by my sister and brother-in-law in a carefully laid ambush. Zenobia had become the more beautiful of the two and by far the most intelligent. She already had many suitors chasing her, she enjoyed teasing them and playing the field, but had no intention of marrying the first man brave enough to ask me, unlike her sister. Zenobia hated Ildiger and regarded him as nothing more than a leech who had bewitched her sister and was using her to raise himself in society. Yet, she always had time for her younger brother, Phocas, and her half-sister, Johanna. Phocas, now a rapidly growing young man, remained quiet throughout the meal. I think he preferred to let his sisters do all the talking and was happy for them to steal the light. He was still very close to his mother, while he and I, well, as he grew into a man, whatever bond we may have had once seemed to have faded. The supper passed pleasantly enough, and soon family banter and laughter took the place of any serious talk. The tables were cleared, and before we dispersed, I said, "I am returning to the capital tomorrow. I need to sort out the new house and prepare for the next posting. I hope the rest of you will stay and enjoy your holiday here with your mother." There was a general agreement. Antonina thought she would be ready to move completely within a month, and the family seemed happy to move as well. Antonina and I left the others to chat, and we headed back to our rooms.

The whole family assembled in the courtyard as I made ready to head back to the capital. I had an extra packhorse loaded with my personal gear, enough, Antonina said, to last even me the rest of the month. Those of my personal guard who were travelling with me had already assembled outside of the courtyard with their own small baggage train. For some reason, Phocas seemed most upset at my leaving and refused to hug me when I came to him to say goodbye. Instead, he held his younger sister's hand. Johanna was happy and still too young to understand what was happening. Zenobia stood there in an elegant silk dress and looked at me with a hard stare. Something wasn't right, but she hadn't said anything, so I assumed it was an argument with her elder sister, Melissa, probably concerning Ildiger, again. She at least allowed me to hug her and say goodbye. Then I was up in the saddle, I gave one last wave and trotted out of the courtyard, one hand holding on to the reins of the packhorse, and I was out of the gate and heading once again to the capital.

The first meeting was arranged for the evening after I returned to the capital. Mundus's former residence was well guarded, and the cook I had inherited was working away, preparing a meal for us. A room had been prepared, and a large table surrounded by chairs was ready. Mundus was the first to arrive, and the military commander of Illyricum was escorted by a small number of his own personal guard and headquarters officers. His guards joined mine in securely sealing the house. Mundus and I sat next to each other, and his headquarters staff sat on the other side of the table. Maps and documents were unpacked and neatly placed on the table. Peter arrived just as the sun was slowly sinking below the western horizon. He came directly from the palace and was accompanied by ten of his personal guards and officials. Peter and his officials joined us at the table, and it occurred to me that any casual observer would question why so many officials were entering the house of Mundus in the evening. Were we planning a coup? Hopefully, any spies might come to the same conclusion and so obscure the true reason for our meetings.

Before the meeting commenced, supper was served, we ate and drank in near silence as we had much to discuss later. Once the food had been cleared away, and the maps and documents put back on the table, we sorted out the logistics of the meetings, such as who recorded the meetings and where these records would be stored. Mundus and I left this to Peter as he was more skilled in dealing with these types of meetings. Once we had agreed with Peter, I formally opened the meeting and welcomed all present and reminded everyone that whatever was said or heard here was to go no further than this room. Peter then indicated he wished to speak first.

"Gentlemen, our emperor sends his greetings to you. He has written a letter he wishes me to read to you." He paused and opened a sealed letter which had rested on the table in front of him. "General Mundus and Belisarius, before you begin planning, I am forced to add certain limitations on your scope of operations. Firstly, I cannot release any troops from the Eastern frontier for the campaign in Italy. General Mundus, I cannot allow you to deplete the north-eastern frontier of men either. Unfortunately, you both will have to operate with small forces. I know you, Belisarius, can achieve much with little and I will be relying on you. Good luck with your planning. Signed, Justin son of Justin, Emperor of the Romans."

Peter finished reading the letter and looked across at me, his face strained, while at the same time appearing to be deep in thought. Our hands had really been knotted together, and it would mean that Mundus and I would be paying for most of our armies. I also suspected that John the Praetorian prefect's shadow was also now hanging over us. Financial constraints from his office would be his means of keeping power and forcing us to be beholden to him for any extra money we would need, not the emperor.

The conversation for the rest of the meeting entirely revolved around the question of the constraints imposed upon us, and so limiting our freedom of action. The meeting broke up a little after midnight, and we agreed to meet again the following week. Mundus left first, then shortly after, Peter returned to the palace. In the meantime, we agreed to work privately on an outline of how we saw the campaign going forward. Then we would discuss each other's ideas and, hopefully, over a period of time, come to formulate an agreed plan.

I assembled all the officers who had since returned from Africa and any other officers who were in the capital that I had served with. I brought them together at my house, and without telling them the real purpose, I had then conducted a planning exercise involving an invasion of another country. I already had some ideas, so I divided the group up and gave each a part of the plan to work on and come up with solutions. In some cases, they could work on their own or in pairs, but they were told to work in secret from each other otherwise this would ruin the purpose of the exercise. Then, the solutions of each team would be given to another for them to go through with a fine-tooth comb and detect any flaws or make suggestions as to how to improve it. In this way, I could cut down on the time it would take to formalise my overall plan. Once we settled on an agreed plan at the main meeting, my teams could then redesign it to fit Italy. It took the rest of the week to complete just the basic outline.

We met several times over the next month, but we failed to agree on any one plan. On the fourth meeting, Peter and Mundus arrived separately as usual, just as it became dark, and we followed the same ritual as before and then settled down to the matter at hand. Peter again was the first speaker, and he outlined his plan for dealing with Gothic Italy. As a diplomat, his plan emphasised this aspect. His plan was to bring pressure to bear directly on Theodatus in several ways. First, and not unexpectedly, he was going to bribe Gothic officials to undermine Theodatus's authority and ferment discord. This was nothing new, and it sounded like a rehash of what had gone before and proved very unsuccessful. The next part was to pay the Franks, who resided in the region of Gaul and Lower Germania, to invade Northern Italy and apply direct military pressure.

I could see real dangers with this idea if the Goths proved weak. Who would stop the Franks from staying and expanding their lands into Northern Italy? It could leave us with a new and dangerously experienced barbarian enemy. Peter though considered the time was right as the Goths and Franks were in conflict over the control of South-eastern Gaul. The Franks had an incentive to fight already, thus pulling out part of the Gothic army from Italy. Thirdly, a naval blockade of Sicily and Italy to stop trade and the closing of the land frontier with the Empire.

With all three working together, he hoped this would pressure Theodatus at the minimum to sell us the southern half of Italy in exchange for dropping the third part of the plan. With the Goths and Franks fighting, only the Romans, he insisted, would be acceptable as honest negotiators, and so remove the Frankish military threat. Whereas all of these would amplify the effects of the first part and so weaken Theodatus's position so that he would either flee or come to a more enlightened agreement with us, if the Goths backtracked, then the trade blockade would be applied.

Again, my main concern was that we had already tried something similar, and it had backfired, and it would take time. More importantly, there was no role for either Mundus or me. I could see from Mundus's face, that he didn't think much of the plan either. Then Mundus gave his presentation. His plan was simple and straightforward in concept and easy to control. He planned an invasion of Gothic-controlled Dalmatia using his army already based in the region. His plan involved capturing all the ports on the Adriatic coastline such as the old capital of Salona and Split. This would ensure the fleet had permanent access to the region. Then he would move north along the Dalmatian Way, heading along the coast to Aquileia at the head of the Adriatic. The fleet could support him on his way north, and once in Italy, he would march to Ravenna and lay siege to it by land and sea. With a successful outcome, he would use the fleet to land his army along all the ports on the eastern coast of Italy all the way down to Brundisum. From Ancona, he could cross the Apennines and strike directly at Rome.

I liked the plan as it was simple and used what was already available such as the road system and ports, and more importantly, it had precedence. Emperor Theodosius the Great had reconquered Italy following a similar route. Also, the Goths had recently made an incursion into the Empire while fighting what was left of the barbarian Gepaedes and attacked the town of Gratiana. But the main problem was the size of the army Mundus would require. Even if we combined the army of Illyria and the central field army, we would have but a small force compared to what Theodosius had led into Italy. Secondly, they would be expecting an attack in revenge for their incursion, so most of their army would be close to Ravenna. We already had limitations on the size of the force we could use. Even with the limits imposed on us, the plan had merits.

I then gave my plan. I intended to invade Sicily — we already had a pretext for meddling on the island. When the Vandal Kingdom surrendered, it had, in theory, handed over to us the fortress of Lilybaeum on the west coast of the island. The Gothic government had refused to surrender it to us, probably seeing it, rightly, as an issue of security, as it would give us a toehold on the island, and a firm base to act as a jumping-off point for Southern Italy. So, my aim was to capture the island as quickly as possible and use it as a base for the African fleet to blockade the Western Italian ports. With Sicily lost, the Gothic government would not only lose face but would also have grave difficulties in finding a new source of food to replace what it imported from the island. I then explained the advantages of my plan, in that a small expeditionary force was all that was required. I also had visited the island, and we knew it was relatively poorly defended. With that, I finished my presentation, and my colleagues had made notes concerning the other plans.

I had a steward serve wine, and then we started devising, as each of us defended our plans to the others. We continued late into the night before we managed to find some consensus between the three of us. I called for a break sometime in the pre-dawn light, Peter and Mundus agreed and together we decided to sleep on what we had discussed. The following afternoon we would reconvene and formulate an overall plan.

I went to bed, my head aching, the wine hadn't helped to calm me down. I lay on the bed and looked up at the ceiling, the room was in semi-darkness and cool, and I soon became more relaxed. I had just fallen asleep when my mind woke me as a nagging worry came to the fore. I managed to calm myself and put the matter to rest, or so I thought. Just as sleep returned to take control, I was awoken again as a new problem entered my mind and played havoc with whatever calm I had just obtained. There was no point in even trying to rest now.

I got up, found my clothes, and dressed and went onto the roof and watched the first streaks of red crack open the eastern sky. The sun rose high enough for me to clearly see the glistening sparkling yellow ball of fire. I sat down in the shade provided by part of the roof and listened to the city. This house lay close to the Golden Horn, so it never really got quiet. Workers and slaves were busy in the fish and meat markets readying goods for the morning and accepting deliveries of fish. Live animals were kept in pens, waiting to be slaughtered as required. I must have eventually fallen asleep on the roof as I felt myself being shaken hard, and I opened my eyes. Standing over me was my orderly, trying to wake me up.

"Sir, it's nearly time for your meeting. If you hurry, you can wash before it starts. I am sorry for the delay, but the servants couldn't find you inside the house."

Now, almost awake and lovely and warm from the heat of the sun, even in the shade, I roused myself and stood up, my mouth was dry, and I felt hungry.

"Thank you. I'll wash right away. Has the cook arranged anything for the guests?"

"Yes, sir, she has fresh lamb and fish ready to cook, and bread has come from the bakery," he said, as he reached out and steadied me, I was still more asleep than awake. Once I was balanced, the orderly led me back down from the roof to my room. Fresh water was in a bowl, and clean clothes were laid out on the freshly made bed, I washed and dressed and went down into the house. The orderly was waiting for me and led me into the conference room where my officers were waiting for me. Peter and Mundus arrived simultaneously with their staff in tow. We sat down and picked up from last night. The discussion soon turned to argument as we each again defended the merits of our plans. Mundus still wanted to invade Northern Italy, Peter wanted diplomacy, then war, and I wanted to invade Sicily. We stopped for a meal and this time we discussed while we ate the food, during which, Peter clashed with Mundus over his main sticking point, besieging Ravenna. He didn't want the capital touched as he explained the marshes that surrounded it made it difficult for a besieger to get close enough to the walls with enough men. The causeways over the marshes effectively restricted how many men could be brought before any section of the wall, and all the while, the Goths would be assailing them with missiles. Eventually, Mundus agreed to reconsider besieging Ravenna and Peter made concessions on his plan. After a good more negotiation, I felt ready to summarise our joint plan to deal with the Goths.

"I think this is the general outline of our plan. First, a campaign of internal subversion will be undertaken to destabilise the Gothic government by Peter. Second, a diplomatic mission will then visit Theodatus and peacefully try and persuade him to relinquish power over to us. Third, if this fails, then we go for the military option. We will bribe the Franks to attack Northern Italy — this should draw part of the Gothic army to the west and bring what remains into North-west Italy to defend the region. Then, Mundus will seize control of the Dalmatian ports, we reapply diplomatic pressure and offer a way out. If this fails, then I invade Sicily, take control of the island and cut food supplies. Hopefully, this will cause a collapse of Theodatus's government and then we should be able to walk in and take control." Peter and Mundus nodded in agreement as I continued, "Peter, as you will be seeing the Basileus,

283

please tell him that we have the outline of a plan, as he requested. Then can you arrange a formal meeting for all of us, with him?"

"I should be seeing him tomorrow. I will tell him then," said Peter.

"May I suggest that we start our staff planning our parts on the assumption that this will be agreed to by him." added Mundus. I paused as I thought it over. This was going to need everyone to be very coordinated and no one daring to leap ahead as this could cause more trouble.

"If you don't object, Mundus, I'll concentrate on Sicily and leave you to deal with Dalmatia, and you, Peter, to your area of expertise."

"I agree with what you have said, Belisarius, what about you, Peter?" Mundus said, glad to hear he would not be having anyone interfering with his plans. But as he looked to Peter, the figure looked oddly pensive still.

"Yes, I agree. But may I add, we will need contingency plans, as we can't predict the future or how Theodatus will think." He grimaced, rubbing his chin with frustration as if he felt that no matter what, there was still so much that could not be guaranteed. Mundus and I nodded. The more we had discussed this, the more I thought we had an outline that depended heavily on Theodatus's actions. We needed to think, What if?

Peter stood up, his staff did likewise, and he shook hands with us and then left the conference. Once he had left the room, Mundus turned to me and beckoned me over to a corner of the room, dismissing his staff. I did likewise. Once the room was empty, he spoke in a half-whisper to me.

"You must be careful, Belisarius. Your recent success has gained you, new enemies, and principally, John the Cappadocian. He is very jealous of the trust Justinian places in you. Peter may be one of them and not for the obvious reason of gaining power, as is the case with John. No, Peter is jealous of you because you have the favour of Theodora. I think he has feelings for her and sees you and your friendship with her as a threat and hindrance to him. Why, you might ask, do I say this? The Augusta has a past, you know that, and I think Peter featured in that past and has yet to get over it. Us older men can be strange."

Following that comment, I was on even more guard and said to

Mundus, "Do I need to fear you?"

"No," he laughed, glad to see I was reacting well, and then continued, "Like you, I am a soldier and as loyal to the emperor as you. But I am older and wiser and know that the greatest threat to us comes not from the battlefield, but from those who eat and drink with us."

"God, I hate all this palace intrigue. Give me a battle any day, at least they fight fair. I have one advantage at least, my Antonina to watch my back," I sighed after he paused, but I was shocked by his next words, my heart trembling that it could be the case.

"Your Antonina has more enemies than you do, and a lot of tongues have been spreading rumours about her such as claims that she keeps your army loyal by looking after more than just their *needs* if you know what I mean." Mundus looked directly into my eyes. I looked back, but his last comment had hurt me badly. Then he smiled and his hands slightly trembling gripped my shoulders. "I must go now. I will see you again when we present our plan to the emperor. Take care, my friend, and double your guard, especially when your family arrives."

I remained silent and walked out of the house with him; there, his guards were already mounted and awaited him. One held his mount, an elegant Arab stallion and then he rode off, but not in the direction of his home but of the city gates. I had heard the rumours too, but I knew they had no foundation, as with the Augusta, not coming from the elite made you a target of vicious gossip. But somehow the thoughts that John the chain and even Peter had mentioned squatted in the back of my mind and I knew I should indeed take heed.

The next day, Antonina and the children arrived at the head of a small convoy of wagons full of our belongings. Within a day, they moved into the house, we quickly grew into the house, and it was filled with the comings and goings of young women at court and the sounds of children growing up. One evening, while I was working away in my office, reading over documents my staff had left with me to consider before I met them again in the morning, Antonina snuck into the room and moved quietly behind me. I only realised she was in the room when she placed her hands over my eyes, so I could no longer continue working. She whispered to me and said, in a mocking hushed tone, "Shall I tell you your secrets?"

"Go on," I said, pausing for a moment and wondering what was coming next, then I said, "Have you caught me with the cook again?"

She paused, just long enough to let me know she thought my jest was quite unbelievable, especially if you had met the cook.

"You are planning a long sea voyage to an island where grapes grow. There you will persuade the islanders to support you, and then you plan to cross a small stretch of water and visit a city founded on the Tiber."

I was stunned for a moment, bemused to think that all my planning and meetings in secret had been pointless. Now, everyone knew what we were planning and more. I looked carefully at my desk, just in case one of the documents had spelt this out, and she had simply learnt it by looking at my desk. No, nothing on my desk even remotely hinted at the plans. Oh, wait a minute. Antonina and the elder children frequently left the house and visited the palace, and who lived there and was my wife's greatest friend.

"I see you have been speaking to the 'all-seeing and hearing' mistress of the world," I teased.

Antonina's hands dropped from my face and slapped my shoulders as they were removed, and she said in a grumpy manner, "Don't be rude about Theodora. You know she has our best interests at heart and protects you from intrigue. Yes, you will be commanding the expedition to Sicily. Oh, by the way, you have an audience with the Basileus tomorrow afternoon."

Who needed an Imperial messenger to inform them, when they had a wife like mine.

An Imperial messenger arrived at the house the next morning with instructions to present the plans in conjunction with Mundus and Peter that afternoon; just as Antonina had said. Just after midday, so many guards arrived in the courtyard that I had trouble spotting Mundus among them. He was, like his guards, covered in dust and dirt from a long journey. I had fresh clothes and a bath made up for him. When he was ready, he joined me in the garden, and we briefly discussed the plans and what we would need to bring with us for the meeting with Justinian. Once that was sorted, we decided, since court appearances were listed, there was no point in trying to be discreet. So, we left together, with just a small number of guards.

Once in the palace, we were escorted formally through the main entrance and directly to the conference chamber where we had met Justinian previously. We entered and found Peter already there, waiting for us. Justinian had not yet appeared, so we used the spare time to discuss briefly, the plans we were going to present. Peter would introduce the overall concept and then move onto his part of the plan, then Mundus and finally myself.

The Imperial doors to the chamber were opened. We stood facing the open doorway as a number of Imperial guards entered the chamber and took up their normal positions. Justinian then entered, and we all prostrated ourselves and waited for the command to rise, which was quick to follow. He greeted us informally, as was his style, and took his seat at the head of the table, then he spoke.

"Peter has already outlined the basic plan to me, and I am happy with it. Now, I want to hear it in detail. Once I am happy with what you say, then you will present it to the war council, and then we can begin the real preparations."

Peter turned and glanced at Mundus and me before he outlined the strategy and his part of the plan to Justinian. He gave a detailed account of how he planned to destabilise the Gothic government at Ravenna by using his agents and members of the church to ferment discord with the nobility with whatever means were available. Further to this, he had already entered into negotiations with the Franks, to test the water, and the results looked promising. One of his agents was already feeding back good intelligence on the Gothic army. Members of the church, even though the Goths were still mostly heretics, could move freely around Italy and into the Empire. They had become not only a good source of intelligence but a safe means to courier documents to us. Already he had learnt that Theodatus's motives for murdering Amalasuntha were for internal purposes to curry favour with the hard-line nobility who were anti-Roman. Theodatus, though, was sitting on a tightrope, trying to balance the pro and anti-Roman camps. He was trying to discreetly court us but feared an alliance would cause his downfall. Neither party in the Gothic court was strong enough to seize power, Theodatus held the centre ground and had just enough support. Peter believed that Theodatus would be susceptible to external pressure, and this would force him into one camp or the other. The Roman camp offered Theodatus security and a safe exile, while the other camp only offered war.

Mundus then took over and detailed his plan, while emphasising the constraints placed on him by Justinian. He expected to be able to achieve his overall objective in one campaign season and have at least half of the field army back inside the Empire before winter came, thus ensuring none of the northern barbarians could take advantage of the absence of most of the army for one summer. Mundus then began to explain in detail his plan; first, he intended to launch a lightning strike into Gothic Dalmatia and seize Split and Salone. Then, march north along the main road seizing towns and ports as he moved, while the fleet sailed from Greece and joined up with him at Split. As he moved north, the Goths would fear an invasion of Northern Italy and an attack on Ravenna. If the Franks also attacked the Goths, the Goths would be forced to defend on two fronts and so must bring all their troops north. Once this had occurred, Mundus would have no need to enter Italy and could retire and garrison the new frontier with Gothic Northern Italy. This would apply plenty of pressure on Theodatus and could ensure he switched camps quickly, to join us.

Finally, it was my turn. I emphasised, from the first, that I envisioned a force of no more than what I had landed in Africa being available for me to use. Once Mundus and Peter's plan were operational, and Peter had confirmed the movement of the Gothic army to the north, I would invade Sicily. I expected to meet some resistance from the Gothic garrisons in the major ports, but not enough to hold up my conquest of the island. Once established there on the island, the fleet would then begin blockading the Italian coastline. We would wait on the island close to Syracuse for word from Peter as to when and where we should land in Italy and take control of the southern half, following Theodatus's surrender to us. I would then have the easiest task of marching along the coast road to Rome, liberating all the cities and the port of Naples as I advanced. We could achieve this in one campaign season if it all went to plan. We had agreed that an opposed landing in Italy was improbable, as we didn't have the resources available to mount such an ambitious task.

With that, my presentation was over, and we all waited for Justinian to speak. He remained silent for some time as he contemplated what he had heard. Then he spoke in his normal mild manner.

"Yes, I like the plan. Its main merits are the limited use of our resources and their use just on two fronts, thus making Gothic manpower less of a problem for us, as they will be divided between three fronts. Only by us all working together do we stand a chance of succeeding. Too many campaigns of the past relied on one approach. I see we have learnt from that, good. The carrot and stick approach, is the most efficient way of using our limited resources. Good, the war council will meet here shortly. So, stay and present your plans as you have for me. The council will then agree with me and supply the necessary resources to undertake the campaign."

All three of us thanked Justinian, and he departed back the way he had come, and his guards left the chamber. Once he was gone, we discussed the plan again amongst ourselves and the approval we had been given.

The door we had entered through was reopened, and the members of the war council entered. We remained seated as they were of the same station as us. John the Cappadocian led the group over to the table and sat, he in the empty space next to the emperor's chair. We remained silent, awaiting the return of Justinian to head the council.

Justinian emerged from his chambers, accompanied again by his guards; we all performed obeisance. Justinian instructed Peter to repeat his part of the plan to the council. Then Mundus and, finally I, finished the presentation. We waited for the questions to follow, but instead, we were greeted by silence. John sat there and looked over some notes he had brought with him into the chamber. Then he cleared his throat, looked at Justinian, who nodded his approval and John spoke.

"I can afford to pay for a force of no more than eight and a half thousand men and a fleet to carry them. The field army of Illyricum would cost no more to us in the field, then having them exercise during the summer. It is Peter's plans that will cost, and I can't really see the value of paying the Franks good gold for them to do something they are probably planning to do anyway. As for the capture of Sicily and the ports in the Adriatic, they should, in time, more than compensate the treasury for the initial outlay."

Justinian listened, but his face showed a degree of displeasure in what John had said. He allowed John to relax after his comment, then he said, again in his mild voice, showing none of the displeasure he had earlier shown, "John, you lack vision. You doubted the viability of my plan to conquer Africa. Belisarius proved you wrong and the treasure he returned with has more than compensated the treasury. Belisarius will succeed again, and Mundus's and Peter's plans will work. We are dealing with greedy gold-loving barbarians, not civilised people. If this works, we will be one big step closer to our goal of unifying the Empire. God will grant us success as it is his wish that all nations should be ruled by us, in his name."

John's face turned a hint of red. He didn't enjoy being shamed by the emperor in front of the council. John allowed a moment to pass before replying. "Yes, Basileus, I was only thinking in terms of money, and I lacked the correct references to see the campaign as part of God's divine plan for man. My apologies, my Basileus, and I assure you that I will give the campaign my full support."

It was not a pretty sight to see John grovel in public, and also a problem. He would be out for revenge for the humiliation he had just suffered. I could just see him, personally weighing each gold coin we were given to ensure we received the exact amount and no more. Whenever I thought of John, the parable from the gospel comes to mind of how difficult it was for a rich man to enter the Kingdom of God compared to a camel passing through the eye of a needle.

Justinian looked around at his council. None had anything to say. They clearly understood that he had made his mind up, and John's example had solidified that quite clearly. He then spoke. "Peter, Mundus and Belisarius, we approve of your plan. We will begin preparations straightaway. Mundus, you must be ready to move by late March, depending on the weather. Belisarius, you need to be ready by late spring." He paused, then continued, "Peter, I want you to use the pretext of the failure of the Goths to hand over Lilybaeum to us, the sacking of Gratiana, as well as the murder of Amalasuntha to push Theodatus to uphold his promise to us. Squeeze him as much as you can. Lastly, any mention of military pressure must be limited. The Persians will quickly hear of it and know we are interested in the West again. They may begin to re-examine their need to keep the peace. The army of the East will need to be active next summer, manoeuvring in the region, just to keep the Persians more interested and concerned as to our real intentions, as by then, they will have learnt of the movement of some of the central field army to the West. By then it will be too late to do anything, so it's the year after next, that we need to be on guard for. But if everything goes well in the West, we will be back to strength and the Persians won't have any advantage over us."

Again, no one had any questions or comments to make. Justinian was far too interested in his overall aim of retaking the West to brook any vocal obstacle from the council. Only the Persians could interrupt his plans. After a short pause, he spoke again.

"Belisarius, you will command the invasion of Sicily and hopefully of Italy. You will again assume your powers of military master of the West, and again your orders will automatically carry my authority. Mundus, you will command your army as military master of Illyricum, you will only become subordinate to Belisarius should you and your army cross into Italy. Peter, you will act in your normal role and assist both of them with the diplomatic aspects of the campaign as well as keeping me informed as to what is afoot with the barbarians. Gentlemen, thank you for attending this meeting. Whatever is required, within reason, for the campaign, the council will do their best to assist and not to hinder."

Justinian stood up, and we all did, and as he turned, we all bowed, and accompanied by his guards, he left the chamber.

John turned and spoke to all in the chamber, his expression a scowl even though he was maintaining his duties. "Have lists drawn up of your requirements and have them sent to me as soon as you can, and I will coordinate your logistical needs."

All three of us thanked him. The council then broke up, and the others followed John out of the chamber. The three of us waited, then followed them out, then Peter turned to us with a soft grunt.

"I will keep you informed as to any developments as they occur, now I have a trip to Ravenna to undertake. Goodbye."

Peter left us. Mundus and I stood outside the chamber and grinned at each other.

"If you enter Italy, there is no way I can be your commander," I stated, "how the hell would I get orders to you through Gothic territory. You act as you see fit, you are the more experienced, I trust you," I said. Mundus nodded in agreement. I needed to say that — he was older, and as I said, more experienced, and he had his pride. He knew that I still respected him, and this would ensure that we worked together, not against each other. I wondered why Justinian had made the point about me commanding Mundus in Italy. It was impractical, but I suppose it was politically correct and befitted my title.

Mundus gripped my shoulders, then turned and left me standing outside of the chamber. As I was about to leave, one of Theodora's ladies-in-waiting approached me out of the shadows of the corridor. I hadn't noticed her there. She instructed me to follow her, and she took me deeper into the palace complex and into the Imperial quarters of the palace. I was led up some winding stairs, and it occurred to me that we were taking a very roundabout route. We also hadn't seen any other servants so far. My sense of adventure overtook my sense of danger. We finally emerged outside the apartment belonging to Theodora. The lady-in-waiting knocked on the door and left me standing there. I suddenly felt danger. If I were found here, how would I explain my presence in this section of the palace, which I had no right to be in. The door to the apartment opened, and another lady-in-waiting ushered me inside. The apartment was huge. I hadn't been in here before; it was more like a barrack block than an apartment. It was beautifully decorated, silks hung from the ceiling, carefully dividing up the apartment into sections. Elegant bronze lamps were suspended by delicate chains from the ceiling and cast a yellow light into the apartment. The furniture was of the finest quality and crafted by the best in the capital. The floor was draped with thick woollen rugs, and the walls were covered in images of nature; the sea, farming and food. They differed in aspect, as their styles were drawn from around the Empire. I had seen examples like these in Antioch. The air of the apartment was scented with perfumes and incense; this was one of Theodora's very private rooms. The sound of giggling and laughter broke my concentration, and then I began to recognise the source of the laughter. A voice came from behind one of the silk drapes.

"Belisarius. Explain your presence in the Augusta's apartment? Have you come to seduce me?"

I quickly answered with my face utterly pale. "No, my Augusta, I was led here by one of your servants." I could have leapt out of the window at that point; some jokes were just too dangerous.

Theodora, the owner of the voice, then said, "Don't you love your Augusta?" That was followed by more laughter.

I replied, I had to and knew I was in a serious situation even if it was the lady's joke. "Yes, my Augusta."

"For what purpose then, were you summoned here?" she said.

"I have no idea, Augusta?"

Then, Theodora spoke not directly to me, but loud enough for me to hear quite clearly. "You are very trusting of him, Antonina. He seems to follow any woman who lures him away."

Antonina laughed and did her best to reply between the giggles, swatting at the air with some silks over their seeming joke. "I know, Theodora, he is far too trusting. Look at the trouble he could be in if our enemies had set him up."

It was one of my faults. I was always far too trusting of women. The pair, still giggling, emerged from behind the silk drape. Antonina came over to me and gave me a big loving hug and a playful kiss, then Theodora spoke.

"Well, Belisarius, you have your new command. I know you will succeed with your campaign. I am sorry for teasing you and luring you here, but you must be more careful and not allow yourself to be trapped so easily."

"Lesson learnt, Augusta. If you dismiss my wife, I will then set about seducing you, my Augusta," I said in a playful manner, with a big smile on my face.

They both laughed at that comment, though my wife made a point to give me a push in the shoulder for my trying joke. Antonina said in a playful way, "You couldn't seduce a citron, my darling. Theodora would have grown old before you mastered the skill."

They both laughed, and Theodora added, "I'll be in my bedroom awaiting you, General, to advance and make contact."

They both broke into even more laughter. When they had both recovered, Theodora, in a serious voice, returned to the situation. "Belisarius, do you remember what I said to you before you left for

Africa?"

"Yes, if I need anything to ask you and you will arrange it, why?"

This was curious and generally meant that I was here for a very important reason, but that they'd also been drinking a little more wine and eager to tease me for not listening about being more careful.

"I fear John will try and sabotage your campaign. While you are here in the capital, he will do all he can to appear to help. But once you are on campaign, he will begin to undermine you. Then he will try and have you removed for any incompetence he can find against you. You must be careful. Seek my help first," she stated firmly, and my mind was quick to remember the rotten biscuits from the voyage, the way so many had been sick, and I nodded my head firmly, thanking her and insisting I would call upon her should I need it. She nodded her head at me, glad I understood. "Antonina tells me, she plans to accompany you again. I will miss her company. You are to ensure that she is looked after and that all her needs catered for. I will enjoy the presence of your children while you are both away."

"Of course, Theodora, we could be gone a long time, maybe my wife would like to reconsider her decision?" I replied, but Antonina pinched me. She was coming, and nothing was going to stop her — she had made her plans.

Theodora just grinned. "You both had better leave. Antonina knows the discreet way out of this section of the palace. Goodbye."

I bowed in respect, and Antonina led me back down the staircase and through the labyrinth of the palace, and out into one of the closed gardens. From there, we walked openly among the palace officials and servants till we reached the main courtyard, it was late in the day. My guards had already been summoned and were waiting for us. I ordered an extra horse be found for Antonina and borrowed a large cloak for her to protect her clothes. We then made our way back to the house, the streets were busy, and I was glad we were on horseback as they had to make way for us.

We arrived home just before sunset, a meal had been prepared, and we ate it together. Then we retired to our bedroom. Lying on the bed, Antonina said in her softly spoken alluring way, "If I hadn't been in Theodora's rooms, would you have allowed yourself to be seduced by her?"

"Certainly not." I paused, then decided to stir the pot a little with Antonina. After all, the pair had enjoyed teasing me earlier on. "Only if she had commanded me to, would I have, and then I would have refused to enjoy myself. Afterwards, I would have felt cheap and used."

Antonina twisted and delivered a perfectly aimed kick into my back, and it almost knocked the wind out of me. Once I regained my breath, I just couldn't help myself and laughed. Antonina joined me in laughter, as the whole situation, on reflection, had been quite comical. Antonina moved closer to me, and we kissed.

The rest of the autumn was taken up with the planning of the invasion and the logistical requirements. Unlike Africa, the southern Italian ports would be closed to us, so the jump from Northern Greece to Sicily would be longer and require more supplies. Once ashore, I hoped that Africa would be able to supply me, but it would depend on how well Solomon and Procopius had done in rebuilding the grain supply in such a short time. Surprisingly, John was proving very helpful and provided me with whatever I required. We would need fewer transports than last time, and I would also be allowed to draw from the central field army, and he also had money to pay for mercenaries. With my extra wealth, I could pay for a further five hundred men to add to my personal guard.

Peter sent regular reports on the situation in Italy, and with the information he supplied on Sicily, we were able to gradually build up a picture of what the Gothic military infrastructure in the area was like. Apart from the reports, I saw nothing of Peter. Mundus had headed north to his headquarters and begun recruiting more men to his field army to build up its strength, as well as planning for his spring offensive. I think we had both acknowledged that we would have to fight the Goths. Peter, for all his skill, wasn't going to bring down Theodatus and his government without a fight. The Goths, like the Vandals before, had nowhere to go. In the past, when we had fought them, they had the Badlands beyond the frontier to retreat into. When they were advancing, it was we who were pushed further back into the Empire with nowhere to go, and we gave ground but never surrendered to them, so I expected that they would react in a similar manner.

At the end of December, which was wet and cold even by the

standards of the capital, I was summoned to the palace for a private audience with Justinian. I left the house early that morning, taking only a few of my guard. The streets were slippery thanks to the continued rain, so I decided it would be prudent to walk to the palace rather than risk a slip on the cobblestones while riding a horse. A fog lay carpeting the streets like a thick grey fur, it was cold and damp at the same time and tasted of smoke from the numerous fires lit by the populace in an effort not only to keep warm but also to cook and work with.

If I felt chilly and damp, a quick glance at my guards proved they were just as miserable. If I had to live any longer in the capital, I was determined to buy furs for not only me but also for my guards. They would keep the cold and damp out if worn with the leather on the outside and the fur on the inside. Perhaps too some fur-lined boots for when it snowed here. I was missing the warmth of Carthage; it may have been wet, but it was at least warmer. With that thought, I hoped Sicily would prove a better climate, especially at this time of year.

The main entrance to the palace loomed out of the grey as we crossed the empty forum. At the gates, my guards were escorted to the Imperial guards' barracks, and I was taken into a waiting room outside of the Imperial apartments. It was busy inside the palace; the room was full of dignities and pleaders hoping for an audience. I waited my turn penitently, others paced up and down, grumbling, stopping any officials and asking when they would see the emperor. Others, more adept at working in these conditions, led the official to one side and a small bag of coins moved from one to the other, in an attempt to speed matters up.

The chamberlain entered the waiting room, and suddenly everyone was standing and moving towards him. This was the man who made the appointments and then collected you for them. He simply brushed aside anyone who dared to come too close with a practised swish of his right arm. He came over to me, greeted me and directed me to follow him. Although the room was silent, one could feel the atmosphere change after the chamberlain had spoken to me, rejection replaced hope.

I was led through the outer rooms of the Imperial quarters to where the doors of his office halted any further progress. I was left standing while the chamberlain knocked hard on the door and entered. The door was closed behind him by an armoured figure. Shortly, it opened again, and a very familiar voice called from within.

"Come, Belisarius." I entered the office, saw the chamberlain standing next to Justinian and immediately prostrated myself on the floor, as the door was closed behind me.

"Basileus, how can I serve you?" I said from my position looking up at him from the floor. He signalled for me to stand and approach.

Once I was standing in front of him, he turned to the chamberlain who was holding a tightly rolled scroll and said, "Chamberlain, present the insignia of the consul, to our new consul." The chamberlain passed the scroll over to me, I took it in my outstretched right hand, which I kept in the same position while I replied.

"O, Basileus, you do me and my family the greatest honour by rewarding me with the honour and prestige of this most ancient symbol of Rome. Thank you."

I had been raised to the most senior rank of the senatorial class, without having been made a senator or attended one of the occasional meetings of the Senate. I never, in my wildest dreams, ever thought that I would share the same rank as Scipio Africanus had, though it would take some beating, as he had been consul numerous times and continually during the war with Hannibal. My father and uncles, had they lived, would have been overjoyed at this privilege and recognition of my service to the Empire, but then Justinian spoke.

"Well, Consul Belisarius, you will be consul for the next year starting on the seventh of January, following the customary six days of games, paid for by the outgoing Consul."

Well, at least I would be away for most of my consulship, but I would have to leave money to pay for numerous events and the six days of games, marking the end of my consulship. It was a great reward, but it came with a price and a victory in Sicily would at least reduce the personal cost to me and my family. Justinian would be the other consul, as had been the practice since the time of Augustus. The chamberlain then begged to speak and said, "My Basileus, Consul Belisarius, may I announce the names of the new consuls as is customary with notices throughout the world?"

"Thank you, Chamberlain, please do so and will you excuse us?"

The chamberlain bowed to the emperor and retreated out of the office, and the doors were again closed to the outside world.

Justinian relaxed, slapped me on the back and said, "Well, Consul, I expect you know how expensive the consulship is. Especially the six days of games and the largesse given here throughout the capital during the year?"

"Yes, the thought had crossed my mind, Basileus."

"Well, my friend, there is a good reason for granting you the consulship now and not later. Firstly, it officially rewards your victory, and secondly, you will not be in the capital come this time next year, as you will be in control of Sicily. So, have no worries about the cost of the games, I will cover them, and you can use your money to pay for local events in Sicily. But more importantly, this gives you a rank equal to that of Theodatus, so you can deal with him on equal terms. I think this will make any local negotiations you may have with him much easier for him to accept," he said with a chuckle.

"Thank you, Basileus."

"You may leave, I will see you at the consular games, eh, Consul Belisarius?"

I bowed to him and made my way out of the office and was escorted by an official back, I thought, towards the main entrance of the palace. Instead, I was led to the office of the Praetorian prefect, and I felt my stomach drop. The door to his office was already opened, and he sat waiting for me, a smug grin on his face. He signalled for me to enter.

"Come in, come in, Consul Belisarius."

I was a little taken aback by his call, but I was slowly getting used to the way the palace worked. A promotion was already known to all but the recipient. I glanced around his office as I entered; nothing much had changed since the last time I had been here. He pointed to a spare chair, and as I sat down in it, I said, "How is the Prefect this morning?"

"Very well, Belisarius. How is your beautiful wife and your equally charming daughters? I see more of them every day, now that they are ladies-in-waiting for the Augusta."

Oddly, that comment made my skin crawl, yet I remained calm. "They are very well, thank you, Prefect. And to what do I owe this surprise and much-welcomed invitation?"

"Belisarius, always direct. I wanted to discuss with you the

298

forthcoming campaign in Sicily." He paused, waiting for me to make any comment, I just nodded my head for him to continue. "I wish to confirm with you the expected numbers of men you intend taking to Sicily. Also, to let you know that I have appointed my most trusted officials to accompany you and deal with all your financial transactions and the running of Sicily. So, leaving you free to concentrate on the campaign."

He was being very forthcoming, and I noted he seemed very confident of the success of my upcoming campaign. Had I misjudged him? With John, until the knife was in your back, you couldn't be sure. He was a slippery character, perfect for operating in the labyrinth that was court politics.

"That's very generous of you, John. I presume this means that I can expect my men to be paid on time," I stated, perhaps a little too brashly as he just seemed to chuckle.

"Have I ever let you down, Belisarius, my friend."

"You did," I stated rather bluntly, a familiar bitter taste coming to my mouth as I recalled how sick Procopius had been and just how much I hadn't been careful about John's seeming kindness beforehand. "Remember the uncooked biscuits you dumped on me, causing the death of a number 'of good men."

"General, surely you don't hold me responsible for that. I personally had the culprits executed for making money out of your rations. How else can I prove my friendship to you, my dear Belisarius?"

He seemed to cough through his teeth, reminding me oddly of a crocodile. I shrugged my shoulders. I wanted to tell him to his face what I truly felt about him, the 'Chain', but he held the purse strings, so I brushed over the matter.

"Just ensure that my men receive their pay on time and don't hold back, should I need to request extra funds, my dear John."

He smiled back, but he had the smile of a snake that was resting in the heat after eating a meal. "Belisarius, trust me, I am your friend."

There came a knock at the door, followed by a light voice with a heavily Persian-accented tone to it.

"My lord, I'm Narses of Armenia, you requested my presence, may I enter?"

John grinned at me and called out. "No, Narses, wait outside, I am speaking to my good friend, General, soon-to-be Consul Belisarius."

I recognised the name. But was this him? He had been my opposite number in the Persian army when I was commanding Dara in the East. I had learnt that he defected to us later on over his failure to achieve a victory for his monarch. But the man I heard didn't sound like a soldier let alone a general? We had never met, until now, perhaps? So, was he now a protégé of John's; that said it all. I turned to John, and we shook arms.

"John, don't let me hold your work up. I'll leave, unless you have anything else, we need to discuss?"

John's grin became a little wider. He was up to something, and for some reason, he wanted to show his hand to me, and perhaps this Narses was that hand.

"No, no, we are quite done, Consul."

We parted on good terms, well, at least I thought we had. I couldn't comprehend that man. We both served the same cause, well, at least I thought we did. I turned and went out of the room, through the now open door and passed Narses, as he stood waiting to be admitted. He was a short, lean well-dressed older man, with a goat-like tuft of a beard of dark hair on his deep olive-skinned face. His facial features were sharp, and his dark eyes darted around him, alert to anything and everything that was going on. He looked more than forty, but as he was Persian, it was hard to tell his exact age. One thing was for sure — I wouldn't want to turn my back on him in the dark and not expect a dagger to be slid between my ribs. He saw me and immediately made a deep, respectful bow.

"My lord, Belisarius, a pleasure to meet you at last."

I bowed in return, and as I passed him, I slowed down to speak just a little. "Narses, I have heard a lot about you."

"All good, I hope, my lord?" he mused, and I nodded my head, insisting it was a pleasure to meet him. But then he turned to enter John's room, and I was led out of the palace. I was thankful to leave, but I could not shake the unpleasant feeling I had over this whole promotion already.

If I had known then what I now know of that Eunuch, I would not have been so polite and instead should have run him through with my

300

sword. John had already then been planning my downfall and Narses was to be his weapon of choice. But that lay in the future, and I will discuss that in the correct place, my dear Procopius.

Chapter Twelve

I met Peter again at the end of February when he attended one of the planning meetings within the palace. We were all assembled in the chamber, and he entered, accompanied by Justinian. Once the formal greetings were completed, we sat at the table and Justinian spoke.

"Peter returned early this morning from Italy, and I know you will want to hear his report."

Peter, for a change, looked scruffy and worn out. I later learnt that he had ridden from the Adriatic coastline directly to the palace, with very little rest during his journey. What he next said explained his condition.

"Thank you, Basileus. Gentlemen, stage one of the campaign, is complete."

We all sat bolt upright at that comment. We, as one, turned to look quizzically at him. I had many questions I wanted to ask, and I was sure I wasn't the only one. This had come out of nowhere.

"I have sealed our pact with the Franks, and the gold has been paid. They, as I speak, are massing on their frontier with the Goths, ready to strike when the time is right. I went on to Rome, where Theodatus was holding court, and I had a private audience with him." He paused and had a sip from one of the goblets of wine that had been left for us on the table. He tried to rush his sip, knowing we were all waiting with bated breath, but as he settled the goblet down, he coughed heavily.

"I presented him with the usual gifts and gave him our emperor's good wishes to our loyal ally. Then I said to him, that the emperor was most upset to learn that his servant was no longer willing to abide by his word and keep to his agreements. This caught him off guard, but being a barbarian, he failed to understand clearly what I had said. Instead, he announced that he considered himself no longer bound by our agreement as he had a special responsibility to his people. Which I took to mean, he had no intention of remaining loyal to us, much as we had expected of a barbarian. He then demanded to know why Mundus had moved his army closer to his frontier in Dalmatia. He demanded to know if the emperor was threatening him. I made no reply to those comments, which infuriated him, so much so, that he declared that he now considers himself at war with us. He then ordered that I leave his kingdom forthwith, also demanding that we remove all of our forces from the frontier. Only if Mundus's army returned to its winter camp, would he consider the matter over."

Peter paused and allowed his words to sink in with the council, giving us time to understand what had happened. The silence which followed his statement reverberated around the chamber. After a short pause, he continued, "The result, gentlemen, is that the first part of the campaign has failed to force Theodatus to hand over his throne to us, let alone Southern Italy. I also failed to find any barbarian willing to mount a challenge to Theodatus. It's my consideration that Theodatus, by taking such a hard line in killing Amalasuntha and the young heir as well as defying you, Basileus, has actually for the first time in many years, managed to unite the Gothic nobility behind the throne."

Peter sat down and finished his wine, keeping his eyes on the goblet rather than looking around at us. He had failed in part of his plan, but deep down, I wondered how much he ever thought he would achieve with the barbarians. Mundus and I had both suspected that we would have to fight, and it looked like we were going to have our turn shortly. All the time the Prefect sat silently. Justinian, out of all of us, didn't look shocked or even surprised. I imagined that Peter had already prepared him, and together they had already moved to the next stage. Peter, I think, was putting on an act for us. Justinian looked around the table at us, thanked Peter for his efforts, and then he spoke.

"So far, so good. I didn't expect Theodatus to be so resolute. No matter, we will now move onto the second phase of the campaign. Peter will be basing himself in Dyrrhachium, so to be close to Mundus and able to cross back into Italy when Theodatus recalls him. Peter, I believe you visited with Mundus on your way back to us?"

Peter nodded and took his cue. "I met with General Mundus, and he reports that the field army is up to strength and he is ready to advance in either late March or April."

"Good, and if God allows it, by Easter, he should be advancing into

Gothic territory." Justinian paused, then announced to all of us. "Peter, before you leave for Moesia, I will have written orders for Mundus ready. I want you to deliver them to him personally with my compliments. Tell him we will all be awaiting his achievements."

"Yes, Basileus."

Justinian then turned to look directly at me and said, "Belisarius, how goes it for you?"

"Basileus, the fleet has been recalled and will be assembled in the Golden Horn by May. I have assembled my command and drafts from the field army will be made ready to take up positions in camps outside of the city in the spring. John's office has already assembled enough logistic support for a campaign of six months."

John the Prefect remained motionless at the table at the mention of his name.

"Belisarius, how many soldiers will you have when you sail?"

"I'll have two thousand two hundred infantry, one thousand five hundred cavalry. I have also expanded my guard to two thousand men. Solomon in Carthage will send me three hundred Berbers once I am ashore. I have also hired three thousand Isaurians and two hundred Huns. With engineers and command and support staff, I'll have a force of about ten thousand men, enough to take Sicily."

"Good, has John assigned any staff to you? To assist with logistical problems?"

"Yes, he has, I have had no problems with the assistance from the prefect's office, Basileus."

Justinian then turned to look at John. His face had changed since we had entered the chamber. "John, any problems?"

Only now did the prefect smile as he replied. "Yes, Basileus. The continued revolt by some of the Berbers in Africa has reduced the amount of taxation I expected to receive this year. I expect a lower amount next year as well. This will pose problems if the campaign continues into the following year. I wanted to send Belisarius's money directly from Africa, to speed up the process, but the problems there may mean a delay as I may need to send money to him from other provinces. On top of this, the continued gold payments to the Persians, had already dented our reserves. And the subsequent payment to the Franks has made matters a little worse. I may not be able to pay for two armies next year unless I can make up for the shortfall. I propose that as soon as Sicily is returned to us, I introduce, as speedily as possible, the current system of taxation to the island, this should help to reduce the current and estimated deficit, my Basileus."

So, this was why John was being so helpful to me — he just saw Sicily as another land to tax to death. Of course, underlying all this was the unspoken truth that Justinian's building programme for the capital was proving more expensive than expected. No one, not even John, was prepared to cross him over this. I replied indirectly to John.

"Basileus, if we treat the Sicilians like that, they will not be willing to assist us. We are desperately going to need their co-operation once we are in control. I would ask that such measures be only slowly introduced as the island recovers from Gothic domination."

John's face remained stoic, and he said nothing, Justinian instead replied.

"Belisarius and John, I will consider the matter once we are in control of Sicily. Gentlemen, thank you for attending the meeting." He stood up, we followed and bowed as he turned to head back to his apartment, accompanied by both Peter and John. The meeting was over, and I clearly realised that John had won that round. I returned home and was escorted through the now-busy streets by my guards.

By the beginning of April, my command staff was assembled at my house, which had now become my headquarters till we sailed. Peter continued to supply me with whatever information he could glean from Italy. We now had a working knowledge of the Gothic garrisons on the island, and with that, we could begin to plan in more detail our invasion. So far it appeared that only the major ports had a garrison of any size and Palermo had the largest.

I planned to land the fleet in the bay of Catania, as the shoreline was clearly undefended, and the size of the bay could easily accommodate the whole of my fleet. More importantly, Mount Etna marked the northern end of the bay. It was clearly visible out at sea and would thus act as a natural marker to assist in our landing.

We would be sailing directly from Greece to Sicily, avoiding Italy. The element of surprise would be maintained the longer we avoided coming into view of the coast. Although I had given the impression to Justinian and company that the campaign would be easy, I had lingering doubts, so I decided to include more engineers. History had taught me that Sicily had never been an easy option. Syracuse, the largest city and port, always had been the hardest nut to crack. The Athenians, under Nicias, had failed, but a Roman army under Marcellus, after a prolonged siege, had finally taken the city. The city's defences then were formidable, but it needed a huge garrison to defend the walls properly. The Goths lacked the manpower to defend the city adequately, but it was the conditions of the walls that really concerned me, and hence my reason for deciding to bring the extra talent for breaking them with me.

In the middle of April, the first dispatches arrived from Mundus via Justinian's office. From them, I learnt that he had crossed into Dalmatia at the start of the month. Heavy rain had slowed his advance at the start, but with a break in the weather, he was making better time. He had already defeated a small Gothic garrison that had tried to block his advance on Split. Peter also sent word that Mundus's advances had drawn what remained of the Gothic reserves from Ravenna towards Dalmatia. This meant that the Gothic garrison on Sicily would have no reinforcements available to call on when we attacked. But there was bad news as well. He had heard rumours that Theodatus had undermined the Frankish alliance. Apparently, Theodatus, if the rumours were correct, had offered the Franks what remained of the Gothic land in Southern Gaul in exchange for their military support if we invaded Italy. These were what was left of the old provinces of Gallia Narbonensis and Alpes Cottiae. Peter reported that he was trying to verify the rumours, but the ban on his entry to Italy was hindering his mission as he was unable to speak to his church sources, who would know what was being hatched in both courts. From all of this, it seemed that Theodatus feared Mundus's advance and was concentrating his forces to deter him, which was in my favour, as they had no idea that I was going to land in Sicily.

With my preparations now complete and the forces assembling at the capital, I had a little more time for the family. I took advantage of the warmer morning to walk around the city and clear my mind after evenings spent entertaining my officers or court officials. The early mists from the sea quickly evaporated as the sun rose earlier each morning. I aimed to catch that period of the day, just after the mist had cleared and before the sun's heat built up, to stroll down to the water's edge. The air was fresh and smelled of the sea, the poor fished at this time of the morning, they knew the best places and crowded around those spots. Wooden poles with bait dangling by string were hung over the surface of the water. Every now and again, a pole was whipped skywards, and out popped a fish dangling from the string. The owner quickly grabbed it, and he was off to his meagre lodging to cook it for himself or his family. His place was instantly taken by another man. Once the heat arrived, the men moved down to the markets looking for work or to the building sites. Come evening, they would return to fish for more food.

Antonina began to accompany me on these strolls, which entailed bringing a few guards with us. I then avoided the fishermen and headed out to the gardens and parkland which lay between the main walls and the old walls of Constantine. We both enjoyed viewing the spring flowers and the crops bursting into life and producing their bounty. This was best seen just before the mist lifted when the flowers would be coated with a silvery layer of moisture. Any later and it would have gone, walking through it left a trail of dark patches where we knocked off the moisture. Once summer arrived, there would be no more of the silver coating as the sun would rise too early to allow the mist to settle. Those were enjoyable times we grabbed each morning that late spring.

With the time rapidly approaching for our departure, Antonina hit my purse hard as she made her preparations for the campaign. While I worked on the final details, she and the family went into the markets looking for whatever she thought would be necessary for living in Sicily. Slowly, one room of the house became packed with chests full of whatever it was she was buying in the markets. She became her own quartermaster, packing and repacking her supplies and then buying more and filling another chest. She intended to make herself as comfortable as possible, not only on the voyage but in our new *palace* in Sicily. She hadn't decided if it should be in Syracuse or Catania.

It had been hot, all day. Finally, the sun began to dip towards the west. A cooling breeze began to slide in from the Golden Horn; the air in the house became a little more bearable. Living on the estate in Asia, I had forgotten how uncomfortable summer could be in the capital in

Europe. The month of May tended to get hotter as we moved through it, till June heralded full summer and the intense heat that would last till the autumn. Only the outbreak of a storm could ease the plight and smell of the city. So far, no storms, just hot and humid air. I dismissed my staff around noon, as it was too uncomfortable to work in the house. So, instead, we started meeting at dawn, which had ended my early morning strolls; they were also becoming too early even for me. The meetings had become informal, as the planning was complete, and now we awaited the first of the transports, which was due to dock anytime. It would then be loaded with the dry stores, food for both men and animals. The warships were here already and had looked after themselves. Now all that was needed was prolonged calm weather, and the loading of men and supplies could proceed at pace.

I had found a nice couch on which to rest during the afternoons. It lay in the only bit of shade in the small area of a garden. Space was a premium in this part of the city. The soil was dry, the flowers seemed to survive somehow, and insects flew around them, but the best was watching the small hummingbirds as they appeared to stand in the air as they picked at the flowers. Below, where the foundations of the house met the ground, an ant hole had been opened. The ants were busy scampering in and out in relays as they gathered whatever food they could find. I wondered if the lizards fed on the ants — they sat around the garden or on the walls soaking up the sunlight, never seeming to eat.

A shout came from within the house. My name was being called repeatedly by one of the servants. The sound of hobnailed boots on the stone announced the imminent arrival of either one of my guards or a soldier. I looked up from my observations of the ants and lizards towards the house. I could see one of my guards walking with purpose in my direction. I stood up and walked towards him. When he saw me, he saluted and informed me that a messenger from the palace had announced that the Basileus required my presence. I told him to inform the messenger that I would be on my way shortly. I entered the house to find Antonina and Zenobia chatting in the anteroom. I excused myself from their planned evening of socializing. After making my apologies, I kissed them goodbye. I had already ordered my guard to assemble a detachment to accompany me to the palace. Now the guard was calling for me, as they were ready to go.

We rode to the palace as the message was urgent. The streets were full of people out again after surviving the heat of the afternoon. Being on horseback was a good choice as we made better progress as people don't like offending horses, as they do men. I entered the palace and was, as usual, escorted to the Imperial apartments and Justinian's office. Inside he was waiting for me, seated at his desk, which was always covered in the documents he was working his way through. He looked up and smiled as I paid him homage and went over to him at his desk.

"My dear Belisarius, thanks for coming so quickly. I have just received two pieces of good news. One is from Mundus, and I think you would want to hear this straightaway."

I did and remained standing in front of his desk.

"Mundus is pleased to announce that he has completed his capture of Split, and the fleet has joined him there. Peter has also informed him that a large Gothic army is on the move out of Northern Italy and is almost certainly marching towards him. Mundus says he intends to seek battle with the Goths and is marching north to intercept them. This, he says, will make your task even easier."

"That's excellent news, Basileus. But anything from Peter regarding Theodatus's real intentions?"

"That's my second piece of good news. Theodatus has begged Peter to return to Italy and speak with him at once. Peter says that he believes that Theodatus should be left to stew. He thinks if he were really desperate, then he would have also mentioned his intentions to abide by our agreement. Peter has also asked that he only return to Italy after your landing in Sicily. I think he is right this time about Theodatus. What do you think?"

"I agree with your decision, and as far as the campaign has progressed, Theodatus does not yet appear amiable. But if Mundus defeats his army and I succeed in Sicily, then he will agree to your terms."

"Unfortunately," said Justinian, pausing, as he pondered the rest of his response.

I also realised that, so far, the campaign had produced very little in the way of forcing Theodatus to come to terms. Would it have been better just to have had Mundus and I attack, then begin negotiations?

Justinian continued, "The campaign, so far, has failed to have any effect on Theodatus. So, you must now attack Sicily. I note the fleet is almost assembled and your allied troops have arrived. To promote secrecy, I will have it known that your mission is to Africa and the completion of your conquest and destruction of the Berber revolt."

"Yes, Basileus, it would seem the most plausible reason for the assembly of an expeditionary army. Only my staff know the real target, and that's how it will stay till we reach Catania."

Justinian waved his hand at me to signal the interview was at an end. I bowed and said, "Thank you, Basileus, I will bring you Sicily and hopefully Southern Italy the next time we meet." I finished with a bow and left the room and returned with my guard to our house in the capital.

Antonina finally finished her packing on the twentieth of June, and her baggage was taken to the flagship and stowed, ready for our departure the next day. We were both invited to the palace that evening for an informal evening meal with the Imperial couple. By then, the army would have finished embarking and all that would remain to do the next day was for us to board and catch the morning tide and wind.

The meal was highly enjoyable and the company, as always, most pleasant. Once we had finished eating, Theodora and Antonina left us to discuss the forthcoming invasion. Justinian and I both relaxed on a pair of couches once they had left.

"Belisarius, while we are in private, please no longer address me so formally. Justin will suffice, after all, we have been friends for many years, have we not?"

"Yes, Basili… I mean Justin," I replied.

"Good. I received a dispatch from Peter today. He informs me that the Franks have betrayed us. They have sided with the Goths in exchange for the land. But most importantly for you, there is no Gothic army south of the River Rubicon. Mundus is proving the greatest threat to the Goths."

"That is the best news I could take with me. That means the Sicilian garrisons will now know they are on their own. Theodatus can't help them, even once we land it will take him weeks to send troops to the island. But he can't if Mundus appears ready to strike towards Ravenna.

When Mundus defeats the Gothic army, Theodatus may even be forced to recall his garrisons from Sicily to help defend the north. He will also be forced to call in the Franks. Those thankless barbarians might even decide to snatch more territory rather than help him. In any event, the conquest of Sicily seems assured, and Southern Italy looks inviting."

"Well, I think all that is left is to wish you every success. It occurs to me that you might even be in Rome this time next year. Can you imagine that? Rome, our ancient capital back within the fold again after all this time. The Empire almost whole once again. God willing." Justinian and I were both quiet after his last comment. If we only had more troops, then we could possibly cross into Southern Italy at the same time as we were completing the reduction of Sicily. Perhaps we were both thinking the same thoughts. Then the conversation started again, and we talked about old times, such as when we used to visit the inn and our girlfriends. Then, Theodora and Antonina returned as if on cue, and the dinner party broke up. We made our informal goodbyes and headed home for our last night in the capital.

Chapter Thirteen

As the sun slowly descended on its voyage into the night, we had our first sight of Sicily. A small column of wispy white smoke rising gently upwards on the horizon announced clearly the presence of Etna and our landing site. The smoke contrasted with the brightly glowing red sky as the sun bid a final farewell to the world. The sky gradually grew dark as we continued our course westward — by dawn, we would be off the coast of Sicily.

I went back to my cabin to have supper with Antonina. I opened the door to our cabin Antonina looked relaxed, reclining on the bed. She gently picked at a dish of fish, and her scowl expressed her feelings for the mouthful she had just consumed. One of utter distaste. Once she had swallowed, she quickly washed her mouth with a glass of wine and then forced the next morsel of fish into her delicate mouth. She looked up from her unpleasant task and forced a smile at me.

"Looks good, the fish," I said in a jovial voice. She looked at me as if I was completely mad.

"No. I am sick and tired of dried fish, salted fish, smoked fish. For two weeks that's all we have had to eat, apart from those biscuits."

"Well, I have some good news," I said with a smile, as I considered playing with my current information and seeing just what mood she was really in.

"Tell me then what news have you?" she said in that disinterested way of hers.

"Ah. I expect payment first before I reveal my news."

She looked at me, her eyes tightened into their sockets, her mouth also changed shape, and there was no trace of a smile on her face. She was certainly in no mood to be toyed with, and yet I couldn't resist toying with her a little bit. "No, I can't, you will have to force it out of me after you have finished your fish supper."

The remains of the fish still attached to the plate sailed in a graceful arc towards me. I stepped to the side, and it continued its path, all the time dropping flakes of fish as it turned and twisted in the air, finally crashing to the floor in the corridor. I dived towards the bed and caught her around the waist, and we both rolled around the bed. I tickled her till she screamed for mercy. I stopped, and she grabbed my left ear in one hand and my other ear in her right, and she twisted both till I pleaded for mercy.

"Only if you reveal your news," she said triumphantly.

"All right, let go," I pleaded. She released my reddening and throbbing ears. She always had a vicious ability to find any bit of flesh, lock on, and make it hurt. "Tomorrow, we land in Sicily."

She let out a whoop of joy and kissed my sore ears, I twisted around, and instead of my ears, she was kissing my face.

With the aid of a breeze and the tide, we were gently moved closer to the sandy shore. The sun behind us lit up the beach, making the sand glimmer. Everyone was on deck, watching the coastline as it crept closer. The waves flowed with us, each with a light coating of froth as they swept us along, then left us and headed towards the beach. Gulls circled us, hoping we were fishing boats and they would soon eat. They were right. The captain ordered all the remaining stocks of fish to be thrown over the side, rather than have to dig holes to bury them once we had landed. Ahead, Mount Etna stood to our right, a massive peak still with a coating of snow at its summit even in summer. Slightly to our right and below the bulk of the mountain, lay the city of Catania. A few fishing boats were within sight of us. They made no effort to approach and instead continued with their tasks.

We entered the bay, and behind the beach, the plain of Catania, with a layer of green, was now clearly visible. We could now easily see our landing site with the mouth of what should be the River Simeto, pinpointing the location. One of my commanders, Constantius, stood next to me. He was around the same age as me. He was a native of the capital, and his family had a long history of military service. He was well built, fit and had the look of a native of the capital with dark hair and olive skin and deep-set brown eyes. He had joined my staff in the capital on the recommendation of Mundus, as had several other commanders.

"Constantius, I want you to take command of the beachhead and have a camp set up as soon as you can."

"Yes, General." He turned and headed to the centre of the ship and then down the gangway, while a small rowing boat was lowered down to meet him. A crew followed him, and they boarded the boat and made for the beach. Once ashore, he would start the process of unloading the transports. I looked around and spotted Bessas. He was a tough, fierce Thracian, shorter than me, but heavier built, with arms like the branches of an old tree. He wore his long red hair up and with a reddish-grey beard, he looked more like a barbarian than a Roman commander. With him was Peranius, a prince from one of the many royal families of Caucasian Iberia. He had been attached to me by Justinian as he needed to learn the art of war before returning home. He held himself with some esteem — his clothing was refined, and he looked like a prince. For all that, he had a good reputation as a fighter. He had the region's thick dark wavy hair and a small beard centred on his chin. They were quite a pair, the complete opposite of each other.

"Bessas, when we are ashore, I want you to organise the engineers and their artillery, so it's ready to use as soon as the army is ashore and ready for combat. Peranius, you take two companies of cavalry and follow the river upstream till you find a ford or a bridge. Take control of it and report back to me. Then send out scouts and see what they can learn, especially about any Gothic troops in the area." They both saluted and asked the captain to prepare a boat for them to be taken ashore. They did not have to wait long as the need for a small boat was curtailed by the sounds and shudder of the ship rolling up the sandy and gravelly beach. Then the ship made one last heavy jolt, and it announced we had arrived on the shore of Sicily.

We were still a little short of the beach. A ramp was dropped from the front of the ship, and it splashed into the surf and dipped under the surface. A few sailors headed down the ramp, carrying cables and stakes. The water reached up to their waists, and they struggled for a short distance, then the height of the water rapidly dropped, and they were on the sandy beach. The cables were laid out and run back up to the ship while the dry ends were attached to stakes freshly hammered into the beach. A small detachment of my guard made their way down the ramp, carrying their armour in bundles on their heads and made their way ashore. Bessas and Peranius followed suit as other ships came ashore and were similarly tied up, and then began unloading. This was one landing in which I had no fear of an enemy fleet intercepting us, as what was left of the Gothic fleet had gone north into the Adriatic in an attempt to hinder Mundus. Antonina joined me on deck, we both looked at the now-busy beach as men and horses were unloaded. The horses were carefully walked down the ramps and taken up the beach and rapidly corralled in the green grass.

"Well, my love, welcome to Sicily," I said.

"Thank you. If you don't mind, my darling, I'll stay on board till our household is established in the camp."

"In that case, I will see you later when you come ashore. Now it's my turn to go ashore." I kissed her goodbye. Removing my boots and hanging them around my shoulders, I began my descent — everyone else so far had made it look easy. Well, it was, until I stood on the ramp and felt it moving up and down in the surf, I felt a bit unsteady. Memories of the earlier incident of using a ramp like this flooded back and hindered me for a moment. I hurried down it and into the warm water. It was quickly up around my waist as a wave washed around me, and I felt myself slightly lifted off my feet for a moment. My feet touched down onto the soft sand. I was able to walk with some effort, till the height of the water dropped below my knees. Then it became easy, and I was out of the surf and onto dry land again. Bessas was waiting for me, along with my guards. They were putting on boots or other articles of clothing they had carried onto the beach. The scene around me was remarkedly relaxed for an invasion of an enemy shore.

I sat down on the beach and put my dry boots on, a bit pointless as everything below my chest was wet. Once I was ready, I walked over to Bessas and my guards who all stood ready. Even though it was midday and hot, the transports and my men continued with their work. I turned to Bessas after surveying the scene.

"How goes it with the engineers and artillery?"

"General, they are already ashore and have begun assembling their equipment, ready to move."

I nodded my head firmly and then I looked around and saw Constantius approaching me, a big grin on his face.

"Constantius, how long before the rest of the army is ashore?"

"By noon tomorrow, as long as the tides are smooth. The camp should be ready by tonight," Constantius replied.

"Has Peranius gone on patrol yet?" I asked.

"Yes, General, he took the first group of horses and mounted up and was away soon after he came ashore," he replied.

"Well, I don't know about you, but I could do with some shelter, that sun reminds me of Africa."

"General, your tent awaits. If you'd follow me."

We all set off following behind Constantius, who led us to the outline of a marching camp. A light barricade had been assembled along the perimeter, using whatever was available. Only a few tents had been set up within the perimeter, and in the centre of the camp lay a group of tents and one of those should be mine. Constantius led us to the central one. A table had been found along with a number of chairs. My guards assumed sentry duty around the tent, while the rest of us went in under the shade and sat down.

"Gentleman, so far we have met no resistance or any sign of it. I intend to move from here within two days. We will take Catania as soon as possible. I intend to make it my headquarters and station the fleet there. The last intelligence I had on the city was that there is a small garrison and the city's walls are in bad condition. Parts of the city are also in disrepair. I understand the mountain had erupted when the city was still in our hands; the ground shook and did all the damage. The Goths hadn't bothered to do any repairs. So, Constantius, once we enter the city, I want you to survey it with the engineers and see what needs repairing first. Bessas, I want you to lead the column with the artillery in front. That should put the fear of God into any thoughts the Goths might have about resisting us. The road should be in a reasonable condition, judging by what we found in Africa. Send word to the fleet to blockade Catania and Syracuse. In the meantime, I'll wait to hear what Peranius has for us." I paused. I looked around the table. Everyone looked keen and eager. So far, we had no problems, and this gave them confidence in me and the plan. "When Peranius returns, I need a large cavalry force ready for him to lead. Then I want him to ride north, bypass Catania and layup till the next morning. He will then advance south along the road to

Catania, as we advance up the road. That should complete the surprise. If word gets out of the city to the rest of the island, they will be confused as to how many there are of us and where exactly we landed."

"General, what if we or Peranius make contact with any Gothic forces before we reach the city?" Bessas had been nodding along before he gave a soft cough in consideration. His words encouraged Constantius also to look curious as I responded.

"Fight and destroy them. If there are too many, don't risk a defeat and pull back to the main force." I then turned and looked at Constantius. "That goes for you as well, no heroics and no setbacks. We have surprise still, and we need to keep them guessing till it is too late for them to do anything about us."

Antonina came ashore that evening, and I escorted her from the beach up to the camp and then onto our tent. Her household had already arrived and unpacked fast and made up the interior of the tent as per instructions. We entered, and the floor was covered in heavy rugs and was very comfy underfoot. Couches had been assembled and made a very comfortable bed.

We decided to sit on the floor with a small table between us; there wasn't much to eat yet, a few biscuits and stale wine were on the table and looked a pretty miserable fare. We both looked a bit despondent at the table, somehow once on dry land one expected the food to improve. It was at that moment that Peranius, Constantius and Bessas entered the tent. They were carrying baskets of food and wine. Peranius grimaced at the sight of the food on the table and said, "First, get a servant to clear that muck from your table. Here. Here. Servants clear this away." At the sound of his royal and commanding voice, servants rushed in and cleared the table. Peranius, Constantius and Bessas sat down beside us and placed the contents of the baskets on the table. It was soon stacked with bread, cheeses and dried meats. The wine was in small clay containers with rope tied around the top, allowing them to be easily carried. Peranius spoke again. "Belisarius and the Lady Antonina, we couldn't let your first night ashore go uncelebrated. So, we found local wine and food for you to enjoy."

"Thank you, you all must stay and enjoy the meal with us. I won't hear no from you," Antonina spoke first and in that sweet voice of hers.

She slapped her hands together several times, and the servants reappeared as she gave them instructions. Couches were found and brought in, and goblets were also obtained and filled with the local wine. We sat around eating and drinking as Peranius informed me that they had seen no sign of the Goths and the locals were overjoyed to see a Roman army here again. They had heard about Africa and wondered if they would be released from the barbarian captors. He was happy to lead the cavalry the next day north of the city.

The wine flowed freely, gradually, we all relaxed, and we began to learn more about our colleagues. Peranius informed us that he had lost everything eleven years ago when the Persians swept through and destroyed all vestige of the pro-Roman aristocracy in his part of the Kingdom of Iberia lying on the eastern shore of Pontus Euxinic. He had fled into the mountains and spent the next six months making his way north, first to the Pontus Euxinic and then along the coastline, till he reached a Roman trading post and had been able to take a ship to the capital. Since then, he had served in the army and gradually been promoted.

Bessas had a similar upbringing to mine, except his family wasn't as wealthy. He had started his military service in the frontier troops. He'd proved himself more than capable, and his local commander thought he was wasted on the frontier and sent him to the field army. From there, he worked his way up the ranks. Later, he had commanded the field army of Thrace, before being sent to the capital and then onto my command. Constantius admitted that his rise to prominence had a lot to do with his family name and whom he was related to. He had begged to serve on my staff as he saw it as his only chance to prove his ability, under a commander who was well known for rewarding ability, not birth. The talk moved onto war and tales of individual bravery. At this point, Antonina excused herself and went to bed. We continued talking well into the night when finally, tiredness and wine forced an end to our chatter.

The sun was already creeping further into the cobalt-blue clear sky, breathing its heat down onto the already parched Sicilian plain. The heat of the Sicilian summer, even this early in the day, rivalled any heat the Syrian desert could produce. Dust filled the air and got into my clothing and then into every crease of my skin, making me feel even drier than the landscape. We had begun assembling at dawn, and finally, we moved out of the camp for the short journey up the road to Catania. We filled not only the road but either side of it. Ahead, dominating the horizon, the snow-tipped might of smoky Etna, and below in its shadow lay our destination.

So far, I had received no word from Bessas at the head of the column, which meant everything was going to plan. The pace of the column increased with the distance from the camp as the column found its length and adjusted itself. Peranius had also reported no problems so far, and the fleet had completely blockaded the port. Now it was up to the defenders of Catania as to what happened next. The camp had already been collapsed, and wagons had been "requisitioned" from local farms to enable it to be moved with us. I remained at the rear of the column with my guards. Behind us came Antonina who had decided to ride on a wagon with her household, as it was her time of the month. She had lost her humour since last night, and during this time, she was prone to mood swings, so I tended to agree to whatever she had in mind as it saved an argument.

The front of the column reached the city's walls and main gate a little after noon and halted. The rest of the column moved up the road and then dispersed around the accessible sections of the perimeter of the city. Bessas sent word of the situation, and I rode with my guards to his position. The infantry, with little to do, had moved off the road and stood facing the city wall, outside of bow range. While they waited, they took the chance to eat and drink. There was an air of anxiety, as well as expectation, in the faces of the men I passed on the road. None of us knew if we would be fighting to get into the city or if the gates would be flung open, and in we would march. I preferred the latter option — it was the easiest and spared bloodshed on both sides.

Before we could reach Bessas, the mood of the men in front of us changed, and they became very excited. They pushed and shoved their way to where I had been forced to halt with my guards. They began clapping, cheering and waving spears and bows in the air. Shouts of congratulations filled my ears, but in all the excitement, I could not make out what was being said. I had no idea as to why, all of a sudden, excitement gripped the men, and by now, there was no point in trying to force my way through my own men, so I called a halt to our progress. I removed my helmet, so I could hear a little better what was being shouted. Above the din, I could hear my name being shouted by a familiar voice. I looked around for the speaker, and it was then I saw Bessas. Pushing his way forward through the men, his horse acting like a battering ram to any who refused to budge, he was waving his free arm in the air in an effort to catch my attention. He finally made his way to me, gingerly avoiding a few of the more reckless spears waving in the air in front of him. He got within shouting distance of me and bellowed, "My lord, Belisarius, the city is ours."

"What you say, the city, the city is what?" I shouted back, leaning as far towards him as I dared.

"Yes, yes, the city of Catania is ours. They surrendered to us without a fight."

"Is Peranius inside the city?" I managed to catch that but still had to holler my questions back and strain to hear the next part.

"Yes, he took the surrender from the city elders."

"Great, go back to him and have him signal the fleet to enter the harbour. Then I will enter once we have our men better organised." I took the greetings from the soldiers gathered around me, shook hands with any hands that were thrust towards me, and patted shoulders for a good part of the afternoon. I was glad that I had brought one of my own horses with me, the Arabian stood her ground well, even under all the pressure of the men pushing and shoving to get close to me. Eventually, the officers and senior non-commissioned officers regained order and had the men line up in companies. Once order had returned, I moved to the head of the column. The artillery had been unloaded and looked strangely out of place now as the city gate stood open, and no defenders looked down on us from the shabby walls. I turned and addressed those troops close enough to hear me, and slow enough for my words to be passed back to those who couldn't directly hear.

"God has been kind to us today and granted us the city of Catania. This is the first of many victories we will have together, and I promise to share with you my victories, as long as you follow my orders. Now we will enter the city in an orderly manner as liberators of the people, not conquerors. You will march in through this gate, then out of the city by the north gate, and you will camp outside the city. Fresh supplies will be brought to you. Only those who I order will be allowed to enter the city."

I waited while my message was carried down the column, then I turned and ordered the advance in through the city gates. The walls of the city rose to a good height and were dotted with the normal number of protruding turrets. Unlike the bricked walled cities in the East, here the walls were made from local cut stone. Inside, the city's buildings were also made from the same stone, very little brickwork was to be seen. But the damage the city had suffered all those years ago was clear — even the walls had one or two very large cracks running up their face. Many of the municipal building showed signs of these cracks too.

Following the main road in the city, I saw the stadium and then the forum, where Constantius and Peranius had formed up some of their cavalry in a guard of honour, ready to welcome me into the centre of the city. They looked impressive. The sun made their armour shine every time a horse or rider moved. The troopers sat smartly at attention with lances held vertically and shields strapped to their left sides each with their unit's distinct insignia displayed in bright colours. Around the square, some of the more curious of the inhabitants had come out to watch the spectacle. Others, I imagined, had locked themselves inside, fearing the worst from a conquering army. There was silence as I entered the forum, apart from the noise of the horses. I dismounted and walked over to where Peranius and Constantius and now Bessas stood waiting for me, alongside them stood the usual group of well-dressed city dignitaries. My officers saluted, and I saluted back, Bessas stepped forward and turned and pointed to the civic leaders.

"Consul Belisarius, may I present the elders of the Roman city of Catania."

"Thank you, General Bessas." I paused, then moved closer to the group of men. "In the name of Justin son of Justin, Emperor of the Romans, I welcome you back to the fold. I wish that you all continue in your present positions and reform a city council. I am governor here, on behalf of the emperor. Roman law and order is restored to you, and of course, final appeal is with the Senate and emperor. Now to business gentlemen. I require from you: accommodation, food, and other supplies for my army, as well as any information you may have on the Gothic garrison of the island."

The best dressed of the elders, who was about my age, acted as their spokesman and stepped forward to address me.

"My lord, we are only too pleased to feed and accommodate your officers and supply your men outside of the city. As to the Gothic garrison, it fled on the day you landed and headed inland towards Palermo, which is their main base on the island." The rest of the group nodded in agreement, and the speaker continued, "My lord, we have been expecting you and have prepared a feast in celebration of our return to the Roman fold. My home is your home for as long as you need it."

"Gentlemen, I am honoured by your kindness, and I will try and make my stay as short as possible, till suitable accommodation can be found for my officers and my household. Thank you for your kindness."

All the time, I wondered why they hadn't sent a messenger to welcome us straight into the city once the Goths had fled. Again, I suppose it was fear of the unknown. How would we react? Would we plunder the city? But, with their pandering to us, I wasn't overly concerned about their actions. We had the city and were safe on the island.

The feast continued into the night; it was good to eat freshly cooked food again, even fish. Antonina seemed to be cheered by her arrival into the city and a real bed to sleep in. After all, she was now being treated as a consul's wife, which made her the most important woman on the island. When we finally reached the bedchamber, for a chamber was what it was, it was huge, airy and cool. Antonina almost cooed with delight as she moved around the luxury room and finally laid on the bed. It was covered with skins — even a lion skin was draped at the foot of the bed. She leapt on it and wrapped herself in it and pretended to growl like a lioness. A breeze full of scents, accompanied by coolness, flowed in from the open windows. I left the drapes open as the air was pleasant compared to what we had been through during the day. We both relaxed on the bed, and soon, moonlight cast a silvery veil through the windows, and it was so bright, that we blew out the lamps as there was no need for their light. The room was like a piece of heaven compared to the previous months. I don't remember who fell asleep first, but it was one of the most comfortable night's sleep, I ever had in Sicily.

I awoke to the sound of gulls flocking over the harbour, a slight smell of sulphur in the air reminded me that Etna was close by. If it was calm, then there was no smell, but when it was angry, the smell came. Ash and dust could follow if the wind was in the right direction to blow it down from the mountain. Antonina was still asleep next to me, so I left the bed carefully, so as not to disturb her, and tiptoed over to the open window. I thought I might close them to allow her to sleep longer. I glanced out of the window, and over to the right, I could just see the harbour. The gulls were swooning over the houses and dropping down into the water looking for food. Then they would suddenly rise above the houses and buildings with food in their beaks, only to be attacked by other birds in an effort to seize the food. I suspected that the first catch of the day had arrived, and the fishermen were in the harbour gutting their catch ready for the market.

I could have watched the aerial warfare all morning, but I had work. I quietly left the room and found a servant who took me down to the luxurious bathhouse. For non-Goths, these people seemed to live very well and would easily slot into the niche the rich of the capital existed in. I enjoyed a good scrub, and a fresh uniform was ready for me when I was dried. My guards were already billeted in part of the house and were waiting for me when I emerged into the courtyard. I decided to take a brief tour of the city, and a detachment of my guard accompanied me towards where I thought the harbour might be. Catania was alive already, the inhabitants, after a quick glance at us, paid little attention from then on. Instead, they got on with their lives, much the same as they had under the Goths. The buildings ended abruptly and there we were standing on the quay, and in front of us, filling part of the harbour, was part of the fleet. The transports now floated high in the water as they were now devoid of cargo. A few warships were tied up, and one was being dragged out of the water, ready to be inspected and, probably, repaired. Part of the fleet I knew was outside of Syracuse, and the rest were in the bay. I had already dispatched three back to the Greek mainland with dispatches informing Justinian of our safe arrival and capture of Catania.

My nose caught the smell of freshly cooking fish, I hadn't eaten since last night, and the smell made me feel very hungry. I followed my nose and came upon a group of fishermen who had a brazier on which they were cooking part of their catch. They looked up at my approach, slightly alarmed at first, then I reassured them that I would like to pay for some of their cooked catch. Their mood changed, and they became friendly and brought another brazier over and began cooking more fish for my guards and me.

"I am General Belisarius and these, my guards." I indicated to the men behind me. "This fish is really good," I said to the fishermen, who smiled in response.

The oldest of the group, stood up and passed more fish over to me and said, "We caught it this morning. Nothing tastes as good as food you have caught and cooked yourself, General."

"Thank you."

We sat down on the quayside and enjoyed a good breakfast, and I chatted with the fishermen. They were relaxed and seemed not to care about who I was. One of the other fishermen, a grey-haired, shrivelled-looking man had been in the sun all his life, and it had semi-cooked his skin, was speaking. I couldn't quite understand what he was saying to us, but a few words sounded familiar. His colleagues nodded in agreement at his sage words. I looked over to the fisherman who had first spoken and said to him, "I don't understand this man, can you tell me what he said?"

The man nodded and spoke to the lizard-like old gentleman, who smiled a knowing look and paused his speech.

"I am sorry, General, he is from the island of Malta, as are some of us, he speaks no Roman, but he says that you must now go to Syracuse. He says the Goths have only a few men there now. Yesterday, when he was there, the fishermen told him that the city is waiting for you to enter. The Goths will run as soon as you approach."

I was shocked by this. Could it be true? The man had no need to lie; no money had been offered to him to induce such a response. Could we be so lucky and walk into the great city of Syracuse virtually unopposed?

"Is he sure of this?" I asked.

The man spoke in the tongue of his island, and the old lizard nodded and spoke more. The translator nodded in agreement as did the rest of the fishermen, then he turned to me.

"Oh yes, General, you can trust him. The Goths are afraid of you. The name Belisarius frightens them. You destroyed the Vandals."

I smiled at that. My guards were also grinning with pleasure at the news they had just heard. I reached into my purse and pulled out several silver coins and gave them to the old dry-skinned fellow. He thanked me profusely and tried to hand the coins back, but I refused and instead gave some more out to the rest of the fishermen. We had found friends, and they knew the waters around the island and would now act as our eyes and ears. So far, the day had been very rewarding. I stood up and left the harbour, my men in tow. Now all I had to do was find our temporary headquarters. I suspected that if we walked back to the forum, it would be close by, or we could find someone to guide us there.

In the forum, we found a sentry who pointed to the old fortress, and we headed for it. I entered through the main gateway and passed a number of soldiers who were unloading carts and taking the contents inside the main building. They saluted as I passed them, and I went into the main building through a well-secured gate and up a stairwell to the main room. Constantius and Bessas were already at work dealing with the logistics of just staying in the city. At the same time, they were arguing the case of the quartermaster with the representatives of the Praetorian prefect who, as per usual, were not happy with any use of monies from the city that the prefect had first call on.

On my arrival, the argument ceased, and the prefect's men left the room, muttering loud enough to be clearly heard, about having to increase taxation to cover the costs of the armies increased need for food. Bessas and Constantius both stood as I entered the room, I signalled for them to sit and joined them at the table. I asked for a map of the eastern side of Sicily, which was brought over, and I laid it out on the table. I pointed on the map to where we were and said, "Gentlemen, we are here." I paused as I moved my hand down to where Syracuse lay, noted the mile references and made a quick calculation. "I have received word that Syracuse is awaiting our presence and that the Goths are afraid of us."

"It would take me a whole day to have the engineers and artillery ready to move. The infantry and cavalry can be ready within hours," Bessas grunted in response.

Constantius had already moved closer to the map and added, "Belisarius, why not send the cavalry by road and put the infantry on the transports along with the artillery and engineers. They could reach the city in hours rather than days if the wind is right."

"Good, that's what I had in mind, a lightning strike south to Syracuse catching the city before any relief force can reach it from Palermo. If God is kind to us, they may well run for it as they did before, otherwise Syracuse is going to be a tough nut to crack. Its defences are still formidable and some of the best, apart from those at the capital. A second easy victory will give us complete control of the east coast and two secure ports to work from. Bessas, organise the fleet and infantry, take only a few hundred and some artillery and engineers, that should speed up your leaving time. Constantius and I will take the cavalry straight to Syracuse. Send word to Peranius to take command here and continue consolidating our position."

They agreed, then Constantius added, "We can be ready by midday if we take your guard and some of the cavalry. The rest can follow."

"The sooner the better. I need to get my armour. I'll meet you back here before midday," I stated, excitement gripping me.

We reached Syracuse that evening and made camp well outside of the walls along the coastal road, close enough for the campfires to be seen from the city. Looking at the cliffs, I realised that the transports would have great difficulty landing here and would have to storm into the harbour to land the infantry. At dawn, part of the fleet reached us and linked up with the ships that had already been blockading the harbour.

We moved down the road in a column till we reached the first fortress which guarded the entrance to the city, as well as the harbour. We weren't challenged as we approached, the gates were unsecured and with effort were swung open by my men. We investigated the fortress. The stables were recently emptied, and the fortress had a ghostly feel to it as if something horrible had appeared and swallowed up the garrison without leaving a trace. Judging by the barracks area, it had hardly been used in years. Maybe a few hundred men had lived inside it, and of them, there was no sign.

We continued on the road, and we reached the last section of the walls and the last gateway into the city proper. The walls were silent and abandoned. This time, the gates were wide open; I sent two scouts ahead to check. They returned shortly with word that the gate was undefended, and we had unhindered access to the city. On the parapet of one of the gate's towers, we could see movement now. Constantius noticed it first and called my attention to it.

"Belisarius, can you see there on the parapet, they seem to be waving something in the air. I can't quite see what it is, can you?"

I looked, but the sun was at the wrong angle and blinded me as I tried to focus on the location. "No, the sun is blocking my view. Let's take a risk and move closer and enter the city and see what happens. So far, no arrows. Do we think the Goths are that clever to risk allowing us to enter the city?"

No one even bothered to react to my comment. I gently eased my mare forward, and the column joined me, my guards, fearful of attack, surrounded me and raised their shields as we entered through the beckoning gate. On the inside, the people on the parapet were now cheering and throwing flowers down over us. I turned to Constantius, who had joined me once my guards had relaxed their shield wall. "God is truly with us this day. Once inside, make your way to the harbour and have the chain dropped, so Bessas and the fleet can dock. Then send a messenger back to Catania with news and order the rest of the army, minus the garrison, to join us here."

"Very good, Belisarius," Constantius was grinning once again, he slapped my shoulder and shouted, so that he could be heard over the noise and excitement of the population.

We moved slowly through the city as the population celebrated our entry and wine, fruit and bread were passed up to us. Eventually, the crowd became too large to try and force our way through so I ordered a halt, and I dismounted, as did the rest of the cavalry. Then we were swamped by the population. My guards quickly moved around me and kept the people at a safe distance. So far, this was the grandest celebration and most welcoming by any liberated city.

Eventually, the usual group of city dignitaries made their careful way through the plebeian mob and halted in front of me. The senior member left the group and made his way to my guards and asked to be allowed to speak to me. I agreed, and the tall, well-dressed man in his fine silks was let through. He had the natural air of one born to wealth and nobility. He carried himself with an air of dignity; his grey hair and beard only reinforced his patrician looks. Then he spoke in clear Roman, without a hint of an accent and said, "Consul Belisarius, I am Timothy of Syracuse. I wish to speak to you."

The name sounded familiar to me, but I couldn't quite place it. Timothy spoke again. "My lord, you sent your legal secretary Procopius to see me when you were last in Sicily."

It all became clear to me, and I remembered exactly who this man was and the importance he played in my campaign in Africa. I moved forward and shook Timothy's now-outstretched arms.

"I am very pleased to meet you. But I was told you were from Chios?"

"My lord, once, now I live here, the city is yours as the Goths ran away last night after they saw your campfires," he stated firmly, and I thanked him for the information. "My lord, will you do me the pleasure of staying in my humble home in the city?"

"Thank you, that would be very kind of you. I am sure we will have much to discuss."

"The men, with me" — he pointed to the group he had approached me with — "they are the leaders of the city and wish to formally surrender the city back into the Empire. They also extend the city's welcome to you and your men."

Timothy turned and led me towards the group who were standing patiently awaiting me. He introduced the group, and the senior one of them handed over to me the symbolic keys to the city.

"My lord, Belisarius, I present you with the keys of our city and thank you for bringing us back to our beloved emperor. The city is yours, and we offer all that we have for you and your men."

"Thank you on behalf of my master, the Emperor of the Romans. He sends you fraternal greetings and welcomes you back into the fold and bosom of the Roman world."

The group escorted me into the city, and a section of my guards followed me. Constantius and the cavalry settled into the welcoming crowd and attempted to make their way to their new barracks. The crowds continued to cheer us as I was led along the main thoroughfare to the palace and our new seat of power. There was so much cheering that I suspected that the civic leaders had organised and paid for the welcome to ingratiate themselves with me. I suppose it worked as I needed willing locals to enable me to return the province to being an integral part of the Empire. For the time being, I was happy with the welcome and allowing these men to run the city and surrounding countryside. It would be up to Justinian and his court how the province would be run in the future. Outside of the palace, the group of elders bowed respectfully to allow me to enter the building first. I bowed back and said to them before I entered, "I wish you to continue to run the city. All the laws of the Goths are to be rendered useless, and the law of the Romans is to be used once again. As soon as I can, I will arrange for a copy of the new laws to be sent to you. Thank you, gentlemen. My quartermasters will no doubt be calling on your assistance soon. I know you will be friendly and helpful to them as you have been to me."

They signalled their agreement and bowed again. I turned, and Timothy followed me into the palace. Once inside the typical government building, I turned to Timothy and said, "I am glad that is over. Will you be kind enough to lead me to your house? I imagine there is another exit from this building?"

Timothy smiled and pointed to a passageway on the far side of the entrance hall. "This way, Belisarius."

We began walking out of the palace in the direction of the harbour. The streets were still filled with revellers enjoying their "liberation". After a short stroll, we came to Timothy's house. It was set back from the street, and we entered through a guarded gateway. My guards followed, and a number joined the guards at the gate. The entrance consisted of a small courtyard with a connected garden in full summer bloom, and a few citrus trees, with developing fruit, lining the path to the house.

The door was opened by several well-dressed servants, and we were led inside to what can only be described as a luxurious villa. Once inside, Timothy directed his servants to show my guards where to stay. Timothy and I were led through the house, out into a partially covered garden. He took me on a short walk on a well-tended path, the stones carefully cut and fitted together. A small fountain marked the centre of the garden;

clear water poured into the collecting bowl beneath. The roof of the villa was designed to slope inwards onto the garden, and a set of piping collected the rain, when it came, and diverted it into the garden. Timothy obviously liked flowers as he proudly showed me those in bloom. He informed me that he personally tended this garden and regarded it as his pride.

Under the Goths, the garden had not interested them as it was unmoveable and not made of gold and silver, which they could take. He had wanted a library, but books were rare and dangerous as the Goths wanted to ensure that only their heretical views should be accessible. The garden, again, offered safety and therefore no threat to the order of things. Timothy pointed to the fountain and pointed out the broken plinth. He thought that a goddess or god had once been mounted on it, but sometime in the past, it had been removed. Tastes had changed with the times, he remarked as he led me under a shaded section where a table and chairs had been set up.

Cool white wine was served, and a bowl of freshly prepared fruit was placed in the centre of the table. We sat in silence. I was still absorbing the beauty of his private garden and the peaceful atmosphere it gave to this section of the house. After a while, I broke the silence. "Timothy, I would like to thank you for your help, but I need to ask for more from you."

"Peter has already been in touch with me and asked me to assist you in any way I can. First, while you are in the city, please use my house as your headquarters. My servants are all trustworthy, and as you may have noticed, it's nice and secluded here."

"Are you sure you don't mind? My wife, Antonina, would really appreciate the offer. Thank you," I stated, a little relieved that she could have somewhere comfortable to rest up and be safe.

"I wouldn't have offered unless I meant it, Belisarius."

"My wife will be here by the end of the week when the rest of the army arrives." I paused for a moment. I preferred Catania, it was less self-important than Syracuse, but this city had the larger port and was closer to Africa and much easier to defend as the walls were in a very good condition and I would prefer to be besieged here rather than in Catania.

Timothy then spoke. "Now to business, Belisarius. My sources tell me that the Gothic commander almost dropped dead when word reached him that you were on the island. Apparently, he met you when you were in Caucana. You seemingly put the fear of God into him."

"You don't mean that wretch of a town governor?" I grimaced, recalling the fellow that had appeared on the boat with us so pompously.

"Yes, the very same. Well, once you took Catania, he really panicked and withdrew all his men to Palermo, and he intends to sit tight till relief is sent from Northern Italy. He is unaware of Mundus's campaign and the lack of any Gothic reserves. So far, I haven't received any word on Theodatus's reaction to your arrival."

"Well, that is good news. I hope Peter is paying you handsomely for your work. You have plenty of connections on the island and the mainland?" I queried.

"Being a merchant, I have agents in all the ports, and I am allowed free movement here on the island and the mainland. I sell luxury goods to the Gothic nobility, and they so desperately want to be like us. So, they need an expert on us, and what better than a Roman merchant. I could sell them anything, if I add that the Romans always had this, wore this or ate this. They wine and dine me in an effort to impress me on how Roman they have become. Their Roman is so poor it makes your ears bleed. With only a little wine, they talk freely and do their best to impress. Those who are a little unwilling suddenly become more willing after a few gifts."

"Corruption is everywhere, luckily for us, especially in the Gothic camp," I added.

Timothy stood up and signalled one of the servants to come and clear the table. "Belisarius, would you like to eat?"

"An excellent idea. It feels like it has been a long day."

Timothy picked up a small bell, I hadn't noticed it, and a servant ran over to him. He spoke casually to the servant. "Tell the steward to prepare some food for the two of us and bring some fresh cold water and wine."

The servant ran off into the house. Timothy then told me about the city and how it had changed under Gothic control. He had obviously researched the subject because once he was done with that, he recounted for me the history of the island since it was colonised by the Greeks. The food arrived later, beautifully cooked lamb, sliced after being roasted over a fire. Fresh bread and a light salad accompanied it and red wine. By the time we were done, the sun had set, and the lamps had been lit. I was full, satisfied with my day, and I made my excuses and was escorted to my room and fell asleep quickly.

Antonina arrived at Timothy's house as expected at the end of the week and easily eased herself and her household into his villa. My command staff also set themselves up in the house. The next day we held our first conference to discuss the next part of our campaign in Sicily. The room had been cleared of all the expensive furniture apart from enough chairs and tables for us and our maps and documents. On the largest wall, I hung a map of the island. Timothy had kindly lent me one of his own. I had placed a marker close to where we were, so we all had an idea of our location on the island. The other marker I placed close to Palermo, so we all knew where the enemy was. I opened the conference.

"Good morning, I hope you had a pleasant time and have enjoyed the delights of Syracuse."

There was a general murmur of agreement from my audience at this comment. I moved over to the wall and began pointing to the locations. "As you can see from the map, we now have complete control of the east coast of Sicily, we control the two main ports, here and here. I have received intelligence on the Gothic defenders—"

"Are we sure the Goths know what island they are supposed to be defending?" a voice called out from among my officers and caused a general outbreak of laughter as he spoke.

Once the laughter ended, I continued, "We have been very lucky so far and have met no resistance from the Goths. There is a good reason for that; their commander has pooled all his forces in an effort to defend the city and port of Palermo. If he manages to hold on to the city and port, he can eventually expect a relieving force to sail and land there. The city's defences are good, and it is not going to be easy to take. Palermo is going to be our next target, and this is how I intend to achieve it. First, Constantius, with half of my guard and half of the cavalry, will return to Catania and then continue up the coast and take Messina. Once you have garrisoned it, you will then move along the coast road to the northern coastline and head west towards Palermo. At each town and city, ensure that enough men are left in each location to secure your route. I am afraid you will have the longest and hardest task of all of us, but I know you are well up to the task. Bessas, I want you to load up all the artillery and engineers onto the fleet and sail along the southern coastline. I have recalled Peranius, and he will be here tomorrow. He will lead the rest of the cavalry along the southern coast road, and you both should meet up and take Lilybaeum. Garrison it, then you and the fleet are to head directly for Palermo. I, in the meantime, will take the rest of my guard and the infantry and march inland directly for Palermo. It should take us about nine days to reach the city. I will surround the city and prepare sites for the artillery. We will then all meet up outside of the city and then lay siege to it, from the land and sea. I hope the city surrenders quickly, but we need to take it before the autumn storms halt our ability to use the sea. Any questions?",

Constantius raised his hand. I nodded, and he spoke, "General, should we encounter resistance, do we stop and clear it up, or bypass it and deal with it later?", it was a good point as I gave a soft sound of approval.

"Constantius, I have it on good authority that there should be none. But if you come across any, deal with it on the spot. If you encounter any, it should be on the roads, making their way towards Palermo. My information is that Messina and Lilybaeum no longer have a Gothic garrison. But you raise a good point, and I am going to alter my plan slightly. We need Messina taken as it stops any Gothic troops crossing from Italy to the island. So, Bessas, you will hold back your departure till Constantius sends word that he has taken the city otherwise you will need to sail to Messina and assist in its capture. Then you can sail to Lilybaeum and then for Palermo." I paused, waiting for any more questions. There was silence. "Gentlemen, I aim to leave within three days. May God grant us a swift victory. Thank you for your time, and I look forward to meeting you all in Palermo. If any problems arise before I leave, come and speak to me at any time."

My officers stood up, and I left the briefing and headed out to the garden. There really wasn't much for me to do now, my officers were now well experienced in preparing their men for the forthcoming adventure. I trusted them to do the job correctly, and by leaving them alone, it gave them more confidence in their own abilities.

The garden was slowly losing its brightness as the last of the summer flowers dropped their petals. While the autumn flowers were still developing, Timothy informed me they would be of much greater colour and smell. The air, meanwhile, around the house was still scented by the citrus trees and their fruit ripening for the second crop. I found a secluded spot and sat on the warm earth and soaked in the calm of the scene around me. I felt a slight chill on the back of my neck, a cool breeze coming from somewhere. Suddenly, it became warm. I turned to see what the cause of the alternating air might be and squatting behind me was Antonina, face tightly contorted in a valiant effort to control her laughing at my predicament. I looked directly into her eyes and made a silly face. The floodgates gave way, and she exploded in laughter that was so infectious that I was caught up in it. We both laughed so much that we ended up rolling on the earth together. Finally, we both managed to control our laughing. I looked at her, and she looked deep into my eyes. I kissed her lips and embraced her, she locked arms around me and returned my affection a thousand-fold. We rolled, intertwined, on the warm earth, under the spreading leaves of a fig tree.

For the first time since we had reached Sicily, it began to rain, and it steadily became heavier. I retreated into the warmth and dryness of my tent and stood close enough to the entrance for the odd drop of rain to hit me still. When the rain eased again, I was able to see Palermo clearly once more. At anchor, off the harbour, were five of my warships mounting an effective blockade, nothing had been able to enter or leave, and that included fishing boats.

We were camped on the lower slopes of Mount Pellegrino. Its wooded slopes provided both shelter and fuel for us as the temperature gradually had become cooler as autumn slipped towards winter. Wherever one stood in the camp, the smell of horse, burning and burnt wood was overpowering. We had been encamped now outside of the city for two months. We had arrived at the end of September, and it had taken twelve days to reach this point. The march had been a lot tougher than anticipated. The road on the map failed to show the terrain of the mountainous interior of the island. For most of the march, we had gone up and down one mountain after another. We were exhausted by the time we reached the outskirts of the city.

My first move had been to display our forces to the defenders of Palermo. We paraded outside of the main gate to intimidate them. I sent one of my junior officers to speak with the governor and offer fair terms of surrender. The governor had greeted him from the parapet of the main gate's guard tower. After listening to my terms, he had shrugged and replied that he was quite happy to accept our surrender, whenever I was ready to offer it. So that night, pickets were placed all around the walls of the city. Each gate was heavily guarded to ensure no one left the city, or for the Goths to try and mount a surprise attack. All the guards were told to light fires every night so that the city knew it was surrounded. It also served to keep the sentries warm as the nights became cooler.

So, we laid siege to the city. The next day, Bessas and his forces landed at Mondello, and within a day the artillery had been brought up to our perimeter. We conducted a survey of the walls and deduced where to place our artillery for the best effect. We counted fourteen towers on the three main walls of the city, each close enough to provide covering fire, and they were in good condition, as was the wall itself. The fleet ensured that the fourth side, the sea, was blocked as well. In places, a dry moat had been maintained, and this provided a further obstacle for us to overcome. But the main advantage was that we occupied Mount Pellegrino and could see directly into the city, and we could watch any movement of Gothic troops within.

The city of Palermo was laid out in an almost rectangle shape, typical of old cities founded by the Greeks. A central thoroughfare could be clearly seen running from the western gate straight to the harbour area, with the forum lying to one side of it close to the centre. The largest buildings were centred close to the forum area. Now, all we could do was build up our forces, entrench close to the city gates, and set up the artillery; this wasn't going to be a quick fight. With control of the small village and harbour of Mondello, we could receive supplies directly from the east of the island and even Africa. It also provided a base for the navy flotilla to operate from.

Once the artillery was installed, they could begin the process of wearing down the defenders. We had two types of artillery. The smallest was the type still called, 'Ballista', and two men worked it. It was a very large bow, laid on its side and mounted on a stand. To operate the weapon, the crew used levers to pull the bowstring back till it was held on a catch. Then a metal-tipped bolt was placed on the guide rails, one of the crew aimed the device by looking along the guide rails, spotting his target and releasing the string, which shot the bolt in a straight line at great speed. It could pierce a heavily armoured Persian cavalryman at three hundred paces. We had forty of these set up around the city.

The larger weapon called the 'onager', was transported on wagons in kit form and assembled when required. It had a crew of five, and before it was assembled, the site had to be pointing towards the target. A base was constructed, then a heavy upright form was assembled, then an arm was bound to the base of the upright, using animal hair. A tackle and block were then used to pull the arm backwards till it was almost touching the rear base. Once the arm was secured, a sling was attached, and a large rock placed in the sling or many smaller rocks depending on what type of target was being fired at. It worked by the crew releasing the tension in the arm, as it was pulled back upright, it lifted the sling and threw the rock forward and upwards, before the arm was halted by the upright stand. It was a slow weapon to fire, but its job was to hammer the walls of the city, in roughly the same place, continually. The effect was the same as if the engineers had stood next to the wall and continually hit it with hammers.

It took four days to fully construct the firing pits and assemble the artillery. With the experienced advice of Bessas's officers, we sited the weapons around each gate as these looked to be the weakest points in the city's defences. Constantius joined us after completing his conquest of the northern shore of Sicily. I ordered him to gain an interview with the Gothic governor, as I considered that his bravado may well have come down quite a notch after watching us assemble our siege around his city. My terms this time were simple, the complete surrender of the city and, in exchange, I would deport him and his men to Italy.

Constantius was greeted by the governor from the gate tower, and he refused our terms again. Once Constantius returned with the negative message, I had the artillery fire on the gates for a long period, just to let the defenders know we meant business.

So, each day we fired rocks and bolts at the city, and they had to sit there and take it. All the while they were eating up their supplies, and we, on the other hand, just got cold and a little wet. My officers joined me inside my tent, and we sat around to discuss the ongoing siege. The siege itself was not the problem, it was the weather, and so we needed to end the siege quickly.

"Gentlemen, we must take Palermo before winter arrives. I have no intention of abandoning what we have gained so quickly and retiring back across the island to Syracuse to winter and return in the spring and start again. In that time, Theodatus might be able to send troops to Palermo. A direct assault on the city seems to be the only option we have. It is going to be costly, and we might not take the section of wall or gates in the first wave. Does anyone have any suggestions to make it easier?"

There was a disturbance outside the tent, the sound of men arguing. This was followed by the sound of water being shaken onto the floor of the tent, then Peranius stepped into the meeting. He was soaking wet and covered in mud. I could see why my guards tried to stop him at the entrance to the tent — he didn't look like a Roman officer of rank.

"Belisarius, I apologise for my lateness and state of my clothes."

"Peranius, good to see you. I have just been outlining our current problem of how to storm the city while reducing casualties," I stated, trying to hide a grin for the way the mud had flicked across the floor at his salute.

"May I suggest something and explain my condition at the same time?"

There was a general murmur in favour of Peranius speaking first, so I nodded to him. Where he stood, a small pool of water and mud began to form.

"Firstly, I am sorry for being late. Earlier on, I was speaking to some sailors, and from what they were saying, I realised that there may be a much easier way into the city. So, I took a small boat, and we slipped into the outer harbour. I went over the side and swam into the harbour and up to the walls there. Thank God for the rain, as it kept the Gothic sentries inside. That's when I discovered that we could bypass the land walls and sail directly into the city through the harbour. The harbour is virtually undefended, and the walls of the city are much lower there than the land walls. At about twenty to twenty-five feet."

The tent was completely silent, only the sound of rain hitting the leather made any noise, as each man present inwardly digested Peranius's comments. Then Bessas spoke. "Belisarius, we could do it using the transports to sail straight into the harbour and storm the walls there."

At his excitement, Peranius spoke again. "I suggest that we have the engineers mount some form of tower on the boats, with a ladder assembly so we can climb easily over the walls."

The commander of the engineers then spoke as the excitement in the tent began to grow. "General, it may well be possible to construct siege towers on the transports as well as mounts for the small artillery. In fact, I am sure we can do it and storm the walls quickly before the Goths realise what has hit them."

Then the flotilla commander spoke, realising just what was being proposed and eager to get a word in just as almost everyone else in the tent was, but he was far more grounded and his words cautious. "General, there are two problems. Firstly, the tides — we will have to enter on a high tide. That means we will only have one chance during the day, and that is around midday now. Otherwise, the transports might not be able to reach the walls, or they might become stuck. And the weather. Storms can blow up quickly here, so we need to act fast."

"Gentlemen, I think we can do it. First, we need to know how many transports can fit into the harbour and how stable they will be with towers mounted. Will the towers be high enough for the ramps to reach the top of the walls? The artillery should do the job of keeping the sentries' heads down while we storm in." I paused and looked at my slightly wet comrades. A murmur had developed as I had been speaking, as each man had ideas, this led to quiet discussions among them. I now knew we could do this. They too believed it was possible and this would make its way down to the men. Once the men believed it was going to work, then it would. "I want you all to work together and have the ships ready to go as soon as possible. We will use Mondello as the staging area. We must be careful and gently move the assault troops back to the port without alerting the Goths. Bessas, let me know as soon as you are ready."

I stood on the quarterdeck of one of the following transports and watched as the first six transports gently slipped into the harbour. The remaining ships waited outside of Palermo's port. Only at the last moment did the warships, manning the blockade, weigh anchor and make way for the transports. Archers had been placed in the masts and rigging to provide increased firepower and support the assault troops. The high tide pushed the transports into the harbour; the sails had been lowered to stop fires spreading too quickly on them. The oars had been stowed so the transports could come as close to the walls as possible and each other. Light artillery, protected by shields, had been placed on the bows ready to fire at the Goths. The decks were covered in soldiers — we could only squeeze a thousand men onto all the ships before they looked in danger of sinking. Each ship had one tower, about thirty feet high, placed in the centre to balance the weight. The ramps on the towers were tied up, ready to be cut and dropped onto the walls.

The noon sun was not bright, and clouds dominated the horizon, and we all feared a storm could be on its way before we had made a landing. The first transports rounded the harbour mole, and then we heard the alarm being sounded from within the city. The sound of trumpets carried across the waves to us, and we knew they were preparing to defend themselves against us. The sound of the heavy thud of the artillery was the first real sign that combat had begun. I ordered the rest of the transports to follow in and jam themselves up to the assault boats, so the rest of the army could clamber across them and into the city. We rode the tide but were faster because we still had rowers who increased the speed, and we chased the assault boats into the harbour. We finally reached the inner harbour, and before us, the six transports lay tight up against the inner walls of the city. Lines had already been thrown and tied to the harbour. The towers had dropped their ramps over the parapet of the walls, and a steady stream of soldiers were making their way up the towers, then out and across the ramps and jumping down below the parapet and out of our sight.

We almost crashed into the assault boats, but the rowers managed to slow us enough, so we did no damage to them. We lost a good number of oars in the process before they could be raised out of the way. The crew rapidly lashed us to the closest transport, I led my men over the side of our ship, across planks and into the assault ship. Then we clambered

339

up the tower before emerging on the ramp. It was quite a drop to the water below. I didn't hang around admiring the view and rushed over the ramp, followed by my men, and down onto the solid mass of the inner wall of Palermo. I found the captain of the assault ship already on the parapet. His men had armed themselves and were supporting the assault. He recognised me and came over to inform me of the action so far.

Once the alarm had been raised, they had received arrow fire, light at first, but the closer they came to the walls, the heavier it became, along with other missiles. They suffered several casualties before the ramp could be dropped. Constantius had led the charge off the ramp and onto the defenders, then fire had rapidly decreased. I looked around. There weren't many bodies up here, mostly they were Goths, as I didn't recognise their clothing. I looked back at the tower I had climbed. We had covered it with rough wood, and it had many missiles sticking out of it. It had done its job, not only protecting the men but also allowing them to breach the walls.

I made my way along the parapet with my men — there was no resistance. We descended the wall and finally entered Palermo proper — judging by the buildings we were in the merchant quarter. We walked through the street — still no sign of the Goths. The street was empty of life; a few bodies lay where they had fallen. Then we entered a square. In the centre was a group of prisoners, lying or squatting on the ground, surrounded by a thin line of my men. The Goths looked pitiful and lost, not capable of putting up much resistance. I still couldn't hear any sounds of fighting since we had boarded the assault ship. The square was bright, as the clouds had moved away, and the city looked peaceful and was also devoid of noise. The shops were boarded up — the market had never opened. This section of the city was ghostly quiet; even the prisoners were silent. I left the square and headed into the city with my men; we moved carefully. My personal guards had surrounded me with the usual shield wall, but there was still no response from the Goths, not even a single arrow fired in our direction. No doors or windows were opened as we passed, the inhabitants, fearful of a sacking army, awaited their fate in silence. The city was in good repair from what I could see as we continued with our ghostly patrol. We reached what looked like the palace — the framework of this part of the city was similar to that of Syracuse. Outside of the palace, I found Constantius looking very pleased with himself. Squatting on the paved surface next to him, bound up like a criminal, was a most wretched-looking creature. Constantius gave him a good kick and the man fell sideways.

"General Belisarius, may I present the last Gothic governor of Sicily."

The man looked up at me. Yes, it was the same arrogant man I had met before. But instead of strength, I only saw fear in that face. His face was slightly bloated, and blood dripped from a fat lip. We had taken the city within a short time with very little resistance. I think both of us were surprised by how easy it had been compared to the time we had spent standing outside of the city, looking in. We had taken the island of Sicily in one campaign season, and we now had a secure base to overwinter. Unfortunately, it was too late to send a message to the capital to inform Justinian of our success. Instead, it would have to wait to the end of the winter storms. We were in for a peaceful winter on the island, and I looked down at the man who thought he could hold out against us. If this was the standard of Gothic commanders, Mundus must have also found the going easy.

"Well, Goth, still feel able to refuse my terms for surrender?" I queried.

He shut his eyes and made no sound. Constantius kicked him again. The governor just mumbled something.

"We caught him trying to hide in the palace. He was dressed as a servant woman. What shall we do with this disgusting wretch?" Constantius growled. "With all the time we have wasted here, not to mention the cost in lives, I should, by rights, cut his head off."

The Gothic governor made a pleading noise through his still swelling lips. Constantius reacted and gave him another kick, this time in the ribs. That shut him up as he rolled around in pain.

"Cut his nose off and send the rest of him to Theodatus with a message that Theodatus is ordered by the Consul Belisarius, governor of

Sicily, conqueror of the Vandals, to present himself and surrender in person to me in Syracuse forthwith, or it won't be just his nose I'll be cutting off."

I expected the messenger wouldn't live long enough to know the answer.

To be continued...